THE
PROUD SERVANT

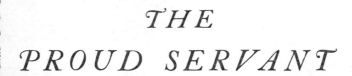

THE
PROUD SERVANT

THE
STORY OF MONTROSE

By

Margaret Irwin

" From the pride of the Grahams,
Good Lord, deliver us ! "

Old Saying.

" I never had passion upon earth so strong
as to do the King, your father, service."

*Letter from James Graham, Marquis
of Montrose, written Jan. 28th, 1649,
to Prince Charles, two days before the
execution of the King, his father.*

1934

CHATTO & WINDUS

LONDON

To

CHEVITHORNE

Contents

*

*

Note

WHILE I was writing *Royal Flush*, I read John Buchan's *Montrose*, and was so much impressed by it that for some months I could not go on with what I was doing, because I was thinking, reading, and occasionally writing about Montrose, though I had then no intention of making a book about him. But as I could not get him out of my head, I have made this venture, which I would never have done had it not been for Buchan's book.

My novel is naturally from a different angle than that of a biography; and this I hope justifies the attempt.

N.B.—All letters and documents quoted in this book are from the original.

Introduction

"The King sits in Dunfermline town
Drinking the blude-red wine."

THE King's face is ugly, puckered, nervous and comical. He spills the blood-red wine when he drinks, to the disgust of his wife, who is a Danish woman, fair, with no thoughts beyond her next new dress. The King is James VI of Scotland, the inappropriate son of Mary Queen of Scots. Daggers flashed in front of her eyes just before he was born; and he was born frightened. Swaddled in padded coats against any possible assassin's steel, he played a cannily cautious part all his life, fought neither on his mother's behalf nor on his own, content that her imprisonment, followed by her execution, should give him the Scottish throne.

And now he has only to wait for another throne to fall into his misshapenly padded lap. While the King of Scotland sits in Dunfermline town, the old Queen of England lies dying at Richmond. The old Queen with a nose like a witch and a golden wig and a face red and white like a dish from China, sits on the floor in her palace and refuses to go to bed; because she knows that when she does she will never get up again, and that that half-century we now call the Elizabethan age will then be over.

She dies, and now King James VI of Scotland is also King James I of England. He travels south through his new possessions, slowly, royally, receiving homage from his new subjects; and with him go his Danish wife and his two elder children, and later the youngest, Baby Charles, a child nearly four years old, but so sickly and backward that he can neither walk yet nor talk, and as all prophesy, is not likely to see more than another year or two of life.

Lucky for England that the King's elder children, the Prince Henry and the Princess Elizabeth, are a splendidly strong up-standing pair of young rascals. They make friends everywhere, they get into scrapes, they get into debt, they run a farm of their very own, they demand plays, picnics, water tournaments for their entertainment; they fall into the river and are not drowned, they ride horses too wild for them and are not thrown,—the like of them has as many lives as a cat, say the nurses, who are daily expecting Baby Charles to die.

If he had died, or if Prince Henry had not, then the story of James Graham, Marquis of Montrose, would not have been the same. But it was Henry who died, of a feverish chill, caught when heated after tennis, in the midst of the preparations for his sister's wedding to the Elector Palatine.

Henry died, Elizabeth sailed away, and Baby Charles was left alone to fight his way up to manhood as best he might. And because of a dim, obstinate courage that never forsook him, the sickly child managed to grow up to be King Charles I of England and Scotland. Before this, and more wonderful still, he made himself a master of horsemanship by the time he was twelve.

At which time, in the year 1612, the Lord James Graham was born at his father's house of Old Montrose, on the east coast of Scotland.

BOOK I
THE GREEN YEARS
1612-1636

I

NO baby, unless it were heir to a throne, could have been more eagerly welcomed. The Lord James Graham was indeed heir to a family of almost royal importance. His father, the fourth Earl of Montrose, was made President of the Privy Council. His grandfather had been Chancellor and Treasurer of Scotland, then Viceroy,—kicked upstairs, said his critics, because he had not enough learning as Chancellor. His great-grandfather had fallen in the famous field of Pinkie; his great-great-grandfather in the still more famous one of Flodden; a yet remoter ancestor, at Falkirk by the side of William Wallace. There was even an ancestor that had had something to do with the Roman wall of Antoninus. In short, of all the families that guarded the Highland line of Scotland, the family of the Grahams was foremost, so that there was good reason that the Lord James should be born, the only son among five daughters, three of whom had been born before himself.

His father led the placid life of a country gentleman as few of his forbears had done—shooting, playing golf, smoking and breaking hundreds of clay pipes and sampling every known variety of tobacco. He ordered his estates with the thrift of a careful husbandman, had full accounts kept, never backed bills nor pledged his land nor speculated in the new commercial companies in soap or tanning that were springing up everywhere in this new crazy search for wealth that had seized on the country in these peaceable times.

He married the Lady Margaret Ruthven, sister to the mysterious young Earl of Gowrie, on whose murdered body had been found a little parchment bag, full of magical characters and words of enchantment. He had been killed by King James' servants, in defence of their royal master, it was said; and the dead body was propped up at the delinquents' bar in Edinburgh to stand its trial for high treason. Small eloquence could it show on its own behalf; it was found guilty, and its head condemned to

3

be set on the Tolbooth, 'there to stand till the wind blow it away.'

This was done on the very day in the year 1600 that Prince Charles was born at Holyrood Palace; and some thought it an unfortunate omen, both for the royal baby and for the new seventeenth century.

From then on, the Lady Margaret Ruthven walked with a defiant carriage and looked out on the world with implacable eyes. All the friends and relatives of the gentle Graham, who became the fourth Earl of Montrose, expressed wonder at his rashness in marrying her.

Only once before had he had occasion to show the courage of his race, and that was when he had set on Sir James Sandilands in the High Street at Edinburgh, and avenged a kinsman's murder by a fight to the death with broadswords. And in this, his single act of violence, he also avenged the fact that King James had given to young Sandilands, in token of his fatuous affection for him, the lands that had belonged to the late Earl of Gowrie.

Into whose disgraced, disinherited and dangerous family, the fourth Earl of Montrose was bold enough to marry. For not only did he make himself brother-in-law to the head of a warlock on the Tolbooth, but his wife's grandfather had been noted as a necromancer. The lovely Queen Mary,—bred up as she had been among the Italian sorceries and juggleries of the French Court under Catherine of Medici,—fearless and curious as she was in all matters,—had yet not dared in her youth to accept a ring from Lord Ruthven, the Lady Margaret's grandfather. So she had said to some of her suite while hawking near Kinross, " for," she said, " I know him to use enchantments,—and yet he is made one of my Privy Council."

But nothing untoward happened in Lady Margaret's marriage, —" as far as one knows," the gossips added hopefully.

She was inhuman, said the many women who rather feared her —a coolly indifferent wife, a careless mother. She had the eyes of a mermaid, and the step of a young stag; there was no man who could keep up with her when she walked over the hills, and often she would walk alone, as no woman should,—till far into the night, no man knew where. So that she did not allay the uneasy reputation of her family; and the old, dreadful stories began to be told again when at the birth of her son, the Lord James, it leaked out that she had consulted witches as to his future. This in itself was chargeable as a crime.

No one knew what Lady Margaret learned from it of her son's fate; whatever it was, she faced it in greater and lonelier pride than ever. She gave birth to two more daughters, Katherine and Beatrix, but she lived less and less in the present; the company round her would slide away and become invisible to her clear and intent gaze. She died rather suddenly, without warning, when her son was just six years old, and left her cheerful and kindly husband very melancholy. He would sit for hours puffing at his pipe, staring through the clouds of smoke with round, sad eyes.

But there were his estates, his children,—he wrote letters to hurry the dressmakers who had not finished his youngest daughter's frocks;—and he had so many friends, he had always given so many shooting and hunting parties, hospitality could not be neglected, any more than his cattle and crops, the best tended in Scotland. His castles at Mugdock and Old Montrose and Kincardine were fast taking on the character of country houses, with antlers on the walls, and fishing rods and golf clubs stacked in the corners, and rows of tobacco jars and pipes beside the chimney corner.

His two elder daughters were well married to rising men,—the eldest, Lilias, to Sir John Colquhoun of Luss, who had lately been given the new title of baronet; and the second, Margaret, to Archibald Napier, soon to be created Lord Napier for his wise and useful service at Court to King James. The younger children, Dorothea, Jamie, Kat (for Katherine) and little Beatrix (whom her father always called ' the bairn ' as though he had not had five other bairns before her), stayed with their elder sisters in turn, and with their father.

*   *   *

At twelve years old, Jamie was old enough to go and study

with a tutor in Glasgow.   He lodged with the Lord Justice-Clerk
and his wife, Sir George and Lady Elphinstone, in one of the old
canons' houses near the Cathedral; and his two cousins, who were
his pages, and his sister Kat, who was a year younger than he
but would never obey him, lived there too.   The little girl and
the three boys all did lessons together with Master William
Forrett, M.A., in a room with red curtains and a red table-cloth,
on which Kat at once made a large ink blob, to Master
Forrett's regular lamentation whenever they sat down to lessons
—though Lord James assured him that that was what it had
been sent for.

All his treasures were crowded into that little red room in the
old canonry, his golf clubs jumbled up with his fencing foils in the
corner, and on the walls hung his cross-bow, inlaid with mother
o' pearl, and his brazen hagbut and his new gilded sword, his first
real sword, a present from his brother-in-law, Archie Napier, in
a silk and silver scarf with belt and hangers, a present from his
father, and a gun with which he had shot several roebuck on the
shores of Loch Lomond, when staying at the Colquhouns' house
of Rossdhu near Luss.   And there were a whole shelf-full of books
that his father had chosen for him from his own library, and silver
spoons and cups for his table, carefully packed and sent by his
father's orders, and linen napkins and table-cloths, and counter-
cloths red and green, and cushions of red embroidery and green
velvet and two of tapestried peacocks and one of plain brown
velvet to kneel on in the kirk, for all that the Kirk was beginning
to call it a Popish and heathenish superstition to kneel at prayers.

" But let you show as good manners to your God as to your
father," said the Earl of Montrose, when his son Jamie knelt to
receive his blessing before riding back with Willy and Mungo
Graham to the narrow streets and wynds of the little country
town of Glasgow.

In spite of King James' passionate efforts to suppress the vicious
new habit of smoking, the back streets managed to wink at
prohibition, and drove a thriving trade with America in tobacco.
Jamie loathed the smell of these back streets, for he had once

tried to smoke a pipe, and it had made him very sick ; but he was drawn to them by the sight of sailors from the Port of Glasgow standing about their low doorways, with black beards and gold rings in their ears, chewing and spitting out the Indian weed. Then if he were lucky was the time to hear tales of savages who were painted blue and scarlet, and emperors who wore crowns of feathers three feet high, and mountains beyond which there lay nothing but the setting sun. One day he too would see these things; in the meantime it did not seem that this life at Glasgow would ever end.

But it ended on a day early in November, when for a whole month Jamie had been fourteen, and Kat was staying with her sister Lilias and Sir John Colquhoun at Luss, twenty miles away. There came a servant from Kincardine to say that the Earl of Montrose was very ill, and that his son must come home at once. His white horse, Torrey, was saddled for him; with his pages dressed in scarlet and he himself in dark green and mulberry, he rode out of the Elphinstones' gates. The gardener was waiting there to hand up a bunch of late red roses and sweet-smelling thyme to pin between his horse's ears. He was always there on Sundays to hand the Lord James a nosegay on his way to church to pin into his cloak, against the smell of the congregation. To-day his sense of the occasion amounted to a bouquet, and the young lord's, in response, to a tip of twelve shillings Scots.

So Master Forrett anxiously ascertained, spurring his nag after him to inquire, and also how much he had given the blind Highlander who sang the time of dinner last night—and how many coins he had just flung to the group of ragged poor children that always gathered as fast as crows round a corn stook to see the young lord mount his horse and clatter away up the narrow street. All these uncounted alms to the poor at his mounting and dismounting, and tips to the servants at his numerous visits, to say nothing of the endless expenses of stray drummers and pipers and fiddlers and morrice-dancers and ballad-singers and jugglers, whose services Lord James commanded, not merely for his own amusement in the old monastic house at Glasgow, but all over the country, wherever he happened to be staying,—no wonder the methodical and thrifty Master Forrett often felt he had been put in charge of a dragonfly.

The Lord James darted here, darted there, on visits to his three homes at Mugdock, Kincardine or Old Montrose, visits to his married sisters and to friends and relations, at what seemed an absurd distance and often for only two or three days. He wore out his horse's shoes unconscionably, and sadly had Master Forrett noted down the charge every time his young lordship's nags were shod since he was seven years old.

The little tutor's thinly covered bones got very tired with all the jolting over rough roads; and his irritably sensitive ear could not abide the pipes which Lord James would order first of all the musicians. He could already imagine their barbarous skirling at Kincardine and the eldritch keening of the women, if the old earl should indeed die.

Would he die?

"Shall we never jog this road back to Glasgow again after all? Will my lord give up his studies there and go straight to college at Saint Andrews, and I have to find a new pupil?" thought Master Forrett.

All at once he knew that he did not care how far or how often he jogged on the road, or how shrilly the pipes assaulted his ears, if only he could continue to see his young lord's puzzled frown over some difficult passage in Caesar's commentaries break into a dazzling smile as he triumphantly construed it wrong,—so fantastically and ingeniously wrong, that Master Forrett sometimes doubted whether his pupil's intentions were serious.

Willy and Mungo Graham occasionally talked low to each other, and their tones and looks had a new respectful awe in them when they addressed their young lord, which pulled him up short whenever he began to whistle. He began again and again, for he always wanted to whistle with pleasure when he heard the rhythmical creek of the saddle under him answering to the throbbing, willing muscles of his horse as it sprang forward beneath the press of his knees.

But he must not whistle when everyone around him was thinking—" The old lord may be dying, and then the Lord James will be Earl of Montrose." He tried to think it himself—" My father may be dying."—To die, to go under the earth,—" To bear the red rose company," the ballads called it, but he could not believe it, for the sunshine was so bright, the shadows that chased it were so sharp and sudden, the hills in the distance, brilliant as blue icebergs, looked so close that he could distinguish every scar of rock and stream upon them.

Then up came the big grey clouds again, shouldering their way up over the round-shouldered hills that stood surly now and black, humping their sodden backs against the rain, until in a flash they were blotted out, invisible. And here came the rain on themselves, marching over the mountains, dipping and trailing its long grey skirts over the plains, till it fell plump on their heads, and turned his pages' scarlet sleeves to purplish black on the windward side.

He flung back his wet, stinging face to look at the scarlet berries of a mountain ash that glistened above his head. The mountain ash flew past him; there was nothing ahead of him now but moorland peat and heather, dark in the flying wings of the storm that had begun to outstrip him. In a watery break of the clouds there tossed a broken banner of iridescent light, the bitten-off stump of a rainbow that sailors call a wind-dog; there were iridescent lights in the rain on his eyelashes as he blinked them against the wild and fugitive loveliness of the scene.

He felt his horse share his happiness, gallant, responsive,— " On with it, Torrey, gallop through it now—with a fol de diddle lalley,—fol de diddle lalley——" But there he was off again, forgetting it all, while his father might be dying—and he would have to go up into his room and stand by the great bed and hold on to the curtains and prod his finger into the threads of a woven beast or fruit and say the right things that must be said to someone who was very ill, while all the time that cloud of nauseating smoke would wreath above his father's good-humoured face that curved chubbily above its beard, and puff slowly up into his own nostrils. Perhaps though, if his father were so very ill, the doctors, who were apt to call tobacco a dangerous drug, would not allow him to smoke this time.

But at this possibility, which should have cheered him, the young Lord James was so much dismayed that for the first time he really understood the meaning of the words he had so often repeated to himself, " My father may be dying."

And something very curious happened. For instantly his life at Glasgow with his tutor and his pages and his impertinent younger sister, receded, and became small, bright and remote, like something seen on a clear day very far away. The suite of little dark rooms made over to his use and coloured with all his possessions, turned into a set of painted boxes; his life in them, self-contained and seemingly eternal, became suddenly childish, unreal, like the life that he and Kat used to imagine for their toys.

Yet never had he seen every detail of those rooms so clearly— the leaded panes of the windows that had shown them one tiny square at a time of the narrow street where carts and riders went racketing over the cobbles—the flowers that the gardener was ordered to put always on the tables—the yellow curtains in his bedroom, and yellow counterpane sewn with red (for he liked always the brightest colours)—and the dancing to fiddlers and pipers on the noisy boards—yes, and the lessons too, and old Forrett's puckered face, always worried about something until one had chaffed that slow unwilling smile on to it,—good old Forrett now riding far behind him and counting up expenses on his nobbly fingers,—all these things suddenly floated up into the air, and a hundred years away,—all finished—all over.

For he knew at this moment that he would never go back to it, and that his father was dying.

II

THE old lord lay in his great bed. He was not really old, but he looked it now. His round rosy face had fallen suddenly into bluish folds, and his smile as he greeted Jamie was wavering and uncertain.

Even his son, even his youngest daughter, Beatrix, who gazed at him in childish, frightened solemnity, were now remote from him; he was withdrawn from them, intent on his own business of dying. They could not accompany him.

Time shifted round his bed. The present faded, grew invisible; someone from the past came forward to bear him company; they saw him look up into her face, and heard him murmur, " Margaret."

Then he died, and his heir was the next Earl of Montrose.

III

HIS children, his sons-in-law, his neighbours, his relatives and connections by marriage to the fifth and sixth degrees, gathered together to do honour to the old earl and to greet the new. The funeral began, and went on for weeks.

There came to it the Grahams of Claverhouse and the Grahams of Morphie, the Grahams of Braco and the Grahams of Fintry, the Grahams of Orchill, the Grahams of Balgowan, the Grahams of Inchbrakie; there was Jamie's cousin german, the Earl of Wigton, and Jamie's brothers-in-law, Lord Napier of Merchiston and Sir John Colquhoun, the Laird of Luss; there was Thomas Hope, the fussy family legal adviser from Edinburgh; there were his five sisters, there was a sprinkling of lesser relatives and connections, an army of pages, valets and servants. And there was room for them all, since the Castle of Kincardine was a hundred and sixty feet long.

On the open hearths glowed huge fires of peat and logs and sea-coal. The meals were prodigious. Most of the guests brought contributions of game or venison, but that went nowhere. The housekeeper provided beef and mutton, veal and ham; poultry and game, ptarmigan and partridges and plovers, were bought or slaughtered in hundreds for the occasion.

Claret and white wine and Easter ale were reckoned by the puncheon in the cellars, and cheese by the stone in the 'petty larder,' where butter and eggs were kept cool, and herrings preserved in salt barrels, and confectionery in spices. Kincardine was famous for its savory-amber and pistache-amber. Salmon was so plentiful that it could only be given to the servants, who objected if it were served to them more than five times a week.

Over barley and mutton broth, and mountainous pies of venison and blackcock and capercailzie, and horn and silver and leather cups of French and Spanish wines and March ales, the funeral guests told the new young earl how they remembered his doing this or that ridiculous and undignified thing when he was a baby.

He had roared so when put back in his cot that his father had declared so lusty a young rebel would trouble all Scotland.

Old John Graham of Balgowan insisted that the boy, when a few weeks old, had swallowed a toad. Jamie's kinsfolk took his part in denying this unnatural charge, for it bore a possible taint in it of witchcraft, such as he might well have inherited from his mother's side of the family.

A woman of a dangerous stillness,—many remembered the old earl's rather timid pride in his beautiful wife. On the whole they were well content that she had died first,—the funeral feast would not have been so comfortable with her in the house. As it was, it all went as pleasantly as if the cheerful and kindly spirit of their dead host were still presiding; and happy, friendly and intimate was all their talk of him.

They praised his management of his farms and pasture lands; told how he had improved the tillage of 'red land' in his wheat fields with so many bolls of common salt, and half as much in sandy ground; how particular he was about the grazing of his cattle on fresh grass, turning them from one park into the other, and instructing his herds to clean the ground of dung after them, so that his acres fed twice as many cattle, and his cows yielded twice as much milk as those of his more careless neighbours, and Jamie's estates had come to him twice as prosperous as in his grandfather's day. So his uncle, Sir William Graham of Braco, told the young earl who sat at the head of the table, holding his head very high, because now at last he was a man, and the head of his family, sitting among the men of the family, and must be as tall as the rest of them.

His eyes looked out on his kinsfolk, clear and grave, but his mouth turned up at the corners, giving it the shape of a half-moon, as though he were smiling. But he was not smiling, he was far too full of the importance of the occasion. He heard his elders talk of his fields and barns and byres—the talk of grown men, admitting him to their fellowship. But it was long and often prosy ; and the stuffy air, breathed by so many, heavy with the smell of peat smoke and roast meat and ale and wine, was soporific.

He must not nod nor yawn as though he were a sleepy child, and so he sat very straight, his eyes bright and alert. On his walls burned dozens of candles that had been made in the kitchens out of animal fat and perfumed with lavender oil to try and drown the smell of the tallow. In the strong draughts they guttered and dripped grease down their beautiful silver sconces; sometimes, to the secret delight of the new earl, a scalding drop blew outwards and fell on the head of a servant passing with a dish, or, better still, of one of the various family pipers who played in turn at each meal. They were more majestically jealous than their masters about precedence, so that it was pleasant to see their stately pace startled into an undignified hop.

The candle-flames blew this way and that, lighting up here a ruddy nose, and there a combative bright eye, as one Graham contradicted another, and here a Graham spat on the floor, and there a Graham delicately bit the last pieces of meat from the fowl's leg between his fingers before throwing it to the dogs, and all the lords and masters of this few-week-old world discussed the ever-disturbing politics of Church and state.

Lord Napier was telling an old story of his father's.—" And I heard them tell King Jamie to his face—' You must make us all bishops if you make any! ' "

There was an assenting roar of laughter, through which Sir Robert Graham of Morphie could be heard agreeing solemnly, a trifle bibulously.

Sir John Colquhoun, who was tipping back in his chair and picking his teeth with a long elegant silver toothpick, shouted out, " Because we have been good enough to give England a king, is that any reason why she should give us bishops ? A bad bargain, I call it! "

He rolled his black eyes round the table to see how it had taken; for whenever Napier made a hit, his brother-in-law had to go one better.

Archie Napier was a very good fellow, he frequently declared, but he did hope that his brand-new peerage would not go to his head. Sir John had just been made one of the Nova Scotia baronets, who had been created by King James as a means of raising money for his new colony. Sir John had had to pay an appalling amount of money for his dignity and for thirty thousand acres of useless land on the other side of the world, but it was worth it, he would say with a deprecating smile, just to prove that adventure was not yet dead in the hearts of Scotsmen. And, though he did not mention that, it would ensure him further promotion when the new young King Charles came north to be crowned King of Scotland.

But when would that be? King Charles had been on the throne of England a year now, and still it was only talk as to when he would come to Scotland. All the Scots lords who hoped to make their way in the world had forsaken their lands and people and were busy currying favour down at the court in London. That was no way for a young man of spirit,—" let you remember that, my young lord," said Graham of Fintry to Jamie, who tried to look profound over his baked sugar comfits, and wished that dinner did not last three hours.

They all said to him the things that his father had said, and told his father's stories, as they sat at his father's table, and drank his father's wine. Down went his head, down, down, then up with a jerk.

Why, out of all his long family of fighters and heroes, had the lot fallen on him to lead the peaceful life of a farmer? Why, when his ancestors had fought the English again and again, had he been born just after it was all over,—so that everyone should tell him that the best way he could serve his country was by seeing that his cattle grazed a different grass on Tuesday from that which they had grazed on Monday?

There were no more Border raids nowadays, no more midnight fordings of the river Tweed, no more sudden attacks on impregnable castles. Kinmont Willie had been the last of the raiders; the Border ballad was nothing now but an old song. The King no longer sat in Dunfermline town; he had gone south to London. There was nothing left to do but to go to the English Court and be a toady, or stay at home and mind his farms; nothing left but peace and profit and fat pastures and interminable meals and old men talking.

He crumbled his bread into pellets, marshalled them into armies, pushed them this way and that in positions of attack and defence. Behind the rise and fall of the voices round him, other words were forming lines and forming rhymes, until a couplet leaped into his head—

> " So, great attempts, heroic ventures shall
> Advance my fortune or renown my fall."

IV

ONLY Kat was ever allowed a glimpse of his verses, but she was not appreciative. She never could see why one wanted to put words into lines of a certain length and sound,— and anyway the poets could do it better. That was what they were there for, weren't they? So she demanded, shaking back her defiant, tangled head.

When he expostulated, all she would say was, "Show them to Dorothea then."

Dorothea would have cooed her pleasure over his verses almost before she had read them, she would have set them to a tune, and sung them to her lute. He did not want that. It was just the difficulty in winning Kat's attention that stimulated him to seek it. She would never try to express anything she did not feel, and there were few things that she felt except animal high spirits, the joy of exercising her strong young legs over the heather, either in riding or running, and the most exquisite thrill of danger.

The more mettlesome a horse, the more determined she was to ride it ; and her wildest pleasure had been a sail in a coracle on Loch Lomond when a storm had suddenly sprung up and all but wrecked the fragile craft. Those who had seen her then, said that of all the family she was the only one who truly resembled her mother. Kat had overheard this and was very proud of it.

She said she could remember going walks with her mother at night and being carried in her shawl; but Jamie would not believe it, as he could only just remember their mother, and Kat was a whole year younger.

"What *do* you remember? Nothing, I know, so that proves it. Where did she take you? Tell me that."

"To the churchyard wall," she answered, grinning, her eyes glinting at him.

She was like a little wild black cat. He guessed her to be

making it up, playing with the notion of their mother's witch blood in order to try and frighten him. The tall nettles in Kincardine churchyard, black and ragged against the moon, plants plucked from a grave at midnight, Kat's elfin face peering out from the folds of the shawl, and above it his mother's clear, implacable eyes,—the picture rushed across his brain, and would not be exorcized.

He swore at Kat for inventing it, warned her she might find her tricks recoil on her own head, since her noble blood might not prevent her being burnt at the stake if she insisted on fastening the charge of witchcraft on herself.

But one could not frighten Kat, only excite her to further mischief; she danced up and down, chanting a silly mumble-jumble she pretended her mother had taught her.

" Liar! " he shouted, and catching her at last, as she dodged and writhed away from him, he hit her hard, so that she squealed and bit his hand. The fight was regrettably undignified,—and just as he had begun to feel himself so much a man.

He had stood beside his father's coffin, and seen it lowered into the vault of all their fathers; he had heard the wailing and the keening, and, above all, the piercing desolation of the pipes; he had been torn by memories of his father's gentle and understanding humour.

He had received acknowledgment and deference everywhere as the head of his house; King Charles himself had written to show his interest in his young kinsman.

Yet he was squabbling and sparring with Kat again just as they had done since they were small children. He could thump her harder than she could thump him, but that was all,—he could never make her acknowledge his superior judgment as elder brother, not even now he was head of their house. Dimly he had begun to see that it was not in Kat to acknowledge any authority; but this did not lessen his desire to dominate her; it was so poignant that when, as in the old childish days of their quarrels, she cried, " I hate you, I hate you," he answered with tears of impotent fury in his eyes, " And I hate you."

She flung away from him into the woods. She would never speak to him again. She would run away and die in a ditch, and only Moffat, her baby donkey, would be sorry, and he only because she would no longer bring him carrots. All her tenderness was reserved for Moffat, whose demure nose and furry forehead and soft, bulging eyes roused her to ecstasy.

She rolled over on the damp leaves and stared round her at the lovely Glen of Kincardine. Above her hung the castle on its crest, its vast grey bulk seen here and there like a thundercloud through the thinning golden trees. Below her, the river of the Ruthven (her mother's river) tossed and tumbled its rocky way, now white and sparkling, now mysterious in its black depths. She never looked at it without thinking of her mother. Some said they had seen her ghost just before the old earl died, and that she had come back to earth to fetch her husband; others said the spirit had been that of the lady in green who, when misfortune was coming to the house, walked under the Tree of Dule, the great yew that had been the Graham Justice Tree in the ancient days when all the family charters were signed beneath it.

Now her brother was head of their house; he would go to college at Saint Andrews, she would do lessons with him no longer but would go and live for good with Lilias and Sir John in their home on the wooded shore of Loch Lomond. She thought her sister silly, and her brother-in-law too, and that his foreign servant, Carlippis, was the only person worth talking to at Rossdhu,—so she told her brother, with the priggish conceit of thirteen, when they next met.

Jamie told her she ought not to talk to Carlippis, who was a rascally fellow,—and she seized the opportunity to say that there would be no chance for her to do so, if only he would agree to their going back together to Glasgow again. Why should he not go to college there, now that Glasgow had started a university too?

But she was told that girls did not understand these things, that it was unthinkable that he should go to Glasgow, or anywhere but to the college of Saint Salvator's which his ancestors had helped to found at Saint Andrews.

So she brooded, savage and miserable, and clenched her fists into hard round balls to keep herself from sobbing as she lay in bed with her two sisters, who talked, talked, talked, all the night, she thought. The three younger girls, Dorothea, Katherine and Beatrix, all slept in one bed with their favourite dogs, and complained of fleas.

It was Beatrix who missed the old earl most. Stolid as she seemed with her round, rosy cheeks and placid eyes,—spoilt by her father as everyone declared her to have been,—there was enough sensitive perception in her round brown head to tell her that never again would she be so tenderly and royally important as she had been to her father. At ten years old she ceased to be a queen, and became a doggedly courageous child who was yet far more of a woman than her three-year-older sister, Kat.

For it was she and not Kat who sympathized with Dorothea's love troubles. Sir James Rollock, the young laird of Duncruib, had fallen in love with her from the very beginning of the funeral; but her younger brother, now the head of the house, had not been sympathetic, saying that he liked Rollock's brother, William, the best of that family. It was the Napiers whose opinion would really count, but even dear Margaret had not understood how important it was,—she had said that Dorothea should not marry yet, and had better live with them at Merchiston for another couple of years, until she had grown stronger and more capable of bearing children.

" But many women bear children at sixteen," sobbed Dorothea, " so why should I not do so? "

Kat kicked contemptuously up at the sheet on her side of the bed, dislodging a brace of spaniels. All this talk of bearing or not bearing children, and growing old enough and strong enough to do it—was there nothing else for a woman to do? Jamie would go abroad and finish his education in Italy and France, living in strange countries for years and years, like her tragic uncle, the Earl of Gowrie, who had studied for seven years at the University of Padua, and was supposed to have gained his knowledge of the Black Art there in a fencing class conducted by the devil himself. Certainly he had come back an excellent swordsman, which in some sort proved it.

One was never allowed to mention the Earl of Gowrie. For that reason, the rebellious Kat thought of him more than of all her other relatives, with the exception of Jamie. But now Jamie would be going out into the world, and she would be left behind with nothing to look forward to but bearing children or not bearing children. Her passionate egoism revolted against it; she vowed to herself she would show Jamie that she was as capable of having adventure and seeing the world as ever he could be.

The funeral rolled on merrily enough. Young Rollock vowed to wait for his Dorothea; the guests made up old quarrels and started new; several of them fell in love with Lilias, and soon forgot it; one or two fell in love with Margaret, and did not.

And Jamie got his guardian, Lord Napier, to agree that he had best now go straight to college at Saint Andrews and start life in earnest,—" as I knew it would be," muttered Master Forrett, his face puckered up like a withered yellow apple.

His young master would not ride that road back to Glasgow, but he must do so to collect and pack all his treasures to be sent after him to Saint Andrews.

And he must find another pupil when the funeral party would at last break up, and his young lord ride south this time instead of west, and Kat ride to Rossdhu with the fair Lady Lilias and Sir John Colquhoun and his servant Carlippis.

arrogant fancy. There they all were, discussing some tedious, outmoded subject. Could they never realize that John Knox was dead?

" Would that the cardinal virtues had gone out with the cardinals! " he exclaimed, but old Graham of Balgowan had to ask him twice over what he had said. He should have said it to Carlippis.

And under his feet, Carlippis, finding the kitchens as full of theological argument and stale beer as his master found the hall, stretched his arms above his head, and yawned.

" Hell mouth yawns! " a pert page exclaimed, who alone had stared unabashed into that red cavern, at the pointed tongue curled back till it touched the gullet, at the domed roof of the foreigner's mouth that made his voice like a bell, at the thick lips, curled back far over the red gums beyond the strong sharp teeth.

Those yawns of Carlippis', cracking, derisive, splitting the air with their titanic boredom, such as had made Satan and his angels burst the bonds of heaven, rent the contented merriment of his company of fellow servants, their harmony of little jokes and gossip, friendships, love-making and rivalries, so that each member of it stood dismembered, no longer a confident part of the company, but a separate, shivering rag of contemptible humanity, uneasily conscious of something ridiculous in himself.

But now not even his yawn could appease Carlippis' insatiable disgust with Scotch broth and argument. He got up, stamped, spat on the floor and lounged out into the courtyard, dragging his heavy feet after him like a tree walking, or a troll. He knew and hated his ugliness, especially the chubby, cheerful aspect of it. What did he see when he looked in the glass but the face of a foolish, good-humoured sot, such as all sensible fellows would want to split open?

He stood there for perhaps an hour, scratching his thigh, blinking his eyes contemptuously at the pale Northern sunlight. The wet dead leaves, swept in heaps into the corners, stank in his nostrils; the year was rotting into decay, like everything else in this dank, sleepy place where nothing happened, nobody amused him, and there was no one to fear but God.

In the laundry yard, maids were stepping out of the doorway with wet clothes, which they hung upon the lines for a brief hour or so before they had to come scampering out again to take them in from the next shower. The wet shirts flapped and dangled in the breeze, slack arms and flighty tails, a depressing parody of humanity that at once appealed to Carlippis' fancy. Damp souls they were in this chilly climate, snivelling, disconsolate, always shrinking back in godly fear from the fluttering of their lusts. Only dim uncomfortable emotions like religion could get any grip on them.

He thought of Italian sunlight, sharp and strong, that cut the narrow streets into stripes of white and dark, of hot and cold,—of the pungent smell of wine booths, and the heavy sweetness of orange trees, and the sickly perfumes of brothels,—of plots and conspiracies that called out all a man's cunning, and danger bright and amusing as a play, and companions into whom he might easily find it necessary to stick a dagger the next night, but who spoke the same language as himself, figuratively as well as literally, knew when he was sneering, and what he was sneering at, in short were his companions, as these thick muddy wits of the North could never be.

His master came through the archway in company with one of his younger sisters-in-law, and stood laughing and talking to her in the exaggeratedly courtly, chaffing manner that men are apt to use towards very young girls; while she stood silent, straight and slight as a hazel rod, with the embarrassingly critical air of thirteen.

A groom led out their horses, Sir John held his hand by the side of her pony, but Lady Katherine ignored it; placing one foot in the stirrup, she swung herself into the saddle and cantered round the yard, calling to him to be quick and mount. He had got one foot into the stirrup, when his horse, eager to follow the pony, danced sideways, and Sir John had to hop after him on a long lean leg, clinging to the saddle with his cloak flapping, looking like a lame crane. He flushed and swore, the stable-boy grinned, Kat laughed clear and high.

The Italian-bred German who stood in the doorway, heavy with discontent, eyed the vanity of the man and the wildness of the girl, and thought, " There is material there—raw stuff, and slight—but something might be done with it. What use can I make of it? "

The emotions of others were his stock-in-trade; his art was to play on them and turn them to his account. And a plan began to shape itself in his mind, whereby he might be relieved of the tyranny of his boredom.

VI

*T*HE funeral feast was over, but some of the lesser and needier family connections showed a tendency to "sit on, picking their teeth, until the next funeral in the family," said young Patrick, the son of Graham of Inchbrakie, known to his still younger cousin of Montrose as Old Pate. Only three or four years his senior, this shrewd, gawky lad seemed to Jamie the complete man of the world.

When all the guests had ridden their different ways, Pate escorted his young lord to college with his two pages. On a grey January day they rode into Saint Andrews, and were installed in their lodgings; and Pate unpacked Jamie's books with his own hands, because servants were so careless with books. He placed on a shelf, nailed on to the new light panelling, all the small vellum volumes, and here and there some monster folio,—among them, Jamie's chief treasure, Sir Walter Raleigh's *History of the World.* He hung up his young cousin's weapons on the walls, and stacked the golf clubs and fencing foils all together in a corner just as they had stood in the Canonry at Glasgow, instead of primly separated by the servants; and then they sat on the familiar yellow and red counterpane, flung over the box bed that had been built into the wall, and thought the room looked rather less strange and empty.

Jamie stared at the red table-cloth with Kat's ink blob on it, and tried not to think he missed her. Old Pate glanced sideways at him with a wise and friendly grin beneath his perceptible moustache, and gave him a word or two of good advice, but not too much, and promised to send him one of the black setter's pups as soon as she should be delivered, and gave him now as a parting present his own flat powder horn, scratched all over with a queer scroll pattern, that he had bought from a Highlander at a fair. At that, Jamie was near disgracing his new college manhood and admitting his homesickness, but Pate, not waiting to be thanked, was looking up at the slit of window which squinted

27

oddly upwards at the great tower of Saint Salvator's, so that a section of it could be seen slanting distortedly through the greenish bottle-glass.

"Your old tower is drunk," he told Jamie just as Willy and Mungo came into the room, and the four boys all hooted at it, while the three who were to remain felt a secret pride in their mockery, already regarding the tower as their own personal property.

So the new Earl of Montrose was left in his lodgings with his companions, a grown man with no one in the house in charge of him, a scholar in a scarlet gown, but more frequently a sportsman. He hunted and shot, he played golf on the links by the sea, he betted at the races at Cupar; and he rode races himself along the wide sands until he and his companions turned at last, scrunching the innumerable sea-urchins' shells beneath their horses' hoofs, and looked back through the mist of sea foam at the little smoky town of Saint Andrews, its dark towers shooting up into the clouds. Above the splash of the waves came the long thin cry of the sand-piper; a spreading wind-dog made lines of coloured rain,—green rain, yellow rain, rain rose-pink, running into red—and behind it all that grey town, to which these riders to the sea must return in time for the lecture in Latin given by a famous foreign scholar.

For a bet he climbed the ruined arch of the Cathedral which Bruce had consecrated as a memorial to his victory over the English at Bannockburn. It still dominated the town that had destroyed it, as though the despairing cry of its murdered Cardinal would remain frozen in stone for ever. "All is gone," he had cried,—and well he might, for John Knox, who had joined his murderers, returned from the galleys to complete his work so thoroughly that now if a Papist wished to marry he had to do so in some wild and secret place by candlelight, for no priest dared do it in the open.

Yet all was not gone, for the colleges remained, and the scarlet scholars, and even the thorn tree that Queen Mary had planted in the courtyard of Saint Mary's College, which burst into as fresh a white and green this spring as though its queen had never been beheaded nor her Church driven out of the land.

Young Lord Wigton, the first of Jamie's many college friends, would have taken Queen Mary's side, and that of her Church, just because it was hers; but Jamie would not go so far.

Rome was the intruder, the interloper, that had helped England to trouble Scotland, she had been the unseen arm behind those fingers that always poked into their pie. Rome had refused to acknowledge Robert Bruce as Scotland's king, until the Scottish nobles had written to the Pope to tell him that neither Rome nor England should dictate to them,—" and neither Rome nor England ever shall! " cried Jamie.

" Not for glory, nor riches, nor honour, but for liberty alone we fight, which no honest man will lose but with his life." Three hundred years ago, his most famous ancestor, Sir John Graham, the friend of Wallace and of Bruce, had helped write that letter. Now his sword hung on the walls of Jamie's college rooms, beside his own, for Jamie had insisted on bringing it from home, now that he was the head of his house. On its blade was an inscription, added a century after its owner had fallen in battle :

> " Sir John the Graeme, very wicht and wise,
> Ane of the chiefs relievit Scotland thryse,
> Fought with ys sword, and ner thout schame,
> Commandit nane to Beir it Bot his name."

" 1405," read out Jamie, running his finger nail along the thin lines on the steel, " and even then this sword was a hundred years old. That is to be famous."

And his eye fell from the old basket-hilted weapon to his own light, gilded rapier, hanging in the silk and silver scarf his father had given him, as he wondered what chance he would ever have to make that, too, famous.

But little Kilpont, who was going through a course of cynic philosophy, remarked that his friend had better gaze hungrily at his pretty pearl-inlaid bow rather than his dainty sword,— for his best chance at present to win fame both for himself and his college was to win the archery medal that would place him as the best marksman in the university of Saint Andrews. So let Jamie come along with him now down to Butts Wyand for half an hour or so of practice at the butts. It was high time Saint Salvator's again won the medal.

"And high time," added Jamie, unhitching the bow from its hook on the wall, "that a Graham won it rather than a Campbell."

VII

ARCHIBALD CAMPBELL, Lord Lorne, the eldest son of the Earl of Argyll, had won the archery medal for all Saint Andrews when he had been up at the University six years before. The victory had given little pleasure to anyone, even the victor. For Archibald Campbell (whom nobody called Archie, as they called even the wise and elderly courtier, Lord Napier) had never been popular at college. His success therefore at the butts and at golf had only added to his bleak sense of grievance against his fellows; for it had only served to remind them that he preferred these peaceful accomplishments to riding or hunting, wherein he was apt to show nervousness.

He was slightly lame,—just enough not to impede his walk but to disfigure it, since it robbed his step of all the buoyancy and confidence of youth. Also he squinted a little, and his face had a crooked twist to it that was likely to increase with age. And this man was destined to be the chieftain of the most important clan in the Highlands, where bravery and beauty were as necessary to a leader as to the hero of a fairy-tale.

Lord Lorne had been unlucky in other ways; his mother had died in his infancy, his father had married again, his step-mother had been unkind to him, had even, he firmly believed, tried to poison him so as to make way for her own children. His uncle, the Earl of Morton, had taken the unhappy little boy into his own household for safety, and brought him up with as much care and affection as his own sons.

But unkind had been young Lorne's early impression of the world; and unkindness would always have more power over him than kindness. He thought of his cruel step-mother far more than of his kind uncle, with that intensity that only hate and fear can give.

He had reason to fear her, for she influenced his old father so much that he became a Roman Catholic for her sake. That flung young Archibald into a panic lest he should lose his patrimony. With precocious prudence he wrote to all his kinsmen, entreating them to stand by him against his father, and see to it that he should not suffer by his father's folly.

He was only twelve years old, but had already gone to Saint Andrews, as he did not get on with Morton's children, and only his tender-hearted cousin, Margaret, would take his side against them. Also he had shown himself old beyond his years; and now this letter was to prove it damnably in the eyes of his fellows. Someone of his college made a copy of it and stuck it up in the banqueting hall, with an additional note, asking everyone to send round the hat and subscribe a few shillings (Scots) for the poor little starveling. And wherever he went, he heard chanted behind him the ancient prayer against his race:

> " From the greed of the Campbells,
> Good Lord, deliver us ! "

Even the loyalty of his own clan was slightly shaken. This lad to be MacCaillan Mhor, the greatest of the Highland chieftains, and lead his clan into battle? Why, he was a cringing clerk, who put more faith in a legal bond than in the fighting power of his men to defend his patrimony!

He understood the situation, and they did not; that only added to his bitterness. Brains then counted for nothing. Any good-looking swaggerer could get appreciation and applause, but not he.

And so it was in love. At nineteen he went to Court in England, he was kindly received by the new King Charles, who arranged a splendid match for him with his own cousin. But the Lady Elizabeth Stuart eloped on the eve of the wedding, with an attractive but penniless fellow,—she preferred a crooked sixpence to a crooked man, people said, laughing,—and back went the slighted lover, to marry his faithful cousin, Margaret Douglas, within four months of the injury. But all her tenderness for him could not wipe it out.

There were furious disputes with his father over money, and the allowances to be made to his step-brothers at college, and the dowries to his step-sisters. Archibald complained that he had been neglected, he had not been consulted; his half-brother James treated him like a stranger; his kind uncle and father-in-law, Morton, like a slave; he would not put up with such contempt.

King Charles himself took his side; he won every point, and was made guardian to the rest of his family, instead of his Papist father. But let King Charles expect no gratitude for that, said the angry old Argyll. He knew his son, and though Charles had helped him, that would not prevent his doing the King an ill turn; for he added the miserable indictment,—" he can love no man."

This then was the Campbell who had won the silver medal for archery six years before James Graham, Earl of Montrose, did so, when only in his second year at college.

The winners had their own medals made; the Campbell's, with the galley of Lorne on its coat of arms, now hung in the porter's lodge; where Jamie was determined his too would hang when he had left college,—and he would have his made much bigger.

He won it; and commemorated his victory with an uproarious supper party, at which songs were sung and toasts were drunk, and the only flaw was that he had to ask Archibald Campbell, Lord Lorne, as he was up at Saint Andrews for the moment on an admonishing visit to his young step-brother, James Campbell, whom he kept painfully short of pocket-money, and lectured as though he were his uncle,—so that gay lad complained, who had none of his youthful guardian's priggish inclination to ' swat ' as he called it, using a Saxon word long obsolete, though still preserved like a fly in amber in schoolboy slang. But he had good wits, and when Montrose asked him to the supper party, he advised him to ask his step-brother, Lorne, as well, " or he might turn it against you,—he is sure to grudge your winning the medal, anyhow."

These were the last persuasions he should have used.

" Why should he grudge it me? He won it himself when he was up. Is he such a dog in the manger that no one can have what he has done with? "

" Yes," said James Campbell, rather comically, but Montrose

was rushing on that he did not care a farthing what Lorne might do against him,—he had never met the fellow, never wanted to, and certainly would not do so now, merely in order to propitiate the future head of the Campbells. They had been the hereditary enemies of his family,—and the present Lorne was nothing but an usurer. He lent people money and got them to mortgage their lands to him, did it even with his own brother-in-law, the Marquis of Huntly. Montrose would see the usurer damned before he asked him to supper,—and his peaked eyebrows knit.

James Campbell, who had learned diplomacy between a Papist father and a Presbyterian step-brother, regarded his heated young host with the eye of a watchful parrot,—then put it to him that he personally must not risk offending his guardian, and would be grateful if Montrose would ask him for his sake.

So Montrose did, and Lord Lorne came; and the two looked at each other across the low dark little room, where the candle-light shone on so many flushed and youthful faces, with the instinctive antagonism of dog and cat. A long, tallow-pale face, freckled only just under its straight red hair, looked with crooked and uncertain gaze at Montrose, "—and *which* eye is looking at me? " he asked himself in unreasoning annoyance. While the future Earl of Argyll, accustomed to dislike from childhood, knew at once how his hesitating speech, his cautious step, his tentative, self-conscious manner irritated Montrose.

As he watched this boy of fifteen, who had so quickly taken the place of a leader among his fellows,—who had already and so easily won the only honour in sport that he himself had ever obtained, and then after such obstinate efforts, Lorne felt his sense of the injustice done him more bitter than ever he had tasted it in all his injured life.

This boy's unconscious carriage of himself,—his happy certainty that he and all these good fellows round him were one and the same good fellow,—his freedom from any doubting, hesitating, hindering thoughts (—" thoughts are cripples, like myself," he discovered, with some satisfaction, for he sought his chief amuse-ment in his worst enemies, self-analysis and self-pity),—so might he himself have been, had he, like Montrose, been spoilt by an adoring family from his cradle,—instead of blighted by a cruel step-mother, a neglectful father, ungrateful brothers and sisters. His uncle and wife slid out of his mind, as always in these categories.

But in the folly of his company he found consolation. What he had cared for at college had been argumentative discussions lasting till far into the night. The present generation had plainly degenerated.

His oblique vision flickered with distaste over the flaunting scarlet curtains and all those bright embroidered cushions,—gifts from adoring sisters and other silly girls, no doubt. He was disgusted with the noisy rowdiness of the company, their idiotic songs, some of them feeblest doggerel, made up on the spur of the moment,—with the travelling tumbler and his performing dogs, ordered in from the town to amuse them, who made low jokes and stood on his head, and so did his dogs, in the middle of the table, and capered about among the wine-cups and flagons without upsetting them, but with such a clatter and a din that Lord Lorne's head nearly split with it.

Yet he would not be the first to slink away from the company. He dreaded what they would say of him as soon as his back was turned,—and his own brother, whose interests he guarded, would never stand up for him,—not he ! And still more than their unheard criticism, he dreaded the actual fact of going. How should he say good-bye? What compliments must he make to this new insolent young rival, who had won his own great distinction? And what hidden sneers would greet his congratulations, insincere as he now knew they would be?

So, miserably, self-consciously, he sat on, when,—horror upon horror! two pipers marched in and strutted up and down, magnificent as fighting cocks, while their music went wheedling and teasing through the room, swelling louder and louder; and all those boys and young men rushed to push back the table, upsetting cups and smashing bottles with as much delight as though this were the cleverest part of their performance, and started to leap into the air and utter shrill, inarticulate cries, and to dance up and down and round and round and in and out in an intricate pattern of good-fellowship,—and now there was no help for it, Lord Lorne had to show how out of it he was, for there was no reel nor round that he could dance.

"Now I *must* go," he thought, and tried to say the words aloud, but still stood uneasily in his corner, while the whirling of hot faces and flying curls and outflung arms and stamping feet and hoarse shouts against the fierce music of the pipes went whizzing on in front of him, ignoring him,—until Montrose suddenly stopped it by challenging all of them to see who could shoot the highest over Saint Salvator's tower.

Out they trooped into Butts Wyand with their bows and arrows,—and there stood the tower, vast and black in the moonlight, while the air blew cool on their cheeks after the stuffy heat of the crowded little room, and the noise fell into a hush as wide as the ends of the world. And in the friendly dark, Lorne got his chance to slip away.

Montrose did not see him go. He was shooting his arrow. All life, all thought, all effort left him in that instant, and became one with its soaring flight. High over the tower it rose, only just under the moon. It disappeared; and thought, released, came back to him, singing in his head.

He, too, slid away from the company, that was now capering like goblins in the moonlight at his superb shot; and he too went up to his empty room, but not to brood over his rival, as his rival was doing, for he had forgotten all about ' old Lord For-Lorne.'

He pulled out of its shelf the vellum-covered copy of Caesar's Commentaries that he had been reading that morning in discontent with this smaller, safer age in which he had to live; and wrote in the margin of the little book:

"Though Caesar's paragon I cannot be,
    Yet shall I soar in thought as high as he."

VIII

IT happened that some of the Saint Andrews citizens were passing in the street on their way home from a belated wedding party, on the night when young Montrose celebrated his victory as a marksman. As they went past Saint Salvator's, they were alarmed by three or four arrows that came whizzing down through the still, moonlit air, as though they had been shot from the top of the tower. The company scampered to their homes for safety, their footsteps thudding along the cobbled street, awakening terrified echoes of the old lawless days of raid and killing affray.

The ruined tower of the Cathedral, which had seen the town rise to murder the last of the Cardinals, looked grimly down on the citizens that fled from a prank of the scholars. Not till they were safe at home did they have breath or time or wit to discover that that was all it was. And it naturally only inflamed the rage of the Provost at the discovery that the high crown of his hat was neatly pierced by one of the arrows like a jaunty feather. He carried his complaints and demands for justice, together with his hat and arrow, to the Principal next day. The arrow was proved to belong to the young Earl of Montrose, who was ordered to make public apology and promises of future good behaviour.

He did so, hat in hand, in token of submission, but as he put it on again, it was seen that he had stuck an arrow through its crown; and so had all his fellows. The derisive fashion caused a riot between Town and Gown; and Montrose, as cause and leader of all the trouble, was sent down for a short time. In his absence, a new statute appeared in Saint Salvator's rule-book— viz. 'That students may not vie one with another in shooting arrows over the college tower.'

*　　*　　*

Montrose's many holidays were scattered widely over the country, so that he had a large choice of where to go in his disgrace.

There was excellent sport to be had with gun and fishing rod at Rossdhu on Loch Lomond, where he often stayed for weeks together; and Sir John would be sure to laugh his loud, rather determined laugh over his prank, and Lilias would croon murmurs of that flattering amusement that pretends to be shocked, and that little dare-devil Kat would envy and long to emulate.

Or, if he felt studious for a change, there was the best library in the country at Balcarres, where the gentle old Sir David Lindsay had pointed out to him no less than ten different works on the Philosopher's Stone, which must surely now, after all this modern research, be within an inch of its certain discovery.

And there were the six pretty, lively daughters of Lord Carnegie at Kinnaird; and all his cousins to the ninth and tenth degrees all over the country, who would rush out into their courtyards, proud and eager to welcome him with a stirrup cup of ale, and another for his horse,—for it was my young lord's arbitrary fancy that he would never dismount till his horse had been given as good as himself—" and see how well he carries it! " he would cry, as he caracoled round the courtyard.

Among all these indulging and admiring friends, Archie, Lord Napier, his chief guardian, was the person most inclined to disapprove of his escapades, and to be disappointed at their hindrance to his studies. Yet, rather oddly, it was to the Napiers' home at Merchiston just outside Edinburgh that he chose to go this time. He was, to tell the truth, a little tired of all his popularity and good-fellowship, which after all never gave a fellow any chance to be alone.

And every now and then through the fun of this latest bicker with authority, there had been a disturbing glimpse of the thrawn face and limp red hair of Archibald Campbell, Lord Lorne. He knew that his usual high hospitality had shown itself as little as possible with Lorne; irritated by his presence, he had done his best to ignore it,—with the result that he had been uneasily conscious of it from time to time ever since.

Now he wanted to be with his sister Margaret and Archie Napier, even though they made him feel a child again. He slept, as he had always done, in the little room above the battlements, where years ago Archie Napier's learned father had invented logarithms. So strange a pursuit had given the room the name of the magician's chamber, and some of the female servants were afraid to go down the three huge stone steps that led into it. But Jamie felt it more his room than any in his own castles. He could see Arthur's Seat from it, like a crouching lion, and the jagged outline of Edinburgh Castle cut sharp against the sky. When the King came to Scotland, he would ride with him out of that castle, down the long mile to Holyrood, and see him crowned.

Napier helped him with his mathematics, and bought a swine's bladder solely for the purpose of trying a mathematical conclusion, which made the hated study surprisingly interesting. He took him hunting and shooting; and in the evening, as they sat in the room with the carved ceiling that was always called Queen Mary's room, Napier told old stories to him and his own children, of Wallace and of Bruce, or, older still, of King Arthur and his knights, who sleep even now in full armour, hidden within those three hills, the Eildons, that rise so suddenly by the river Tweed, until they shall hear the bugle that will awaken them to life.

" But that bugle," he said, " will only be blown when Scotland again has need of them."

" Then why was it not blown at Falkirk or on Flodden Field? " asked Jamie.

" I do not know," said Napier, " but the time had not come, and they still sleep, and it is time now for you to go and do the same, if you are going to get up at dawn to go duck-shooting to-morrow."

Jamie picked himself up from the sheep-rug on the floor as reluctantly sleepy as his very small nephew who had gone off hours ago; he wished that, since he had to go to sleep, he might do so as Sir Launcelot had done by the water called Mortoise, ' awaiting the adventure that should be sent to him.'

" What adventure will be sent to me? " he asked himself, as he said good-night to his brother-in-law and his sister; and she bade him good dreams, and he, good sport next morning,—their faces smiling at him like the reverse sides of a coin, so much at one did they appear to be, and yet so different; for his was long and fine, shaped like a fir-cone with its pointed beard and the domed forehead that spread smoothly up from his arched eyebrows; and hers was tender and rather tired, with irregular lines and angles running here and there in it, which no one who knew her noticed.

She was sitting in the wide window-seat that ran inwards at an angle to the window, looking out over the orchards and farm buildings; the late evening light of summer still clung about that corner, so that her head showed dark against it, bent over her loom. She was weaving fine white linen, a favourite occupation of hers, and this a favourite pattern,—" the hundred rose knot," she called it.

" What is it you are making? " Jamie asked idly, as excuse to linger.

" A pillow-case for your marriage bed," she told him, putting up her face to kiss him, " I shall have at least a dozen ready for you by the time you are seventeen."

*   *   *

He knew he would probably marry by then, before going abroad to finish his education at Rome or Padua; it was the correct procedure that he, the head of his house, should provide it with an heir before he saw the world. But it was not till the marriage of his sister Dorothea to Sir James Rollock of Duncruib that he knew who it was that he himself would marry.

Dorothea's wedding took place, as Margaret had promised, after the two years of waiting; and her young brother opened his castle of Kincardine again for the early days of the wedding festivities; then moved the whole house party on to his house at Old Montrose, near to the little harbour and fishing village of Montrose on the broad estuary of the South Esk. This was not very far up the east coast from Saint Andrews, and within four miles of Kinnaird Castle, the home of Lord Carnegie, who had been a close friend of the late Earl of Montrose.

So that those of Carnegie's daughters who were not married at too great a distance (like Catherine, who was Lady Traquair now, and down at the Court in London), or who were not already staying with one or other of the Graham sisters (like Marjory and her husband, William Haliburton of Pitcur, who had come over with Lilias and Kat from Rossdhu), rode out every day by the path that had been built up through the bog, and met the party from Old Montrose for hunting or hawking over the flat uplands, or sailing at high tide over the smooth waters of the estuary.

Here it was, in the placid landscape of her home, a landscape of grass and water and waving rushes, with the hills no more than a blue line in the distance, that Jamie grew aware of Magdalen Carnegie, and knew that she would be his wife.

She was the youngest, some said the best-looking, and certainly the quietest of the Carnegies. As an infant she used to sit by the hour together in her favourite shelter under the table, silently nursing some stump of wood or scrap of leather which she had chosen to represent the glories of the universe; and her big brothers and five elder sisters and whichever of the elder Graham sisters who happened to be with them, would duck their heads under the table, calling her, coaxing her. But not all their imperious affection could dislodge her; if anyone used force she would yell and kick; nor did she allow anyone to caress her but their nurse. Before she could walk, she made her own world, and hoarded her secret treasure.

She grew older, and " like a heron " her sisters told her, for her head and nose and legs were all rather long; but her deep-set eyes were very large and blue under their black lashes, and her arched eyebrows, which had given her a deceptively plaintive look in childhood, thickened and darkened in effective contrast to the clear pallor of her face. A lily of the valley hiding beneath its leaves, was the comparison made by prospective suitors when she reached her teens. She was a little younger than the Earl of Montrose, who now swept down on his neighbouring house, and filled it with gay company for his sister's wedding.

He had given a grand house-warming last year at Kincardine

to celebrate his succession to the title; now he must glorify this occasion. Without telling anyone why, he suddenly rode off one day to Edinburgh, and all to get presents of necklaces and embroidered gloves for each of his sisters. His page, Willy, protested that he could have got them, but that would never do, for he might not have chosen the colours right,—blue and green for Margaret, and carnation for Lilias, and mulberry for Dorothea, and orange tanny for Kat, and cramoisy for Beatrix. There were slighter gifts too for the rest of the girls in the party,— silver buttons and painted Italian boxes and plaits of ribbons hung with little bells.

Back he came with his presents, and stood in the hall with the girls all crowding round him, circling and swooping and shrilling over their spoils—" like a pack of silly seagulls," cried Kat, suddenly swerving out of the group.

Her brother came up to her with her present,—" orange tanny for you, Kat, because your hair is so dark."

She had brought him too out of the group, to where she stood apart,—erect, alert, ready for anything. She ran one hand up through her hair as he spoke of it, and it crackled, and sparks came out of it, as when she brushed it the wrong way. She held up the necklace in her other hand, a little stream of orange light between her fingers; and laughed and said she did not care for jewels, and never would wear gloves,—she would rather have a new riding whip—and suggested in her casual way that Jamie should transfer her present to Magdalen, and dropped it in his hand again, and ran off, singing.

" What can be the matter with her? " asked Margaret, and Lilias shrugged her shoulders and murmured that she was always being difficult. So ungracious too, when the poor lad——

They were all looking at the ' poor lad,' wondering anxiously what he would say or do to show his anger. But he only stood looking after her for an instant, and then as he turned, he saw Magdalen; his face flushed, he hesitated, then said with grave, boyish dignity, " I would like to give you her present, but you will not want to take it now."

Magdalen did not want to, but neither did she want to hurt his feelings by a second refusal. She took his jewel in her hands, and the colour flooded her pale face. They were both angry with Kat, it was a strange thing to illumine their passive, childish acceptance of each other, with the possibility of future passion. She wished the Grahams did not matter so much to each other. *Her* brothers would never mind the rudeness of a younger sister, except to reprove and punish such intolerable manners. But then her brothers would never ride off for three days to choose their sisters' presents. The Grahams all thought each other too important.

It was a flash of prescient jealousy, but it was also a warning of the unwilling adoration that she was to suffer, when it would seem to her that all other people led safe, enviable lives, because they did not love Jamie.

IX

*T*HAT evening she sat by his hearth, wearing the fiery jewel that he had given Kat; and knew that he was looking at it, and at her.

All the party from Kinnaird were staying the night, for as there was no moon, the path would not be safe by night over the bog; and the beds were large enough to hold two or three extra occupants apiece.

Lord Carnegie's eldest son was with them. He had lately returned from six years at the university at Padua, transformed from a slight youth into a swarthy, stalwart stranger, with a decisive nose.

His forcible manner and downright speech, giving only the briefest answers to all the questions on his travels, made him the most dominating person now in the wedding party; it made Sir John Colquhoun feel guilty that he had never travelled, and Lilias anxious as to whether Italian women were more attractive than Scots; it made Jamie burn to prove himself a man, and Magdalen all the more uneasily conscious of Jamie's impulsive nature.

She was thankful that her brother's keen black eyes had not watched their childish follies that afternoon; and she grew hot with shame for Jamie when Beatrix, with the indiscriminating pride of a younger sister, insisted on telling David Carnegie all about her brother's college escapade of shooting over the tower and wearing an arrow in his hat. Even at twelve years old, Beatrix should know better than to try and impress this man of the world with such silly schoolboy mischief. She thought he had a harsh, contemptuous air as he gave one glance at the new young Earl of Montrose, then turned to talk politics with Willy's father, old Sir Robert of Morphie, while the pipes spun and shrilled their indefatigable music, and the young people danced reels,—Beatrix with young Drummond of Madertie, Magdalen with Montrose.

When they were tired out they flung themselves down on

44

benches, stools, and the few high carved chairs, into a brief pool of quiet, broken only by Sir Robert's plodding voice, saying— " The young king does not know his own country, that is the whole trouble. Once he comes up for his coronation in Scotland, we will settle the matter,—we will show him it is no use to think he can do what he likes about the church tithes."

" Poor king," said Lilias to David Carnegie, " I thought kings could do what they liked."

" Only in England," he answered her.

" That is true," said Sir Robert. " The Tudors were a bad education for kings. Here in Scotland we have always known how to deal with them."

" By murdering them, usually," said a sweet girlish voice, which was not at once traced to Kat. Sir John applauded her with his loud laugh. Jamie turned impatiently away, his resentment with her flaming up in a hot desire to express scorn for something or somebody, it did not much matter what.

" The English have always been slaves," he said. " They are used to being conquered by other nations,—now they change their religion whenever their sovereign tells them to."

" That has ceased to be true," said Carnegie curtly.

The boy bit his lips, seeking a retort that would not sound too rude from a host, but before he could find it, Sir John snatched his opportunity to rush into the conversation.

" The church tithes have been our property for generations———"

' Property '—' tithes '—Magdalen had noticed that no other two words in the language had such power to stir the company. She had also noticed her brother's tone to Jamie, and the boy's angry look in return. Men talked politics, but they thought other things behind them.

Before David had gone to Padua, Jamie had given him the silent worship of nine years old. Why should David snub him now? Jamie was as good at sport as David had been, and better. He had won the archery medal for Saint Andrews. His college friends here, Wigton and the lively Kilpont and the studious Madertie, all adored him. Her father liked to tease him, with

that attentive chaff that elder men so often use to cloak their
admiration for a brilliantly promising youngster. Her mother loved
and petted him.   Her sisters treated him with friendly superiority, to show they recognized that he was too young for them
matrimonially,—an attitude that Magdalen wished in vain to copy.

She was not really at ease with him, but then she was not often
that with anybody.

She was glad when the talk ceased, and the travelling minstrel,
or Dusty-foot, came forward with his harp, and the scattered
company spread out into a wide semi-circle round the fire.

The gnarled logs lay piled on the hearth, hoarily encrusted with
lichen, grey-green, primaeval, like monsters that had survived
another age; their red-hot noses met together, pointing into the
flames, they blazed and roared, hissed and spat out showers of
burning sparks; they sucked all the air in the room into a dozen
draughts that blew out the curtains from the shuttered windows
and whistled up the great chimney; whirlpools of white wood ash
fluffed out and danced in feathery, fan-shaped patterns over their
surface.

There, in the glow of the candlelight,

> "And the charcoal burning red,"

the faces of the company, turned towards the harpist, heard the
story of the wife whose former lover came back after seven years
and enticed her away from her husband and children, telling her
how

> "I'll show where the white lilies grow
> On the banks o' Italie."

So off they went in his ship,

> "With mariners and merchandise
> And music on every hand,"

but they had not sailed a few leagues from the shore when a
frightful storm sprang up, and the face of the lover changed to
that of the devil, and he stood over the poor woman as high as

the mast of the ship, and with a shriek of splitting wood the ship
was rent in two, and she heard his voice mocking her:

> " I'll show where the white lilies grow
> In the bottom o' the sea."

The harp crashed through the close of the nightmare to a
sudden, unearthly silence. Dorothea screamed, and said she would
be afraid to go to sleep to-night for what she might dream; but
her bridegroom whispered to her and made her smile.

Dark and intent, Kat's eyes, alone among those of the girls,
showed no fear, but resolve.

Then Margaret asked for something with a happy ending; and
Jamie called for the ballads he liked best; and the harp twanged
a gay answer, and the harpist's voice rang out in the tale of some
bold ruffian whom his friends had loved. Back they bore him in
triumph on their shoulders from the English prison whence they
had rescued him, chaffing him about his weight, as he chaffed
them about the roughness of his steeds, until they had placed him
again by his own fireside, and there knocked the fetters from
his wrists, and

> " ' Now Jock my billie,' quoth a' the three,
> ' The day is come thou wast to dee,
> But thou's as weel at thy ain ingle-side,
> Now sitting I think 'twixt thee and me.' "

Jamie's voice had joined in the last verse, Madertie's and
Kilpont's with him. What a happy ending was that, to sit at
your own fireside with your friends all round you, on the day
you had been condemned to hang! What friends, what triumph
of courage and loyalty and laughter, equally ready with a joke to
greet the hangman, had he called for him that morning instead
of his rescuers! They were bad times, those of the Border raids,
—all the older men said what a good thing it was that they had
passed away,—but then what great-hearted friendships they had
bred, what things worth living for, more than life itself!

For like all youth that lives intensely, imaginatively, Jamie
could only think of life as a splendid thing when it was disregarded,

and cast away. And so the happy or the unhappy ending
made little odds to him, whether the raid or the day's hunting
ended by the hero's fireside, or with—

> " Now Johnnie's gude bend bow is broke
> And his gude grey dogs are slain,
> And his body lies dead in Durrisdeer,
> And his hunting it is done."

" That is how it will be one day," thought Magdalen, " he will
die and lie under the earth."

But she saw that even though he sang it, he did not believe
it,—who could believe it, who looked as he did now?

The music ceased, releasing her from that flash of troubled
fancy. A spell had been broken, people were talking, telling
queer tales to cap the ballad-monger's marvels.

Witches had sailed on the sea in sieves on the eve of the late
King Jamie's wedding; they had danced on the shore at North
Berwick, led by a black-haired girl, playing on a jew's-harp.
No one had ever made a ballad about that. No one had dared.

A schoolmaster a few years ago had loved the sister of one of
his pupils, and had promised the boy never to birch him for the
rest of his schooling, if he would but bring him three hairs from
his sister's head. But the cunning boy, suspecting mischief, yet
anxious to close with so good a bargain, brought instead three
hairs from a heifer's tail. On these hairs the poor schoolmaster
wrought a love charm, so that the heifer pranced after him everywhere, even to the church door, leaping and dancing upon him,
to the scandalized amazement of the congregation.

They all laughed at that, and Jamie said that it was a pity
old Forrett had never fallen in love with Kat, or they might
have tried the experiment on him.

" Queer tales," said Sir John Colquhoun a trifle portentously
as he stirred his punch, " you all tell queer tales, but they
are none of 'em as queer as what my man, Carlippis, could
tell you."

And he summoned his servant forward within the fire-lit circle, with a snap of his plump, well-kept fingers, and a " What are you doing back there in the shadow, you rascal? "

" Looking at my young lord's books," said the man, shutting a great tome upon the shelf as he came forward.

And instantly Jamie knew that it was his Sir Walter Raleigh's *History of the World* that Carlippis had been looking at ; it was the only book of that size that he always troubled to bring back with him from college, for he would have it with him wherever he went, it was his talisman against defeat or depression or minds like Carlippis',—not that he knew this, any more than he knew defeat, depression or Carlippis' mind,—only that when he heard the heavy sound of the book shutting, and knew that Carlippis had been grasping it with his spread hands, peering into it with those little eyes enclosed in fat, he wanted to tear it from him, kick him out of the room, choke him round the throat till those eyes goggled.

He half rose, not knowing what he would do in his rage, he had time only to say, " You have been looking at my Raleigh! " and then Colquhoun said pleasantly, " Yes, tell us of Raleigh."

And then Carlippis was talking. His fierce and restless mind disguised itself in a bitter-tasting good-humour. It found in all men something to laugh at; it found in all deeds, heroic or terrible, virtuous or vicious, the little grain of commonplace, the trivial motive of vanity or self-distrustfulness or fear, which linked the doer of them with one's most shamefaced thoughts, or with those of any schoolboy who is anxiously striving to show off.

Was Sir Walter Raleigh really one of the greatest men that ever lived? Carlippis, who knew everybody, had once, long ago, seen the superb adventurer at Court. That story of his throwing his pearl-embroidered cloak in the mud for the old English Queen to tread on,—that showed the man all over—the servile gesture that was yet magnificent, like the fawning caress of a wild beast. " But to see that, you should have seen the man, the great shoulders, the long nervous hand of the adventurer,—and then the earrings, the rosebud mouth to please the women,—but then the eyes—of a startled hare! Does he not write of ' Death that

D

doth pursue us and hold us in chase from our infancy?' That was himself, longing, but not daring to glance back at his pursuer. Even a Court painter could not conceal it; he has painted him afraid,—as he has painted himself in the preface to this book you read so often, my lord, the book he wrote in prison, and would have dedicated to Prince Henry, in the hope that his young highness would get him freed, since he liked to come and listen to his travellers' tales, to glance at his scribbling. But his young patron died on him,—and there he was, a rat in a trap, walking up and down the Tower grounds, and hearing the men calling to each other in the dockyards below, at their work on the new ships that he would never sail,—and going in again to write into his preface fresh praises of the infinite justice and clemency of that merciful monarch who kept him mewed up there. All to what purpose? That the merciful monarch, King James, should at long last strike off his head, as a pretty compliment to the Spanish ambassador."

The magic of that deep, foreign-sounding voice, guttural yet musical, snapped off in a brittle sharpness, as though that were the end of the life of man, even of the greatest,—a contemptuous flick of the finger of fate.

But Jamie could not endure to admit it. Envy, not pity, was his tribute to Raleigh. In that very same preface wherein Raleigh had made his piteous bid for life, was a passage that Jamie had never known he had by heart till now, when he found himself saying it aloud, while all those listening, wondering faces turned towards him:

" ' Only those few black swans I must except, who behold death without dread, and the grave without fear—and embrace both, as necessary guides to endless glory.' "

" Who said that? " and—" Jamie, who is that? "

" The true Raleigh," he replied, a little shamefacedly, not daring to glance at Carnegie.

Yes, Raleigh, despite his apprehensions, had been one of these ' few black swans.' Above all earthly ambitions Jamie prayed that he too might prove to be another.

But how grave the company had grown, and—" can you not tell us of something more cheerful, Carlippis? " asked Lilias.

And at once he gave them something more cheerful, gave of good measure, broad and running over. Had her ladyship heard the latest gossip of the fair young Queen of France, whom everyone called Anne of Austria? The Duke of Buckingham had fallen madly in love with her, but Queen Anne's Spanish etiquette had made her excessively prudish, until lately, in a garden at Amiens——

In that icy room, where the draught blew under their chairs and froze their heels even as they roasted their toes at the fire, the garden at Amiens grew before their eyes,—the scent of jasmine and of orange trees in tubs, the music, the coloured lights in the warm darkness, the titters and whispers of faithless maids of honour, the shriek of a frightened queen, the strong English oaths of the Duke of Buckingham, discovered, dishevelled, enraged.

There was a touch of insolent contempt in the agility with which Carlippis' mind leaped down to the level of that of his mistress and gave this tit-bit from the outer world. So might a great ape leap to the lower branch of its tree and offer its discarded nut-shells. His splayed features, widening yet further in a mechanic grin, the expansive gestures of his broad hands, on which the thick red hairs glistened in the light of the fire,—here indeed was the servility of the wild beast, of which Carlippis himself had spoken. But with it was the scorn that belongs, not to beast, but to devil.

His little light eye flicked out from under the red lid and round his company, and in that cold flame each one seemed to have withered a little. Even David Carnegie's silent disapproval of the scandal, of this glib, insolent fellow of Colquhoun's, made no good case for virtue, so sagging and sullen was his expression.

Kat alone of the company seemed unaffected by Carlippis,—did not even listen. She sat on a cushion, clasping her knees; she never stirred; nor laughed; nor looked up when the others spoke. The firelight on her pale face made it like a cameo carved in amber; it turned her dark hair to copper, and the shadows in her green dress into rivulets of purple and black; the dress flowed out into a circle round her; it might have been an enchanted circle, imprisoning her, removing her from their company.

So had she sat and stared at the fire as a child, sphinx-like, remote, yet not quite like this. Jamie forgot his anger with her in a sudden apprehension. She must not sit so still,—too still. He leaned forward and touched her on the shoulder. She did not start at his touch, but raised her eyes, and for an instant he looked into their bright, blank gaze.

" You stare so hard you are squinting," he said. It was what they had told her as a child, but it was not true at the moment, and he said it only because her gaze made him uncomfortable, and he wished to force some expression into it. But it did not alter, and he added, " You have not heard one word."

" I heard the sounds." And suddenly she laughed, the eyes flashed, the whole face seemed to open, widen, soften. The spell was broken, she was there again. " Carlippis is my musician," she said, " I have no need to listen to what he says."

And as the servant bowed his mocking gratitude to her, once again there was that disconcerting glimpse as of a primitive beast, for all his superior subtlety, holding them under his red and hairy paw, condescending to pretend at playfulness the while he waited to use them for what he wished.

Then the music began again, the music of the gayest dances and the saddest songs in the world; it went on until even this company had at last to go to bed.

X

DAVID CARNEGIE hurried the rest of the family home at an early hour the next morning, because he must walk all round the policies with his father, who wished to consult him on the new gardens he was planting. Their young host, who did not know how early they were leaving, was not down to say good-bye,—surprisingly for him, since he had been out each morning earlier than any of them, to fly his hawks over the uplands above the marsh. But just this morning he was late,— " it *would* be so," thought Magdalen, watching her brother's contemptuous glance at Mungo Graham, as he came running into the hall with apologies for his lordship, who had been rather sick in the night, explained the page.

" Over-eaten himself," was Carnegie's comment, somewhat justified by the weeks of feasting and over-exertion and excitement of the festivities.

Magdalen rode back to Kinnaird beside her brother. It was pleasant to see her father waiting for them, full of plans about his orchards. Years of peace and prosperity and settled home life would be necessary to bring them to maturity; he could count on them, for he had always had them. His confidence in the future had expressed itself in the planting of a rare silver fir which would take more than a century to reach its full growth. And there were the three young ash trees that his children had irreverently named Adam and Eve and Samuel.

" Why Samuel, and not the Serpent? " Magdalen had asked as a child, and was told not to bring the devil into *this* garden.

Round the new gardens, that were being banked up out of the surrounding marsh, she walked in the wake of her father and brother,—an obedient girl, moving as softly as one of the fawns in the park, in and out of the spring sunshine and the shadows of the trees, slender, silent, attentive to the weighty masculine pronouncements on the property,—thankful that for this once they did not mention the tithes question.

Old Daniel Muschet, the gardener, joined the peregrination; solemn as a church ceremonial of the old days, they proceeded over the holy ground. ' Honour thy father and mother that thy days may be long in the land which the Lord thy God giveth thee.' This it was to be safe, to be settled, to be firmly planted in the soil,—wild soil, reclaimed from the bog, which was once useful only in warfare, as a defence from invaders. That was why Kinnaird Castle had been built here in the old evil days.

Wars with England, or civil wars, they were all over; even family feuds and killing affrays had practically ceased since all the laws passed in the last reign; only the Highland clans were still untamed, and carried on their lawless raids upon their neighbours. But that was in the mountains, and here at Kinnaird, only a wave of blue on the horizon marked their outposts.

From there, along the Grampians, right across Scotland, from that great loch that lay at the beginning of the Western Highlands, the young Earl of Montrose came riding when he had been staying at Rossdhu, where lived his sister Kat, and that man, Carlippis. Kat, Carlippis, Jamie himself—there was something disturbing to Magdalen in each of these. . . . Perhaps her brother was right not to take to Montrose; he was generally right. He belonged here to the plains, and Montrose to the hills; you never knew what he would do next.

Now they had nearly reached the rise in the ground, covered with scrub and bushes and wind-twisted thorn trees, where Montrose had always ridden and waved in signal on his way to the uplands, to see if any from Kinnaird would join his party at hawking. But to-day there was no horse standing on the hill, and no scarlet scarf waving like a banner in the breeze,—and that although he had not been down to say good-bye to them. But you never knew what he would not do next.

And when she looked at his necklace, chosen to match Kat's tawny eyes, she wished she had not worn it,—she would not wear it again,—nor share his presents nor anything else with Kat.

It was a pleasant encouragement to her resolve, to remember that young Ogilvy, the Master of Airlie, was riding up from

Saint Andrews to pay them a visit of some days. He was one of the admirers of the Carnegie sisters in general who had begun to concentrate his attentions on the youngest,—so that there had even been some talk of his hopes from his father, the Earl of Airlie, to Lord Carnegie. Here then was an offering indubitably Magdalen's very own, not to be shared with her sisters, nor with his. She awaited it with a pleasant sense of the balm to be laid upon her injured vanity, which no one could have guessed who saw her calm demeanour.

But young Ogilvy did not arrive that day, as expected; nor the next. Later they heard that his horse had stumbled while crossing a river, swollen by the April rains, and that he had had a ducking. Young Ogilvy was a self conscious youth; horsemanship was his most tender spot; he had on a new suit of black velvet, which was ruined; and he could not face the laughter of the sisters. The grave and gentle Magdalen would not laugh, he thought,— but the others. He shuddered in spirit as well as body, and returned to Saint Andrews, where he had a bad cold.

" But why did the young fool not come on up to Kinnaird and get dried? " asked Lord Carnegie.

" I would have given him a brandy and black currant posset that would have snipped off his sneezes before ever they began," said Lady Carnegie.

" And I would have lent him my new rose-coloured dress to wear while his fine mourning suit was drying," said her daughter, Agnes.

" Whatever should he come courting for in black? " asked Agnes' sister, Elizabeth.

" To show he could have been faithful unto death, if only he had been drowned," said their youngest sister, in a voice so small and still it was almost a whisper.

The others were delighted that that little mouse Magdalen could laugh herself at her silly young lover. Who would have thought she had it in her? They repeated what she had said; Magdalen tried to stop them, but it was too late, and her sarcasm soon reached the Master of Airlie, whose streaming cold now had a fresh bitterness added to its salty rheum. He recovered within two or three days, but did not ride again to Kinnaird; and now Magdalen felt far more bitterness against herself than she had uttered in that first impulse of annoyance against her suitor.

" I shall always say things I am sorry for," she had discovered. And added to this came a fresh discovery,—that of her injustice to the young Earl of Montrose, who must have been really ill on the morning of their departure from his house, for no sooner had he returned to Saint Andrews than he had fallen very ill indeed,—not with just a cold, like that silly sulking young Ogilvy, but with first one doctor and then another, at double the fee of the first, (the worst possible sign), and then a barber to cut off all his long curling hair, close to his head, because of the fever.

And it took so long to get news, and her father, the only one who noticed she was more pensive than usual, told her not to pine for that foolish young puppy, Ogilvy, (when she had quite stopped thinking of him), for he would get her the best match in Scotland; and by his smile and indulgent shake of the head she knew he meant Montrose,—but what was the use of promising her Montrose, when nobody knew how he was getting on, or if he ever thought of her, as he lay there tossing in his bed?

But at last there came news from the factor at Old Montrose that my lord must be sitting up, for he had sent for his chessboard and packs of cards, and had ordered trout from his river at Kincardine to be sent to him, for none of the doctors had known how to cure him until he had told them to order him aleberry and claret and his own trout.

Whereupon Magdalen in her relief remarked drily that Montrose seemed altogether too cock-a-hoop to have been really ill, but her mother (who never ceased lamenting the loss of the boy's lovely shining locks) ran herself in indignant refutation to the kitchens, to prepare a great jar of chicken and calves-foot jelly from her own particular recipe, that she might send it back by my lord's servant to Saint Andrews.

Fruit and flowers and eggs and cream and wine and jellies,

presents of all these things came showering in on the popular patient, where he lay sick to death of convalescence. Nearly three weeks he had lain there in his room that looked on to the street; it had been May when he fell ill, and now it was June, and summer was slipping on past him, and he not there to enjoy it; and there had been something he wanted to tell Magdalen Carnegie, but before he could do that, there was something that he must say to his sister Kat, and at first it had all been clear in his head what he was to say to them both, but it grew less and less clear as his head grew hotter and the room buzzed round him more and more rapidly. That had stopped now, but his head was empty, he had forgotten what he had wanted to say.

Down below his window, carts rattled over the cobbles, horses neighed and stamped, clanking their harness, voices called to each other in the burring, unhurried tones of the Lowland Scot. Often when he woke, he lay for an instant, unsure of his condition, not knowing why he felt so slack, so disinclined to jump out of bed, until the heavy pad, pad of a football and the shouts of boys at their impromptu game in the street below, reminded him that he was ill, that he could not get up, he could not play.

He opened his eyes once again on that slightly crooked new curtain, that had been hung across the window since his illness, and had become an irritating symbol of it. The curtain moved only a little in the draught, but to his fevered imagination it was bouncing and fidgeting, and the voices of the boys below in the street surged up and filled his ears with a confused drumming sound.

A queer little scene came into his head that he had imagined, or else had quite forgotten. He was first of all standing in the orchard at Rossdhu (and this he had done a hundred times) when the apple-blossom had just begun to sprout in tight rosy buds on the gnarled grey trees, and the blue of the loch shone behind them. Cow-parsley and buttercups grew in the long grass; and the twisted shadows of the branches lay very faintly across it. He was waiting for Kat, but she did not come, so he went back into the house, and without thinking why, he turned towards the west turret and went up the narrow winding stair and into the little round room at the top of it that had been given to Carlippis for use as a study in his experiments in chemistry.

There stood that gross man, leaning over a small table that was crowded with objects; his fat hands moved dexterously among them, his under lip was sucked in, his red bushy eyebrows met together in a frown of intent absorption. Behind him stood Sir John Colquhoun, for once remarkably still. The pale last rays of the sun slanted in at the window, and lay across the edge of the table, lighting up three short dark curling hairs.

This scene now presented itself so vividly in Jamie's mind that it became clear enough to wonder what had happened next, or if indeed any of this could actually have happened,—for how could he ever have come to forget it?

Nevertheless, when he was well, he forgot it again, so that years afterwards when it stood again in his mind, he could not be sure that it was not only a dream of his delirium.

XI

MONTROSE was not yet seventeen, Magdalen Carnegie a few months younger, when they became betrothed in the easy effortless fashion in which such matters were arranged among a host of other important matters. For he was back again at college, winning more medals and silver arrows at sport, and losing his money at billiards,—and acting as Lord of Misrule in the holidays in a Christmas play at Balcarres, where he led the whole company on hobby-horses, improvised out of broomsticks and painted cloths, playing on drums, and on trumpets made of cows' horns, and whistles of elder stems, led them through the house and into the church and churchyard, where the villagers waited to offer him ale and cheese and cakes, and the company crowned him with silver paper, and then chased him back into the house, tore his crown from him, his bells and his ribbons, and cried that he was deposed.

For it was the law of Misrule that its Lord, chosen for a day, should be condemned at the end of it; so had the Boy Bishops, in the days of the old religion, led the tomfoolery in the church, and been kicked out at the end; so had the appointed victim of a still older religion been crowned and hung with garlands as king and god, and sacrificed in grim earnest at the end; so now did the young Earl of Montrose, after leading his merry company on his wild-goose chase, bend his neck before his page, Mungo Graham, to be executed with a sausage.

And from Balcarres he came to Kinnaird, and he and Magdalen ate their Twelfth Night cake together, searching in it for the tokens that would tell them their future,—a bean for a king, a clove for a knave, a rag for a slut,—which of these things would they become?

Now, among all these activities, matrimony presented itself, but not startlingly. He was so intimate with the Carnegie family that Magdalen seemed to him very much like one of his own sisters, whom he did not know quite as well as them, only because she talked less. But since their betrothal, which happened without their quite knowing how, and had more to do with their guardians than themselves, she became more remote to him, rather than less; and he was suddenly shy of her as never before.

No one, least of all himself, knew what she thought of the matter; as of old, she guarded her secret treasure. But it was characteristic of that guardianship that the only thing she wanted from her betrothed was a portrait of himself; for then, she thought, wherever he went, she would always keep his image with her.

So Montrose rode to Aberdeen for a couple of sittings with Jamesone, since, luckily for the restless youth, the artist was a lightning portrait painter; and his cousin and curator, Sir Robert Graham of Morphie, told him to send the bill of £2, 4s. 5d. sterling in to him, and that would be his wedding present to the young couple.

And at Aberdeen, in the intervals between his sittings, in his wedding clothes, and buying new buckles for his spurs, and elegant new gloves of Spanish leather for his wedding, he was made a burgess of the city, entertained at a great banquet given in his honour, and had all the bells in the town ringing to greet him.

With the peal and clash of bells in his ears, he rode from one gay visit to another on that last week before his wedding, staying with his bride's relations,—Friday night with her married sister, Marjory Haliburton at Pitcur, and Saturday to Monday at Halkerton for an energetic week-end of hunting and shooting, and back to Montrose on the Monday for a couple of rounds of golf with Colquhoun, and on after them to stay that night in the Mearns with Sir Robert Graham of Morphie and his wife, who was Marjory's Aunt Euphemia, and would be Jamie's after to-morrow. For this was now the afternoon before his wedding day, a month after his seventeenth birthday.

*   *   *

Perhaps it was because Sir John Colquhoun pronounced Italian too well, or flourished his hands, or looked too eagerly for applause; but Jamie was never very happily at ease with him.

That Monday afternoon in early November on the rough sheep-nibbled turf above the town of Montrose, only widened the gulf between them—perversely so, for all the time Sir John seemed to be trying to lessen it, to treat his young brother-in-law as a fellow-man and a brother, perhaps even as his confidant.

The sun had not shone all day, and now there was a dark wind blowing, which did not clear the sky but sent dead leaves scurrying into the air, where the plovers whirled and harshly cried. The fore-caddie stalked ahead of them through the grey air to mark the next hole, a scarecrow figure with the gesture of an avenging prophet as he stopped and flung out his arm.

Jamie was playing with a slender spoon-faced wooden club, but Sir John, with his superior height, had chosen for his first club a long-shafted heavy 'putter-faced' bludgeon. He complained of its weight, that its face was not sufficiently lofted to grip the damp leather surface of his ball, which had skidded at his first stroke. Why could they not discover some way to make the surface rougher? He would speak to James Melville about it—a pretty thing it was for a man to have the monopoly of making golf balls, and never do anything to improve them!

"Yours are wet, that is all," said Jamie, who had bought a new lot in Montrose that morning. But Sir John had neglected to do that, and his had been drenched while playing in the rain two days ago, every feather in them was sodden, heavy as lead,— "How can a man hit a hatful of wet feathers?" he exclaimed in fury at the third hole, and disproved his words by swiping the ball off the toe of his club so that it sailed away to the right in an unfortunate curve that landed it right off the course in the deep heather among the whin bushes.

A lost ball meant a lost hole; Sir John tried to dispute it,— if the ball were struck into the water, the penalty, according to the most ancient rules of Aberdeen, was only a lost stroke,—and he held it more than likely that his ball had disappeared in that puddle over there, which the rain had enlarged into a pond. A game should be a game, not a contest with the unreasoning forces of nature. And when at the fifth hole (the whole course measured six) Jamie laid him a stymie, he coupled the unreasonable forces of nature with those of chance, and damned them together with the inclemency of this hideous climate, which alone could have bred such a barbaric and old-fashioned sport.

His long nose shone blue in the raw air; but Jamie, who had a good circulation, and never wanted a warming pan in his bed, like his luxurious sisters, was exhilarated by this sour wind whistling in his ears. He strode on in pursuit of his ball, while behind him, like the negligible croakings of a ruffled crow, Sir John's protests fluttered up against the wind, and by the wind were carried away — " Monstrous — damnation — may the curse of God——"

A few dead leaves raced past from the blown bushes, and ' *crash*—suck back and surge, surrrge forward, *crash*,' came the sound of the sea ahead of him. ' It is the Lord that ruleth the sea; the voice of the Lord is a glorious voice.'

He thought of Magdalen, silent among her chattering sisters, embroidering with them the blankets that had been woven in the cottages from the Kinnaird sheep and dyed scarlet and green,—scarlet for him and green for her, the sisters said, holding up before their laughing faces the enormous rugs of rough bright homespun wool that would lie on the great bed, made for them both. They sewed at clothes that were to make her yet more beautiful, for him. ' The king's daughter is all glorious within; her clothing is of wrought gold.'

Words from the Psalms and the Song of Solomon shouted in his heart and made it throb so that the blood stung his nostrils as though he were fighting. He thought of peacocks prancing before the gate of a sultan's palace, of their strut and pomp, the glitter and the rattle of their spread tails. ' Thy neck is as a tower of ivory. Thy two breasts are like two young roes that are twins, which feed among the lilies.'

" I am most damnably off my game," said Sir John.

" And balls at three pounds Scots a dozen," muttered Sir John's caddie, as he searched the whins in vain for yet another lost ball.

And having lost the match as well, Sir John went back with

his young brother-in-law to John Garn's for a drink; and they sat on a rough bench with their cap ale in wooden bowls, and smelt the peat smoke and the pig-styes behind the door, and saw the firelight leap on the rafters, and heard John Garn's opinion of the beastly and superstitious practice of surplices for the clergy; which interested Jamie, not in John Garn's opinion, but in the wild light it lit in his eye, transforming his heavy, animal face into that of a passionately thinking man.

But Sir John waved the tiresome fellow away, for he had only a few minutes now in which to say all he had not said on the links, and he had so much to say, so much good advice,—his young kinsman must not waste his life in dull domesticity, as he perhaps had wasted his; he must go about and see the world, go to England and get the ear of his King—or perhaps it would be best to wait for that till the King came up here to be crowned in Scotland, and *then* would be their chance—his and Jamie's— when the King would see them in their own place and all their native importance.

Jamie could not quite make out all the things that he must do, which were in some way to remedy the things that Sir John had left undone. For when Sir John inveighed against the dangerous sluggishness induced by matrimony, then he broke off in delighted envy of those very dangers.—" Oh! to be seventeen, and on the eve of your wedding, and your bride as young as you! "—how exquisite was youth in a woman, the freshness, the abruptness, the very crudities of youth so pure and absolute that one could hardly distinguish it from the youth of a boy, (" But Magdalen is not a bit like a boy," said Jamie, and was not heard) —the freedom, the gay courage, the passion for adventure— " You have no idea what a passion that can still be to some of us even in these days of money-grubbing and joint stock companies,"—and, yes, he would take another drink.

" Eating and drinking, the pleasures of the flesh, it is all we have left to us," he cried.

John Garn replenished his bowl with cappie, and made the severe remark that he had best not let the Lord overhear him.

But Sir John was talking far too hard to hear John Garn. He had discovered that it was the curse of this age to be unhappy; the old Church had been destroyed, and all the old guides and safeguards; people were left rudderless, blind, separated from God, all trying new things, each struggling with his own fate.

And by the time he had persuaded himself of the general unhappiness of modern man, he had made himself quite happy.

His nose now warmly purpling with the cappie, his eyes shining like dark plums, arrogant, self-conscious, he was well pleased with himself once again. The Black Cock o' the North, he had been nicknamed from his complexion;—" I've seen him practise his ' dark glances ' in the glass," the wicked Kat had once told Jamie.

But through all his florid and uneasy talk, it was odd how that important-looking face became blurred and as it were thrust aside by another, which was not there;—by a bloated, battered face, with a look of purposeful joviality, a bright light eye and round hard red cheeks, as though made of crudely painted wood, like a dummy set up as a cock-shy at a fair; and like that dummy, battered and buffeted, so that beneath all the jolly good-fellowship of its exterior show, one felt the disillusionment, the deadness of spirit.

So that Jamie, not listening to the rich dramatic voice of his brother-in-law, but remembering the face of his servant Carlippis, thought how sad sin was, though his thought found no words.

He rose and paid John Garn, as he had won the shillings they had laid on the match, and went to the door, and saw it was nearly dark. A bleak tree, already bereft of its leaves, tossed its spidery twigs against the torn black clouds. Magdalen would be sitting snug in the firelight at Kinnaird; perhaps she was looking at his portrait, which should have reached her by now. Suddenly he knew that he himself must visit her this evening, if only for one moment; he could not wait till to-morrow, when he would see her as his bride.

XII

HE rode over the dark and windy landscape, through the park gates, then pulled up sharply, seeing the crouched figure of the lame boy who held them back. He was as old as Jamie, but much smaller, for he was mis-shapen. Jamie leaped off his horse and handed him the reins.

"Hold him till I come back," he said; "that will make me come in time." He put six shillings with the bridle into Lame Tom's hand, and ran up through the little wood. Above the black network of the branches the sky still glimmered grey. Some big bird, probably a wood-pigeon, clattered through them, startling the still air; the sodden twigs and leaves crackled and squelched beneath his feet, the damp air clung to his face; he did not know if it were raining or not, he would not have known if it had been pouring.

All that talk just now, sound and fury, rolled out of his head,— and his golf, and the grouse shooting yesterday, and the stag hunt the day before, and the banquet at Aberdeen with all the speeches and toasts,—but not the bells, for they were still ringing in his head, ding *dong*, ding *dong*, and his heart was thumping in a loud, wild song, that seemed to break into a shout when he saw the lights of the castle.

Now he was inside it, and Magdalen before him, looking at him, speaking to him, showing him something, his portrait.

"Do you like it?" he asked.

"Yes."

"What have you been doing?" she asked.

"Nothing. You look so——"

"Yes?"

"Grave," he said, to tease her, for she had shown that she knew he was going to say, "so pretty," or was it, "so beautiful"?

But their laughter echoed into silence; an odd hush fell on them both; they who knew each other so well could find nothing to say, and stood as if enchanted. She was no longer somebody that he had known from childhood; she was a princess that he had rescued from her lonely tower; a white pillar of a ruined temple that he had found standing alone in the wilderness. For always there would be this touch of the austere and the desolate in his images of her beauty, always he would think of her as unattainable, —as she would always think of him.

So that she turned her eyes from him to his portrait, a possession so secure that it would outlast them both by hundreds of years. Yet even in the painted presentment of her lover there was something that eluded her. What right had any eyes to look so hopeful and yet so secure? Especially when his hopes were so likely to be fantastic. And on an impulse of real humility that underlay her distrustfulness of herself and others, she prayed that she would not be one of those to disappoint him (" not more than is necessary," added her ironic conscience). The boy's grave yet smiling face looked out of its frame on her and past her,—into what future neither he nor she could guess.

And the boy beside her, who would wear at his wedding to-morrow that new velvet suit in the portrait, with the sleeves slashed with oyster satin, was telling her he could not stay, or he would never get to Morphie and her aunt Euphemia by to-night.

It was far too late to go, said Lady Carnegie—was there ever anything so wild as this lad, to come miles out of his way merely for one glimpse of Magdalen, whom he was going to see for the rest of his life when he came back here to-morrow.

But it was Magdalen Carnegie he had come to see, he said, and her he would never see again. He would go, he was far too restless and excited to stay, and he wanted to hear again the song that his heart had sung when he was alone.

He went back through the little wood to where Lame Tom was waiting for him with his horse in the rain that was now falling. He mounted and rode through the rain and the darkness, and he heard his song, but no words with it; there was no rhyme nor reason in his head; only a wild music, clear and high, like the

single shrilling of the pipes when they play without the drones,—
like a thin air that he had once heard on the sea-shore at Saint
Andrews, when there had been no man on all that wide shore to
play it; and he had gone home wondering if he had indeed heard
fairy music.

XIII

IT IS childhood had passed without his knowing, like one of its own endless midsummer days when he had been asleep before that late Northern twilight at last stole up to veil the midnight sky.

Even matrimony made no sharp break in his tutelage, for his father-in-law had made it a condition in the settlements that the young Earl should stay at his wife's home for the first three years of their marriage, and continue his studies until he was of age and ready to go abroad. He was spared the growing pains of adolescence; and only added to the boyish activities of sport and study those of a proudly adoring young husband, and, before very very long, those of a still prouder father.

In discovering the ardours and powers of his body, he felt that he had discovered Magdalen—and moreover rescued her, as if from cruel guardians—though all that her guardians had done was to bring about their match so easily and comfortably that Jamie now found himself established in yet another welcoming home.

Now her laughter was an echo of Jamie's, free of criticism whether of people or of life, bubbling up from some irrepressible source of enjoyment of all the world. There was no holding him, when, barely nineteen, he wrote to his old tutor, Master Forrett, M.A., to tell him that he must prepare himself to be tutor to his son and heir with all speed, since the boy at two days old was already showing remarkable intelligence.

" And see it that he does not swallow a toad in his cradle," he instructed the young mother, who looked as anxious as if it were a likely accident, for she hated any reference, even in joke, to the supposed uncanny propensities in her husband's race.

At present surely there was no one and nothing that could harm him, not even himself. There they were safe in the home of her parents, who loved Jamie as if he were their own son. But everybody loved Jamie,—was it in that lay her fear of losing him? But his loyalty came too naturally to cost him any effort or her any question. Her only impulses of jealousy were those that she was ashamed to admit even to herself. And they were for his sisters, to whom he was always riding off,—and what could she fear from them?

She walked in the new garden that her father had planted at some distance below the castle, snug and sheltered within its stone walls, while outside the wind raced over the bare landscape. It tasted salt when it blew from the sea, it was sharp and bitter then from the east, and old Daniel covered up his precious new vegetables with flannel as tenderly as if they were his infant children.

But the wind that disturbed her most blew from the west, with a scurry of soft raindrops, and clouds piling up above the garden walls as huge as mountains. And that wind came from the mountains, from the Grampians that traverse Scotland; and there on the other side of them, in a hollow among the hills, lived Kat, who was alive and free as Jamie was, and as she herself could never hope to be, except when carried away by his bold and laughing spirit. And there Jamie had ridden yet again.

*   *   *

While the wind blew at Kinnaird, in the west it was so hot that even Jamie was content to sit still for once. He had joined his sisters at their Italian reading on the smooth white pebbly shore of ' our little Mediterranean,' as the Colquhouns liked to call it ever since a traveller had compared Loch Lomond to that foreign sea.

With Carlippis to correct their pronunciation, they sat under the silver birch trees and read Boccaccio's amusing stories. Lilias took a simple pleasure in the resemblance of their *al fresco* gathering to that smiling and worldly company of the *Decameron*, who had sat in a ring on the olive terraces above Florence, seeing nothing but the fair silent towers of the plague-stricken city below, escaping from the reality of sickness and death into the airy bawdry of novelists' imaginings.

The resemblance was nearer than Lilias knew. She and Sir

John had come to feel themselves as spiritual exiles, and all because of Carlippis' pride in the lead that Italy had given to the world these last two centuries. His passion was that of a convert—of a German for the land of his adoption; he rationalized it, compared the glories of her Renaissance with the dreary theologies of the Reformation.

"Sermons instead of pictures, arguments instead of plays, John Knox instead of that holy trinity, Leonardo, Raphael and Michael Angelo,—that is the best these poor Northern savages can do with the New Learning."

His master shared the foreigner's sense of superiority; his mistress read, listened, or forgot to listen, wove daisy chains and cast them on the smooth waters of the loch, thinking—"Shall I ever go to Italy?" And both escaped in day-dreams from the knowledge of what was slowly happening round them, bringing them nearer and nearer to disaster.

It was Jamie whose attention was first awakened.

He had been lying on his elbow, trying to play ducks and drakes in that difficult position; and then on his stomach, staring first down and then up the loch, for they were at the end of the little peninsula of Rossdhu, nearly at the middle of the loch, and had a long view in both directions. But he never much cared to look down it, for there there were only the low, peaceful pasturages round Glasgow, where, in the old days, he used to have to ride back to school. He would look in that direction only for the satisfaction that it gave him to turn to the other, and see the heather-covered hills rising higher and higher, until the mighty head of Ben Lomond, flushing blood-red in the sunshine, over-topped them all. There, round the bend of the loch beneath Ben Lomond, the gleaming water disappeared.

That gap in the hills had always invited him to go through it in search of adventure. There, where Ben Lomond looked towards Ben Nevis, lay the true Highlands, whence from time immemorial the wild mountain clans had rushed down in torrents to raid this sheltered land and carry off its fat cattle. There at Inveraray, to the west of Ben Lomond, lay the heart of the

Argyll country, whose elderly young lord, the future MacCaillan Mhor of the great clan Diarmaid, had supped with him at Saint Andrews, and shown how he hated to taste his salt.

" I'll sup with him in his own country yet," thought Montrose. He was getting bored with these sly little stories, mostly on adultery and never on fighting, and all in a mincing fashionable language that sounded like a lot of baby talk. He pulled out of his pocket an elf-bolt he had found that morning, a flint spear-head such as was believed to have been made by the fairies, and certainly used by witches, for Maggie Blandilands, the potter's widow at Luss, had exhausted all her neighbours' cattle before the fair by driving them round and round the fields, shooting at them with elf-bolts.

But Archie Napier, who was as fond of history as of algebra, said they were the rude weapons of some incredibly early race that had lived here before the Romans came, in houses underneath the earth,—but in houses so small, as Jamie had seen for himself, that only goblins could have lived in it. He had found one with Kat when they were children, playing that they were William Wallace and their ancestor, his faithful friend and ally, whose sword they possessed.

She had crawled into the house on her hands and knees and called out to him like the woman in the fairy tale, " What are you doing, sitting on my house? " For he had stayed on the grass above, and when he saw she had gone inside that green hump, he had jumped down and pulled her out by the heels, for how could he know that she would not go further and further into the earth, until there came a skirl of laughter and shrill music, and she would never come out again, but be heard sometimes under the earth like the lost piper of the Mull of Kintyre, crying:

" I doubt, I doubt
I'll never win out! "

As he remembered that hollow mound and Kat's heels sticking out of it, he stopped examining his elf-bolt, and rolled over and looked at Kat, and noticed for the first time that she was wearing a jewel. It was an intricate piece of gold work, fretted in circles and pentagons in as ingenious and complicated a structure as a spider's web; and set in it here and there, in positions that even Jamie's unpractised taste could recognize as inevitably right for the pattern, was the burning eye of a ruby.

"What is that thing?" he asked as soon as the reading was finished, and he had seized the chance to stroll off apart with her on their way back to the house.

"It fastens my dress," said Kat.

"Your dress was fastened before, I suppose." His brusque reversion to schoolboy rudeness was unusual. "I thought you did not care for jewels," he said. "You would not wear mine, I remember."

Magdalen had worn his jewel instead. He bit off his corollary, "and I am glad."

Kat had been determinedly aloof, defiant of late—her attitude saying, "you are a married man now," as though it were a barrier that he had set up on purpose between them. If there were a barrier, he would break it down,—he would not have this silly, unnecessary coldness; so he continued casually and reasonably. "But you were almost a child then. Are you beginning to like jewels?"

"I like this one," said Kat.

There was no continuing. She was on the other side of the bars, glaring at him. The jewel on her breast winked its sultry eyes at him.

It grew in his mind, it became of irritating importance. It spoilt his pleasure in his visit to Rossdhu, because he found his eye caught in its circular maze, following its pattern round and round, found himself wondering who had given it her, why she would not tell him (though that indeed was only too likely to be from a wish to tease him), thinking it was undignified of him to ask, and then that he was the man of the family and it was his duty to do so.

A dread of his own temper prevented him from again approaching Kat. He asked Lilias, who was as usual rather vague, had noticed Kat had taken to wearing that jewel, thought it pretty though too elaborate for her taste, for she did not like ornaments to look like mathematical diagrams. She and Sir John had given it her quite a long time ago.

" Did *you* give it then? "

" He suggested we should give it together—I believe it was her birthday. Did you think she had a suitor? I am sure I wish she had, I have done my best, but I am afraid she has no charm for men. We shall have to arrange a match in the ordinary way, and that is so unusual in our family."

She smiled in a sweet, abstracted manner at somebody behind Jamie's head, so that he looked round, startled, and then saw that it was at a mirror. She was thinking how Sir John had demanded her hand from her parents, having fallen headlong in love with her after one glimpse of her riding through the streets of Montrose; her thoughts had rocked so comfortably away that she was bewildered for an instant to hear Jamie say—" Do you know where it comes from? "

" Where — what — oh the jewel? How should I know? Carlippis got it, I suppose—he gets everything like that."

As he heard it, he realized that he had known all along that would be the answer.

" I hate that fellow," he broke out.

She looked at him, startled, and for that instant it seemed that his exclamation had opened a door into her mind,—and what he saw there was bewildered and terrified. But in a flash it was shut again; she was telling him that though Carlippis' appearance was repulsive, and his reputation not very savoury, yet he had always been a good and faithful servant, would do anything for any of them, was devoted to the children and so good for their modern languages—and in any case, she added rather wildly, it was no use saying a word against him to Sir John, she had discovered that, and she begged Jamie not to try, for it could only make trouble.

This sudden flurry left her as quickly as it came. She was stitching placidly again at her embroidery picture of Queen

Margaret and the Robber, seated on her Italian chair with gilded and painted carving on its back. Behind her bent head with its mass of fair curls were two old family portraits of the Colquhouns, —Sir John's grandfather in an Elizabethan ruff and pointed beard, and his grandmother's keen face, looking out of a big white ruff of delicate lace. They gave a settled, reassuring air to the background; so, in a way, did the new portrait of Sir John that had lately been placed beside them.

For surely that prosperous and complacent man in his rich but sober suit of black, lightly touched with dark mulberry, was not going to do anything or have anyone in his house that might endanger either his comfort or his reputation.

But what really reassured Jamie was that the day before he rode back to Kinnaird, Kat flung her arms round his neck and told him she did not know why she had been like an ill-natured hedgehog all his visit, for there was nobody in the world she loved as much as he,—but she knew that Magdalen did not like her.

He told her not to be so foolish, to go and stay with the Napiers and Beatrix at Merchiston, and not to snub the young men she met there as unmercifully as she had done last time,—all excepting young Madertie, and was that, he asked, suddenly remembering some promptings of his elder sisters, just because Madertie had been paying court to Beatrix?

Then, feeling very wise, elder-brotherly, and relieved, he rode back to the flat pastures of Kinnaird, to Magdalen, and his young son, Johnnie.

XIV

*T*HERE was no air moving by day over Loch Lomond; the hills and green islands were as clear upon the shimmering water as in the air. But at night a little breeze stirred the surface of the loch, and Kat could hear the ripples plainly from her window just above it. They curled over, sighed, sucked back the pebbles, then came again. The night was alive, never quite dark, as though it were always watching. She got into bed, she slept, she dreamed.

Scurrying through her dreams came a host of hunched figures, black on a moonlit sea. Shrieking with laughter (and yet she could not hear them) they tossed and waved their arms, brandishing flagons of wine from which they drank, then urged each other on, nearer and nearer the shore on which she stood. Each of them was whirling round and round in a tiny circular boat,— but it was not a boat, it was not even a tub, and there was something very strange in it holding anyone upon the water for it was full of holes, and she could see them now as though she were sitting in it,—and she was sitting in it, looking down through the holes to the black whirling waters below, far, far below, beneath their blackness, to the still and lovely forms of flowers.

> " I'll show where the white lilies grow
> In the bottom o' the sea."

Suddenly she laughed, for she saw that what she was sitting in was the old sieve, the big one made of punched sheepskin that hung upon the stone wall of the kitchen at Kincardine. Round her were two hundred other sieves, and in them all were women, drinking from flagons of wine, and laughing. Now they had reached the shore, now they were dancing in a ring, and their long black hair streeled out on the night wind.

Her bare feet tossed and scattered the sand, it rose in a cloud beneath her, and she rose on it, higher and higher, leaping as she had never leapt in a reel before, her body dancing of itself, blown by that singing wind as a dead leaf is blown, round and round on a whirlwind of sand, now backward, now forward, on, on, pursuing someone in front of her, a girl who, as she danced, played the mad tune of the reel on a tiny jew's-harp.

All that whirling company came dancing after, and Kat in front of them, nearest to that figure with the jew's-harp against her lips, who led them with thin bare feet and white legs flashing in and out in the moonlight, whose short black hair blew straight up from her head, whose face Kat knew, did she turn and look back, would be the same as her own.

This is a nightmare, she thought, I must wake up, and there she was lying in her own bed,—but am I asleep or awake? she asked. The darkness inside the curtains was thick round her, but she could see a glimmer from the linen sheet where she had thrown it back. Yes, she was awake, she was here safe in bed, but where had she been a moment ago? Out on the sea-shore miles away, right across Scotland, on the east coast, dancing with a company of witches.

It was true then; she was a witch; and she laughed softly in the darkness. It gave her an odd sense of power, as though that in itself were witchcraft, that she should be lying awake, listening to the silence of the great house all round her, and the little whispering sounds outside, to be lying there so still, yet tingling with excitement, wakefulness, the sense of adventure.

Who else is awake in this house besides me? she thought. Someone knows that I am awake—someone is thinking of me— speaking to me—calling me.

Out of her bed she got in her white linen smock, pushed back the curtains and saw a criss-cross pattern of dull light falling from the small, leaded panes of the window on to the boards;—then stepped from those clouded squares to the window, and pushed it open, to see the flood of unearthly light outside.

There was the world she had always known, transformed and magical. A white foxglove had grown by accident in a corner of the courtyard; it stood there like a spear of ivory; like a gallant knight in white armour; and now as the wind blew, like a swaying, feathery ghost.

> " I'll show where the white lilies grow
> On the banks o' Italie."

" That is where I will go," she thought, and remembered the company of story-tellers on the hillside above Florence,—but they were dull to sit and tell of what they had never seen. She would do more, she would go further, she did not know what, nor where. She turned her head, as though she were listening for a sound within the house, the sound of her own name called in a voice she could not hear, and yet it was ringing in her ears.

A dark circle whirled and wound round and round in her head; she knew that she must move round and round, up and up. She turned and went up to the door and lifted the latch and stepped into the passage, where only a grey glimmer showed in the direction of the wide staircase. But she went in the opposite direction, deeper into the darkness till her bare feet felt the shock of stone and her hand reached out for the touch of stone, and then she began to walk up a narrow winding stair, up and up, round and round.

Until above her head she saw a thin stripe of yellow light, and her hand felt for the latch of a door, and opened it, and there, inside Carlippis' room, all alone, stood Sir John, staring at her as though she were a ghost.

A lighted candle stood on the table before him; its flame glinted upwards on his dark chin and the white of his eyeballs, giving his face a flickering and distorted look; he seemed even taller than usual, leaning forward over the candle, with the top of his head disappearing in shadow,—as tall as the mast of a ship, she thought —and with that a giddiness swam over her, so that she felt the little round room whirling, and herself in it, as in a little round boat, and beneath her the black, whirling waters of the sea.

" I am walking in my sleep," said Kat to herself, " and now I must wake up."

But as in a nightmare, she could do nothing. She stood there as if bound hand and foot; her tongue could not move, it clung to the roof of her mouth, which was dry and hot; and then a sudden trembling shook all her body, her hand dropped from the latch and hung by her side, powerless to fling out as she wished, to thrust away the man who was now moving towards her.

XV

KING CHARLES I had been on the throne over seven years now; and still he had not come up to be crowned in Scotland. His loyal Scottish subjects were burning to do him homage,—and still more to get the royal ear, and explain the tithes question to him. Church lands and Church tithes, the happy windfalls of the Reformation, were now sacred to the nobles' private pockets, said the jolly Lord Rothes, with his enormous wink.

This good-humoured man of the world, a friend of Napier's and the Carnegies, put his fat finger on the money side of the troubles.

" Says he's restoring them to the Church—to pay their stipends out of it! Restore his grandmother! The King's short of money like the rest of us, and that's all there is to it. Because he can't fill his revenue out of the stingy English pockets, he comes down on us for it."

" Small blame to him," said Archie Napier, " with money not worth one half its old value,"—and at once Lady Carnegie, her blue eyes fierce with excitement, broke in with sad recollections of her mother furnishing her whole wardrobe with a sum that she had now to give those extravagant hussies, her daughters, for a single dress and cloak.

Napier's economics, as befitted the son of the famous higher mathematician and inventor of logarithms, were more impersonal than hers, or yet Rothes. In his opinion, the vast influx of gold from the Indies in the last century had half ruined the world. Look at Spain. They looked surprised, for Spain was as much the El Dorado to the rest of Europe as South America was to Spain. But all her wealth and wide empire was nothing but a hollow shell, declared Napier, and it had shown but another instance of old King Jamie's short-sighted wisdom that he had always longed to marry his son Charles to the Spanish Infanta. A good thing for England that Charles had so bungled his wooing of her.

" And a bad thing for England that he chose the little French cat instead," said Rothes.

What a tartar! What a termagant! They all had stories about Queen Henrietta Maria—how she had refused (at sixteen) to be crowned according to the Church of England, and even to walk in the Coronation procession; how she had chattered as loud as she could with her ladies in the hall of a country house, to show her disrespect for the Anglican prayers that her host was reading on the other side of a thin door;—how she still could not talk English properly, and the poets were writing long pieces of poetry for her to say in the masques at Court, so that her vanity might be a bribe to her industry.

But she was sure to settle down into a good, sensible little queen, the loyalists finally decided; and King Charles would settle down too, would stop all this nonsense about the tithes, and his wish to reform the churches of England and Scotland. How many more reformations were they to stand, in the name of God? and hadn't John Knox, God rest his soul, given them as many knocks as they needed for a century at least?

King Charles apparently was to settle down from the moment he came to Scotland. That would teach him everything. Some Englishman had been so ill-advised as to suggest that the Scottish regalia might be sent to London, so that Charles could be crowned King of Scotland in his English capital. There was an outburst of indignation. Doubtless the King would like to keep the Scottish crown under his coronation chair at Westminster, where the Hammer of the Scots, King Edward I, had placed the immemorially ancient coronation stone of Scone.

Did King Charles then think the Scottish crown not worth the trouble of a journey? The old king had been a Scot first and an English king afterwards,—but his son must be English in every bone of his body.

But at the time he left Scotland, Charles' bones were so soft that the doctors doubted as to whether he had had any at birth at all.

And softness, or lack of backbone as it is called, prevented the young king from making the effort to come to his native kingdom; though he looked forward to it with all the vague optimism of a sentimentalist who believes that in any change of scene, certainly when it be to the scene of his infancy, will lie the best way out of his difficulties.

For England was being very difficult. Pirates from Turkey and Algiers infested her coasts, to the great harm of her trade; and she was in danger of losing her herring fishery to the Dutch, who were now the real masters of the sea. But when Charles tried to restore the Navy to its former importance, he could get no support.

To him it seemed that the English were the sentimentalists; they sang sea-songs with the best of them; they loved to recall the great days of the Armada, when the old Queen had waved her hand from Greenwich Palace in greeting to the ships that came proudly up the Thames with sails of blue damask, and loot from Bokhara and Canada, the Russian galleys and the navy of Japan.

" Ah, those were the days," they said, when Captain Drake was served in his cabin off silver plate, and every man of Cavendish's crew wore a gold chain, and violins played on the decks of the *Golden Hind.*

Now a man would as soon be in the galleys as in the King's Navy, so wretched was the pay and the food, so lousy and rat-eaten were the ships; and so powerful the Barbary rovers, who sold English mariners as slaves at Sallee to grind in their mills; and so insolent the Dutch herring fishers, who landed without leave to spread their nets on the English shores.

But for all their bitter shame, the suggestion of paying ship-money made every Englishman's blood boil. Let the sea-coast towns go on paying for the Navy. What had it to do with the rest of England?

In regretful contrast Charles remembered all that his father had told him of the logic and reasonableness of Scottish minds, and longed to revisit his native land. But it took so much trouble, it would be such an expense, the English nobles were always opposing it, and it never seemed to be the right moment.

F

Now at last it was all settled, the coronation was to be held at Holyrood next year, and the King, with a train of Scots and English nobles, would make a tour of the principal Lowland towns, who had been preparing for his advent ever since his accession. Odes of welcome were written in English and Latin; masques were rehearsed; the company of glovers at Perth practised a particularly complicated sword-dance; a pretty young lady in Edinburgh, chosen to represent that city, spent hours before the glass, trying on an immense castellated headdress so as to look like a stone wall.

And Lady Carnegie organized a fire-screen in appliqué work to be sewn in various pieces by the leading ladies of Scotland and assembled together for the King's use in his Palace of Holyrood, which had lain empty so long. She worked the centre piece of the Crown herself, together with her daughter Magdalen, and briskly disposed of any feebler clutches on the Crown made by rival female ambitions.

It was now the autumn, and all expectations would be realized (or not) early in the next year, 1633. Some timid and fanciful spirits added up the numbers that make that date, deplored the fact that they came to thirteen, and demanded why King Charles could not have chosen any other year in which to be crowned in Scotland. But such complaints smacked of that worst superstition, popery. It was the Last Supper of Our Lord and His apostles that had made thirteen an unlucky number; and the Scottish divines were growing more and more disinclined to allow Our Lord any apostles at all.

Apostles—apostolic succession—the laying on of hands—bishops. Such was the sequence of ideas; and its apotheosis was the next important question (after the tithes) that King Charles did not as yet properly understand, but would be made to do so as soon as he had reached Scotland. He was to give the nobles their tithes, and he was to take away the bishops.

Of all those who expected advancement at the Coronation, none had better reason to do so than the young Earl of Montrose, the head of one of the finest fighting families in the land, young, good-looking, an athlete and a superb rider—a sure help to Charles' favour. And Montrose would be splendidly sponsored at his introduction. His brother-in-law, Lord Napier, was arranging most of the details of the Coronation, and would himself be one of the bearers of the canopy over the King's head in the Procession. His father-in-law, Lord Carnegie, was to be made an earl at the Coronation, and had chosen for his title the broad and placid waters of the South Esk that flowed past Kinnaird and into the estuary by the town of Montrose. One of Carnegie's three brothers was also to be honoured, so that it was inevitable he should choose the upper river of North Esk. And the new Lord Southesk's son-in-law, now at Court, who had been first Sir John and then Lord Stewart of Traquair, would also be made an earl, and probably the next Treasurer of Scotland.

Among all these family honours, what would fall to Montrose? The lion's share, thought at least one poet in his Coronation ode, who recommended to his sovereign the merits of:

" That hopeful youth, the Young Lord Graham,
James, Earl of Montarose,"

(inserting an extra syllable into his title for the sake of the line). There were also the merits of his ancestors:

" Whose hearts, whose hands, whose swords, whose deeds, whose fame,
Made Mars for valour canonize the Graham! "

Mr. William Lithgow's previous publication, ' Adventures and painful peregrinations of long nineteen years travel from Scotland to the most famous kingdoms in Europe, Asia and Africa,' had been presented to Montrose at college, and rewarded with a large sum of money, but Mr. Lithgow had ill rewarded the patronage, for he asked leave to submit his next work in manuscript for his noble patron's private reading, and it bore this title:—' The gushing tears of godly sorrow, containing the causes, conditions and remedies of sin, depending mainly upon contrition, and they seconded with sacred and comfortable passages, under the mourning canopy of tears and repentance.'

But the author abandoned his pious mood in time for the Coronation. Nothing seemed to exist, thought Montrose, except for the Coronation.

When Napier told him that he, Montrose, was to be one of the King's train-bearers, his guardian's pleasure surprised and rather depressed the young man. Were these the aloof ideals of the man whose father had invented the symbols of an unknown quantity of indefinite value?

What could all this fuss lead to but a place at Court?

" And you yourself are sick of Court life, and only long to retire from it altogether. You are always saying so."

" That is because I am growing old, and Margaret is not strong, and it is time we had a rest together. But you are young. Have you no ambitions? "

Yes, he had, overweening ambitions, beyond any Coronation honour. But he was too shy to speak them. He growled instead that he wished to God that sour, sallow, tallow-faced fellow, Archibald Campbell, Lord Lorne, was not going to be one of the other train-bearers. " If I get the chance, I'll trip him over it."

He was not always so contrary. Sometimes he would imagine the conversations he would have with his sovereign, in which he would convince Charles of exactly what was needed to settle the Scottish question. Walking beside him on the links above Saint Andrews, where of course the King would wish to play golf as his royal father had done thirty years ago, Montrose would describe the pride of his nation in its own peculiar half-religious, half-political creation, the Kirk. Had the King forgotten that England was a foreign country? that his Bishop of London, Laud, who wanted to meddle with Scottish as well as English Church services, was a pedantic Oxford don who had never set foot on a tuft of Scottish heather in his life?

But then the day-dream, floating past him in the hum of the heather bees and the honey-sweet smell of the yellow bed-straw flowers where he lay that hot, late autumn afternoon on the links near Saint Andrews (which was why he could not imagine talking to King Charles anywhere else), would turn its darker side, and he would wonder how he should ever speak so freely, with Lord Lorne, who had already been to Court and made friends with the King, looking on, and with him the insolent English lords, despising as a raw country lad anyone who had not been to London.

All his pride rose in revolt, that this was the best opportunity his manhood should give him, that he should make a good impression on a foreign-bred king. *That* was not how he wished to prove himself.

He could talk to none of his occasional uneasiness. Even Archie Napier had found his scruples finicky. Napier was as upright and honourable as anyone could wish, but he was a man of the world, and his world had been built up by royal favour, or at least recognition. So had the world of his father-in-law, so soon now to be Earl of Southesk.

As for Magdalen, had he confided such fancies to her, he could well imagine her despairing gaze. " You do not *wish* to meet the King—to gain his notice—win his favour? "

And her eyes would fall on the wooden cradle, wherein she rocked the heir to all her hopes of himself, and say nothing more, but he would feel how he had dashed them. No woman could understand, since her fate was to be cautious, careful of the future, thrifty and watchful of any opportunity that might advance those she cared for with such unceasing patience.

No woman in the world, he repeated to himself,—but a wandering thought that had strayed in a direction forgotten of late, answered—" Yes, there is one." Kat, whom he had forgotten while he worried about the coronation, and of whom he had had no news for many weeks, Kat would understand his desire not to be dependent on any man's opinion. And with that there came so sudden a desire to see her that it throbbed in his breast like terror.

" I must ride to Rossdhu," he said to Magdalen, and her eyes fell before his. What could she fear or wish to reprove, that her eyes could not tell him? Would she like to bind him always to her side? It must hurt cruelly to be a woman, he thought, stung to an unusual power of perception by his own conflicting desires and perplexities. He held his arms round her as if to protect her, and whispered to her, " My dear and only love."

" That sounds like poetry," she said, with her ironic smile.

XVI

ON his way from Kinnaird, he met Archibald Napier, who was riding to meet him, and only then remembered that he was that day to go with him to Edinburgh for a state banquet with the Lord Chancellor. But he could not, he said, he must go to Rossdhu. Why then? demanded his brother-in-law. Had he had news? No, that was it, he had had no news for a long time, he was anxious, and Archie must let him go. The boy looked oddly, Napier could not think what had come to him.

"Then I can give you news," he said, "for Sir John is at Edinburgh, and had a letter from his wife only this morning, and they are all well at home."

Jamie began to feel he had been a fool. Of course they were all well. But the real factor that reassured him was that Sir John was at Edinburgh.

So he went there, and rode in the Chancellor's coach with his gilded state sword at his side; and went to the banquet and there saw Sir John, who drank a good deal and talked more than ever, apparently to cover his nervous apprehension. It was all because of the Coronation, Archie Napier told Jamie with a smile. If he worked himself up into fits like this, months before the time, what would he be like at the actual event?

"That is a sick man," said Napier. Colquhoun was eagerly forming a group round himself, breaking off the story he was telling so dramatically to a couple of men, in order to pluck the cloak of a third and draw him into his audience; to whisper a hurried joke into the ear of a fourth as he passed by; to wave, as he did now, in exaggeratedly friendly greeting to his brothers-in-law, the lords Napier and Montrose. He seemed very gay, his roving eyes sought those of everyone in the room, his flexible eyebrows puckered and contracted and one went up and the other went down, as though they could never agree whether to wink or frown.

Behind him the candlelight slid over the dark panels, cut this way and that by the shadows of men passing.

Jamie wondered what should have prompted the wise Napier's remark, and then heard himself say, without intention, " What is driving him? "

And a thin little shadow of fear fell on him for his brother-in-law, who was held to be so brilliant, so popular, so likely to win the favour and success he craved for; and who yet, as Jamie watched him now, the laughing centre of his little crowd, seemed oddly alone, clutching at all who passed as a drowning man might clutch at the twigs that drift down-stream.

In candlelight, then, in company, " man walketh in a vain shadow, and disquieteth himself in vain." And Jamie considered if he should go over and speak to him, but was discomforted by this glimpse he had had of him, as though he had seen him naked and unaware among the crowd. Sir John's worries, if any, had nothing to do with him.

And here was Wigton, whom he was longing to tell of the salmon as long as his two arms,—well, nearly—which he had caught with one of the new artificial flies instead of sticking to Wigton's favourite old ground bait. He would see Sir John next day.

But next day he had first to call on the family adviser, Sir Thomas Hope, who had been promoted to the proud position of Lord Advocate. A solemn, crotchety old fellow, he recorded his dreams every morning as carefully as he entered his accounts at night, to see if they would not come true, since he had once unquestioningly dreamed in June of the left-hand shoelace that he would break in September,—a clear proof of predestination, said Montrose, to tease him.

The Almighty had condescended to speak to Sir Thomas in the middle of last night, saying in a loud voice, not unlike the sound of the yard-dog barking, " I have done it." What the Almighty had done, Sir Thomas could not say. But he had made his wife get up and record the marvel, saying to her— " Spouse, did you not hear One speak a word? "

" She said one on her own account, I suppose," murmured the sympathetic listener.

His wife, a cross-looking woman, with sagging cheeks and down-drooped mouth, had to show the notebook, muttering that it had been a sin and a shame to trouble the Almighty and herself like this, when a pinch of peppermint in hot water would have settled Sir Thomas' stomach troubles for the night.

But her husband, who was slightly deaf, happily followed divine messages with obscene devilry, telling of a hag who had given a young girl a magic trinket, and so enticed her into the embrace of the Evil One, which, according to the report of her confession, she had found ' very cold.'

" The world has grown too old," thought Jamie, " it is full of old men grumbling in their sleep."

But for all his gossip and dreams and diary of private informations straight from the Lord's mouth, Sir Thomas showed his shrewd business side as soon as he settled down to the legal business of his patron's estates. It was indeed the patron who went back to the subject he had despised.

" Can a trinket be made to bewitch its wearer? " he asked idly; but paid no attention to the answer. Once again, and this time not to be delayed even by a visit to Sir John, he knew that he must go to Rossdhu.

XVII

HE rode into woods that were dripping with the early November mists. The trees never stirred; the silver trunks of the birches had a naked look through their mesh of purple twigs. The hoofs of his mare, Bess, squelched through the sodden bracken, making the only sound in that drenched red place. All but the birches were red; the bracken a dark crimson, the hillside blood-red in the shadows, wine-purple in the long stretches of wet dead heather.

This dim and glowing place took possession of him, wrapped him in a cloud of silent obscurity. A squirrel ran across a clearing in the trees, stopped close in front of the steaming horse, scrabbled through the leaves into the brown earth, and there buried a nut. Its wary glances shot to right and left, more full of alert intelligence than seemed natural in so tiny a creature. All over the mare that stood there so still, up to the human figure that sat on its back as if carved from stone, over the face, and straight into Jamie's curious eyes, went that intent, terrified and watchful glance, stared, yet saw nothing.

Then Bess shook her head. Straightway the squirrel disappeared,—jerk, flicker, jerk, its rippling brown tail repeating all its movements, as silent as the trees that received it into their midst. Jamie rode on.

Now he saw the loch through the trees, and realized that he had through his preoccupation missed the way that he knew as well as his own home, and had to follow the curve of the loch along the shore. The outline of the near hills was flattened in the mist as though smudged by a giant thumb against the air. There was no sky, there were no shadows, no distant shapes, only on the water there glistened a faint silver radiance.

Suddenly Bess pulled up, plunging; he patted her neck to soothe her, and felt that she was trembling. He knew, before he raised his eyes to the rocks on the hillside just before him, that Kat stood there. How long had she been there, watching him coming?

His nervous beast throbbed and fussed beneath him, telling him that no human being had a right to stand so still. Even now he could not see that she was looking at him, though her head was turned his way, and that reflection of invisible light from the loch glimmered upwards on her face, making it clear like water in the darkness of her hair.

As he called and rode up to her, he saw her eyes on his face, scanning him, and was reminded of that wild creature of the woods that had looked at him just now, and had not seen him. He swung off his horse, threw the bridle over his arm, and held out the other to her.

"Kat," he cried, "what mischief are you up to, standing there to frighten Bess?"

She said, "Now I have made you come at last. Why did you not come before?"

"I came as soon as I thought of it. You did not make me. Did you send for me then? Why did you want me? I am here now. Tell me."

His words rushed over each other. He moved up to her, pulling Bess's bridle with the one hand, while he pushed the other over Kat's head, jerked it up under her chin to make her look at him, dropped it on her shoulder and shook it a little in the old affectionate, exasperated way; and all the time the hand was saying, "This is my sister Kat, she is just the same as she always was, round head and bushy hair and sharp small shoulder, what is there in her that can make you afraid?" and all the time his eyes asked more than his hand could tell.

A flight of crows went skirling up into the grey air, beating on it with the black sweeping strokes of their wings. He watched them helplessly while odd, disconnected thoughts flew into his head and out again,—until he noticed that she was wearing riding boots beneath her skirt, which was looped up through her belt as she always wore it when on the moor.

"Where are you going?" he asked. "Where is your horse?"

He caught a fleeting look, askance,—the next instant she was boldly facing him——her horse was a few yards away, she said, and why should she not be riding at twilight, so near home, as she had done often enough before?

" I do not know what has happened," he said. " We can never meet now without quarrelling. I used to think I loved you more than any of my sisters, but you do not want me to love you, it has all gone."

He could not bear to go on talking with her. He turned Bess's head from her, and began to move away. He heard a sob, but he would not believe she was crying. Only women who were gentle and tender-hearted, cried. There came a rushing movement through the wet bracken, and she was there on the other side of Bess, pulling at the bridle to stop them.

" I have always loved you best," she said, " but now you love Magdalen best."

He stared at her. " She is my wife." He did not know if he said it or not.

" Well, I have tried to love someone else too, to love him better than you. But I cannot change as you have done. I love you better than the whole world. I know it now."

Some strained quality in her voice startled the mare, who reared and plunged her head, but Kat, still holding the bridle, paid no attention to her; she was crying, " It is not too late, now you have come at last. Jamie, take me away from them all. Let us run away."

She had often said that, years ago; and now the childish cry came again, but with how strange an echo! The cry of a thing lost and frightened,——but she was never frightened, she would not let herself be so now,——her voice came pantingly, and yet she forced it into the casual off-hand tones it had always worn. It was he whose voice faltered as he demanded who it was that she had ' tried to love.'

" And who would it be? One of the Fleming brothers or my young Lord Wigton, because you tried to arrange matches for me with one or other of them? That is how you think of love, something that comes safely and dutifully after marriage."

" Answer me," he shouted, the words rushing like blood into his mouth, " have you lain with any man? "

She stared at him an instant, then turned and fled from him among the trees. She had answered him. He dared not follow, for fear of what he might do.

He still saw her face before him, a white, distorted thing in the murky air, distorting his vision of her, mocking his love for her, making it hideous. A grinning mountebank, counterfeiting love, such as Carlippis might act to draw their uneasy laughter, so their relationship tumbled and twisted itself.

He buried his burning face against the mare's neck, pressing it against that strong skin, cool and damp from sweat. Soothed by his touch, but still quivering, the beast stood still. Last winter he and Kat had taken the mare to be shod on a white and breathless morning when the frost was melting all round them in the sun with a faint crackling sound like that of a million tiny flames. The hills had shone pale blue like skimmed milk, the spire of smoke from John the Smith's cottage had been iridescent as a rainbow, a thrush had sung on a bare tree, and ' tink tonk, tink tonk ' went the clang of John the Smith's hammer through the thin and sparkling air. They had held hands as they used to do as children, staring at the blacksmith's forge; then they had mounted and ridden up through the heather over the crisp white moor.

Like a song that no one yet had written; so he had thought of that morning. Now he would never be able to think of it again,—never,—never.

And with the lost vision of that pearl-coloured morning, the thrush's song and their ride together, the little flames of melting frost leaped up into a roar and blaze, devouring his whole childhood.

He hated to think of anyone who loved him; he now saw an unnatural force in the reproach in Magdalen's grave eyes, when he told her he must go and see Kat. And he had lain in such deep, unspeakable content within her arms. Now there would be Kat between them. His lips moved against that clean, rank skin, muttering, " Never—Never—I will never touch any of you again."

He raised his head, and stared at the birch trees where she had disappeared, and gradually his anger melted into anxiety. What could have driven her to this madness? She must be bewitched.

At that he cursed himself, and leaped into the saddle.

" Can a trinket be made to bewitch its wearer? "

Only last night he had asked that of Sir Thomas Hope.

Surely he would have noticed it if Kat had been wearing that twisted jewel? Yet only now did he fancy he had seen the wink and sparkle of a ruby as she had stood there in that last moment, facing him, before she fled.

She had been bewitched, and he had known it, and then he had forgotten it, he had let himself be angered, when all the time it was Kat who had been hurt, and he had discovered nothing of it, not even who had been her lover—but that he would not think of,—not yet.

He was urging Bess forward among the ghostly trees. He called her—" Kat, come back, come back. Kat, I am not angry now. Come back."

His voice trailed through the muffled air. He seemed to be groping through a cloud, a dream. The mist had deepened. No voice answered him. And presently, he began to hear the whispering, pricking sound of the invisible rain.

XVIII

IT was late at night when he came at last to Rossdhu. The grooms who took his horse, the steward who came forward to greet him in the hall, looked at him with scared faces. He asked to be taken straight to the Lady Lilias, and found her walking up and down her room. She turned on him with her hands outflung.

"You!" she cried, "what news do *you* bring, brother?"

The gesture was dramatic, the small hands were white and beautifully kept, covered with rings. He found himself staring at them sullenly, unable to speak. One of them fluttered up to her face, armed with the fresh weapon of a lace handkerchief from Brussels. He watched her hold it to her eyes. There was bad news coming.

"Kat has not returned, then?" he said at last, slowly.

"Kat! Are you mocking me? Oh, then, you know nothing!"

She sat on a stool, looking up at him just under the silver candle sconce so that he saw her face plainly, and that she had been crying. She said in a small, pitiful voice, "I am the most unhappy creature in the world. My lord has left me."

Now he should exclaim and swear at Sir John, and vow to avenge her; or lay his hand on hers and show his sympathy and admiration for her,—for all these demands were in the air, though he did not know what it was, soft and persistent, that clung about his mind, preventing him from thinking clearly, when it was more important than it had ever been for him to do this.

He blinked his eyes against the mellow light of the candles. So long had he been peering into the darkness, distinguishing only the rugged shapes of the trees, as he rode and ran through the worst hours of his life.

In this carefully lighted, pretty, modernly furnished room, with its new Flemish tapestries and its French chairs covered in rose-coloured velvet, and its one good religious picture from Italy, he was in an alien world from that wet wood, where only the

95

hoots of startled owls had answered his despairing voice. He stood squelching his toes in his sodden boots, uncomfortably regarding this beautiful woman who wore her sorrow as elegantly as a rose.

" How do you know he has left you? " he said. " I saw him at Edinburgh, only yesterday."

Lilias stiffened a little. She told him that Sir John should have arrived home that day. He had never come,—but now instead had come from Edinburgh a scared servant of Sir John's, who said that his master had gone, this morning, south towards England. His tale had been so confused and rambling, Lilias had not been able to disentangle it. It was enough to know that she had been deserted, she who had always loved him so devotedly, and was the mother of his children.

" How do you know," her brother kept saying. " How do you know he means to desert you? "

The real issue of all this, the chief cause for anxiety, was sliding past him. Sir John left Edinburgh this morning, Sir John went south,—well, but Kat stood by the loch this afternoon. What had she to do with this?

He asked to see the servant and knew him at once, one Jock Finnie, a weak-headed, clumsy youth he had always thought him, who never knew what he should do next, torn as he was between his desire to get on in the world and his terror of the minister. Montrose had noticed his subservience to Carlippis, whose favour it was almost more worth while to win than that of Sir John. But he had to keep in with God as well as man, even when, as now, he had inconveniently to do it in turns.

He had been bribed to go to London with Sir John, and had eagerly consented. But his conscience smote him, he was afraid of the powers of darkness, at the last moment he had escaped and fled back to Rossdhu to disclose the plot. For Sir John meant to leave his family, he had laid all his plans with the greatest secrecy, he was going to London first, and then to Italy.

Still the reason for it all hovered just out of sight. Had Lilias never even wondered what it might be? Her brother looked at the red, twitching hands of the repentant informer; they kept catching at his handkerchief, that absurd luxury for a servant, and then thrusting it back into his pocket.

" Did Carlippis ride with him? "

Yes. No. That is, Carlippis had left Edinburgh a day earlier than Sir John. He was to go on in advance, get lodgings, order fresh horses, prepare the way.

" Did you see him start? "

No. Yes. That is, he had this very morning spoken to a countryman who had yesterday brought in his sheep into Edinburgh, and had met the German on the road.

" What man was this? " asked Jamie.

" Oh, what can it matter? " wailed Lilias, wringing her hands. All these tedious questions, beside the point, how men loved asking them, just to show their pompous wisdom! If only her young sons were men! Her brother was the only man now of the family, and not one word of help or sympathy had she had from him, only stupid questions.

She turned aside, chilled and lonely, and with a little tremor of fear, inexplicable, unnamed. What were all these questions leading to, what worse evil waited there in the darkness to be discovered? And what evil could there be worse than the betrayal of her true and tender heart?

She stared out of the window, for in the confusion of this evening no one had closed the shutters nor drawn the curtains. Black night, the swish of heavy rain falling, of trees in the rising wind, and the waves of the loch falling louder and louder on the shore,—these were heard even through the new well-fitting glass panes. It was working up to a wild night. How often she had heard that said, and hated it. She began to cry.

The farmer was Pennycuik from The Croft over by Fernhaugh.

" But that," said Jamie's clear voice, " is not on the road into England. If he were driving his sheep, he was coming straight from the west, for Fernhaugh is on the way here."

Lilias stopped crying to say, coldly, " Carlippis has never been here to-day."

G

Jamie did not speak. His silence fell as heavy as a stone. She looked at him, and cried, "For God's sake tell me, what is it you fear?" Her cry had snapped discordantly. She had forgotten to be beautiful, or even sad.

But still her brother did not look at her, he was staring at the raw chapped wrists of Jock Finnie, thrust well beyond his coat sleeves; they were all that was now visible of his hands, which were clutched together, his handkerchief wound tightly round them, and yet even with this support, the wrists were shaking as though the man had got the palsy. His eyes were downcast, almost shut, but the stare of the young lord gradually forced them to rise and meet it. He flung himself on his knees, raising those clutched hands, and sobbed hysterically, "My lord, he is a warlock, all the world knows it, he is the devil himself."

"What do you know of him in this matter?"

"He has persuaded my master to go to Italy, he has enchanted him. And not only my master——" He stopped, was whimpering, his head down again.

"Who else has been bewitched?"

The whimpering stopped, but Jock Finnie did not answer at once.

The silence was all round them now, no longer a stone dropped between them, but a chain uniting them, drawing their thoughts together, nearer and nearer, unwilling prisoners, forced into the same dungeon.

"My young mistress," came at last in a whisper.

XIX

OTHERS had to be questioned; the steward, a tearful incoherent chambermaid of Kat's, one of Lilias' own maids, indignant and on the defensive; each gave separate information, which went to build up that inevitable whole. They gave it in their own ways, but all hesitating,—afraid, not of their master for giving it, nor of their mistress and the young Earl for having so long withheld it, but of their fellow servant, Carlippis. They would not now have confessed what they knew of his doings, but that they believed him to have gone south with Sir John on his way to Italy.

It had been his way all along. That ruthless force of mind had wrecked a great house, merely to escape from boredom. Carlippis himself, villainous and powerful as he was now proving, seemed too small a thing for this demoniac, this monstrous and miserable energy, that was too bitter and hostile ever to create, and so must always destroy.

With all the subtlety of his adopted nation, and the dogged persistence of his own, he had engineered a love affair between his master and his master's young sister-in-law and ward, that would compel Sir John to leave his home and family, the estate that had belonged to that family for centuries, together with the dearly bought new honour of his Nova Scotia baronetcy, and all the hopes and ambitions he had been so anxiously spinning round the approaching Coronation,—to fling them all to the winds, and rush headlong from them,—breaking the law, incurring probably the sentence of death,—and all that Carlippis might get back in comfort to Italy.

The vast selfishness of his plan lay bare at last after seven years of its contriving. He had been successful, he had started Sir John towards London, while he had gone back in secret to Rossdhu to fetch Kat, and join him later on the road.

And Kat must have been on the way to meet him when Jamie had encountered her by the lake. Yet that was strange—for

Carlippis had left Edinburgh yesterday, and Kat should have met him much sooner and ridden away.

Then he remembered her greeting to himself—" Now I have made you come at last. Why did you not come before? "

So she had agreed to go with Carlippis, she had given herself to Sir John,—but now she knew that she hated him and his pander Carlippis, and that the only man she had ever loved was himself. She had wished him to come to her, and he had come, but he had repulsed her. He had driven her back on to those others, by now she had met Carlippis, she was riding with him through the rain to meet her seducer. She had cried, " It is not too late, now you have come to me at last." But he had made it so.

His mind swung from that in fury. These last few hours, that moment of horror-stricken anger, must be wiped out. He would not believe she had gone to meet Carlippis; she had fled from him; why should she not even now be hiding from him?

He sent a messenger on his best horse to Napier, who was still in Edinburgh and might yet have a chance of catching the fugitives on their road to London. He himself determined to seek his sister on the shores of Loch Lomond. For if she were hiding there, as he believed, only he could find her, knowing as he did their old haunts on those shores, and where she was likely to find shelter. So for three days he sought her there, going further and further afield, by the ice-white torrents that gashed the dark surface of the mountains; through the woods that had provided oaks for the roof of Glasgow Cathedral, and yews for the archers' bows at Bannockburn.

And back through his spent childhood he seemed to be searching for her, as he scanned the country for some hut or shelter patched together with bracken and branches and heather, such as they had then made together, and might even now be harbouring her. The granite boulders, perched so oddly here and there, were where they had held their castle against the English, or the robber, Edom o' Gordon. There was the one down on the shore that they had always looked at to see if the waves had reached it, for that meant the loch was at a good fishing level,—and there was the mighty giant that had yet been split apart by a sapling growing up through it. And here was the great stone, stark and gaunt in the midst of a bare stretch of moorland, that had once marked the boundaries of three ancient kingdoms.

Other ages than his own surrounded him in these woods and stones. Unconscious of them, and of their history, he was yet reminded in this sad search back through his youth, that the world was very old, and drawing to an end.

Snow had begun to creep down the slopes of Ben Lomond, a thick white cruddled surface like the skin of a corpse, more sinister than the black clouds that rolled across it. The year was dying round him; the dank smell of decaying leaves and rotting wood hung in his nostrils; something within him too was dying, but this he did not know.

For the happy innocence on the surface of that life at Rossdhu had shivered and broken for ever. Corruption had been at work underneath. There was no security then in his old sunny acceptance of life. Life was not lovely and happy if left to itself to slide along like a boat on summer waters. At any moment it might happen that:

> " When the lift grew dark, and the wind blew loud,
>   And gurly grew the sea,"

—and the boat be rent asunder, and the face of its captain turn into that of the devil.

XX

*T*HEY heard that Colquhoun had been seen in London with the Lady Katherine, then that he had left for Italy. The family conferred, the law was called in, King Charles sent royal mandates to the Lord Justice-General of Scotland and the Lord Advocate, and a weighty prosecution was drawn up against Colquhoun for the criminal offences of adultery and incest. The marriage tie of sister-in-law was considered the same as the blood tie of sister.

There was however no charge against the girl herself, who was regarded as a helpless victim. For there was a still graver charge against Colquhoun, that of using witchcraft to gain his ends, and employing his foreign servant, Carlippis, ' ane necromancer,' to win the girl to him by means of love philtres, and a certain five-pointed jewel in gold and rubies, that had been ' poisoned and intoxicate.'

Once again the shadow of sorcery lay on the family. The victim was own niece to a ' studier of magic and a conjurer with devils ' ; great-granddaughter to a man whose proffered jewel Queen Mary had feared to accept, because he used enchantments.

There were many at Rossdhu to hint that the Lady Katherine had taken kindly enough to magic. She, who could not bear to sit still at her lessons or her needlework and had refused to learn any of the housewifely arts, on the grounds that they kept her indoors, would stay in, even when the sun was shining in summer weather, in the little round room in the west turret that Carlippis had been given as a study.

There, with Sir John, she would watch him by the hour at his doubtless horrible and blasphemous work. That she learned something of it on her own account was more than probable; and the servants now remembered one instance after another of how she had used her powers on them. She had made them obey her in disobedience to their masters, and why, they could not tell.

At one she had looked until his head swam, and he could see nothing but a green pool, and in it her eyes like two imps dancing.

These stories were added to those of her mother, her uncle, her great-grandfather, and considered by the servants as more spicy bits of scandal than even the details of her seduction by their master. They added a note of disapproval of their mistress, who had neglected to shut herself into a darkened room, and there remain until either she died of grief or satisfied decency by a reasonably long illness.

Lilias in fact was showing a quiet fortitude that surprised all who knew her. Her young brother's face had grown so stern that for the first time in her life she did not dare to speak to him. But now for the first time she did not wish to share her sorrow. The shock of this discovery had stunned her. Her vanity had been a glittering shield between her and the world, and now it lay destroyed, since Sir John had preferred Kat to herself. The same simplicity that had upheld her vanity now accepted this fact.

The picture of herself as a lovely and gracious woman, to which she had been accustomed all these years, had been shattered, so that all she could see in it was her cracked image. Not gracious and lovely then, not even trustful, with all her innocence abused, but "a fool—a fool!" she sobbed, alone in her room, "oh God, what a fool I have been!"

And her folly had hurt Kat more than herself. Kat had been in her charge since a child; and now Kat was a criminal, flying from her home and country, because Lilias had thought too much of herself to look after her.

Since Sir John Colquhoun had failed to appear and stand his trial, the young Earl of Montrose, against the advice and urging of all his friends and advisers, decided to go now to Italy in search of him and the Lady Katherine. It had always been agreed that he must go abroad. But how, said all his friends, could he possibly think of doing so at just this moment, when in a few months King Charles would be in Scotland for his Coronation? What would become of all his chances to make a good impression on his sovereign, and lay the foundations of his career? It was bad enough that this family scandal should happen just now, for King Charles' domestic life was irreproachable. But Montrose's own married life was also above reproach; it was all the more important for him to bear testimony to this fact by his presence in the bosom of his devoted family.

So argued his father and mother and brother-in-law, his guardians, Archie Napier and Graham of Morphie, chief among a score of others. Only Lilias did not try to persuade him, and that not because she wished him to seek her husband and sister.

"What difference does it make?" she said. "Kat would come back if she wished. She can do anything she chooses."

Magdalen's haunted eyes said "Yes" to that. She sat very still, except for her hands,—twisting her long fingers, she said, "She has done this on purpose. She knew you would follow her. She knew the Coronation was coming, that it would ruin your whole life. Why do you let her do with you what she chooses?"

He stared helplessly at her. Women were mad, he thought, especially when they spoke of each other. Magdalen and Kat, the thought of the other made each of them 'poisoned and intoxicate.' He turned in revulsion from his life among women, his sisters, his wife, his mother-in-law. They talked round him, they told him things about himself, and things about each other. Little points of bitterness, of too acute perception, barbed their tongues.

Their dreams were all of 'favour and of prettiness,'—of a new title, of a place at Court, of silk dresses by candlelight. On the reverse side of this was a ceaseless vigilance, a clutch as with claws on all that they held as their possession,—yes, even on thoughts and affections.

He told his wife he would have no word against his sister; and a paralysing silence grew between them.

"There is no real love in the world between a man and woman," he thought; and she, "I am driving him away, I am losing him, and if I lose him, what will I do?"

But she did nothing. Between her brows was a little strained look of expectation, rather than fear. For where there is fear there is hope, and not for one moment did she allow herself to hope that her husband would stay in Scotland until after the Coronation. In proportion as it drew nearer, she could feel Jamie's attention waver and recede from it. It was natural to him to fling away his advancement in order to pursue and save his sister from dishonour, unwilling though she be. And Magdalen had seen this coming, before even the occasion that caused it.

So, early in the year whose spring was to end in the Coronation at Edinburgh, the Earl of Montrose left his country for Italy, in company with Willy Graham, the son of Graham of Morphie, and a small retinue.

When it came to the parting, Magdalen did not weep nor cling to him; it was he then who held her to him, spoke little broken words of farewell, tried to cheer her with his own sorrow at leaving her. But she gave no response; it seemed to him that she had frozen within his arms.

Then he went; and she stood still and stared after him, until she turned to quiet the crying of young Johnnie, who was hanging on to her skirts and had become as much aware as a puppy might be of the unnatural chill and tension in his mother.

Her own movement broke it. She went round the house, looking on this and that which Jamie had left behind; his golf clubs, his silver arrow and other trophies from Saint Andrews, his great folio of Raleigh's *History of the World*—and on that her eyes rested in a dull wonder that he had not taken it.

" But he must know it too well by now to need it with him," she thought, with that faint acrid flavour that tinged her thoughts of all those things in which he escaped from his home, his safety, his self-interest, and her.

These lifeless objects then were all that were left to her of that fervent body that had lain and laughed for joy within her arms. For three years she had had him with her, had borne a son to bind him to her, and now he had gone. Why had she always known this would happen? If she had not known it, she would have been so happy with him all this time, as happy perhaps as he. But her memory of his eyes, of his step on the stairs, of his voice when he teased her many fears, gave her the lie.

> " I know my love by his way of walking,
>   And I know my love by his way of talking,
>   And I know my love by his eyes of blue,
>   And if my love leaves me, what will I do ? "

No, whatever happiness in life came to her, she could never be as happy as he would always be, whatever of darkness and sadness came to him. Her nurse's old song rang in her head, mocking her:

> " And still she cried, ' I love him the best,
>   But a troubled mind sure can know no rest,'
>   And still she cried, ' Bonny lads are few,
>   And if my love leaves me, what will I do? ' "

At the echo of that refrain, some long imprisoned thing broke loose in her; in a release that was agony, she rushed to the window, flung it wide, and cried out into the empty air, " Oh, Jamie, come back, come back, and take me with you! "

But the wood below was still, where once she had heard the startled pigeons rise and clatter in the branches at his approach, as he ran up to greet her the evening before their wedding.

XXI

EVERY morning he was unsure for an instant where he was; the strident sounds that came into his waking dreams were so unfamiliar, even the footsteps sharper than those he had known, and the voices twanging and resonant as a violin string, knowing exactly what they had to say. Always there was the sound of bells, church bells pealing, bells on harness and mule carriages tinkling and clattering. Shutters rose before his opening eyes, each bar a luminous green, dark above and melting into pale below, like the scales of a dragon's skin held up against the sun. In the top corner a tiny finger-point of that intrusive light burned crimson, then gold, then white.

Outside, a blazing world awaited the young Earl of Montrose, where towns that looked like flowers smelled more strong and strange than even the slums of Glasgow; and the sunlight cut the streets into patterns. Bright glances met his, keen and conscious, quick in appraisement, learning all that could be learned about him by sight, while the busy intelligence behind them catalogued it securely.

Was it the sunlight that cut the mind too into such sharp patterns, divided God from man with such neat efficiency, parted the body from both mind and soul, so that neither need be troubled by the other? Here, one knew where one was. The street or the palazza and the sunlight was the place for man; the dimly glittering darkness of the church, where the light of day never entered, was the place for God. He never troubled the mind of common men as everywhere in Scotland. But here, the mind was not God's place. It was for Him to be; for His priests to give His orders; for the rest of mankind to accept.

And to accept was the lesson Montrose learned of Italy, as millions of northern foreigners have learned it since. Relationships were put in their places. Magdalen became more distinctly his wife, the mother of his children, the guardian of his home; and Kat his erring sister, who had brought disgrace on his family.

That she had shaken him to the depths, so that he had thought he could never touch any woman again, was a half-forgotten nightmare.

And the quest for her did not absorb his whole self as it had done in Scotland. His home was no longer in the centre of his life. News of what happened there came to him vaguely and belatedly. Not till three months after he had left Scotland did he learn that Magdalen would bear him a second child in his absence.

She wrote that she was glad to have something to do, and she would leave Johnnie wholly to his father, if he would let her have this new one all her own,—which was only fair, since Jamie would not be there when she was born. For 'she' it was to be, since Magdalen, unusual in her age, wanted a daughter more than another son. And Jamie guessed that this too was because a daughter would be the more ' all her own.'

Both family and country remained dear to him, but were growing a little foreign. England-Scotland—an island up in the north—remote and mist-enshrouded, even a trifle barbarous— so he now began to see it in the light of his new companions' questions.

Was it true that in his country they had only lately began to use forks at dinner? that in spite of the frigid climate the inhabitants of the northern mountains went about half-naked? that there were neither gardeners nor sculptors in the whole island? since their great lords, when they wished to adorn their estates, had to send for them from Italy? And the compliments Montrose received on his own table manners and knowledge of modern languages, the surprise which greeted his remark that he had not travelled before, unflatteringly revealed the general opinion of his country.

Even his standard of sportsmanship had to be readjusted. No one here had even heard of golf, and when he tried to explain it, it was regarded as an incredibly crude and childish game. Archery was out of date in warfare, and therefore in sport too. Montrose buried his pearl-inlaid bow at the bottom of his trunk, and learned all that he could of modern gunnery from the progressive Italian engineers.

So he did in all things. No sternly active dreams of what *he* would do, now came from him, as they had done in his northern home, where the bleak air, the frowning aspect of the rugged heath against the sky, the draughty corner by the fire, invited all glow and comfort, all prospect of life and variety to come from within. But here, sensuous and teeming life surrounded him, from the lover serenading his mistress in the warm darkness of the summer night, to the lizard darting like a living emerald across the sun-baked rock; and here, for the only time in his life, he relaxed, received, let life flow round him and into him.

But he did what he could with the guess-work which was all he could make of Colquhoun's movements. He wrote letters and sent messengers to one town after another, he went to Rome and made inquiries of the Ambassador and the English college there.

In Rome there was a colony of Scots and English, more immediately friendly and fluent than any he had known. How they talked! It must be the sun, which disinclined one to do anything else. But the talk of these witty connoisseurs, these cultured men of the world, was by no means all of art and letters, still less of the events that were racking Europe,—of the war that was devastating Germany, the death of the great Swedish conqueror, Gustavus Adolphus, at the height of his triumphs, and the growing danger to Protestantism all over Europe.

To the handful of Protestants in this alien city close under the Vatican, whose shadow was advancing with its armies over Europe, what mattered most was the relative value of the Italian money to pounds Scots or sterling.

Detached from the responsibilities of their estates, they clung to slighter personal relations, were quickly pleased or annoyed with new arrivals, gossiped, quarrelled, took sides, split into factions, drank enormously of Italian wine while complaining that it was not English ale, and did all they could to provide themselves with worries, so that they might not be too much cloyed with the unwonted amenities of their life.

So young Lord Angus explained to Montrose, when he took him to dine at the English college in Rome and expounded the little colony, easily, mockingly, as he could never have done before he had left Scotland. Angus' father was back there, happily expecting his promotion at the Coronation to the Marquisate of Douglas,—but what odds would that make out here? demanded Angus, where one God-damn milord was of the same rank as another. But his father would never understand that; he had just told Angus to increase his retinue on the strength of the new family honour, "and that's all the strength that can carry it, for it has never occurred to the old gentleman to increase my allowance as well."

Did not Montrose find all this family feeling a trifle ridiculous ? Douglas would be delighted with his son for entertaining the head of the Grahams to dinner, but why should they, two sensible fellows living in the present day, care if their ancestors had fallen together at Flodden, or slipped up at Selkirk, or been pinked at Pinkie, as long as this pleasant golden Roman wine could now make them fall together under the same table?

Montrose laughed rather shyly, envying his companion's rapid flow of talk. And yet as he watched the freckled, blunt-featured face that had acquired this new look of conscious cleverness— was this what he himself had wanted to be?

"Though Caesar's paragon I cannot be,
Yet shall I soar in thought as high as he."

But only a prig, a poet, would remember here the lines he had written in the margin of his school books. Once again he accepted the occasion, and soon was merrier than Angus, though never as critically aware of occasions for laughter in his fellows.

But in the opinion of that over-civilized young man, suspicious of the promise of strength, even sternness, in the keen eye and high-bridged, hawk-like nose of his companion's profile, Montrose was too country-bred, too unyielding and reserved, ever to make

his way in this flexible modern world. There was something
aloof and haughty in his bearing, for all the boyish simplicity
with which he relied on Angus to tell him the customs of the
country. His pride was sensitive, not to take offence, but to
avoid any occasion for it, in himself or others. Often had Angus
seen him prevent some silly squabble among their fellow countrymen, as though he could not bear that any standard in his company
should be lower than his own.

The recent disgrace to his family had deepened his natural
sensitiveness; he feared that in talking to him, people would
remember the scandal about his sister, and be thinking ill of her.
This made him unwilling to seek new friendships among his
countrymen. All he met knew that he had come abroad in
pursuit of his sister and brother-in-law, but none dared refer to
this, nor question him. In a society so chattily intimate, this
was rare indeed, and he himself was half aware of its rarity, for
sometimes it struck him how much more at home would Sir John
Colquhoun be in this company than himself. He would even
find himself listening for Colquhoun's voice among the conversation, so appropriate would be the intrusion of those eagerly
social tones.

It was while he was at Rome that a report reached him of a
very tall English milord at Venice, travelling with his young
wife. Sir John was certainly travelling incognito, and would
probably pass as an Englishman to help his disguise. Carlippis
did not appear to be with him, but otherwise there was some
probability that this Englishman might be Colquhoun, enough
to send Montrose hot-foot to Venice.

He reached it on a fierce midday in June. He had been riding
since three o'clock that morning, and had changed horses twice
to keep up the pace. In the last hour of noonday heat he seemed
to have been riding in his sleep, and had to hold on to his saddle
for a moment when he dismounted, giddy and half blinded.
Then he walked down a narrow path beside a roadway of water,
and sat in the doorway of a tavern and drank a glass of wine while
he sent his Italian servant to make inquiries.

He was given a roll of bread, and crumbled and threw some to the pigeons that were cooing and wheeling in long white strokes through the glittering air. His eyes shut against the glare, and black suns came whirling past the red darkness inside his eyelids. They turned into faces, silly faces like those he had drawn on the sand as a child—three dots for eyes and nose, a stroke for a mouth. " I am falling asleep," he said to himself, and opened his eyes for an instant on the pigeons.

They were swooping and curling in a little cloud, round a figure in front of him in a white-and-blue dress, who stood throwing crumbs to them on the edge of the water. It was Kat, bareheaded, with her face upturned to the sun, smiling. Small dark freckles dotted her nose and chin; she wore earrings that shook and quivered in points of light. The prow of a gondola stood up from the water beneath her; a pigeon balanced itself on it and fed from the hand she held out to it. A young man stood behind her, smiling at her.

Jamie blinked furiously, half sprang from his chair, opened his eyes again. There was nobody there, and no gondola. Only the pigeons still wheeled and fluttered, stepped towards him and bowed, cooing. " It was the heat," he said aloud, so that he might believe it.

The innkeeper came forward to tell him that his lunch was ready. Savoury smells of hot pasta and cheese, of cold garlic sausage, of a great bowl of *bouillabaisse*, wherein floated mussels and tiny lobsters and strange red fish of the Mediterranean, conquered all other senses. He sat at the table, suddenly aware that he was starving.

It took him till next day to run Sir John to earth; and that afternoon he came to the house where he lodged. As his gondola came round the corner, he saw three workmen noisily engaged in dragging a great flat package out of a barge, and up the marble steps of a house like a palace. The waters of the canal lapped lazily, lispingly against the marble steps, in ironic undercurrent to the shrill shouts and curses that hurtled above them. The group made the only stir in that shining afternoon; they staggered up the steps under their burden, disappeared through the doorway, and left the canal to its silence of little whispering sounds.

Jamie's guide told him that this was the house of the English milord. He went up the steps and through the doorway where the men had so lately passed, and now he heard their voices on the stairs above him, and then another voice, giving directions, querulous, indignant.

At the sound of it, the blood came rushing into his head, and his hand went to his sword. "Pray God I shall find him alone," he said to himself. He had parted from Kat in anger and horror; he did not want her to meet him now in his bloodthirsty rage against her lover.

He entered a vast, cool, green-shuttered room, blinked his eyes against its sudden darkness, saw the men undoing the package, and Sir John, leaning over it, saw that his sister was not there.

"Tell your fellows to go," he said.

The tall man who was fussing unhappily over his new possession, spun round, straightening his back, stared, then made a panic-stricken movement away from him, towards the window, pushing back the shutter, so that the blinding sunlight flooded in, cutting off that end of the room.

Montrose was astounded. He knew Colquhoun to be no coward, yet his stare had been one of terrified agitation, and his first movement that of flight. He had checked it, however; he now came back to the men and ordered them to leave the package as it was.

They expostulated, waved their hands, looked suspiciously at the new milord who had entered so mysteriously, unannounced, and did what they were told with as much protest as possible. Sir John took refuge in watching them go, in calling after them some slight, insufficient order, in patting and glancing at the top corner of his half-unwrapped picture, wherefrom, beneath a rag of dirty sacking and a splintered lath, there looked out the pale head of a girl, her hair bound with coral.

Montrose saw that this was a beaten man before him, who had been so before he himself encountered him.

H

" Where is Kat? " he demanded in fierce exultation, knowing the answer before the other could be made to confess it.

Colquhoun walked up and down the room, trying every now and then to make a gesture, to induce an ironic tone into his voice, to show that he was still at least master of himself, if no longer of the situation, as he answered his young kinsman's stern questions. He had been abandoned a week ago. Kat had not deceived him; she had told him she was tired of him, that she intended to leave him for a young French gentleman, with whom they had been pleasantly acquainted for the last three months. Not all Sir John's grief and rage could move her,—here he forgot his attempt at aloofness, and sobbed.

Montrose asked the Frenchman's name; he could learn little else of him,—the lad was a son of a noble family, and had seemed a nice intelligent fellow,—Colquhoun had had no suspicion of his treachery until the blow fell on him—and then how cool they had both been about it, how shameless, heartless! He did not understand these modern young people, they had no passion, nothing but cold calculation—and yet Kat had been so mad that she had refused to take any of his presents, or even the clothes he had bought her; she had just stepped into a gondola one day last week, and gone off with nothing but the blue-and-white dress that she was wearing.

" She had been feeding the pigeons," thought Montrose.

Had she projected that image of herself, serene and careless, so that he should know her happy? The young man who had stood and smiled at her, proud, tender and amused, gave greater promise of her happiness than any she could have had with this pricked bladder of a man.

He looked for the first time at the room round him, dim and cool as a cave, except at the end where the sunlight struck upon a table, painted with goddesses in chariots drawn by leopards, its shadow falling on the white floor in a pool of brilliant violet light. Colquhoun had flung open that shutter in his instinctive desire to escape him. Well, Colquhoun had escaped him, he told himself bitterly.

"What of Carlippis?" he exclaimed suddenly. His worst fears were over when he learned that Carlippis had left Sir John months ago for the more amusing and profitable service of a great merchant. So this new escapade had at least not been engineered for his own ends by Carlippis. He had used Colquhoun and left him, as indeed Kat had too. She had never been in love with him; Carlippis had been the true seducer, with his talk of adventure and travel, experiment and freedom, and with the deadly enchantment of his hypnotic powers.

Colquhoun had merely been her gateway to adventure, a make-shift, as he had been to Carlippis. No one had found it worth while to stick to him. His vanity had been so cruelly wounded that no other punishment could hurt him. He would have welcomed death, if it could have been death as revenge on the successful seducer. Now not even death could save his face. That pleasant slippery polish of his was all rubbed off. He had lost his place in the world; and would go on losing it, rather than face the shame of returning, a poor cuckolded lover, to ask the pardon of his wife and community.

Helpless, rudderless, he drifted about the room, coming always to anchor in front of his purchase, as though it contained his single claim to self-respect. It was the first work of art he had dared to buy without the advice of Carlippis. Mantegna was not a fashionable painter, but King Charles of England, a noted connoisseur, had been buying them,—and he had thought it very pretty—and the subject, a Roman triumph, had appealed to him. That girl's fair head, peeping out of the top corner, was that of a captive virgin. If ever he made love again, it would only be to fair women; they were docile, gentle, faithful; to love them would be a sort of loyalty to his poor wife, to whom he could never now return.

But at the thought of Lilias among her pretty, modern furniture at Rossdhu, stitching at her embroidery picture of Queen Margaret and the Robber,—and then of Kat sitting before the fire in a still circle of enchantment that had drawn into it his unwilling soul and chained it so that it had hung quivering in expectation of her voice or glance—at that, his last defence fell from him, he sat down suddenly, and his head flopped forward on to the cold, shiny surface of the painted table.

He never knew that Montrose, who had come to kill him, had left the room; he knew only that he had lost Kat, and had never won her.

* * *

Montrose went down the water steps to his gondola, and told the man to go wherever he liked. The honey-white houses drifted past him, the curved shadows of bridges trembling on the water. Sounds came sleepily towards him through the silence of this city without traffic, in the hour of its siesta,—the rhythmical swirl of the oar behind him, the lapping of the ripples on the marble steps, the occasional long cry of a gondolier, " ohé, ohé! " as the prow of another gondola glided round a corner.

" I am seeing Venice," thought Montrose, reminding himself of the dream of all would-be travellers in his country; he could have laughed at the emptiness that the satisfaction of that dream had brought him. And suddenly, as the triumphant bells pealed out the hour, he asked his gondolier what day of June it was. His guess was right—this was the 23rd, the day King Charles was being crowned in Edinburgh.

On this iridescent shimmer of white heat there impinged a scene of gaunt grey houses huddling into narrow streets, staggering up against a grey sky, of faces peering from all the tiny crooked windows, bunched together under the gables, of people standing in the streets wherever there was or wasn't room to stand, in mud, in rain-puddles, on each other's toes, all crowding, craning, straining to see a little company of men who rode out of the gates of a huge grey castle, their cloaks teased and tossed by the wind that always whistled round that corner.

In their midst rode a man with the ancient crown of Scotland on his head, under a canopy borne by men who were all of them Jamie's friends, and one of them was his brother-in-law, and one of them should have been himself. He had thrown away the greatest opportunity for his ambition, to pursue a sister so wanton that she could not even stay six months with her first lover.

" I have ruined my career," he thought, and for perhaps four minutes was sunk in the rich, egotistic despair of youth.

So had Colquhoun, and his home, country and reputation as well, but his case naturally did not strike Jamie as so tragic. On a wave of passionate homesickness he longed to go straight back to Magdalen and put his head down on her breast, and tell her how unhappy he was, and what a fool he had been. But there, alas, she would agree.

XXII

HE was right. Magdalen agreed with him, so did Napier, so did everyone who knew him. He was right, too, about the weather. It was raining in Edinburgh; the procession might have just missed the rain if it had started in time, but it was half an hour late,—" as well as seven years late," Napier reflected. Later on, he was apt to say,—" It all began with the Coronation."

For everything went wrong after it, and yet nothing went wrong at it. King Charles made a fine show on horseback and the towns welcomed him with roars of loyalty. At Perth, the house of Montrose's maternal uncle, the late Earl of Gowrie, whose wizened head still adorned the front of the Tolbooth in Edinburgh, was prepared as a royal residence; the glovers did their sword-dance in green caps and white shoes with silver strings and red ribbons and as many different steps as possible.

Old William Drummond's masque of *Endymion* was performed, and young Drummond of Madertie told everyone the poet was his cousin, and much better than the English poets Ben Jonson or Shakespeare. Endymion, dressed according to the stage directions, "like a shepherd," in a long coat of crimson velvet with gilt leather buskins, was as splendid as the King himself.

The expense everywhere was enormous. All the town's soldiers in Edinburgh had to be put into white satin doublets and black velvet breeches and silk stockings, with gilded pikes, to form a royal guard to the King. The provost and bailies in furred red robes, attended by the town councillors in black velvet, gave the King a gold basin worth a mint of money, into which the provost shook out a purse of a thousand gold pieces.

" The King," wrote Napier to his absent ward, " looked gladly upon speech and gift, but the Marquis of Hamilton, Master of His Majesty's Horse, hard beside him, meddled with the gift as due to *him* by virtue of his office." Which was not what the loyal townsfolk had intended when they scraped the sum together.

The King had brought five hundred English nobles in his train,

as well as Scots, and Scottish hospitality, poorer but prouder than
its neighbour's, was in a fret not to be shamed before them. The
city gave them a banquet, a great success, as the whole town
could see, for after it they all came dancing down the High Street,
provost and proud English nobles, bailies and councillors, all
holding hands, without their hats, tripping and frisking like lambs,
'with music and much merriment.' In such a mood it was
blissfully clear that Scotland and England were one nation.

But there was always next morning.

And more mischievous in effect than all the pride and greed
of the nobles was a single small conscientious English priest, the
former Chancellor of Oxford and present Bishop of London,
whom the King had brought to conduct the Coronation service
and set the crown on his head. All bishops were suspect, but
worse than a Scots bishop was an English bishop, and worst of
them all was Bishop Laud, with his fussy respect for his cloth,—
'of the cloth clothy, and doubly so,' Rothes had discovered,
since he was the son of a clothier and a clothier's widow. The
Scots took his low birth as an insult to themselves, aggravated by
his conceited Oxford voice and tactless remarks. He had referred
to the English Parliament as 'that noise.' He now gave it as
his opinion that there was 'no religion in Scotland.'

No religion, was there? Let him wait and he would see!
Certainly he 'knew not the stomach of that people,' as Charles'
father, King Jamie, had surmised in one of his many flashes of
pawky native shrewdness. King Jamie would never have been
so mistaken as to make this earnest, honest, restless, provincial-
minded little man the chief figure next to the King in the
Coronation.

But did King Charles ever see what was happening round him?
(and Napier scratched the imprudent question out of his letter to
Montrose)—did he ever see, except in a glass darkly, any motive
or impulse that was not his own?

And his own intentions were admirable. He looked on his
journey to Scotland as a sacred pilgrimage to the home of his
forefathers, and his own most precious infancy; on the eve of the

Coronation he prayed all night in the chapel at Edinburgh, in the spirit of a young knight of old, that God might fit him for his high task as King of this his native land.

But the vigil did little to fit him for next morning's squabbles as to whether the Lord Chancellor, Kinnoull, or the Archbishop of Saint Andrews, should go first in the procession. Everyone was waiting to start, when an insulting message reached the King from the old Earl of Kinnoull, that he would resign his office as Chancellor, for 'never a stoled priest in Scotland should set a foot before him, so long as his blood was hot.'

His tired sovereign, heavy-eyed from lack of sleep, merely answered—" Well, let's go to business; I will not meddle further with that old cankered, gouty man, at whose hands there is nothing to be gained but sour words."

So off they set, more than half an hour late, and by then it had begun to rain; and in the Chapel of Holyrood the English bishop, Laud, set the crown on Charles' head, while the Scots nobles fixed their resentful eyes on him more often than on their King.

Napier, seeing this as he bore the canopy over the King, turned his eyes in sadness from that watchful, suspicious congregation, and caught a glimpse behind him of the long sallow face of Archibald Campbell, Lord Lorne, who bore the King's train.

And his fear for the King became coupled with fear for Montrose. It was wrong that Montrose was not here, not merely on his own account, but to help counterbalance this pack of greedy wolves that howled round the King. It was wrong too that the heir to Argyll was here when Montrose was not, that he was one of the train-bearers, talking to the King whenever possible, with that soft, slightly halting, hesitating voice, that must make a welcome contrast to the truculent tones of all the aggrieved nobles, all furiously concerned with their tithes and their dignities and their properties.

Lord Lorne had been careful to inquire from Napier, in King Charles' hearing, for news of the absent Montrose, and whether he had found his sister and brother-in-law.—" A nasty business that, to have in a man's family,—sorcery and incest," he had added, with pursed lips and an oddly feminine relish, while one of those crooked eyes flickered round to watch the effect on Charles' fastidious moral standard.

And Charles seems to like him, " as he likes any food that is set before him," observed Napier, with a connoisseur's irritation at a duller palate.

But now Napier's disquiet went deeper than the moment.

Whatever game fate intended those three to play,—the King, the man who would be Scotland's most powerful noble, and the youth whom Napier loved as his own son,—it was a wrong move that so early in the game placed the future Earl of Argyll by his sovereign's side, while it absented the Earl of Montrose.

* * *

On the happy news of a birth of a second son (but on the unlucky date of October 13th) Charles hurried back to London, the Queen, and her new baby, James, Duke of York.

The Coronation was over, and the royal progress through Scotland. One relic of its pomp remained. That was the show of a camel, belonging to the King, which was led by tuck of drum through all the cities of Scotland, except on the Sabbath day. So the contemptuous beast continued the procession, shuffling through the grey, chilly little towns, as crowded at the sight of him as at that of the King.

Other results of the Coronation did not give so much satisfaction. Everybody was in debt, and nobody had got all they hoped for. The waters of the South Esk had dried up, and it was thought to be a bad omen both for Scotland and the family of Carnegie. The old Earl of Kinnoull died of a fit of gout, brought on by a fit of temper. So that hot blood of his was cold within a year of his quarrel with the Archbishop of Saint Andrews; and the ' stoled priest ' he had then thrust behind him now stepped forward into his shoes as Lord Chancellor.

It was another step to disaster in the State.

The one happy aspect of the appointment, in Napier's slightly malicious eyes, was that Lord Lorne had applied for it, and was sulking at his disappointment. Otherwise they all, as much as old Kinnoull, hated to be led by a priest in affairs of state. No churchman had held the office of Chancellor since the Reformation. This appointment then was a step ' Back to Rome.'

And there were others. Two months after the Coronation, Laud had been made Archbishop of Canterbury, and had at once appointed a majority of bishops on the Scottish Privy Council. With arrogant simplicity, he believed that devout Churchmen must make the best rulers; but the nobles expressed a blasphemously opposite view, for they found themselves out-voted by the bishops, who were safe to vote only as the King wanted, since they held their appointments from the Crown.

All that King Charles wanted was ' to promote, first, the good and peace of the Church, and, second, the increase of religion.' To do this, he proposed to uproot the aforesaid Church, and remodel it without sanction from Scotland.

He had all the less right to meddle with Scotland, since he was never the formal head of her Church, as he was of the Church of England. But he, the dilettante art-collector, and ' the clothier's son,' with his doubly hereditary liking for a neat and elegant appearance, had both been shocked by the Scottish churches,— not merely by the lack of beauty and music and fine vestments, but often by the sheer filth and squalor, the deliberate disorder, the loud, irreverent voices of people who refused to kneel to their God even when they received communion, but stared critically at the preacher as if challenging him to speak any better than they.

So Charles, on leaving his native country, ordered prayers to be held in the King's Chapel at Holyrood, as in England, with surplices and a monthly Communion, to be received kneeling, that there might be this single oasis in the desert of Scottish self-conceit and stubbornness before their God. He had restored the tithes to the Kirk, and given it financial independence. But of what use was material aid? It was the soul of religion he longed to save, all through his kingdoms.

This he now set out to do, with the romantic enthusiasm of

a Crusader. And beside him, urging him on whenever his dilatory spirit slackened, was Laud, his new Archbishop of Canterbury, of whom old King James had years ago complained that he ' loved to toss and change and to bring matters to a pitch of reformation floating in his own brain.'

A book of instructions in the new form of Church government was published in England and sent up to Scotland. It was called the *Book of Canons;* it promised that a new Prayer Book would arrive shortly, which must be read on pain of high treason in all Scottish churches, in place of John Knox's *Book of Common Order*, or the improved Liturgy of Aberdeen, or any version ordained by the Kirk. And the English Archbishop, ' assisted ' by some English and two or three Scottish bishops in London, had prepared this book, in insult to the national religion.

English bishops were the enemy, Scottish bishops the traitors, and all bishops the villains of the piece.

To threaten a people with high treason for not using a book which was not yet published, struck Napier as a safe prophecy of a national crisis.

He sat down in his house at Merchiston to write to Montrose, with a greater urgency than he had used since the young man had left home three years before.

XXIII

BELATEDLY, as always in the case of any severe shock, Montrose began to suffer the effect of his disillusionment with his sister. He went to France in search of her and her Frenchman, and found no chance to trace them. He lost hope, not only of finding her, but of there being any use in doing so. She had chosen her way, and it was not his; it was the way of Carlippis, who pursued his own ends. His end had been a comfortable passage to Italy; hers had been adventure, devoid of any further purpose. Passionless, except in her wild egoism, she could rejoice in setting out to sea in a sieve, without rudder or anchor.

She had destroyed Montrose's first and best chance to make friends with his King; and this was to affect the lives of both men until the end.

Yet still more important to them both, later on, was her effect now upon her brother's spirit; which had accepted the good things of this life so gaily and unthinkingly, and was for the first time overcast with doubt and question. Kat had chosen her way, and he only wished he knew where to choose his.

But his disillusionment did not prevent him from having a very good time. He distinguished himself in the school of arms at Angers; he stayed at the delightful châteaux on the Loire, joining in the royal hunting and boating parties; he was well accepted at Court, for Louis XIII liked superb young horsemen with good looks, and would invite him to ride beside him in the hunt, reminding him of the close alliance there had always been between their countries. The name of Scotland's lovely and unhappy Queen Mary was still remembered in these woods for her fearless riding.

Queen Anne of Austria, whose beauty had been wasted on a cold husband, and abortive, unhappy love-affairs that could satisfy little more than her vanity, was coyly appreciative of Montrose's qualities. And the Dowager Queen, Marie de Medici, moaned to him about her darling daughter, Henrietta Maria, the only one of her children who really understood her,—" She longs for me to visit her in England, that peaceful and prosperous country, where there are no wars nor troubles, as everywhere else in Europe."

The news from Scotland did not sound so peaceful. Napier, who was a good letter writer, kept him in touch with them from time to time, but it was all a great way off, and all the news had happened a long time ago: and Scotland was not as exciting as ' the rarities of the East,' which he had longed to see ever since he had been a boy.

And now he met his chance of far distant travel in a Genoese sea-captain, who was on business in Paris, and in a few days would join his ship at Havre and set out for India to trade in spices, silks and jewels. He found the young Scottish noble restless and anxious for some new adventure, and persuaded him to join them. Leaning across the rough oak table in the inn corner, lithe, laughing, taut with the continual expectation of danger, the Genoese promised that Montrose should see heathen temples hidden in the jungle, and gods carved out of gold and silver, with a hundred breasts and arms, should ride an elephant and shoot a tiger.

An overland route to India would lead Montrose through Persia and Turkey as well as half the countries of Europe, but when he put this to his new friend, the captain countered him with the advantages of his new galéasse, the fastest flying vessel ever yet built.

" For please," he said, " on the road, it is not convenient that you make something always. The night, he come, you sleep,— or you do not sleep. Ah those inns! The fleas! The robbers! The women! The pox! In any case, you make nothing. But with me, you sleep, and the ship makes something. You wake up, you are many miles nearer India. It is more convenient."

His dazzling smile lit up his lean, dark, rugged face; enormous earrings dangled on either side of his short black beard ; his hair was as stiffly bushy as an Ethiopian's. A son of the ancient Ligurian race, its blood mingled with that of Saracen pirates, he belonged not only to the keen commercial Italy of the present day, but to an age ' when the world had not yet adored Rome, nor the ocean yielded the precedence to Tiber.' That sentence from an adventure story Jamie had read at school now convinced him more than his companion's eloquence. And when he diffidently admitted to talking Italian, the matter was decided, so clear was it that more than all else in life it was ' convenient.'

But when he returned to his lodgings, he found letters come from home, and one was from Magdalen.

She never urged his return, never even asked about it. She gave him news of the estates, and the improvements her father was making in the policies, and news of the children. James the younger (for James had refused to be a daughter, and her reprisal for that was to call him by his father's name, but never by the diminutive that all used for him)—James was growing stronger every day, though he was not near as big as Johnnie had been at his age. And Johnnie, aged five, was so forward that Master Forrett had taught him to read from a horn-book; and he rode his pony gallantly, had good hands and an easy seat; he saluted his father's portrait every morning, and it was remarkable how like it he himself was growing.

Her restraint struck her young husband for the first time. He knew the difficulty she always found in writing a letter, not in the actual writing and spelling, for she had been taught better than many young women of her rank, but in choosing her words, and even her subject. She would sit biting the fronds off her quill, stroking it against her chin, frowning till her brows nearly met together. " There is no need to say that," she would answer to most suggestions.

Suddenly she had felt the need to tell him all this. His sons were growing, and he had not even seen the younger; and all that the boys could know of their father was that portrait that Jameson had painted of him when he was seventeen, just before his wedding.

And in a flash he remembered coming in out of a windy autumn night, and sitting at Morphie's table, and not listening to a word the old man was saying about that portrait, his wedding present to them, but crumbling his bread and marshalling the pellets beside his plate into regiments and emplacements, while in his head there sang a high wild song without words, because he was to be married to Magdalen to-morrow.

He turned sharply to the other letter that the post had brought him. It was from Archie Napier; and for no reason Jamie felt a keen anxiety as he broke the seal. Had Magdalen fallen ill since she had written?

More than a year ago, Napier had written to tell Montrose of the death of his own wife, ' dear Margaret,' as all thought of her. The shock of that news had made Montrose search his letters first for any personal names before reading them through. So that he was immediately relieved to find the troubles he feared were only public, not private.

But then he grew disturbed, as he followed more closely the fine, upstanding strokes of Napier's handwriting. It was not like Archie to be an alarmist, but what was all this about an English book of rules for Scotland's worship? What right had any foreigner to meddle in the way that Scots addressed their God?

" Oh wha dare meddle wi' me? " he whistled, but his anger was grave enough. His ancestor and namesake, James Graham, had saved Scotland three times from the power of England? Now that would be in vain. This bugbear that Scotland had fought against from the beginning of time, spilling her dearest blood to escape it, had come once again suddenly, insidiously near at hand. Was Scotland after all to suffer English rule, to pay her money to England, to have even her religion, the trophy she had won from Rome, dictated by an English priest?

If so, his true adventure lay at home. He would return by London, and at last see Charles, this time in his Court at Whitehall. Napier hoped for this, it was plain, for he told him that the best person to introduce him to his sovereign was the great Scottish Marquis of Hamilton, Charles' closest and most trusted friend.

Now was his chance, far more than at the Coronation; now that he had seen the world, was an experienced man, and not a raw home-bred youth, might he not *now* be the means of reconciling his King with his country, and liberty with loyalty?

Once again the crowded foreground of his life shivered and broke up. All the plans of his Eastern voyage scurried away like so much sea-drift. So did the invitation of King Louis to hunt with him for several days at his ' absurd little box of a place at Versailles ' ; and a more embarrassing invitation from Queen Anne to meet her as by accident one evening in the gardens of the Louvre, and there walk with her and talk of his country, " for she finds the English type extremely sympathetic," said the pretty waiting-maid who so discreetly submitted the invitation, after a preliminary altruistic flirtation that Montrose had ingenuously supposed to be conducted only on her own account.

None of these things needed now to be considered. His narrow Parisian lodgings went whirling about him—that book of Montaigne's essays must be returned to the old doctor at the Sorbonne,—that bill for his new stirrups must be paid at once,— that tedious letter from the French savant, inquiring into his ancestry from Antoninus, could now be left unanswered.

Suddenly he was free again, at large, and starting on his adventure.

" Willy," he shouted, flinging open the door on to the staircase, to be greeted by the rich, garlic-haunted smell of cooking that was so soon to become first strange and then forgotten,—" Willy, are you there? Have you brought all my things from Angers? "

" Why yes, my lord," answered Willy's voice. " Are we to start so soon for the Indies? "

" Not the Indies this time. We start for home to-morrow."

XXIV

MONTROSE'S impression of the French Court had been that of a perpetual family quarrel; his impression of the English was that of domestic bliss. Domesticity was all the fashion, in piquant contrast with the scandals of the last reign. Those obscure, unhappy vices of the old King James, that ugly son of a beautiful mother, whose instincts had been somehow frightened and twisted before he was born, were now in the shade; and the royal nursery held instead the public eye.

The little Princess Elizabeth, the little Prince Charles, the Princess Mary, and the baby Prince James, were continually seen in their nurses' arms in varieties of lace caps, and, later, playing with their spaniels, riding their ponies, running through the Home Park, and being rowed in little boats at their river palace at Hampton Court. Their sharp sayings and engaging pranks were quoted throughout the kingdom.

And presiding over these infant angels was the devotion of their parents to each other. King Charles was so handsome and dignified and so adored his charming Queen, their children were so pretty and quaintly precocious, that it seemed as though this English royal family were that in a fairy tale, who must all live happily ever after.

Charles was indeed like a certain prince in a fairy tale, one that was begun by Kat, and ended at its first sentence: " There was once a prince that was enchanted, but did not know in what respect he differed from other men."

For here was this prince who had youth and looks and courage and perseverance; whose opinions were often sound, and intentions excellent; whose family life was beyond reproach. But was that because he was beyond temptation?

That shrewd Frenchwoman, his wife, had declared petulantly (jealous as she would have been if taken at her word) that she wished Charles had managed to fall in love with some other woman once or twice, whether before or after matrimony,—it would have made him more like other men.

For he never seemed quite to belong to their world, and that not because he created another, as poets do, or seers. He was too facile; even in his dreams everything had to be made easy for him. " If I were only——", " if it could so happen——", with these opiates in the place of any active desire, he would lie on his day-bed, looking out through the little window panes on to the lawns and flower-beds of Hampton Court, and see the trees waving that Henry VIII had planted, and think in some confused way how odd it was that Henry was dead, and he was alive; but indeed he was not thinking,—he was seeing, minute after minute, hour after hour, a picture of that beloved scene before him,—which, if only he could paint——

But no creative pulse throbbed in those sluggish veins. He was not an artist, but a collector. It needed someone from outside, —a friend, or his Queen, always urging him to something, or a despairing messenger, sent to remind him yet again that this or that was waiting to be settled—to tell him that he must do something.

Dully he rose, wishing he were a hermit of old, so that his lethargy could be called contemplation. But kings must be decisive, and he could show himself as good a king as any,—and the result of that was often some disconcertingly sudden action, made without any reference to his counsellors, who knew nothing about it till it was over.

For no man had less of the social sense than Charles; he was a unit, moving blindly in his own circuit, incapable of teaching or learning from others. Someone must stand between him and them.

As a child all his trust and admiration were placed in his brother Henry, six years older than himself. He watched Henry ride at tournaments and take a toss, and spring up muddy and laughing to catch his horse; he heard his gay, conquering shouts at fencing or tennis when he pushed his rolled-up shirt-sleeve across his hot face. The pale timid child resolved that he too would one day do these things, so that Henry should no longer treat him as a baby with rough tolerant kindness, but as a man and a brother.

He did it. The child who at four years old was too feeble to walk or talk, had become a remarkably fine horseman by the time he was twelve. But well before that time, his magnificent brother had died; and Charles had to carry on alone.

He could not do that. All his strength and determination were needed to make a man of himself; he had none over to expend on the world round him. People seemed to him now dark, now light, without reason. He never saw why they said this or that; their actions were those of a puppet show;—and someone must act the showman to him.

After Henry's death, the young Villiers, Duke of Buckingham, came to fill his place. How impudently silly was 'Steenie's' behaviour in Spain, when he and Charles went together to woo the Spanish infanta, incognito, as Mr. Thomas Smith and his servant! And there was his outrageous indiscretion with the beautiful young Queen of France, Anne of Austria!

Yet young Charles, modest, shy, reserved, had been enviously dazzled by it. As long as Buckingham lived, he saw the world only through those bright and dissipated eyes, so unlike his own. But with the same dragon-fly inconsequence as he had lived, Buckingham died, stabbed by an assassin. His death was more sudden than any of his actions.

They brought the news to Charles in the Chapel at Hampton Court; and he continued to repeat the chanting words of the Service, his face unaltered, unaware. By finishing whatever it was he was doing, by refusing to take in what he had heard, his mind could creep back for a little space into the black mercy of unconsciousness.

But the world forced its way in; forced him to know that the rudder of his life was broken.

Gradually, however, substitutes were found.

Henrietta Maria now had her first real opportunity to exert her influence. Slowly, as was natural in a young man of late development, unaccustomed to women, Charles came to observe and listen to his wife more and more. Her petulant sprightliness could always explain what motives, greedy or amorous, lay behind people's apparently simple actions. Like most women, she was a born story-lover, and had the fatal cleverness to enjoy weaving her own plots and translating them into certainties.

" Woman's wit," said he gravely, as he listened to some preposterous theory of hers to explain why it was that the Scottish nobles, whom she had never met, were behaving so troublesomely.

Woman's wit had to be supplemented. There must still be the elder brother to whom Charles could turn for final guidance. His trust in the dash and verve of reckless youth had been shattered. Henry had died suddenly as a boy, Buckingham had been murdered almost by accident. Charles must now choose someone wise and thoughtful to stand between him and the world.

In the unlucky isolation of his mind, his choice was one that scarcely any of his Court could understand. The Marquis of Hamilton did not look like a man who has soared into the sun of his sovereign's favour; on the contrary, his nervous, touchy, over-subtle nature was that of a man under a cloud. But then he was, always had been under a cloud, for he was over-shadowed by his mother.

A wisp of a shadow it was, yet enough to darken his life. Lady Anne Cunningham of Glencairn, tiny, weather-beaten, frosty-eyed, was one of those old Scottish ladies whose ferocious pride and sense of humour could blast any mere man. Hamilton's sensitive childhood had withered under her humour; but her arrogance was the more dangerous to his manhood, for it gave him ambitions that could be carried out only by a greatly heroic villain—or possibly his mother.

But Anne Cunningham was determined that a man *was* his mother, at any rate when that mother happened to be herself. Did not her blood run in his veins, and that, the blood of kings? Hamilton's royal descent was hammered into him so frequently that whenever he looked in the glass he anxiously speculated what his face would look like under a crown. Under a cloud, under a crown, it was much the same thing.

There was too a prophecy that he would succeed King Charles, which Hamilton found very unsettling to his politics.

Something in his self-distrustful nature must have caught Charles' fancy, for here was someone who could appreciate as he did the dangers and uncertainties of life. Hamilton appreciated them indeed so much as to make them twice as dangerous and uncertain as they need have been. Charles would wait with a slight sigh for one illusion after another to be shattered by Hamilton's penetrating wisdom. That secretly bewildered brain was apt to attribute motives that never existed, to be as over-flexible as Charles' was over-rigid, and equally incapable of understanding others.

To this man, the most powerful Scottish noble at the English Court, the young Earl of Montrose had first to pay his respects. The Marquis welcomed him with a great many kind inquiries, but all the time in a state of fuss, so that in spite of his determined frown and air of importance, he struck his visitor as rather an old woman,—a sad nemesis of Anne Cunningham's resolve to make the man his mother.

Hamilton was fussed because he was trying as usual to grasp more of the situation than it really afforded. Would the young man's introduction at the English Court be an advantage to himself, or the reverse? In any case, one must never make an enemy. Like a child's prayer gabbled mechanically at the back of his mind, he reminded himself of the whole duty of a courtier,—" Let me draw him out while I seem to talk most myself, charm him to my side by a warm and friendly manner."

They discussed the latest news. The King's Ship Money had fitted out forty more ships of war, which had secured the narrow seas for English trade, and saved Dunkirk from the recent attack of the Dutch.

Yet Hamilton had his doubts. A very wealthy and influential gentleman called John Hampden had refused to pay this new tax and was even now on trial, and winning the sympathy of the country.

A matter of a few pounds seemed a small proportion of his

thousands to pay towards the upkeep of the navy; but Hamilton shook his head slowly, like a cat licking its whiskers after cream, and said that a question had been involved more serious than the defence of the country's coast and trade,—and that was the question of correct parliamentary procedure.

" The English are idealists. The mere practical value of forty new ships is not to be set above a matter of principle."

" The English are apt to have principles where their interest is concerned," remarked his fellow Scot.

Hamilton smiled with some annoyance. He might have said that himself in another minute.

In compensation to himself, he gave so much good advice as to Montrose's conduct with the King that the young man began to feel as though he were a new lion-tamer being given the charge of a dangerous animal. He must remember this, avoid that, walk warily, speak carefully, and only even smile at stated intervals.

With the Queen, on the other hand, Montrose should be gay and easy, and admire the beautiful eyes of the little Prince of Wales, for she had joked so much about her ugly little black brat of a baby that it was probably to hide her sensitiveness on the subject. Her dogs too were a good topic—if he were clever he would get her to tell him stories of their remarkable intelligence.

Hamilton's air of sly affability, as if amused by his own triviality, then became deep, secret and portentous. Montrose must re-member that the English resented the presence of Scottish nobles at the Court, and were even, so he whispered, inclined to be jealous of the fact that their King had come from Scotland.

" He came long enough ago, then," said Montrose. " In Scot-land, people are apt to think of the King as an Englishman."

Hamilton turned over this questionable remark. Did it smack of treason, or only discontent? But it was always better to agree.

" Just so," he said, " the King has been brought up as an Englishman. It is a pity you have still so much of the Scottish accent. Be careful not to use any uncouth native words or expressions. His Majesty always looked on his father's use of them as undignified."

The young Scot felt his face flaming. Should this man instruct his speech? That Hamilton was a powerful noble and his patron at Court, made the impertinence all the harder to digest. Montrose was easy and familiar enough with those beneath him; with those above him he was on his guard, anxious not to push his way, and therefore sensitive against any attempt to drag him.

" It would be better," continued Hamilton, uneasily aware that the atmosphere had changed, but quite unaware of the cause,— " It would be more politic not to drag in Scotland at all. Speak of Italy—of pictures. Have you seen any Mantegnas?—You can say you have. The King has brought some of his frescoes for his palace at Hampton Court." He warmed into genuine intentions for the young man's good, since it would result from his planning,—" Let the King discover you alone in his gallery, lost in admiration of his pictures—perhaps the new Breughel would please him best. Admire the snow effects."

" Thank you," said Montrose, " but I do not understand art,— nor yet the art to pretend that I do."

His voice was cold with contempt. It was Hamilton's turn to feel uncomfortably hot. Once more had things turned out unexpectedly. He had been doing his best by this raw young cub, and he insulted him. Once more had his mother boxed his ears.

XXV

IN one thing King Charles' artistic taste stood him in good stead. Kings should choose their portrait painters even more carefully than their historians.

The Dutch Court painter, Van Dyck, was acting as a happy interpreter for the Royal Family. Those who saw his groups of the lovely and intelligent children, their baby fingers resting fearlessly on the heads of bloodhounds, their candid gaze gravely answering that of the spectator, had little fear for the heirs to the throne.

And the King and Queen themselves owed much to the witchery of Van Dyck. No one had ever spoken of King Charles as particularly handsome at the beginning of his reign; and the little princess from France had been as lively as a kitten, but sallow, and her teeth stuck out. But now they had the reputation of a nobly beautiful couple; they had seen themselves as Van Dyck had seen them, and could show in their best moments, loyally treasured by the painter, the happy dignity, not merely of royalty, but of beauty.

Montrose had already seen the latest portrait of King Charles before his introduction to him in the gardens at Hampton Court. This meeting-place had been Hamilton's final suggestion. King Charles liked the informality of the gardens; he also liked to be able to observe newcomers there before the actual meeting. Here again, however, Montrose proved difficult. He refused to loaf about in the gardens just in order to be observed. He would meet his King in an ordinary straightforward way, or not at all.

But all the same he had to loaf for a good two hours, with plenty of people to observe him, though not the King, and all of them knowing why he was there; while he strolled up and down, trying to feel nonchalant; and nearer and nearer came the moment that he had awaited and revolted from, ever since he had been Earl of Montrose.

He hated the thumping of his heart, the eagerness with which his eyes turned towards the palace every time some fresh figure issued from it. It was a maddening waste of time on a sunny afternoon in May, when he might have been swimming in that broad slow river, or playing in those excellent tennis courts. The best of opportunities was being offered him—but he hated opportunities.

The wide lawns stretched down to the river side, flower-beds spread their perfume, the wind stirred in the globed chestnut trees, rustling their skirts of green, flecked with white or red. A group of ladies laughed in soft flattering tones round a small, solemn, dark-faced boy, who stared at him as he went past. So that was the little Prince of Wales.

Music came drifting across the river from a boat, bright with people, and the sound of voices calling lazily, clear as voices only are upon the water. He turned to see who answered them, and there were two or three gentlemen of the Court strolling back from the tennis courts in their shirt-sleeves, mopping their foreheads, too hot from their play to put on the splendid coats that dangled on their arms. They talked and laughed with the deep satisfaction of men tired with sport, and Montrose wished he were of their company.

Suddenly they began to put on their coats; the companionable leisure of their voices changed to something alert and wary. He turned his head as they had turned theirs; he saw a crowd of men coming in his direction, a crowd curving inwards to its centre, so that it had some difficulty in progression.

All these men were carrying their hats, flourishing them, bending their bare curled heads; they swayed towards a figure in their midst that made a sombre line among their colours,—an upright, even rigid line among all those glances and gestures, eager to the point of unmannerliness.

And now Montrose's desire to escape touched a strange fear, as though he knew this meeting would bind both him and his King in chains inextricable until the death of both.

Like a man blindly seeking to avoid his destiny, he glanced to right and left into those gardens that shone iridescent and unreal in the evening light. The sunset on the water, the silver drops of fountains in the air, the ladies like tropic flowers beneath the trees, were like the transparent scene reflected on the glossy surface of a soap bubble; they shimmered as if about to dissolve, while through them there came slowly towards him, nearer and nearer, through a buzz of talk and movement, the dark figure of his King.

His moment of panic dropped from him; he looked at Charles, and saw his courtiers pressing on him as hotly as hunters on their quarry.

Then that busy, shifting crowd melted round him; Montrose saw only the two men who now concerned him,—Hamilton, pompous, ill at ease, with his air of trying to remember what it was he had forgotten; and on his arm the figure of his King. He was smaller and slighter not only than Hamilton, but than the impression given by his picture. The curiously appealing beauty of his King that had already been painted in Montrose's mind, shrank as he looked on the reality.

He saw a face like a mask, blank and expressionless; the eyes indeed as beautiful as in the picture, but abstracted; their warm, reddish-brown colour contrasted strangely with their cold expression. They looked through him, as if not seeing him, while Hamilton introduced him; there was an instant's awkward pause; and then the King gave him a hand to kiss, as lovely and lifeless as if it were modelled in wax. Almost as he did so, he turned stiffly towards Hamilton, and made some remark to him that had nothing to do with Montrose; then rigidly, icily, he moved away.

At the listless touch of that cold hand, the disturbing fancy struck Montrose that he was kissing a hand of the dead. It may have been that that sent an apprehensive shiver through his spine, like the first shiver of the wind in the trees that heralds a storm a long way off. Whatever it was, it was echoed in his company; there was all round him a stir, a rustle, a sigh of excitement, an almost audible smile. So the young Earl of Montrose had been condemned to disfavour at first sight by his sovereign. What was the reason for it? Hundreds would be found in half an hour.

But that was the end of it. There was nothing for the young man to do but to return to Scotland.

The scene had not dissolved. The shadows slanted from the yew trees, the fountains splashed, the voices from the boat, now under the bank, called up to the gardens, unaware that the King had come out into them. The courtiers who had been playing tennis joined the crowd round the King; the crowd condensed again, hiding him entirely as he moved away, leaving this new aspirant to the royal favour standing alone, looking after them, until they disappeared.

XXVI

THAT then was the end of it all. The small dull words pressed down on him as he rode back to Scotland, flattening down his mind, which till then had ridden as high as a conqueror's. His pride rebelled at the knowledge that his career could be crushed because any man, however much a king, had neither spoken nor smiled at him, had merely passed him by. Yet this was the disaster that he did not know how to tell Magdalen, or Archie Napier, who had such high hopes of him.

The flat pasturages of the midlands unrolled before him as he rode north; forests spread across the horizon, and swept down to the edge of the common, roughened with whin, and to the fields of fresh green corn that rippled in the breeze like the sea. Brown villages nestled into the countryside; here and there a castle stood up, gaunt and grey, but more often a farm or manor house of red brick, built in the comfortable modern fashion, new any time these last hundred years since civil war had ceased to trouble the land. Then on the fourth day he saw a solid block with square towers in the distance, the first fortified farmhouse, showing he was nearing the Border.

Now the landscape rolled upwards into hills, while the proud woods grew narrow and timid, they huddled into deep hollows as though they had dug themselves in with a spade to escape the wild weather; through the trunks of the fir trees he could see at the bottom the white and black of a tumbling stream. Rocks and rough little walls of piled stones glistened black with rain; the sunset was a torn ridge of fire and white light in a thunderous sky.

And now after days of heavy cloud, he once again saw before him the fleeting splendour of early morning, too brilliant to endure, painting the first of the Scottish hills. The bushes of broom were golden banners; the spaces of pale bent or hair-grass, torn by the north wind, gleamed like flowing silver among the rich bracken.

Tunes he had forgotten for the past three years came bubbling up to his lips, tunes that he had sung among hills like these, on May mornings like this, when he rose at dawn and whistled his dogs to him and ran to the greenwood with his gun, ' to bring the dun deer down.'

> " He's lookit east and he's lookit west
>   And a little below the sun,
>   And there he spied the dun deer lying
>   Aneath a buss o' broom."

He was coming home where these tunes and these hills and these cowering trees and noisy streams and this smell of damp earth and peat smoke all belonged.   Never had he been so glad to be a Scot.

For the first time he had a glimpse of himself as part of these things.   His life had been like a bright morning in a northern country,—he rode out, the sun shone, the streams sparkled on the hills; then the black cloud of his disappointment had swum over him, tearing off all the colours of his hopes, as the cloud shadows stripped the hills of their gold and green; it darkened his early manhood, and so made him for the first time aware of it, and of himself.

Where then had the pageant of his youth been leading him? He had done nothing yet with his life, had failed to find his sister, and had been shown that his King had no wish for his services. He had sought favour, knowing it not worth the seeking.   In that, and not in the caprice of his King, lay his true humiliation.

The youth of the gay cavalier was over; his disillusionment with his sister, his disappointment with his King now led him to the mood of the puritan, who sees his adventure, not in things outside, but in himself.   Was he to be happy, like an insect, only when the sun shone on him?   He had never noticed in the past what others had done or not done to him.   Now that care-free immunity was gone, and he must recover it.   What adventure would be a worthy one?   To travel and discover the rarities of the East seemed now a trivial exploit.   Any boy could be excited by strange

countries.   It was a sterner taste for adventure that bade him
seek it at home.

He longed to serve some high cause, some enthusiasm in which
he could forget himself as utterly as when he had been wont to
forget himself in the tunes to which he sang, in the lovely lilt and
speed of his horse moving in a rhythm more gracious and inevitable
than any dance.

And now he began to see his disappointment, not as the end
to his adventure, but the beginning.   His heart rode high again
with that nameless hope, that bright expectation of he knew not
what, that had always accompanied him.

It was justified, for the need for his service was awaiting him.

XXVII

BEFORE going on to Kinnaird he spent a couple of nights with Lord Napier at Merchiston, just outside Edinburgh.

The grim houses of the Canongate told him he had come home again; there was John Knox's house butting further and further out over his head, tall enough to totter on its narrow base, but stark enough to hold good for centuries yet. The upper window which had served so often as a pulpit, the text carved on the lintel of the door, made him pull in his horse to look at them once again, with the smile of sudden understanding that comparison can give. Here he was back again in the religion of words. In France, the pretty blue-and-white image of a lady would have taken the place of that austere carving, with its appeal to the mind only, and not the eye.

The thatched cottages of England were snug as furry field-mice; those tall harridans, the Italian houses, painted red and white with green shutters, had flaunted themselves against the unreal blue. But this ragged outline of roofs, towering against the stormy sky, was his familiar friend; and he was almost as glad to see it again as to ride through the gates of Merchiston, past Queen Mary's pear tree in its fading blossom, and see Archie Napier come down the steps towards him.

It was eighteen months since Margaret had died; and Napier looked as though he had not begun to get used to her absence. To Jamie she had given more than anyone else of what a mother is supposed to give, certainly more than his queer fleeting memories of his own mother could have promised. It was strange to come into this house without her running to greet him, generally with some piece of sewing in her hand, and her hair a little ruffled, as she pushed it back with that delightful gesture she always used when startled. Her quiet voice, that spoke seldom enough, had left a disproportionate silence.

Napier led him after dinner into Queen Mary's room.

It was very satisfying to sit once again in his own familiar shabby chair, with the leather peeling off the back, and look upwards at the bearded faces of David and Alexander Rex, moulded in the plaster ceiling.

There was the small casket of gold filagree that Archie's famous mathematical father had been given by the Doge of Venice,—a piece of work so exquisite that one could never find anything precious enough for it to contain.

" What have you got in it now? " he asked; and laughed delightedly on discovering the same broken seal-ring and old coin with a hole in it, that had always been there when he had poked into it as a child.

For the first time he was noticing all these things, as for the first time he noticed Archie's face before him, with the domed forehead under the flowing hair, that had grown a little thinner, and the pointed beard and gallant upward twirl of the moustache, that had grown a little greyer. Elegant and precise, he looked as finished a courtier as ever, but there was a new gravity that must have been growing on him ever since Margaret's death.

They both dreaded to talk of that, and spoke of public troubles.

King Charles, said Napier, was in the same position as a poor descendant of a wealthy and powerful family. The Tudors had been high-handed, and succeeded; Charles tried to be, without their backing. The mood of England had changed; it no longer was submissive to sovereignty; the King, as well as everything else, must prove his value, or be disregarded. And no occasional violent gesture would prove it, such as he had attempted here just after the Coronation.

At the Riding of the Parliament after it, he had looked like Charlemagne and Alexander rolled into one; he wore feathers on his head, and James IV's robe royal of purple velvet, furred and laced with gold, hanging over his horse's tail and borne by five grooms in a line; and Rothes had carried the sceptre, and Hamilton was on his left hand, and the whole magnificent train rode out of Abbey Close, in front of Holyrood Palace, and up to the Castle, and there marched into the Banqueting Hall, and seated themselves

under the wooden roof, painted red and gold, to hold King Charles'
first Scottish parliament.

But once there he was badly heckled over the tithes. So he rose
before his Scottish parliament, and held out a list, with these
remarkable words,—" Well, gentlemen, I have all your names
here, and I can see well enough from this day who are to be
counted as my friends and who my enemies."

There it was, done; too late for anyone to prevent it, since no
one could foresee an action so foolhardy or so pitiful. And it
seemed to Archie Napier that the stout ghost of old Harry of
England had stood behind that slight wavering figure. For such
a threat from King Harry would have made men tremble for their
heads, but from Charles, standing there, not quite sure whether
to go on or to sit down,—" Eh, Jamie, but it made me tremble
only for himself! "

" And what happened the next day? "

" Next day he went in a coach, and walked back, and so fast
as to make all his foot-guard sweat. In a royal rage, but with all
the wrong people."

" Has he no judgment? "

" A very fair one, if only he would use it. But he distrusts it,
and takes that of others,—Hamilton's for choice. One never
knows who is behind his actions."

And here Napier's private troubles peeped out; some tangle
of a plot against him at Court, that had led to his resignation of
his Orkney estates. He had had to clear himself to King Charles'
impassive face (' a wax image of a face,' Jamie muttered, and had
the mortuary fancy of a death mask)—to wonder how much of
what he had said had penetrated behind it.

Since Margaret's death, he cared little for his public life, and
would be glad to retire from that hectic and artificial turmoil to
the quiet of Merchiston—a few books, some good wine, and his
own private hobby-horse—he would tell Jamie of that in a moment.
Yet that secret undermining of his power had galled him badly;
the furtive sneers, just not out of his hearing—as on one occasion
when certain gentlemen of the Court were coming slowly down

K

the stairs behind Lord Mar, who was lame, and one sniggered softly to another, " This is like Lord Napier, *who is going down by degrees*."

Through Jamie's angry sympathy went a thrill of pride; Archie was telling him for the first time of his personal difficulties, as to an equal in age and experience. And selfishly, it was some relief to hear of them before he told of his own failure at Court. Where a high official of Napier's standing could have his armour pierced by impertinent thrusts, it was no wonder that himself, raw as he was, should have met with disfavour. Perhaps that disfavour also had been the result of meddling from others ?

" I was told to mind my Scots accent," he remarked with a rueful smile, remembering how little chance he had had to expose it.

" Sound advice," replied Napier,—and Jamie for the first time felt an uncomfortable suspicion that his own proud temper might have helped towards his failure at Court. Well, if it had, he could not help it, nor change himself. Archie might advise his speech, but he was damned if Hamilton should.

Napier did not see what was making his young kinsman so thoughtful. He was busy telling him what good reason the King had to dread these youngsters from Scotland, who were apt to thrust their way into Court as if it had still been King James who sat on the throne. The keeping of state, said Archie, smiling at his fancy, was like committing adultery,—both parties must consent to it. These thrusters could always succeed in pushing to the King's side, however much he disliked them, and thus help their credit by the appearance at least of a confidential talk with him.

" Did you ever hear when you were in Rome of the ignorant but intelligent young man who stuck beside the Pope when he was visiting some Italian city, so as to give wrong answers to all His Holiness' questions? What did that matter? The Pope was just as well satisfied as if he had been told the truth—and the young man had the honour to be seen in close conversation with him—whereas, at the first ' I don't know,' he would have been replaced by someone else. So it is with the men about King

Charles. It is their business to be knowing and effective.—But to talk of them gives one a sour taste. Let us drink instead."

He unlocked the Flemish wine cupboard of inlaid wood, where knights chased a stag over a high curved bridge towards the pointed roofs of a little town. The doors were opened, the scene disappeared, instead there darkly glimmered a row of squat, round-bellied bottles.

He poured out some Burgundy in the thin Venetian glasses that Jamie had brought him, handed one to his guest, and held the other up to the fading daylight from the window,—a long, faintly opalescent bubble on a twisted stem. Jamie had a contrasting memory of Colquhoun's feverish dartings at his new picture, a poor thing to drug a man's lost happiness,—he had been too contemptuous even to notice it at the moment. He was startled to hear his former guardian speak in echo of his own thought.

"We need salves to our wounded pride," he said. "My compensating vanity is that of the author. I am baulked of directing the times as much as I wish, and so I am writing a history of them."

He pulled some sheets of manuscript from a table littered with papers, and the two men bent their heads over the curling flourishes of his handwriting. A Latin quotation caught Jamie's eye; he read it aloud, translating,—"How often is it to the interest of four or five ministers to combine together to deceive their sovereign!"

He had seen such men pressing on King Charles on every side, like hunters on their quarry. Their quarry—their prisoner—whose eyes looked out from their midst, helpless, yet unaware, the eyes of a man sleep-walking on the edge of a precipice.

"He is a fool to trust such men," he cried. "What is Southesk doing, and Carnegie? We must all get together and prevent these men from harming Scotland, while there is yet time."

But the son of the man who had invented logarithms smiled at that last phrase.

"I met an astrologer in England," he said with apparent

irrelevance, " who believes that the world will last a great time yet. He told me that Saturn is now in the ascendant, and will be so for the next three hundred years. Saturn, as you know, is Lord of Death. So that there will be great wars, and, what is perhaps even worse, ceaseless strife, apart from wars."

" Do you believe him? "

" I believe what I have already seen. I do not like the way the world has turned in this century. We have had more than thirty years of marvellous inventions and discoveries,—but of what use is that, if all that this vast new power and wealth is used for, is to enrich clever and greedy men? The world is growing too clever. More and more books flood into it——"

" And you too are now guilty! "

" No author will ever admit that. His book is always the one book that the world needs. But mine, as it happens, is not to be published."

" And so you will prevent others from knowing as much as yourself? "

" Knowledge does not bring wisdom, especially when it is cheaply and easily come by. There was peace in the learning of the past, because men earned it slowly, absorbing it into the very stuff and pattern of their lives. Now any glib fellow can get a smattering of it, and be none the less a fool, only the more dangerous. For his object will be neither wisdom nor peace, but the vulgar determination to make good his own ends, at no matter whose expense."

The afterglow of a sunset they could not see, shone primrose down the deep angle of the window seat, where Margaret used to sit. Only their lace collars were clear beneath the darkening faces of the two men,—a cobweb transparency that would last long after their eyes had been darkened for ever. To Jamie, in this protracted northern twilight that he had missed so long, time itself had stopped, and held them there; as their empty glasses caught and held the reflected colours of the invisible sky. He could only see the hollows of Archie's eyes, and the white blur of his forehead, as he heard the quiet tones of his voice.

" There is a new kind of man in the world to-day. The knight-errant gave way to the adventurer, and now he in his turn to the fortune hunter. The men who stumbled on gold in America have engendered an insane new greed of money—they have given hope to every man, whatever his station, that he may make a fortune. It is that that I fear may destroy the world, more than wars. For the love of an insensate metal, that is death."

" This is the wisest man I have known," thought Jamie, a little dashed, for it is startling to make such a discovery on one's return home after three years of seeing the world. His recognition of it burst from him in an odd form, prompted by a memory of a mathematical lesson that Napier had once tried to give him from the works of his father, that abstruse inventor.

" Did you not say once that the letter ' e ' in logarithms is an unknown quantity, expressive of an indefinable value? What is that value that men must attach to life, if they are to live indeed,—a value that you are more aware of than any man I know? Whatever it is, if the world is losing it, no knowledge, power or wealth that it gains will avail, until it is won back."

The colours had died from his glass; it was now a ghost. He heard the steps of servants bringing candles. The moment that had held them in the past and future as much as in the present, was going from them. In the bright light they would speak of more practical and immediate matters, ask after So-and-So and Such-and-Such.

If it were true that the world, instead of drawing to its end as everyone supposed, were to last another three hundred years under the rule of Saturn, Lord of Death,—what difference would it then make that they two sat here to-night and talked? They could not change the course of the stars, roll back time, and bring a nobler age to the earth. So his mind said.

Yet because he was young, and loved and admired Archie, and was shocked at what he had been told of the self-seekers who ruled the King, his heart refused to agree with his mind, and he believed that they could do this.

BOOK II

THE LEAN YEARS

1636-1644

I

*M*AGDALEN'S favourite picture as a little girl was on the scroll of parchment which lay in the big oak chest in the library. As a treat it would be taken out for her, and unrolled on the table; and herself lifted up to see it on her father's warm knee, his beard bristling against her hair as their two heads leaned over it and his big hands spread over it, flattening down first one part and then another.

There in the top left corner was the cross little old man who looked as though he wanted to ' shoo ' away the two cherubs that buzzed just over his head. And then, moving along to the right of the parchment, though her finger must not touch but only point at its beauties, was the bird as big as the old man, with pink wings and long blue striped body like a fish, and the butterfly almost as big as the bird, and the cherries and corn-flowers and the thistle with a crown over it, and the honeysuckle and strawberries and bees and a tiny blue beetle, going all round the edge till they came up again to where the peevish old man sat in his corner.

In the middle of the parchment was a lot of writing, and that was the part her father liked. It was a long time before Magdalen understood that this picture was the patent of King James I's creation of her father's nobility that had been given to him a year or two after her birth;—and even then she was apt, not unnaturally, to confuse King James and his angelic attendants with God ' who sitteth among the cherubim '; and to believe that King James had created all the fruit and flowers and insects that rioted round those dry words that had created her father Lord Carnegie of Kinnaird.

Because he had ' unobtrusively exhibited singular prudence, sound judgment and zeal towards the King.'—Yes, but is the bird going to eat that butterfly? She refrained from the question; for she learned early to adapt herself to her family's opinion as to what was and was not a matter of importance; and there could be no doubt what that was in this case. There was the new Lord Carnegie as the centre of this creation.

For some generations the Carnegie family had shown a higher and more complex standard of civilization than many of their neighbours. They had played the part of statesmen, combining loyalty to their cause with a rational perception of their own interests, at a time when the barren ambitions of most Scottish nobles were those of isolated robbers.

David Carnegie's father and grandfather had conducted embassies to France and England on behalf of Queen Mary, and her mother the Queen Regent. And of the same type of faithful public servant with a well-balanced brain, was the first Earl of Southesk, formerly Lord Carnegie, formerly Sir David Carnegie, formerly plain David Carnegie, Laird of Kinnaird.

Only once did his ' zeal ' outrun his ' prudence,' and that was when King James VI of Scotland came to stay with him at Kinnaird a few months before he became King James I of England. It was an excusably exciting, even upsetting occasion. The old Queen of England was undoubtedly dying in her palace at Richmond; and half her ministers were sending secret protestations to King James to assure him of their support to him as her successor. And yet she was a wonderful woman, you never knew what might happen next with her—at any moment she might spring up again as though she had only been shamming dead like the fox in the fable, and then what a fury she would be in at any whisper of a successor! Had she not refused again and again to appoint her heir, regarding as treason the implied suggestion that she was mortal?

And as treason now did her subservient heir regard it when his host, David Carnegie, actually dared at dinner to drink to his health as the future sovereign of England as well as Scotland.

" And," added the tactless fellow, " I have forty muskets ready at hand, should your Majesty have need of them."

" For all sakes, man! " spluttered his sovereign, so purple and incoherent that Carnegie at first mistook his agitation for a fit of choking, as was frequently caused by his way of eating, and leaned forward to pat His Majesty on the back. But King James started from the impious hand, and like a restive pony chafed and foamed at the mouth; he could scarcely slobber out fast enough his passionate protestations that all he desired was that Her Majesty should live at least twice as long (" She could hardly do that now she's hard on seventy," muttered Carnegie), that he regarded himself as her subject in everything and never desired anything else,—unless in the due course of time, and without the lifting of a finger in the matter, let alone forty muskets, God should see fit in the inscrutable workings of His Providence to appoint him as His deputy in England as well as Scotland.

But even this admission was too much for his nerves; he checked it to drink greedily, spilt his wine, gulped out that he acquitted Her Majesty freely of the unfortunate circumstance of his mother's beheadal, wiped his bespattered lips with a simple gesture of the back of his hand, rolled his eyes round his company to see how they were taking all this; and then added that he intended to write his thanks to Her Majesty very shortly,— though whether this were, belatedly, for his mother's beheadal, or for what other reason, was not quite clear in the confusion of his loyalty to Queen Elizabeth and his desire to see his cup replenished.

" I have spilt more than the half of it, Davie, the more's the pity, for your wine's better than your daft talk."

King James' panic, though unpleasant, was not unreasonable, for in his train was Mr. George Nicholson, English agent in Scotland to Elizabeth's minister, Cecil; and Mr. Nicholson wrote that evening a lively account of the conversation to his master.

But for all his protested hopes to the contrary, within the year King James VI of Scotland and I of England was on his way south to his new kingdom. He wrote to David Carnegie, entrusting him with the care of ' our said dearest bedfellow ' (for so he referred some four or five times to his Queen) and her children, on their journey down to London. This letter was preserved in the new French cabinet that Carnegie bought in

London; it stood in the newly furnished and newly named with-drawing-room, to which the ladies of Kinnaird now withdrew after meals in the correct new London fashion.

Thus did David Carnegie win his first title; he was knighted for his escort of the Queen and royal children to London, and richly deserved it, considering the trouble given him by those princely young rascals, Henry and Elizabeth—for the task of keeping them out of mischief and danger was far harder than even his subsequent work as one of the Commissioners appointed to consult on the ' perfect Union of Scotland and England.' For which he was, some twelve years later, created Lord Carnegie of Kinnaird.

His public life grew steadily in importance; he was never out of office, always on the bench or in the Scottish Parliament, or a Commissioner, or one of the Lords of the Council or Lords of the Articles. And in the latter semi-ecclesiastic function, he stood up fearlessly for Scotland's rights; protested that there could be no freedom of speech or voting in the General Assembly ' with the King's guard standing behind our backs '; and objected to the King's Acts of Parliament when they actually dared attack some of the Protestants as well as the Papists.

But this courageous independence did nothing to impair his friendship with King James; and when the home-sick monarch, after thirteen years of England, confessed to his ' salmon-like instinct ' to revisit his native country, he stayed once more at Kinnaird.

Very different was this visit from his last, as the royal guest reminded his host, nudging him in a most unkindly manner and giggling over his own discomfiture—" Eh man, Davie, but do you mind the fright you gave me with your bold talk of forty muskets, and Geordie Nicholson sitting there with his lugs flapping open to catch every word? "

Nor was security its only difference. King James I of England and Scotland was a far more important guest than King Jamie of Scotland; and the Lord Carnegie a greater and richer man than the Laird of Kinnaird. The entertainment had to impress English nobles as well as a Scots king, a high standard to live up to, for at one great English country-house a bed had been furnished at the cost of eight thousand pounds for King James' visit. Kinnaird could not equal Knowle. But Carnegie provided some very stately hunting and hawking parties, and three or four poets who furnished rhymes in both Latin and English on all the entertainments and all the virtues of their monarch, including even his appetite, and the gusto with which

"He gladly drinks the heart-comfórting wine."

A grave little girl of four years old watched the proceedings, and was not impressed. King James was very like his portrait among the cherubs and strawberries and butterflies, but now at last she saw he was not God. He was a greedy and foolish old man. He pinched her cheek, asked her name, and told her that a learned college at Oxford had been called after her. Magdalen did not believe him.

She had to dance on to the new-made lawn before the house together with her five elder sisters and the three eldest Graham girls; and she held tightly, not to say stickily, on to Dorothy Graham's hand. The nine girls represented the nine Muses, and wore new dresses of silver tissue which were very expensive and could not be worn afterwards because they were so fantastic, nor used as bed curtains because they were so flimsy. For weeks Lady Carnegie and her daughter Catherine argued this problem, which was somehow connected in Magdalen's mind with a mysterious occasion when Catherine burst into tears and said that Sir John Stewart of Traquair was a bleating bellwether.

Sir John, a pompous, elderly young man, was made Lord Stewart of Traquair as a direct result of the royal visit, and next year Catherine married him, and nobody seemed to remember that she had once called him a bellwether, least of all her mother, who had then answered her by boxing her daughter's ears.

But now they were in close accord over house linen and baby clothes, for there is nothing like matrimony for drawing a mother and daughter together, particularly when the matrimony is not entirely to the daughter's taste. So Magdalen observed in the dry note-book stage of priggishly critical adolescence,—that stage that frightened young Ogilvy from his courtship of her.

All the sisters married men of political importance, furnished their houses in the most modern and comfortable manner, and bore healthy babies. They talked in a knowledgeable way of their husbands' activities, entertained those who would help their careers, and discussed the problems of the public good.

When wives become politically minded, it is a sure sign that the world has settled down; and so it had, for there was scope in it for a man to increase his property and advance his family without murdering his neighbour and raiding his possessions to do so. The stages by which David Carnegie became Earl of Southesk showed that Scotland had well advanced from the age of lawless banditry and desperate chivalry into that of modern statesmanship.

He was now a magnificent old man; his sense of growing importance defeated his advancing age, and his eye grew brighter in command as his beard grew patriarchal. For Magdalen he had an old man's weakness for the youngest; she was not as strong as her sisters, nor as assertive, and this increased his tenderness. He worried more over the births of her two children than he had done over any of the ten born to Lady Southesk and himself. Anxiety has a wonderful way of stimulating affection — and exasperation.

Which was why Lord Southesk was so often angry with his young son-in-law of Montrose, whom he loved, reluctantly, and without admitting it, more than any of his own sons. Why could not Jamie be more like those four stalwart, swarthy young men, who were so like himself? He was as good at games as they, as keen a swordsman, a better rider, had as much fire and spirit,—too much, that was it. There was something unaccountable about the boy; one never knew what he would be up to next.

Nothing had ever aroused in him such baffled fury as he had felt when Jamie absconded just before the Coronation. His experience would have been of such use to the boy at that profitable function. The family had certainly done well at it, with earldoms all round, but it gave him little pleasure that his rather heavy son-in-law, of Traquair, should be ' climbing like a mule,' as he unkindly put it; when his son-in-law of Montrose, for whom he wished most, had deprived him of any chance to help him to advancement.

No, none of his own sons had ever given him such pain, he told himself; and did not know that it was because none of them had ever given him such pleasure.

And now the boy was coming home, having made a mess of things at Court, probably, or he would not be leaving in such a hurry. " But anyway the girl will be happy,"—so he excused his own feelings.

For all that there was of youth in his veins (and there was still a surprising amount) tingled in anticipation of hearing again that note of merry affection, half teasing, half respectful,—and also of challenges and storms to come, advice, rebellions, scoldings, —and even of that far-off, visionary hope, that can beset the wisest of old men, that one day young Jamie would acknowledge him to be in the right.

II

*T*HREE years Jamie had been gone.

For three years Magdalen had helped her mother count the linen and embroider it with the new Earl's coronet, and spin fine wool on her small spinning-wheel while her foot rocked the heavy wooden cradle for the baby, James, and she crooned lullabies, to which the wheel sang a thin, whining accompaniment, and the bobbin on the floor danced on and on, now in the sunlight, now in the shadow, and the tabby kitten watched, and dared not pounce.

> " Oh can ye sew cushions?   And can ye sew sheets?
> And can ye sing Ballaloo when the bairnie greets? "

She could and did, putting infinite and exquisite labour into darns as fine as lace, in sheets so old they could only go to the wash once or twice more before they were torn up for polishing cloths.

" But she has no sense of time," Lady Carnegie, now Lady Southesk, complained of her daughter,—and it was true, for time would race by her, while she stood motionless in eternity, her hand on the heavy iron latch of the door of their room.

The latch clanked up, the door opened, the latch clanked down; and all the silence in the big house (so much more silent since Jamie had gone) surged back on her again, as she stood looking at a bole, or knot, or the grain of the tree in one of the boards, listening for the sound of a step or a voice she could not hope to hear; stood until she had to walk round the room, look into the cupboard, open the pretty painted marriage-chest that had been bought for her from a Dutch merchant, before she could remember what errand it was that had brought her here.

She walked in the walled garden and picked poppy-heads and thyme for her mother's famous sleeping pillows, which had cured even poor Mr. Henderson, the minister, of insomnia, and called to Johnnie and James, who could now trot quite well (though not as sturdily as Johnnie at his age) for it was now three years since Jamie had been gone, and the kitten that had watched the bobbin dance beside James' cradle was now a sleek stout cat, flying precipitately from its sunny corner at the yells of the pursuing boys.

There was no silence when they were about, making murderous attempts to pick off the heads of the flowers, pulling like puppies at her skirts, uttering little greedy cries of supplication as she stood beside her mother at the stillroom table, and pressed apples or damsons through a sieve for cheese, or preserved in dry yet succulent sweetness those delicious plums to which the French queen, La Reine Claude, had given her name more than a century ago.

That simple queen of the most gorgeous of the Renaissance kings, in her passion for bottling and preserving, had bequeathed plums to the world, where François I had left palaces and a race of perverse and diseased kings.

" Plums are the better," said Magdalen, dropping one into each of the gaping mouths beside her.

" Better than what? " said her mother.

" Better than cherries,—bigger," said her elder son.

Johnnie she loved because he was bold and held his head like his father, and James because he had a tiny pale face and clung to her side. He was never called Jamie, because only his father had that name, and no other. He should not go to school with Johnnie, she resolved. All her family said that though he was three years younger, it would be much better for them to start together, it would bring him on, and teach him not to be so much the baby.

But Magdalen, who had no sense of time, knew that James was older than Johnnie in some ways, and always would be.

If she could, she would keep him at home with her and Master Forrett for at least two or three years after Johnnie had gone to school. Only Master Forrett was on her side in this matter, and ' the others ' were such fools as to think that his own interest and desire to stay on as tutor prompted his opinion. She must get Jamie on her side as soon as he came home.

L

" As soon as " was now so soon that her mother's words to her across the kitchen table thrilled through her blood like the sound of trumpets.

" They will certainly be here for dinner," said Lady Southesk. She said " they," because Mr. Henderson was coming up too from his remote parish in the marshes of Leuchars,—and Lady Southesk could remember that, though Jamie would be at dinner. She could even talk about vegetables too,—and the honey sauce she was making for " that new vegetable with the outlandish name I can never remember. Run out between these storms to Daniel yourself, and choose the best."

So Lady Southesk commanded from the pastry board,—for let her be made countess or duchess or queen itself, she would trust nobody else with the short paste, and was telling all within earshot of the fact. Maidservants scurried round her, eddying like a whirlpool, their skirts of coarse homespun flying out round their bare feet which pattered on the stone floors as fast as rain upon the leaves, their faces red and flurried, hot with the anxious certainty that whatever their mistress told them to do next, they would do wrong.

A groom tramped in with a game-bag of woodcock, and unloaded them on the table by the great fireplace. One of them had only been stunned, and as soon as it was out of the bag, shot up to the low, blackened ceiling, skimming and bumping round and round like a gigantic moth.

It might have been the devil himself let loose, by the commotion it caused among the maids. The grinning groom chased the bird past the flushed faces of all the flustered busybodies and over the fluttering white cloths on their heads.

" Let it fall in my pastry and I'll wring your neck with the bird's," Lady Southesk warned him, proceeding imperturbably with her operations on the slab of white marble that made her pastry board. But he caught it without that dire result, knocking it down from the ceiling with a broom, killed it with a turn of his wrist, and laid the limp body on the heap of game.

Their feathers were stained with blood—" Pray heaven she

does not remember the ostrich feathers again! " breathed Magdalen.
For her mother had already told her three times to fetch out the
bunches of precious ostrich feathers, dyed red and purple, to tie
at the top of the four posts of the bed in which Mr. Henderson
was to sleep. Lady Southesk had a great regard for Mr. Henderson,
who had been their minister down in Fife at the parish of Leuchars
for over twenty years, and the one man that they all thought as
wise as Lord Southesk, and still more good,—an opinion shared
by Lord Southesk himself. And Lady Southesk perversely
insisted on showing their regard by treating the minister to all
the favours he was most likely to despise as worldly vanities.

Ostrich feathers therefore were essential to Mr. Henderson; but
his hostess had given so many directions to everybody, including
herself, that she often could not remember what they were; and
so now she could not think what resting-place, safe from dust
and mice, she had chosen for the feathers; and Magdalen could
not think either, and half the maids were in tears,—but at that
Lady Southesk briskly measured out as much cheerful encouragement as she had formerly dealt scoldings, declaring that anyway
it was a great thing the Italian brocade coverlid had been found
and placed on the bed, for that was the first thing that anyone
would notice, and it was only later that the eye would travel
upwards to the four top corners of the bed, adorned (or not, as
the case might be) with red and purple feathers.

And mustering her troops together, she launched them on some
fresh objective, with the happy light in her eye of a general who
is hard-pressed, but accustomed to conquer.

So Magdalen left the community humming like a hive behind
her, and the fierce, strong-smelling heat of the kitchen, and went
out into the rabbit-warren of cold passages, where the stone floors
sweated with damp, and all the old white-wash was darkened with
age, and the heavy doors rose up on either side of her, opening
into the larders and the pantry and the store-room and the cellar
and the still-room and the preserving room; and in the cold gloom
of that sunless half-light there glimmered the huge, pale curves
of bowls and jars and pans of cream, and bags of corn or meal,

made of plaited rushes; and the dark, pendulous shapes of hams and joints hung heavily from the ceiling in sacrifice to the appetite of man.

She felt her way along to the white gleam of daylight round the corner, and ran out into the sunlit courtyard.

III

NOW she was in the little wood, stopped, picked one of the many wild hyacinth pods that rustled round her feet, pinched it in half with her finger nail, and looked intently at the seeds that lay like pearls in their three green cells. She thought of a secret place further down in the wood, where the sunlight slanted like thin spears through the green latticed depths and struck on the dark ground-ivy in points of polished steel.

As she had once nursed a stump of wood or scrap of leather under the table, so these were now her treasures, close-guarded from her family. Only Johnnie and young James were sometimes allowed a glimpse.

The seed pearls dropped from her fingers, she walked out from the trees up to the stone garden walls that her father had built. Field daisies and poppies had sown themselves on the top, and waved like a row of banners from their castle wall. Magdalen entered those tall gates of wrought iron and was once again within her fortress. The fruit trees were splayed against the walls; outside them, leaning over them, trees were tossing and blowing, as big and dark as thunder-clouds; above them, huge clouds, white and black, were riding like galleons high up in the blue sky.

She was looking down a path of flowers and sweet herbs, all tossed and tangled with the last storm that had swept over from the sea. Almost she could hear the roaring of the waves against the coast, five miles away,—or was it only the wind in the big trees? Bushes of drowned roses bowed before her, the campanulas had the wet blue of rain-sodden clouds. Only the new Nancy-pretty was too slight to be battered by the storms, it stood up as feathery as ever, a quivering, dancing pink. The hot sun on the rain had brought out all the scent of the rosemary, the mint and musk.

On either side of the flower walk were the vegetable beds, in which Lord Southesk took more pride than in any flowers. Rich brown earth neatly dotted with green, they were sturdily undaunted by the storm, and there, bent double over them, was Daniel Muschet, digging. He stood up straight as she came up to him, a tall old man who looked at her out of shrewd, small, screwed-up eyes, blue and happy. It was a fine head with a big nose, the Carnegie nose, spare and lean and strong. Magdalen found herself wondering for an instant what was his probable relationship to herself, but passed at once to the more immediate problem of potatoes.

Daniel proudly led the way to the steely blue-green leaves, parted them with his hand, showing the hummocked ridges of earth in which he had planted them,—burrowed in them, first on one side, then the other, and pulled out two or three balls of a purplish brown colour, only a little lighter than plums.

The great Raleigh had ventured to America for this rare delicacy, as they still were up here in the north, regarded as half fruit, half-vegetable; only a few were to be gathered even for honoured guests.

" You'll get none finer than these in England itself," he boasted, " and I hear they are fonder of them there. A dull rooty thing I call it myself, and the first time my lord ever showed one to me, I thought it a lump of earth."

" How did you know how to grow them, then, Daniel? "

" I did not. I stood here with them in my hands, balancing them this way and that, and I said to myself, ' Now, how shall I plant them? ' And I heard a voice from the end of the garden, as though someone had called out to me from behind that wall, ' Plant 'em in rows.' So I did, and I hummocked the earth up a bit as I planted them, and they came up well. But I had no knowledge of how to plant them till that moment, and then I heard that voice as plain as I hear you———"

In country fashion he began to tell his tale all over again, while she scanned those old, keen, triangular eyes.

She had never known he had the second sight, she said,— but he denied it; that was the only time that the like had happened to him; except that if he were to meet anyone on the road, no matter who it might be, he always found himself thinking of them a minute or two before he saw them.

He was turning up the potatoes now in his fingers, filling her basket with them.

" Do you ever see more than that? Do you ever see what is round a person—his weird? "

She had suspected glimpses of second sight in herself—a gift to fear. Was it that that prevented her from sharing as whole-heartedly as she longed to do in her mother's simple happiness in the preparations for Jamie's home-coming?

Daniel turned round on her with the basket full in his hands; his look showed her that he had seen her thought.

He said, " I'll tell you what I see round your young lord, and that is a great glory and gladness,—and stories and songs springing up round him like flowers under his feet. Whatever death he may die, it would be better to be himself than any man in the length and breadth of Scotland."

She turned from him. She was choking back the tears that came so rarely to her. " It is true, it is true," she sobbed in an undertone so low the old man never heard her (—" Whatever death he may die "—*what* death then?—). No, never think of it. It does not matter. There's a strange thing to say of the death of one's husband, but it is true, it is his life that matters, springing up like a flower that never knows nor cares if or how or when it be cut down.

" Give me the basket." She held out her hands, her face still turned away. She felt his gnarled hand placed over hers as in benediction.

" I am seventy this year," he said, " and not a year but I have found life sweet."

" Oh, Daniel, I wish I were as young as you."

He did not understand that, but let it pass.

" I tell you," he said, " when I was as young as you, my heart was like a bird, ready to fly out of my breast, and if I were on the one side of this hedge and anyone were on the other, I would leap over it just for the gladness that was in me. That is how it is with your young lord, and that is how it should be with you, my young lady, for it is a great thing to be young, and to have the love of such a man, and indeed you have little to complain of."

She was smiling now as she met his eyes.

" You know everything, Daniel," she said.

He answered gravely, " I knew nothing when I first worked here, but I have gone on working here in the evenings when my sons have gone to dance with the lassies as soon as work is over, and I know now which plants to plant at sundown, and which at the new moon, and now here is this rare Dutch plant and I must take a cutting from it, and get up out of my bed to-night to do it, for it's best done at the turn of the moon."

She took the potatoes and walked away. Her dress made a blue patch through the iron gates, then disappeared; he heard her singing on the other side of the wall; her voice went up along the path through the bracken and away into the wood. He stood listening until he heard only the wind in the trees.

She was singing a wild song of two sisters who loved the same knight, but she was not thinking of what she sang; the words in her head were—" Jamie is coming home to-day, and I shall see him with my own two eyes."

The old man had given her the courage to be happy; she was no longer thinking of delays in Edinburgh, or disappointments in London, for disappointment of some sort there had certainly been.

But what did it matter? What could anything matter but that he was coming home?

IV

*T*HERE is a special place for women in the Scottish ballads, perhaps because women have always held a special place in Scottish life. Not for them did such home-grown proverbs spring up as those in England on the way to treat a wife, a dog and a walnut tree.

Even the fury of witch hunting that raged through Scotland was a fearful tribute to their power, distorted into a horrible fantasy by the twisted mind of that misogynist, King James.

In the ballads the woman's place is in the home; sometimes an active one, for she ' takes her kirtle by the hem ' and runs through the open country to raise armed men against those who are attacking it; or she guards it herself against her husband's foes while he is away, refusing surrender even when the house is fired and her children are dying in the smoke.

But more often her part is the passive and plaintive one of the adviser, whose guidance is seldom followed, but always regretted. For the man rides out to rob his neighbour's cattle and even so small a spoil as ' three auld coverlids ' off the gude-wife's bed; or else he takes down his bend-bow to go deer poaching,—and little use it is for his mother to wring her hands, and tell him there is plenty of good wheat bread in the house, and plenty of blood-red wine,

> " And therefore for nae venison, Johnnie,
> I pray ye, stir frae hame."

And still less use is it for her to wail over his dead body at the end of the day:

> " Ye wadna be warned, my son Johnnie,
> Frae the hunting to bide awa'! "

That is the sigh of women through all the ages. Behind all these tales of daring,—magnificent or cruel, high adventure or robbery and bloodshed,—there murmurs the voice of the women:

> " *But I wat they had better ha'e staid at hame.*"

When Magdalen saw Jamie, all the three years he had been gone seemed to narrow and concentrate themselves into these last two days. All that she had expected to hear of foreign lands, Italy, France, and England (" yes, but in London, what happened when you saw the King? " But no, she would not ask about that, not yet—none of them had liked to ask yet)—all these things seemed to have been left behind at the Border,—for he would talk only of what Napier had said to him in these last two days at Merchiston.

Like all travellers, he could not tell what he had seen. The sun out there was very hot. He had met Angus in Rome. Queen Anne of Austria was not as beautiful now as they had said.

The treasures that he brought for her, the Italian shawl, the little fantastic shoes of stamped leather with absurd heels, the French enamel casket for her jewels, the Chinese chest of tea from London—these things were so much fairy gold, showing only that he had been where she had not.

But now he was here again, with her and their sons. " Hey, you young rascal, how high have you grown? High as my shoulder, aren't you? Up you go, higher and higher."

And up he hoisted Johnnie on to his shoulder, two small hands clutching at his hair. " I left no one half so big behind me," he said, " I don't know you. Do you know me? "

" Yes sir, I do. You are the man in the picture."

And so he was, the very same, now that he had stopped playing with the children.

What made him so different from those other men at the table as they sat at dinner—from her father and brother with their close-clipped beards and big noses, their shrewd, sardonic eyes,—and then the anxious, scholarly face of Mr. Henderson? They were all so old beside Jamie,—even her brother, who was only a few years older,—they would always be older than he could ever be.

There was Mr. Henderson gravely answering his patron's half-jocular inquiries into the Church question. Southesk was asking if he did not think these English High Churchmen and their fads were like a lot of old women,—no doubt it was all owing to the white petticoats they wore.

"And now," said Henderson, in tones suitable for national disaster, "they are determined to bring their surplices back into Scotland."

"That will further the interests of the washerwomen," said Jamie with a burst of laughter; and she was suddenly conscious with him of the narrow little world to which he had returned after the broadening influences of foreign travel. But even as he was laughing, he remembered John Garn's fanatical rage against popish surplices that autumn evening years ago when he and Colquhoun had drunk cappie at John Garn's inn, and Colquhoun had talked of Kat, and he himself had never known it.

"The tithes," he said, "who cares for them? They affect only pockets, and those of the landowners, like ourselves. The surplice is a symbol for anyone to see."

His *volte-face* was too much for David, who retorted, "I thought it was only a question of washerwomen's wages? Do they matter to you then more than our rightful property?"

The old note of family argument was creeping into the talk. But mercifully Mr. Henderson had taken up the matter, and so earnestly as to abash both the young men.

"Of what account," he demanded, "is either property or symbol, when the primitive truth and simplicity of our religion is being threatened by a papacy as strong as Rome's?"

These prying fingers were those of England, but the brain behind them, the arm that gave them their strength, were those of Rome. So they said, ominously, shaking their heads.

And behind the slow, conscientious figure of the King, was that passionate little Roman Catholic, his Queen.

"Oh tell us of the Queen, Jamie?" Lady Southesk interpolated swiftly. "Does she indeed dance half-naked as a heathen goddess in those masques at Court? What did you think of her?"

"As a very small brown bird, with a twig too large to carry. She took the part of an Amazon, and her bow was far too long for her, and so were her speeches. The prompter said most."

" And what did she say to you? "

" Nothing.   I was never presented to her."

" In the name of heaven, Jamie, why not? "

" What went wrong? "

" What happened at Court? "

Their questions burst round him, and there he sat in the middle of them, shy, angry, determined not to show what he was feeling.   David's question came last.

" What did the King say to you? "

" Nothing."

" Were you not presented to him either? "

" Yes, I was.   He gave me his hand to kiss, and turned his back on me."

" But why——? "

" Who introduced you? "

It all began again.

He answered as haughtily as if he were addressing the man he spoke of.

" The Marquis of Hamilton.   He told me how to behave to the King.   I did not like his advice,—so I suppose he told the King how to behave to me."

Southesk burst out—" I knew it,—you and your precious Raleigh!   They always said he was ' damnable proud '—must you copy him in that too? "

And then David began, but Southesk turned on his son and bit off his words, since it was the lad's first night at home, and he himself may have forgotten it for an instant, but nobody else should.

But his wife, more tenderly concerned than any except Magdalen, could not restrain her laments that he had not at least met the Queen, who would have loved him at sight, declared the partial mother-in-law, " for it's as my lord says, you are over-proud, Jamie, but if a man does not love a lad any better for that, a woman does."

But the Queen could not love him, for she had not seen him. " It was a pity "—" If you had only "—" But why did you? "

—or "Why did you not?"—these were the beginnings of sentences that rose in all their minds, and were choked down, exasperating their sorrow into anger.

"You had better ha'e staid at hame."

But it had to remain unspoken on this his first evening, so they hurriedly passed on to other matters, showed exaggerated pleasure that he looked so well;—he was so brown and strong, his shoulders had broadened out, they believed he had even grown taller, though surely that was impossible.

Twenty-three he was now, and the father of a growing family —high time to settle down and see to his estates for a bit, said his father-in-law, with bluff tact covering the point that since his sovereign had ignored him, there was no alternative at present to rustic retirement.

They were all covering things over now, making them easy. Only be patient and sensible, they seemed to say, and everything would turn out for the best. Even this business of Church reform would all come to nothing in the long run, Southesk was sure of that. And back they were safely on politics,—only they did not sound so safe to Magdalen when Henderson was talking.

For though no man was less of a firebrand than Henderson, with his quiet voice, and dark, disturbed eyes, yet he made all in his presence feel that what he said had a power beyond his own.

That power was the Kirk of Scotland, creating a new mind in the nation, turning it at last from the barbarities of Border warfare and robber raids, giving it a tough intellectual fibre, a passion for argument, theology and education, making a spiritual de-mocracy, that was hardening into bone and sinew in the close and murky air of the parish church.

In the house of God all men were equal; the bulk of the congregation might stink to heaven, but every member of it had equal rights with the young Earl of Montrose himself, sitting in his Sunday finery with his flowers to his nose, but sitting on no more than a stool, as did all the rest, and with no stronger voice than they when they appointed their minister.

There Magdalen had sat beside him while the hour-glass on

the pulpit was turned and sometimes turned again, and the sun shone to no purpose for them through the dusty motes that wafted slowly up and up through the dim and stuffy air, and their still feet grew colder and colder on the stone floor. Life was short, but heaven and hell were eternal, and most preachers preferred to describe the latter.

Not so Mr. Henderson. The goblins that haunted his mind were those of the present situation; he was a statesman, who found the times out of joint and was being reluctantly forced to the conclusion that he must do what he could to set them right.

For what was to happen in the country when this threatened Prayer Book from England should burst upon it? Every congregation in Scotland from the chief elder to the humblest peasant was demanding that their ministers should refuse to be ruled by a few bishops from London.

His company listened with respectful attention; Lady Southesk's indeed was almost a glare; Magdalen suspected her mind to be secretly wandering from the minister's words. Had the red and purple feathers not been found? The thought of them nodding over that earnest, sallow face in bed made a sudden and most unusual onslaught on her gravity; she had to bow her head, pretending attention to one of the dogs, and when she looked up and caught Jamie's eye, believed that he was sharing her mirth.

But no, it was not mirth that made his eyes bright, and flung back his head on his throat as though he were laughing.

What fresh enterprise was it then that stirred in his breast, like a bird finding its wings?

" Oh stay with me," her heart was crying, " you have not been home one night, and are you already eager to be off again? "

Off on some new high enthusiasm that Henderson could share, and Napier too, apparently, that austere though urbane man,— but not herself. She was out of it, listening to a lot of talk about a Book of Canons, when suddenly there was his voice among it all, ringing like a call to arms.

"This Prayer Book is a dead book. It has nothing to do with us. Are we to have a corpse thrust into our living Kirk? It is all the doing of the men at Court,—they engineer trouble as the Campbells do with the clans of Macdonald, for the sake of what fishing they may get in the muddy waters. But these English robbers have a greed worse than Argyll's—they have stolen the King's conscience and put it in their pockets."

A call to arms it was; she could see the spark, that he had caught from Henderson's grave harangue, flash back to the minister, rise and glow between them. That was how he would fire others. Would he, would other men, really be such fools as to start a war over this matter? War—and Jamie riding out with his head held high, and that laugh on his face,—but no, whatever happened, she must shut out the rest of the picture, or it might come true.

"Is this because you met with a snub at Court?" she inserted in a thin little voice through his eloquence.

He stopped dead, his face flamed, he looked younger now than in his portrait. Anguish assailed her, she wanted to cry "Go on, go on," and knew she could never make him. Why did she ever speak? Passionately now she was on his side, for when her stiletto had pierced him, her father and brother brought out their bludgeons.

What was all this nonsense against the ruling authority of the King? There were always corrupt men at Court, and there had been squabbling at the Coronation, but that was to be expected; as long as one played one's own part well, that was all that need concern one.

The trouble in Jamie's case, said his father-in-law, was that he had not played his part there at all. No wonder His Majesty had been offended at so pointed an absence, after odes of introduction had been written for him too, by half a dozen truckling poets. All those odes. Odes. Verses. Wind and hot air. It was not quite clear whether the Earl of Southesk was the more annoyed with the odes for being written, or with his son-in-law for not fulfilling their occasion.

Suddenly his son David, who had been glowering since his father shut his mouth for him, broke into a rush of hot, thick talk, his lips showing savagely in his black beard, for he was a man whom anger affected with a kind of greed; he seldom gave way to it, but when he did he could not bear to forgo the pleasure of tasting his bitter words.

"You talk big of the King and his false advisers when you have flung away your only chance to remedy it,—you have made a mess of it, as you will always of everything."

The blood surged to Jamie's head, to his hands; he stared at David's face and longed to smash his fist into it.

"As big as I talk," he said, "I will make it good. The King shall not crush our liberties. If I failed at Court, I will not fail in the camp, and you shall have reason to know it."

He hated the threat in his own voice. Words had gone as far as they could. He could not fight his wife's brother.

Magdalen did not dare look at her husband's face. "And I began it," she told herself, and—"so this is his home-coming."

Once she was alone with him she would tell him everything that was racing through her thoughts, once they were upstairs, safe and alone together, with all these faces left behind. Families were horrible things—

> "My mother has killed me,
> My father is eating me,
> My brothers and sisters sit under the table
> Picking up my bones,
> And they bury them under the cold marble stones."

They were all at it, tearing her in pieces, first with their scoldings of him,—and now their soothings.

Southesk had recognized a deadlier quality in this, the latest of the young men's quarrels. The time had gone past for them to fight it out with their fists. For the moment they were enemies,—but he thrust the knowledge away with such phrases to himself as 'lads' quarrels' and 'young blood is hot,' and belatedly sought to make the peace.

" Give it time to settle down——"

Behind all he said, Magdalen could hear his accustomed, comfortable phrase. If only other people would ever give it time to come true.

But everyone was rushing along on his own little path—Jamie wanting to prove himself to David,—David wanting to contradict and cross him before he even began,—Lord Rothes greedy for his tithes,—Mr. Henderson anxious for the Kirk,—Lord Napier for the country,—King Charles and his archbishop for " the perfect unity of worship throughout the kingdoms,"—how, in the circumscribed space of Scotland, were these conflicting aims to agree, not only with each other, but with all the hurtling ambitions, private and public,—of ministers who loved to hear their own words,—and patriots who could not bear to hear those of an English bishop,—and nobles who wanted to keep their extra pocket money,—and peasants who thought a surplice hung on the same peg as an inquisitor's robe?

Let them once start pulling the bricks out of the wall, each of them clutching at just his own particular brick, and down would come the whole vast interwoven structure of the state, and each little individual home within it.

Her father could see that. " Add or emend," he was saying, " but never destroy, for there is no end to destruction."

Could no one else see that, would they none of them give anything time to settle down?

But looking at Jamie's face, that had now grown so still, Magdalen mocked the hopes that rose in her whenever her father talked in that majestic, equable voice that had made her feel safe ever since she could remember.

Whatever he might say, Jamie would never settle down,— never, except when asleep and safe in her arms.

The table melted away, the glow of the candlelight on pewter plates and the silver rims of leather drinking-cups, on faces reddened with food and argument.

Jamie was looking at her now across the table, he was sharing this new shy thought of hers, perhaps had lit it in her mind, and

M

was watching it burn there, still and shining, " for his eyes are bright enough to light anything," she thought, and shivered in an excitement that touched on fear.

The voices round them became a blur, meaningless, unimportant, the voices of men talking politics.

V

THE voices had been left behind downstairs. There was silence here in their own room; and there, like an inner room, was their private citadel, the great bed that had been made for them with their interwoven monograms carved on its roof. This was their territory, that none of those voices, critical or argumentative, so like hers and yet not hers, could invade.

If she were always out of hearing of them, then would she be always as free to love Jamie as she was now, free as his own love, that bore him as on wings across the room to her? She had wanted to tell him she was sorry for that thrust she had given him, but he had forgotten it, she was forgetting it. All thought was shut out of his burning eyes; before them, her mind also fell silent at last.

Through curtains of tapestry, green as a forest, they entered their domain. She had woven two blankets for it while he had been away. In a laughing, trembling whisper, she began to tell him this, to taste ecstasy the deeper by postponing it.—" A green one for me, a red one for you,—do you still love the brightest colours, Jamie? "

His arms were round her, as when he had lifted her into the bed; his body was stronger, his shoulders were broader than when he had last so held her; he was now a full-grown man, and his strength crushed her against him, a blind force, even alien,—so long was it since she had felt it, so imperative and furious it had grown, like a gale of wind lifting her, or a wave of the sea over-whelming her; she was lost in it, and all her thoughts and fears and fancies, all that made up herself,—only this remained, that he was a man, and she a woman, whom after three years he now possessed again.

But when his passion was spent, there was his head under her hand again as it had lain so often before; once again her fingers could feel the long, sweeping curves of the skull beneath the soft thickness of the hair; a boy's head still, a proud and lovely head, and tenderly she brought it down to the curve of her shoulder, where it nestled in its accustomed place under her chin.

" So you are home again."

" Where I would always be."

" You lie, dear love, you lie. You would be roving from me all the time."

" A part of me stays here always."

She felt his lips in the hollow at the base of her throat. It is true, she said to herself, there is his head, it has lain there all these three years, it will be there always, no one can take it away. But at that last thought, defiance crept in, and with it fear,—" *no one can take it away*," she repeated to herself, and her hands closed round it, clutching it to her.

He felt the convulsive movement, the shiver that ran through her.

" Dear love, you are trembling, what are you afraid of? "

" I am afraid of nothing, nothing. You are here with me, always."

It was a cry, lost in the night. The thick darkness of tapestried curtains, of shuttered windows, of stone walls, four feet thick, panelled inside with wood, all shut it in to the room where they lay. Her husband's mouth came down on hers and closed it with kisses.

Yet outside the castle where the wind blew and the clouds raced across the sinking moon, Daniel stood within the high walls of the garden, to cut the sprig of the Dutch plant at the turn of the moon, and lifted his head from staring down into the blackness of the earth, and looked up at the overhanging blackness of the castle, and heard a cry that was not from owl or night-jay, and prayed heaven it was not from the wraith of Kinnaird.

But even as he prayed he knew that his mind had heard what his senses could not,—that it was Magdalen who had cried her love and terror to the night; and his prayer turned towards her, that such love and such terror should not in itself forebode disaster.

VI

$\mathcal{M}$ONTROSE'S old college friends were eager to rally round him once again, and tell him all that had happened to their company since he had left. They chaffed him on his foreign appearance, and showed how much it secretly impressed them by asking for the addresses of his tailors and hairdressers in Paris, against the time when they too should make their tour. Were lace collars really as broad as that now, and curls as long? They took an infernal amount of brushing to keep smooth,—and did he put anything on them?

His hair lotion, his new Andrea Ferrara sword, his French book on fencing from the School of Arms, all came in for as serious an attention as his impressions of the slavish state of Protestants abroad, and his warnings lest Scotland might also find the clock put back on her. To ardent spirits fresh from college, no worse indictment could be made than that of an old fashion.

And yet to Montrose these progressive young men seemed all to have remained just where he had left them. The only change he could see was in poor Patrick Graham of Inchbrakie, who had scarred his face in an accident with gunpowder, and was known now by the nickname of Black Pate.

" A good thing it was I and not you," said his cousin, as they went round the stables together, looking at the horses.

He said it with so jolly a grin that the disfigurement on his cheek seemed only an extension of it. " Just think of the loss of employment that would have caused to all the young ladies who write you verses and Arcadian compliments!—What did you think of the Italian women? " he added, seating himself on the stable-yard bucket, and looking up at him with a knowing air, for he was not going to be outdone by his young cousin now he had come back so elegant and Italianate.

Montrose grinned back at him, teasing his curiosity, then replied with preternatural solemnity, " They have to be very young to be pretty. They wear black head-dresses, and walk with a stately, swinging step as though they were dancing." He forgot that his purpose was merely to annoy old Pate, and added, " There always seems to be music in Italy, even when none is to be heard."

" That sounds very poetical," said Black Pate, " and all I can make of it is that you are not going to tell me anything worth hearing of the Italian women. No doubt I am too young," he snorted, pulling the ears of the old black setter, whose head rested on his knee.

It was true that Montrose, on meeting his old friends again, became suddenly aware of having changed and learned so much in his three years abroad that he sadly told his wife how " Travel ages a man,"—and could not think why she laughed so much.

David Drummond of Madertie had not yet married, and hinted to Montrose that he was still brooding over the time when Kat had amused herself with him for a little,—largely, as her brother suspected, because Madertie had first begun to be attracted by her little sister Beatrix.

" Who is worth ten of Kat, as any fool could see," Montrose told him, angry at Madertie's obtuseness, but more at his own perception, reluctantly forced on him at last.

How callow these unmarried youths seemed after the catalogued experience of their foreign contemporaries!

Young Kilpont had some time ago fathered a bastard on the wife of a college pastrycook. Wigton was no longer romantic about Queen Mary and her thorn tree in Saint Mary's College. Her religion would not now fit in with this new enthusiasm for Scottish independence.

" It may come to a struggle with England yet," he told Montrose with sparkling eyes.

At the first mention of England they were all off again like a pack of hounds on the trail of the Coronation; and Montrose was told for the fiftieth time that he ought to have been there, instead of lounging in a gondola.

" You should have heard old ForLorne asking after you," Lord Wigton told him, between puffs at his long clay pipe,—" and as stealthy a sneer as ever I saw looking out of one eye and into the other, for his squint gets no better."

Lord Lorne was all but Earl of Argyll now, for his old father was slowly dying in exile in Spain. His son was showing himself a coming man; had been sent for to Court to advise King Charles on the Scottish question; and was rapidly clearing all the debts on the estate by foreclosing mortgages on his neighbours' lands. His sister had married the extravagant Marquis of Huntly, and was producing children as fast as rabbits, " and with every fresh brat," cried Kilpont, " Huntly mortgages another bit of land to Lorne, so that it is worth his while to encourage copulation,— you should hear him preach to his sister on her wifely duties."

" What side will *he* take, if it comes to a struggle? " asked Black Pate.

" The winning one," said Montrose.

They drowned their opinion of the coming Campbell in red Burgundy. They drank confusion to the bishops and their white petticoats and their retrogressive measures. And not only among these young hotheads, as Southesk called them, but among Southesk's own generation, did Montrose meet everywhere with anger and determination against the *Book of Canons*.

" This book is a bombshell; the peaceable Scots are not used to such cannon fire," said the jolly Lord Rothes, rolling his little white elephant's eye in the vast circumference of his cheek.

Where Henderson was the spirit of the protesting party, Rothes was its brawn and fat. No visionary man of God this, so he emphasized his position, but a sensible fellow, who was not going to have England play any of her old pranks on them. Books of Common Prayer, indeed! Prayers his foot (—or a less elegant portion of his anatomy). These canons were really the first broadside of England's attack on Scotland's national liberty.

A remarkably broad-minded man, for he could appreciate another man's joke, and even another man's character (were it as different from his own as that of the young Earl of Montrose), Rothes was the most popular man in Scotland. Southesk looked on his growing friendship with his son-in-law with less alarm than it deserved, for even if Rothes held advanced views, it would be with shrewd, practical sense and no flyaway notions, and he would keep the boy from taking either them or himself too seriously.

A more alarming ally was his terrible old friend, Lady Anne Cunningham of Glencairn, whose maternal shadow had so over-clouded the Marquis of Hamilton from birth. Small as a wren, with the nose of a hawk and the appetite of a wolf, she had a tireless energy and a wild temper, danced reels as gaily at seventy as she had done at seventeen, swore like a trooper, smoked like a sailor, and flouted Southesk, who had admired her and fumed at her and called her " Daft Annie " since their childhood.

She adored Montrose—" that boy of yours, Davie Carnegie " (for she never would remember his new title, nor for that matter any of his titles—" how can I keep pace with all these skippings from laird to knight and baron to earl? ")—" is worth all your sons put together, and mine too. Given you trouble, has he? And what pleasure could a tough old pair like us take in anything that did not give us trouble? My eldest boy, rot him, is so anxious that nothing and nobody should give any trouble, that he succeeds only in doing nothing and being a nobody."

Her nostrils snuffed battle, she stamped her foot like the war-horse when he sayeth " ha, ha! "; she cried that the Scarlet Whore was winning back all the ground she had lost. That little vixen, Henrietta Maria, meant to shove the Roman Church in on them again after Laud and his Prayer Book had opened the door to it. Laud was a rank Cardinal at heart, ' rank as a fox '—Lady Anne was as sure of it as she was that that foolish doll, Lord Holland, was the Queen's lover,—and in that case who could answer for the succession?

" Lord Holland, apparently," said Southesk's driest voice; but instead of accepting the rebuke to her scandal, she let out a laugh like the hoot of a hunting owl, and raced on with undiminished vigour.

" Only mark my words,—we shall be under Rome again before we know where we are,—and where will you be, *then*, you cautious old courtier!" (for she loved to insult Southesk, and it was her last relic of the coquetry of girlhood that she could still enjoy rapping him over the knuckles:)—"No use then to sit on the fence,—it's on the rack you'll be, for I'll say this for you, if it comes to persecution and martyrdom again, you'll stand by your faith as staunch as any."

And she took a pull at her pipe, and spat, with no relic at all of coquetry. "But you think you can stave it off by fair words and fair play," said she, "and you're wrong, I tell you, you can't see further than your nose, and for all it's as long as mine, that's not enough. That boy there sees twice as far as any of us."

*   *   *

With that singular ill-judgment of time which made King Charles do everything, good or bad, either too late or too early, the *Book of Canons* had been published so long before its accompanying Prayer Book that the nation had time to work itself up into a fever. Nobody dared make plans nor cared to decide anything nor go anywhere, since nobody knew what would happen when at last the Prayer Book should arrive.

What happened first was a riot in Saint Giles' Church at Edinburgh. At the first reading of the new service book, the congregation answered the bishop with yells and catcalls, and one of the women hurled the stool on which she had been sitting. The Provost and magistrates of the city had to clear the church of the mob, in a free fight which only by chance failed to kill anybody; and the service was continued to a trembling remnant of a congregation, while outside grew a deafening clamour of threatening yells and battering upon the doors and crash of broken windows.

"So you have the fishwives on your side," said David Carnegie to Montrose.

It was not quite clear whose side was whose, for the Carnegies as well as Montrose were now saying England was going too far; and were signing protests to King Charles against the interference of the English Church with the Scottish national worship. But at this time, on whatever side they were, even if it were the same, Carnegie and Montrose would differ, irrationally, irrevocably.

Elsewhere, one common impulse was binding people together all through the country. All the different classes, nobles and ministers, lairds and burgesses, formed themselves into a new governing body, called the Tables; and at the Table of the Nobles sat, not only Montrose, but the Earl of Southesk. So all must be well, after all, thought Magdalen.

But she did not feel so sure when later in the winter her brother-in-law, Traquair, now Lord Treasurer for Scotland, arrived from London and paid them a flying and almost secret visit of a few hours, in order to leave his wife Catherine at her home before he went back to Edinburgh. It was clear that this was because he feared trouble there.

All these months, His Majesty had refused to admit to his presence any of the deputations from Scotland, as though by ignoring them he could forbid their existence. Now at last Scotland had broken through this insulting royal indifference; Traquair was to read the King's proclamation in answer to his Scottish subjects to-morrow in Edinburgh.

And this answer was that he acknowledged full responsibility for the new Prayer Book, and ordered all petitioners against it to disperse,—on pain of high treason.

Lord Traquair told this at dinner, and Lord Southesk smashed his fist down on the table.

" Did you point out to the King that *I* had signed that petition? "

Traquair thought he had, but there had been so much to point out,—a place at Court these days was a dog's life.

He drank profusely, and his classic sheep's profile looked the more despondent as he did so. He was one whom wine did not make genial. He was haunted by the dignity of his position, or rather, as the Scots had begun to call it, by " that English devil, the keeping of state." Traquair kept it by half shutting his eyes, pulling out his voice, and climbing laboriously on to a pedestal every time he spoke. For these slight reasons he was fast becoming the best hated man in Scotland.

" He is worn out,—completely worn out," reiterated Catherine proudly in the withdrawing-room, where the ladies of the family had retired, leaving their lords to their interminable discussions. " The King has sent for him sometimes as much as two or three times a day,—always changing his mind, thinking of something fresh that he can add to the Proclamation—as if the people would listen to it all!—Or indeed any of it, once they hear that he has refused them. I am sorry for the Queen, I am indeed. She said to me, about King Charles,—I think I may repeat it——"

Further proofs of Catherine's intimate position in Court circles were produced. Lady Southesk found herself longing to say— " Well, I put Queen Anne to bed when she was drunk, and what she said to me then about King James wasn't fit for anybody to repeat."

But she restrained herself, and offered her daughter tea from Montrose's present of the Chinese tea chest; and admired her complexion, which was smooth as cream from massage and powder; and asked if it were the latest London fashion to have her dress slipping off one shoulder like that, for to her mind it merely looked as though it did not fit very well.

And Catherine gave a little well-bred smile and did hope her father would not tire out Traquair by telling him all his views; Traquair could see two sides of a question as well as anyone, but what *nobody* in Scotland could understand, least of all her dear father, was that *nobody* in London, except those at the very secret centre of affairs, knew or cared anything at all about this uproar of patriotic feeling in the north.

Disturbances in Germany, France, or Poland were the only subjects there considered worthy of discussion,—but as for poor little Scotland, she was not thought sufficiently important for even a tiny paragraph in the *Gazette*.

So she said, smoothing out the new watered-silk material of her skirts as she placed her dish of tea on the table, leaving it half full, because her mother had left the water too long upon the tea leaves.

Magdalen, listening to her sister's thin tones dropping sharp and brittle among the soft burr of Scottish voices, wondered what it was that women who live in London hold against all others,— so that all else beside it, whether of politics or religion or national crisis, loses importance beside the problems that it raises of dress, of speech, of drinking or not drinking tea.

She had never seen London. Would she ever see it?

" Have you danced in the masques at Court? " she asked; and at once her vision of those unknown splendours was obscured by yards of silver tissue, by Catherine's voice, Scottish then, and young and quick and hot in tearful argument, by the memory that Traquair, who was responsible for her present remote glory, had then been to her " that bleating bellwether."

But the half smile froze on her lips, her eyes became fixed and passive, for she heard steps coming towards the door, and men's voices, and as they came in, her husband was looking across the room to her, and saying, just as she had known in that instant he would say, " I am riding with Traquair to Edinburgh."

VII

IN Edinburgh, Montrose went straight to Lord Rothes, who had evidently expected him.

"We all know what is in this Proclamation," he said, "but we have our answer ready. I have found a little nonsuch of a lawyer's clerk who has every statute at his finger-tips from the days of Malcolm the Maiden."

"Of what college?"

"Glasgow."

The Saint Andrews man tried not to look superior.

"Never you mind," said Rothes. "His law is sound enough to prove all we want. And that's not the best of our Mr. Johnston. It's the passion he puts into it—he tells the Lord Himself what to do about it all—and you may be sure the Lord won't dare do contrary. But come with me and see him for yourself. He is worth a visit,—he keeps a private prophetess in the house, a Mrs. Mitchell, who can testify all night on occasion. Sad trial for his wife."

They found the lawyer's lodging down a flight of smelly steps where the keen February wind had concentrated into a draught that blew the dust into a whirlpool of shreds and scraps, rags, straws and rustling onion skins. The two nobles clutched at their cloaks, blew their noses, wiped the dust from their eyes, and peered up at a stone doorway on which had been recently carved the beginning of a text—"Except the Lord build the house——" Here the patience of the inscriber had given out, or perhaps space had, for the letters had got narrower and narrower but were near the end of the lintel.

Rothes began to heave himself up a winding stone stair, and into a dark, small room, inordinately crowded with women and children, so it seemed, although there were only two of each kind. A gaunt grey woman standing by the fireplace looked like a prophetess; the other must be Johnston's wife, a good-looking woman with a courageous head, but a harassed expression, deepened by this early arrival of grand visitors. She had a baby in her arms, and a little girl of four or five hanging on to her skirts with a vice-like grip of her two crumpled purple fists, which tightened to white as her mother whirled her out of the room in her haste to fetch her husband from his writing-closet.

"Fine woman, Helen," observed Rothes, "but these wives of the men of God get a starved look. It would be a charity to put some warmth into them."

The rigid shadow by the fireplace was evidently impervious to any earthly whisper.

"Will she not speak?" murmured Montrose.

"God forbid!" replied Rothes,—"the last time she did, it was from two in the afternoon till three next morning."

He stared out of a broken pane of glass at a pole, protruding from the window, on which were hung some damp children's clothes, slapped here and there by the raw wind.

There were 'alarums and excursions without'; a woman's voice (not Helen Johnston's), thick and whining, it sounded intoxicated; Helen's, hurried, urgent, furious, but doing its best to keep low and to hush the other's; and a man's voice, though at first it did not sound like it, so high-pitched and complaining was it in anger.

Suddenly the little girl reappeared, detached at last from her mother, ran up to the prophetess, thumped her on the knees, and cried in eager tones, "Marg'ret, Marg'ret, Minnie says come quick and put the fear of God into Lisbie for stealing Anna's ale."

A convulsive shudder passed through the lifeless form of Margaret Mitchell—it stiffened its arms, flung back its head, and stalked after the happy and excited child.

"Does she have to be called so to meals?" asked Rothes, but checked his Punchinello commentary as a little man bolted into the room like a rabbit out of its hole, and began pouring out his apology, his distress, his indignation with their idle drunken slut, Lisbie, who had with diabolic cunning pierced a hole in Anna's leather puncheon and drunk all it held, and then denied her fault with lies and oaths, until his wife's temper, being hasty, had flown away with her, and she was even now, God help him, pushing Lisbie out of the house.

He seemed to share his anger impartially between Lisbie and Helen, for so rashly ridding them of their only servant, and also God, for sending this disturbance on his household the very moment that his new patron had called.

Rothes tried to soothe him by introducing Montrose to Mr. Archibald Johnston of Warriston with formal courtesy, and then inquiring after his health, to which Mr. Johnston eagerly replied with intimate details of the way he felt sick every morning, and his stomach wambling within him.

" Lord, the man must be with child. It is the Protestation breeding within you. Well, Warriston, you shall bring it forth out of your labour in a couple of hours now. Lord Traquair is to read the King's Proclamation in front of the Tolbooth at twelve o'clock."

Mr. Johnston's face was contorted with so furious a spasm that Montrose wondered if he were going to give instant evidence of his morning sickness. But it was rage that gushed out against that haughty, self-conceited, lying and malignant devil, the Lord Treasurer.

Traquair's empty arrogance, which so bored his wife's family, evidently gave mortal offence to some. This nervous, touchy creature must have writhed under some probably imagined insult, which he had at once transformed into a national injury.

" The Lord," he cried, " has put it into the King's heart to send Traquair to us, so as to show the King intends evil against us."

The white face seemed to blaze, though it had not changed colour. " It is the eyes," thought Montrose, seeing them clearly for the first time, for they had been misty and blurred, with the red rims and heavy lids of sleepless nights, the eyes of a man weak in sight and weak in health. Yet these eyes had now become windows, not merely into his own soul, but the soul of his people.

This man would take his orders from no man, not from the King himself, not even from God.

" Oh Lord, do it, *do* it! Show these servile priests that you will not be mocked. Your credit is engaged."

And plain it was that he ordered God to do as he himself willed rather than God.

Suddenly he was conscious of Montrose's cool, quick glance upon him, shied from it, became at once suspicious.

" But what is he doing here, my lord of Montrose? Is he with us? For he that is not with us is against us."

" He is with us," said Rothes.

But Montrose had never felt less with them. The white-hot sincerity of the little man convinced but repelled him. And the young noble's rich clothes, carelessly worn, his curling hair burnished with long brushing, his unconscious health and vigour, all made the little sickly clerk miserably aware that the Lord might have done better for him himself.

But he must thank God for all his blessings, even including that torture of indigestion, which was beneficial in keeping him awake for prayer, where otherwise he might have sinfully indulged in more than three hours' sleep. There was the beauty that pleased God, the beauty of holiness, " neither delighteth he in any man's legs,"—and his eye shot down at the red silk stockings so finely knitted, no doubt by some adoring fool of a young lady, on the muscular legs of the Earl of Montrose. Of what good to have a body like a racehorse, if the heart were rotten at the core?

For all his obvious worldliness, Rothes, just because he was gross, talked bawdily, had pimples on his large blown face, did not frighten and therefore antagonize Warriston, as did this quiet young man that he had brought with him. Beauty and courtesy were things to suspect, to beware of, to fight tooth and nail.

His wife, Helen, ' a fine woman,' loyal as well as handsome, who bore him children and did all the work of the house, even when he brought a mad prophetess into it, could never arouse in him that strain of agonized tenderness that he still felt for his very plain little first wife, Jean, a child of fourteen, always ill, and marked with the small-pox. It was a tenderness induced even more by his misery after her death than by the few months they had lived together. He had loved her best and thought her most beautiful when her face was all blotched with crying at her prayers.

The loved face disfigured with tears—earthly love baulked by death—the love of God tried to its uttermost by anger that He should have snatched his Jean from him,—his own tired, tormented body—distrust of even his own sincerity in prayer, unless his eyes gushed forth in weeping—all these things gave him a physical loathing of the easy and pleasant ways of life.

So with pride he told Rothes how he had been up all night preparing the Protestation. And how he, an insignificant and desperately poor clerk, who had worked his way up without influence, would appear to-day in public on behalf of his nation, against the King.

As he turned and twisted his body towards that stout man, who sat heavily at ease even on a rickety stool, his little girl sidled back into the room, and edged her way along the wall up to Montrose. There she stood staring, her eyes round and lovely on either side of a pinched pink nose, with a scarlet drip-line running from it to the open upper lip.

She drew closer and closer to the young man, until now at last she was near enough to put out her hand and touch the blue stone that shone like an angel's eye on the cuff of his sleeve. She touched it, and he had not noticed; she held it tight, so that the cool rotundity of the button gradually glowed as though coming to life within her sticky palm, and still he had not noticed; she stared at her small fist crumpled over it, a chilly bluish-red against the dark velvet of his sleeve; and, near her fist, so near that she was all but touching that too, a long strong slender hand, oddly smooth, and of a warm, even brown, instead of rough and chapped with chilblains, as her father's always was in winter,—a very clean hand, with no dirt nor ink even in the finger nails, and those, too, longer than one would expect, and surprisingly smooth, instead of bitten short and tagged with harsh skin.

And still he had not noticed, or had not shown it, so that now she could look up at his face, and at his eyes, which looked gravely down at hers. All this time he had been looking at her, seeing

N

what she was doing, and had never shown, nor by even a flicker of his eyelid frightened her away. Surely only God looked like that,—God or His angels. This beautiful young man was an angel.

But all in one blinding flash her father had noticed and—" Christie, you wicked child, take your hand off my lord's coat, let go of his button, do you hear,—off with you to Lisbie "—(as a loud sobbing howl arose). " Oh Lord, Lord, send me patience, and Lisbie turned out of the house only this very moment by that improvident fool—*fool*—says she minds the house, and turns all the children loose on me."

Amidst the weeping and wailing and gnashing of teeth, Montrose had drawn his whinger out of its sheath with his right hand, and cut the cord that had sewn the gold and sapphire button to his left cuff, without disturbing the child's grasp on it; then taking her other hand he closed that too over it, and said, " That is my Christmas present to you,—a little late."

The first sound of that low voice stopped her tears.

" What is a Christmas present? " she asked, staring.

" A filthy, heathenish, popish custom," screamed her father.

" The gifts that we still give each other, because three wise men gave gifts to Christ as a child," replied the young man.

His voice was deeper now and sterner; she felt he was angry. When he added, " Take this now to your mother and tell her to tie it round your neck," she began to cry again; but she knew that her father would not now take the button from her before she left the room. Still it was best to get her mother on her side as fast as she could.

At her departure, the three men looked a trifle ashamed. It was difficult to get back to the Protestation, which had shrunk oddly in importance.

" All's well, then," said Rothes, rising with an ominous creak from the stool, which his weight must have broken. " Nothing to do but ram it home on the crowd as you have to us. Well, James, we must go and hunt out that solemn ass, Traquair, and see what sort of late breakfast or early dinner we can get out of him. Politics go wrong on an empty stomach. And you, Warriston, get some food and warmed claret inside you before coming to the Tolbooth."

" Claret? " repeated Warriston in wonder. " I have never had any in the house."

Rothes suppressed an exclamation, and changed the subject tactfully. " I sent you a new client yesterday, a Mr. David Dickson, a virtuous minister, very forward in this work of ours. I hope you found him profitable."

" Oh yes, a profitable speaker to the glory of God and the confounding of His enemies. It did my heart good to hear his wrath against the bishops."

" Confound the bishops, man, and your heart too. What good did he do your purse? "

The furious fanatic looked like an unhappy child. With no hint of malice but the most genuine discomfort, he confessed guiltily that Mr. Dickson had not seen fit to reward him for his legal services with any gold, but had very kindly said a prayer instead, " recommending me and my family to the Lord."

Recommending Mr. Dickson very heartily to the devil, and scolding Warriston for being so unworldly that he could not get a fee out of a client, Rothes stumbled down the narrow steps into the icy air.

" And yet he's an admirable lawyer, by God so he is; and curse this toe of mine—why must one always stub the gouty one? " he added, leaning heavily on Montrose's arm as they walked away. " Mark me, if he does not go clean mad, he'll be the most useful man we can have on our side."

" And if he does, he'll be the most dangerous."

" Why then we'll clear him out. These frantic enthusiasts may get beyond themselves as the campaign proceeds, but at its outset they are invaluable. But you did not like him,—nor he you."

" He was never at his ease with me."

" How should he be, poor devil? There's more intolerance in health than in religion. He can excuse my excesses since they've rotted my body, but he'll never forgive you your strength—and

God knows why I do, unless it is that I'm more of a Christian than either he or you, young James."

"More of a liar," growled James. "You'd never like a man any more than I do, that's got a perpetual pain in his belly. His ecstasies are more indigestible than game pies."

"And praying all night," concluded Rothes comfortably, "will wreck a man's constitution quicker than a brothel."

VIII

LORD TRAQUAIR read King Charles' Proclamation to his people from what had once been the Market Cross, in the square in front of the Tolbooth, where four years earlier the King had passed in his Coronation procession.

Now, as then, every inch of the square was crowded, and of the long street running downhill from the Castle, and of all the little windows in those tall crazy houses under the bleak sky. The white heads of women, tied up in their linen cloths, the curled heads of the gentry, the scrubby hair of poorer folk, of necessity kept shorter, were all craning towards that central point where a small group of men had mounted on top of the stone octagon.

The long-drawn-out voice of Traquair came in a succession of weary shouts through the raw mist. Slowly the grandiloquent phrases of the Proclamation made clear to those in front, who growled to those behind, and so to the streets beyond,—that the King had refused to make himself their champion, as his native country had begged; that he was treating their just complaints as treason. And a deep groan answered the Proclamation, more alarming than the hysterical yells that had greeted the Prayer Book.

This could not be the end of the matter. The people waited; they saw a pale young man in a lawyer's gown mount the octagon and in his turn read a paper, in protestation.

Warriston's hour had come, but never had he felt so unprepared to meet it. Why did the Lord see fit to chasten him thus, just when His own interests demanded the best that he could give?

" Oh Lord, this will be the worse for you," he had warned Him that morning.

His eyes were heavy, his weakened vitality shivered in the raw air, his voice, shrill and whining, was the voice of one crying in the wilderness,—' an evil scraped tongue,' as he himself bitterly recognized. He even lost his place at one point; was a man who lost his place in his own speech to be a leader against a powerful King and Church?

A dull silence followed his, like a wintry fog upon all their spirits. Would nothing more happen then? It was cold work waiting there. One or two began to drift away, muttering that for all the nobility's fine words, the King was bound to win,— it was not going to be worth any man's while to risk his neck in this matter. Their movement was one of acquiescence, the ignoblest form of despair.

But a shout like a trumpet arrested them. " Stop! Are you slaves to sneak away at the first breath that opposes you? "

They looked back, they saw a young man scrambling up on to a barrel, flinging up his arm to them in a gesture of command. The keen outline of his head was above all the people, his raised arm was in a velvet sleeve, slashed with red,—here was another speaking to them, and in how different a voice from that of Traquair or Warriston!

" The young Montrose," said those who knew him by sight, and the crowd pressed forward to see this young man who was one of Scotland's greatest nobles, now returned from foreign lands, a fine personable young man,—and what had that ringing voice to say to them?

A change had come over the spirit of the crowd, a running murmur of excitement.

Montrose was crying to them, " Is England to be our master yet again? Are we to be nothing now but her province? "

The crowd heaved forward like corn in the wind, and like the storm wind came the angry murmur of all those voices in assent. That collection of separate, baffled people was now a single unit, moving as one man and being moved, as that voice called to them, swayed them, bade them look forward and hope, look back and remember how again and again their country had risen to resist England's tyranny,—how Wallace had been judged and killed as a traitor by an English king, but was greater than any king in Scottish hearts.

" Then who need fear the name of treason? " came on a cry of exultation.

And in answer came a roar from the crowd, shouting that

Montrose should lead them, that they would follow him to England, follow him to death. They surrounded him, swung him off the barrel, and on to their shoulders, crying—" Down with the Bishops! Down with the Prayer Book! " and here and there was heard, " Down with the King! "

Bumping and staggering, Montrose swayed this way and that on his uneasy perch, clutching now at the rough heads of his bearers and now at their frieze-clad shoulders, seeing the houses climb up against the sky behind a stormy sea of shouting heads.

Behind them, above them, he could still see the head of his mother's brother on the spike in front of the Tolbooth, a blackened, withered object, unrecognizable as human, which had once been the handsomest young man in King James' country. And here in front of the Tolbooth his father had taken the wild justice of revenge into his own hands, and attacked in the public street the man who had murdered his kinsman. Now he too had taken the law into his own hands, before he had known what he was doing. The people round him had been depressed and sheep-like, dully waiting for a lead; and he had transformed them into this living fire.

His bearers had gone in a circle; he saw the little group of his friends once again; Madertie was laughing with tears of excitement running down his cheeks, and not knowing it at all, as he had done when they chaired Montrose in triumph after he had won his silver medal at Saint Salvator's. He saw Rothes' face, laughing too, but with some concern upon it; and Traquair's, haughty and injured, looking as usual for the insult to himself; and Warriston, that nervous, crack-brained little fellow, who did not count, and could never be a leader of a national movement.

So Montrose thought, misjudging Warriston, even as Warriston had misjudged him.

But Warriston was past judging or misjudging. He was rocking in an agony of hatred. He had failed in his first essay to touch the hearts of the people and incline them to the Lord,—and then this young noble, whom he had instantly distrusted, had sprung up and swayed the silly sheep this way and that, not with the words of God, but with the pride of the heart and the lust of the eye. And every gesture that commanded them had been a personal insult to Warriston, since the sleeve that cloaked it lacked a certain gold and sapphire button.

Montrose struggled from his bearers; in shyness and confusion he was trying to escape through the little group of his friends, when Rothes' heavy hand descended on his shoulder.

The young man looked into the other's twinkling little eyes, half hidden in the surrounding folds of flesh. What was it in his own,—clear and grey, calm in spite of his excitement,—that made even such eyes as Rothes' see something of his destiny?

" James," said the bluff voice, " you will never rest till you are lifted up above us all in three fathoms of rope."

IX

*T*HE whole nation was united, as it had not been since John Knox had bound it together against the Pope of Rome. His spirit was alive to-day, and his Covenant against popery was revived in a new version, drawn up by Mr. Henderson and Warriston, and legalized by the sanction of Sir Thomas Hope, the Lord Advocate, and his judges.

The law, religion, the respectability of old men to whom a broken shoelace is a sign from heaven, were all on the side of the Covenant. Thousands flocked to sign it;—it was a bond of union among men and with God in defence of Scotland's liberty; it ran through the nation like a fiery cross, carried by the clansmen as a call to battle; copies were even sent out to Scots serving overseas as mercenaries in foreign armies, and many of them left their commands and hope of preferment abroad in order to hurry home in readiness to fight for their country.

Sermons were preached on the text of the Covenant as though it were the Bible; it was read aloud from the pulpit, and one minister asked the nobles there present to rise and swear to uphold it by the living God. Montrose was sitting in the middle of the church; he rose, and with him rose that close-packed throng in one movement with upraised arms, in one loud sobbing cry.

There he stood and Scotland round him in a single congregation. He looked on the smooth faces of burgesses, the rugged ones of peasants, two or three of nobles like himself,—on the faces of elderly women, worn into the same tired pattern by the lifelong cares of household and children,—of young women, fresh and eager for those same cares that awaited them within the arms of their lovers.

All these faces were transfigured, set free of their own lives, united in a bond where there was no distinction of class or sex or age. On many of them the tears were running down, but not a hand swerved from its raised testimony to brush them away, for none were conscious of them,—not even Montrose, who was looking on them. The wind of this new spirit had caught him up and was hurrying him along with them. Only long afterwards did he remember those varied faces expressing one emotion, and that his own.

At home he was thought tiresomely exaggerated. His father-in-law would compare Scotland's proud demand for religious liberty with the sordid disturbances in England, caused by grasping citizens who refused to pay their taxes. As if they could be compared!

Yet, said Lord Southesk, " England squeals as loudly now for her purse as we for our conscience," and half the country gentlemen nodded their heads with him. They wished well to the Kirk and disapproved of a forced Prayer Book, but after all there had to be something to trouble about, whether taxes or spying bishops.

But Montrose, who saw justice as a necessity, believed that so little was needed to make Scotland, and England too, the true garden of Europe.

" Take care that in the process you do not make it into a battle-field and graveyard," said Southesk.

Old men were despicable, cautious, playing for safety, believing nothing, hoping nothing, fearing everything.

But he knew Southesk was not despicable, and that they loved each other; and yet, now, whenever they met, they quarrelled.

And Magdalen, who loved them both, knew all the affection and irritation that they gave each other. Her opinions were formed on her father's, rather than on those of this reckless intruder into her father's house,—a changeling she sometimes thought him, when she remembered his own father, her father's old friend,—and the many rounds of golf and pipefuls of strong tobacco the two cronies had enjoyed together.

Often she tried to coax Jamie into a taste for tobacco, which he still could not abide, and he never knew it was because of her early memories of a delightful big man with a long pipe who used to take her on one knee and his youngest daughter Beatrix on the other, when they were very small, and tie their heads together with a piece of red twine he had pulled out of his pocket, because he said they were as much together as a pair of turtle doves.

But Jamie would not smoke, and was always riding on some hot errand of the new Covenant.

" You are never with me now," she said.

" Then do you come with me," he begged. " Be a rival to Lady Anne Cunningham and Lady Pitsligo. They work harder for the Covenant than a troop of men."

" They are as old as sin," she said, looking down on Johnnie and little James,—" it is easy for them to work for it."

" But not so easy for them to draw men to it. Sweet, be a Covenanter, and see how Scotland will follow you. We will all wear your colours. What are they? Blue suits you best."

But he could not coax her into coming. Crowds frightened her, and scenes of strong emotion. She had no great belief in the possibility of a perfect state, such as her husband thought so near to them. Women are seldom idealists in politics.

He answered her doubts and her mother's distressful cluckings with the laughter of one who is so certain of his cause that he can afford to take it lightly; he told them to be ready to sit under him when he too preached for the Covenant, and he would have a cap of molten tar, the extreme penalty for inattention in the Kirk, all ready for their hoods, should he catch them napping.

They heard him whistling one of his old songs as he ran down the stone staircase, they heard a clatter and barking of dogs in the courtyard as he called for Gray Oliphant to be saddled, as once he had called for little Torrey or Bess, they heard his horse's hoofs thudding hollowly over the drawbridge,—and there he was gone, leaving the two women to become conscious of the emptiness growing through the house, as their smiles faded and their faces settled once again into the preoccupied, slightly harassed lines of the faces of women who have now only their immediate material cares to concern them.

And Montrose rode to Aberdeen with Mr. Henderson and Mr. Cant and Mr. David Dickson, who had never paid Mr. Johnston, and answered in nervous haste, " Of course, of course, the moment I return," whenever Montrose unkindly reminded him of it.   It was an incongruous company, the three ministers in their black Genevan gowns and bands, and Montrose's striking appearance as a gay cavalier—" a noble and true-hearted cavalier," so Rothes had written of him, in a most unusual strain, in his letters of introduction.

The ministers preached for the conversion of Aberdeen's citizens to the Covenant; but the young earl commanded their allegiance.   He was angry with their obstinacy, he refused to attend the fine banquet they had prepared for him in the old hall.

Nine years ago in the week before his wedding he had been feasted there as a burgess; he had come cramped from sitting to Jamesone for his portrait, and hungrier from that unaccustomed stillness than from any hunt; his hosts had then been the best fellows in the world, and the wine excellent.   Did the ghost of that convivial youth smile now, with rounded curves of cheek and chin, at the arrogant hawk-like face of the young man who had become so stern a Covenanter?

Yet even in his most puritan mood of rejection, Montrose could not achieve a purely negative gesture.   He asked for the wine to be distributed among the poor instead, and delighted in watching the barrels being broached in the street among the ecstatic crowds.   This was far better than throwing a handful of coins as he mounted or dismounted.   The crowd thought so too.

" Oh bonny Saint Covenant! " sang the free drinkers, not quite clear as to the cause of this happy state of things, and a good deal less clear as the day wore on.

The Aberdeen ministers showed less hospitality than the burgesses, and refused their pulpits to the three visiting clergy, who had to preach from a wooden gallery overlooking a yard. There was a good deal of heckling from below in the yard, in spite of the presence on a balcony of old Lady Pitsligo, in a white gown, who was perched precariously on a high stool, and jerked her head continuously like a cockatoo,—in approval, said the Covenanters,—in slumber, said the others.

A still more doubtful honour was paid by the learned doctors of the town, who had an alarmingly high reputation for theological reasoning, and prepared fourteen points of objection and argument with which to confute their visitors.

Words, words, words,—demands, objections,—fifthly, sixthly, seventhly,—controversely, controversially, contradictorily,—while the clouds raced like ships in full sail across the early summer sky. Montrose hated this solemn self-conceited place with all the astute businesslike faces so smugly set against their company. This Town of Granite had granite heads and hearts as well as houses. Their sturdy logic, their fierce passion for accuracy and hard facts, their contempt of the imagination, bound them, he thought, in a prison of iron complacency. All they cared about was the literal word, the legalizing of every motion of the spirit.

Did not even Messrs. Henderson, Cant, and David Dickson use too many words? On the journey here they had argued until he felt that the high simplicity of the Covenant, which had shone in the spring like a new light on men's hearts, was in danger of being obscured and fussed over and fretted away into little niggling points of mental reasoning.

He was in the unfortunate position of a man who has seen a vision, and has to hear it explained again and again, by those who have not.

His relief was in action, in winning fresh support for his cause. He rode to the fishing villages on the east coast, up the steep and narrow streets of little harsh houses like dropped pebbles of grey stone, their thatch of turf bristling with tufts of long bent and heather as rough as the rawhide shoes of their inmates, and quite different from the soft, mousy thatch of the pretty English cottages. He rode to castles and big houses, sometimes to the very houses he used to visit for summer sports and Christmas revels.

His hosts came out into the courtyards to greet his arrival, half expecting the boy who used to swing himself out of the saddle and call for ale for his horse while he drank his stirrup cup. Then he had come to hunt and shoot and fish and dance, to summon the fiddles and pipes from the nearest town.

But now their sudden guest was an ardent young man who came with the Covenant inscribed on a sheepskin parchment on his saddle-bow,—a man who set them on fire with his own zeal, and that not only because his glance and voice were those of one to whom command came unsought, yet inevitably.

To those lonely houses and little towns his arrival brought something from another world than that of their humdrum everyday. Here was their own youth, riding up to their doors,—their own desire for adventure, beyond the skirmishings of their self-interest,—their own dreams, that they had left behind in their struggle for existence in this workaday world.

Another piece of land, more cows or sheep, bread, meat, clothes, dowries for the daughters, college for the sons, all that they had tried to think their chief concern in life, now slid back into an only relative importance;—as the focus of their lives shifted under the eager and imperious gaze of this young man.

In his world, as in their youth, men served something greater than themselves. And because men breathe more freely in that world than the other, they signed and swore to support the Covenant, as the badge of his knight-errantry as well as of his mission.

They did more, for they even left their homes to give their testimony to his cause. They wished to follow him,—not merely to Aberdeen and Edinburgh, but back to the heroic age, where all men at one time or other, in their dreams, in their cups, or in their lonely walks over the hills, have felt a desire to be.

X

YET Montrose's biggest failure in this part of the country was from the most romantic-minded person in it. That was the Marquis of Huntly, chief of the clan of the Gordons, who bore the proud title of Cock o' the North.

The trouble with all the Gordons was that they were romantic. The father of the present Marquis had so delighted in slender French tourelles with fish-scale slates, that the grim old mediaeval castle looked as though it were decorated with a quantity of inverted mermaids. Every time he took a walk round the policies his eager imagination would be struck by the need of a new Italian fountain or a little Dutch garden or a wall to the deer park. His estates were left heavily encumbered at his death; but that was nothing to the scandal of his burial, according to the rites of the Roman Church. It was done in great state, at night, by torch-light, with hundreds of gentlemen attending it,—an appalling disgrace for the presbytery of his parish, who had converted him in his lifetime at least five or six times.

It was an astounding proof of their power that so arrogant an old gentleman should have had to truckle thus to the ministers. The Gordons of Huntly were men who made their own laws, as the Huntly of the last reign had shown when he killed the " Bonny Earl of Moray " on the somewhat thin excuse of his being " the Queen's love." Said that handsome man as he lay dying, " You have spoiled a better face than your own."

Few could say that to the present Huntly. A superb creature with the body of a Viking and flashing eyes, it took one some time to realize that the bird-like shape of his face was really too thin and narrow to complete him properly. He cuts a fine figure, one would say, but it wants a head. So it was in his life. He cut a fine figure everywhere, with dash and verve and high principles, but never a thought behind any of it.

He complained of living in a drab age, when every year clothes got plainer, life got safer, and more and more tradesmen pushed

their way into circles that used to be reserved for the nobles,—
though, thank God, not yet as much as in England. He was as
improvident as his father had been, and proud of the family debts,
as of a dash of colour in this too respectable world. There was
always that tame, plodding fellow, his brother-in-law of Lorne,
to lend him money when he needed it.

His wife died on the birth of her eleventh child. Huntly was
left with a turbulent family of all ages, a mortgaged estate, and
a world that was beginning to crumble round him without his
noticing it.

He received clear warning of this last when the young Earl of
Montrose rode up to his doors with the National League and
Covenant rolled up on his saddle-bow.

Huntly gave it a dull glance, like a hen discarding a pebble
that it had hoped was a pea, and asked Montrose what he would
drink. Montrose chose ale as usual. The stirrup cup was handed
him in the hall by the eldest Gordon lad, after some delay, caused
by the younger son Lewis, who had been sent to fetch it and
drank it himself instead. A little rascal of eleven or twelve, he
was handed howling to judgment by his elder brother, Aboyne,
and Montrose had a glimpse of a scarlet monkey face, tousled
hair, and an irrepressibly merry eye as if enjoying the fuss he was
making, before his father cuffed him out of the way.

Even the girls of the family kept thrusting themselves forward.
One tiny chit came running down the stairs to ask if the new-
comer was the King's camel, and burst into tears with disappointment when told it was only my Lord of Montrose.

Through her clamour there shrilled the demand of the Lady
Jean, some years older, for seven and sixpence " to go to the
dwarf's marriage,"—and when her father turned his purse inside
out to show it was empty, she reminded him in vicious tones that
he had promised her and Lewis six shillings by to-morrow morning
to buy a cock for the Shrove Tuesday cock-fighting. A roar from
her father blew her out as on a blast of wind, and then young
Lord Gordon said quietly, " If my Lord of Montrose has anything of importance to tell us, sir, we had best go into the library."

Montrose looked at him and liked him. Lord Gordon looked back, and Montrose realized from his dark and thoughtful eyes what it must be to be the eldest son of such a family, and to have, inappropriately, a sense of discipline.

In the library, he unfolded the mighty roll of " The National League and Covenant,"—four feet by three feet eight. The sheepskin parchment was already so thickly inscribed with the names of those who had sworn to support it that the signatures had to wriggle into every corner and finally to descend to initials only, all down the margins, since there was no room for the whole name. But rings had been inked out in the centre of the sheet for the great names of the nobles; and there, between Rothes' name and Montrose's, was an empty ring, into which Montrose now did his best to make Huntly insert his own.

But again that discontented eye rejected it.

" What, am I to sign here between you,—and every Tom, Dick and Harry sprawling round on the top of us! Why should we fight the ministers' battles for them? They harried my father into his grave,—a pack of dirty mice nibbling at a lion. Do you know why he wouldn't go to the Kirk? ' Because,' as he said to their snuffy long faces, ' there are no gentlemen there.' "

" A man cannot answer for his own gentility," said Montrose, smiling, " but my brother-in-law Carnegie is elder for his presbytery at Brechin."

" Yes, and fine friends you are, aren't you! " retorted Huntly with superb irrelevancy, pursing his small mouth into a button.

There was no holding him to any point.

At one moment Montrose succeeded in firing him, and that was when he quoted to him the letter by which their ancestors had forced the Pope to acknowledge Bruce as King of Scotland. " As long as there shall but one hundred of us remain alive, we will never subject us to the dominion of the English."

" By God, you are right, boy," he cried, slapping his hand down on the trews of Gordon tartan that clothed his lengthy legs. " I never hear the tune of the Gay Gordons, if it's only one of

o

my brats playing it on a penny whistle, but I vow to kill an Englishman or two before I die."

And then with a sudden brilliance, " Let this be *our* business. Keep the ministers out of it. Leave it to the nobles. I'll consent then to be your leader.—As Cock o' the North, there can be no question of that."

Montrose explained that as the whole trouble had been started by King Charles forcing an English Prayer Book on the Scottish ministry, it would be impossible to keep that ministry out of it.

The lustrous eyes before him dulled again. Huntly was growing convinced that this young fellow who thought he knew everything, was jealous of his generous offer to be their leader. The Grahams had always been jealous of the Gordons.

" From the pride of the Grahams,—" he breathed,

" From the wind of the Gordons,—" paraphrased Montrose,

" Good Lord, deliver us," prayed both.

Something had to be done. They could not sit on, glowering at each other. Montrose had refused his invitation to stay and dine, pleading the pressure of his business.

Huntly had to give a decisive answer.

" I don't like ministers——"

" I want to be leader——"

Neither of them expressed the nobility of his spirit. He had to find something better. Suddenly he had it.

" All this," he said, laying his hand heavily upon the parchment, " is aimed at the King."

" No, for the King himself does not know the situation. He has only been in Scotland once for a few weeks since he was an infant. It is aimed at those who advise the King, wrongly, for their own ends."

Huntly hardly waited till he had finished, for he had now got his answer ready.

" Same thing," he said airily, " all the same thing. And you can tell your precious ministers this—that my house has risen by the Kings of Scotland, and that if the King were to fall, then I would bury my life, honour and estate under the rubbish."

He looked round him.   Montrose was obviously impressed by the splendid simplicity of such loyalty.

But his own son looked shy and uncomfortable, anxious to avoid both his own eye and that of their guest.   Confound these modern young puppies,—they were so afraid of fine words that they would soon rule out all fine feelings too, and fine actions as well.

"What are you looking sheepish for?" he growled at Gordon, "don't care about your King, do you,—prefer a presbytery in black coats?   Wouldn't lift a finger to fight for him, I suppose?"

"Yes, sir, I would."

Montrose was rolling up the Covenant.   That ring would have to remain empty of Huntly's name.   His hosts came out on to the steps to see him off, Huntly reiterating questions as to whether he were sure he wouldn't take anything more before he went.   His high-stepping walk was that of a peacock.

Gordon led his visitor's horse through the courtyard in a burst of spring sunshine.

"I wish I could join you," said Gordon.

*   *   *

He went back to Aberdeen at the head of his army of converts, back to those theological controversies, in which nothing had been settled, and Henderson's practical wisdom stood no chance against the arid logic of the learned doctors, and Cant and Dickson were so flustered and blown about by the bludgeoning of the contrary arguments that their very gowns flapped about them the more loosely, and their crestfallen faces looked to Montrose like a couple of deflated footballs.

"You do no good here," he told them curtly.   "Better go before their ' fourteenthly ' explodes you altogether."

Back they went to Edinburgh in his wake among the host of his devoted followers, who only completed the ministers' sense of failure, since they testified to this young man's triumph.   The ministers who had not accompanied him called him a lovely and gracious youth, a very David before the Lord.   But Mr. Cant and Mr. Dickson and several others began to complain of his high-handed ways, though not to his face.

And at Edinburgh he met his brother-in-law, Carnegie, who told him what he thought of him, for it was high time somebody did something to stop the young fellow making a fool of himself. Montrose's temper was savage enough after that to justify any of the ministers' complaints.

Nor was it improved by the plum of good news that Rothes had been preserving in secret for him, and now told with a wink and a sly, fat finger held to his jolly red nose.

It was an odd story, Montrose hoped a false one, of Lord Lorne, who had just become Earl of Argyll, and his incongruous friendship with that insignificant little lawyer's clerk, Mr. Johnston of Warriston. No doubt it would be indiscreet for the fiery anti-royalist, Warriston, to be seen visiting the house of the great Earl of Argyll, who sat on the King's Privy Council with the Marquis of Hamilton, and had been sent for to London to help advise the King.

But Argyll had certainly been visiting Warriston, and frequently, though the little clerk had never admitted it,—Rothes had got it all out of his wife, Helen (again that wink)—" more useful that, than your conquest of the daughter. Ah well, you young men can afford to take long views."

And then came the point of the story, pure supposition as it was. Again and again the Covenanters had got wind of the King's plans in time to circumvent them; and no one, not even Rothes, knew what the means of communication had been. But certainly those most possible would be from Argyll to Warriston.

" And Argyll himself has given reason enough to think so, for he has refused to join our side, saying he can help us better in secret."

" Then he can be nothing but a sneaking cur, and I pity the side that has him on it."

" Tut, tut," said Rothes comfortably, " you young men are so narrow-minded, you can never see more than one quality at a time. The new Earl of Argyll has a sincere sense of religion, and would do much for the Kirk."

"Then I say again, the Kirk is to be pitied for such an ally—yes, and for Warriston too. I trust neither of those men."

"And the ministers are blinded by their pedantry? And Mr. Dickson is a low fellow? And Mr. Cant can't say a word but cant. And if David Carnegie had not been your wife's brother, you'd have run him through last Tuesday. Eh, James, James, but you'll never make a party larger than one."

"Give me soldiers to deal with, and see if that is true."

"Oh, you'll have your soldiers before we have done," said Rothes.

XI

*L*ORD SOUTHESK saw more clearly than most the confusion of cross-purposes that had fallen on the land. As mediator, he suggested a General Assembly of the Kirk to express the views of all classes, convince the King that he must not interfere with the Kirk, and convince the Kirk that the King was willing to make concessions.

But what he hoped might be a safety valve proved an explosive.

The Assembly sat in the Cathedral at Glasgow in the November of '37, eighteen months after Montrose had come home; it sat for weeks, and day by day the fog stole up from sea and river, hung about the little cobbled streets, and filled the cathedral with a raw damp in which men's breaths hung like visible sighs of suspense. The crowd was so dense both without and within the Cathedral that the town guard had to fight with fists and sticks to force a passage for the members to their seats.

The great church was ice-cold, stuffy to smothering point, thick with the stench of sweat and damp sheepskin and onion and salted herring, munched with oatmeal bannocks by the onlookers in the galleries, who had waited up there for twenty-four hours to secure their places. This was a national contest, and everyone concerned in it. The excitement reached hysteria; they stamped and shouted; called and whistled and roared their greeting of each member who entered;—booed Hamilton, who had been appointed to preside as Royal Commissioner and representative of the King, and yelled applause of the more popular nobles, among them the Earl of Montrose, whom they had seen in their streets in his schoolboy days, scattering cash to the beggars.

He and Lord Southesk sat at the table of the nobles, just below Mr. Henderson, who had been unanimously elected as Moderator, and Warriston as Clerk. These two sat alone at their table, the focus point of the discussions. Down at the lower end of the church were the representatives of the lesser nobility, the rows of the peers, and on either side the burgess and clerical members. But not a bishop dared show his face, for the main object of the Assembly was their destruction.

At the top end of the church, Hamilton sat enthroned in his Chair of State; and nearest him, the Lords of the Privy Council, who had been acting as an advisory committee to the King,—among them, as Montrose could see whenever he leaned far enough forward, the red hair and pale ambiguous face of the new Earl of Argyll.

The colours of splendid cloaks showed dimly among the massive pillars, and here and there the gleam of a steel pistol butt or the winking yellow eye of a cairngorm in the hilt of a whinger. The King had forbidden any to wear arms; but all wore them, even the ministers under their black cloaks,—for who could tell what might happen at any minute?

November darkened into December, the fogs thickened, the nights lengthened, the church was dark nearly all day; all hope of settlement died, and nothing but war became possible between the opposing parties.

And the immediate cause of that war was Montrose's quarrel with his brother-in-law Carnegie.

Montrose had set aside Carnegie's election as the representative elder for Brechin, and appointed another, Erskine of Dun, in his stead. As Warriston, the Clerk of the Assembly (" only half-awake as usual," growled Rothes) read out the notice of this appointment, he inadvertently read aloud as well Montrose's peremptory message, scrawled on the back of it, saying that Carnegie's election was to be cancelled. It all happened so casually, in Warriston's high sing-song scraping voice, that only a few noticed it.

But one of them was Hamilton, all ready to seize his opportunity to dissolve the Assembly. Here was his chance, in this intolerably high-handed action—the elections had been tampered with, the Assembly ' packed ' by the nobles,—and Hamilton was justified in declaring that he would dissolve it straight away.

But he could not do so straight away, for there was at once a terrible perturbation.

The ministers tried to hush it up, and put all the blame on Warriston.

Mr. David Dickson (who had not yet paid him) rose to apologize for the negligence of the Clerk in leaving a private note on a document that was to be read in public.

Before he could speak more than a few sentences, Montrose was on his feet, hotly disclaiming the apology.

"What I have written, I have written," he said, "and am ready to avow the least jot of it."

The frightened minister actually began to apologize this time to Montrose, pulled himself up, but did not dare go on with his speech. He sat down in a huddle, his head poking out from the folds of his hood like an anxious tortoise.

But there was another lion there who could roar as angrily as my Lord of Montrose. The Earl of Southesk had risen, and fiercely attacked his son-in-law for cancelling Carnegie's election. He spoke for his son, Montrose for Erskine, but they spoke for far more than that.

Here in this arena, set for a national struggle, before hundreds of spectators, they fought out their personal quarrel, saying the cruel things they had never yet uttered in private.

Southesk saw in the young man only the unscrupulous resolve to get his own way, the desire to avenge his pique against his King, and against his brother-in-law. He saw all his work as mediator, in procuring this Assembly, destroyed by Montrose, who had given Hamilton this chance to dissolve it.

And Montrose saw in the old man only the instinct to guard family and property and honours granted by royal favour,—knew himself to be unfair, to have behaved abominably, but was determined to stick to it. Only one thing mattered—the business that they had to do. He was in a fury that this should have interrupted it; he flung out that he did not care what he had done, nor who knew of it, he would have no half-hearted moderates in the Assembly if he could help it.

His cloak swung back with the violence of his gesture, it was seen that he had drawn his sword an inch or two from the scabbard.

The movement had been unconscious, but the blazing anger in his eyes and voice made it deadly. A rustle ran through the Assembly.

Henderson, who loved both him and Southesk, could not bear to look upon their faces. He rose slowly, leaning forward with his long fine hands upon his table to keep them from shaking, and interrupted the quarrel. Since these two elections had caused such dissension, he would annul them both.

Old Southesk turned and rent him. How dare he annul Lord Carnegie's appointment, which had been won by fair election? Not only his son-in-law, but his own minister, who had served him down in his parish of Leuchars for twenty-four years, had turned against him. He had forgotten Henderson's few-days-old office as Moderator.

One of the Lords of the Council rebuked him for rating the Moderator.

The old man sat down, bewildered with anger. He had in his time stood up for reform and freedom against his King, and was now scorned for selfish prudence. His son-in-law had gone mad, that was all that could be said about it. But so had many others.

Like a deaf man watching the movements of a dance, meaningless without its music, he watched the flame of this new enthusiasm leap from one member of the Assembly to another, lighting some in the name of God, and others in the name of Scotland, and others with a strange new belief, which had as yet no name and no confirmation,—the belief that men must be free to work out their own salvation and damnation.

Hamilton had dissolved the Assembly in the name of the King. But the Assembly would not be dissolved.

Hamilton sat waiting, fearful lest when he rose and left, only his immediate supporters would leave with him. Darkness was shutting in on the great church, on the crowds of angry people who were sitting there, waiting to see what would happen.

A boy had begun to go down the aisles, lighting candles, his boots squeaking loudly in the silence of that suspense. In the flickering and vagrant light, a man with red hair rose from among the Lords of the Council, just below the Royal Commissioner's great chair of state, and began to speak in a low, hesitating, and curiously inexpressive voice.

It was the new Earl of Argyll, the head of the great clan of Campbell. People craned their necks to see him, to hear on which side he would enlist his enormous power and estates, as those low, slow, vague words dropped through the candle-lit church, that had lately resounded to such haste and fury of speech.

Argyll was to make himself a good speaker, to acquire even charm in the grave courtesy of his manner. But that was to come with deliberation and practice,—a charm won by sheer hard work. As yet he was untried, a man who looked out on the world, suspiciously, from eyes that could never look both together at anything. And now one looked at worldly advantage, at the probabilities of success in this new, popular movement; while the other looked at heaven, seeing more good than he ever had in his life before, in this Covenanters' creed of a man's lonely communion with his God,—a creed removed as far as possible from that of his father.

But so anxious was he to be cautious and not to commit himself unduly, so strange was it to that compressed mouth to speak freely, that it was clear to no one what he had stood up to say,— not even when he sat down again, his face a pale blur behind the candles.

" It is a ruse," thought Hamilton approvingly, " cunning fellow, how like him! "

But as he rose at last and left the church with all his supporters, he looked back at the table of the Privy Council; and one man still sat on alone at it, and that man was the Earl of Argyll.

" Is he showing himself on our side? " ran the excited whisper through the church.

" Devil take me, but I believe he is! " exclaimed Rothes.

But Montrose felt no such elation.

" Devil take me, but I would rather have that man my enemy than my ally," he replied.

The King's men passed out.   The others sat on.

In this cold cathedral, where respectful protest was hardening into revolution, many fates were being determined; and many of those ardent and arrogant heads that there conferred together would be struck from the neck and held up by the bloody hand of the executioner; as also one that, confused in the extreme, was now waiting unhappily in London for news from the North.

And Hamilton, whose uneasy imagination could see none of this, knew at least that he could write no satisfactory answer to King Charles' question to him as to " what might be the end of it all? "

XII

O F all letters Hamilton had ever had to write, this answer to King Charles' question placed him in the most delicate situation.

Ever since he had been born, Hamilton had been in a delicate situation. His mother then, and now at the head of the Covenanters, was against him. The King blamed him for her outrageous activities, and she blamed him for the King's shilly-shallying.

Every time he had come north, it had been with two royal proclamations in his pocket, one severe and one lenient, to use according to his judgment, but as everyone knew about the first, they guessed him to be only gaining time when he used the second.

He was so discreet that nobody could understand what he meant; he was so sympathetic with the petitions handed to him that he wept in the street in front of the largest crowds; he was so friendly with the Covenanting leaders that he suggested to Montrose, ' as a kindly Scot,' that he had only to go on ' with that courage and resolution you have already shown,' to win his cause.

At this astonishing betrayal, the young man's contemptuous glance had shot in his direction, but only once, as though it found nothing there to detain it. Hamilton rolled away, to waver between the rôles of a kindly Scot and a loyal Royal commissioner, between the conflicting methods of reserve and frankness, sympathy and sternness, to sow suspicion between the nobles and the clergy by warning each against the other in strictest confidence; and thus waste his time very unhappily until the General Assembly burst upon him.

And now he had dissolved the Assembly—but the Assembly sat on—and he had to write to the King and explain why. He could not very well give Mr. David Dickson's explanation—that the Marquis of Hamilton had obeyed the word of his royal master, but that they themselves had to follow a still greater master, and obey the word of Christ.

Who was to say which word that would be for each occasion, chosen out of all the words spoken on such different occasions, sixteen hundred years ago?

The Assembly found no difficulty.

But Hamilton did.

It was easier to write—" Next to hell do I hate this place." His sons should all be brought up in England; none of his daughters should marry Scots,—that should convince his master how little truth there was in his hoping to clutch a crown here for himself.

How little truth was there? Very little—there must be—or he could not think with such tenderness of Charles' last note to him, that began with all its old affectionate intimacy—' James '—and was signed, ' Your loving Friend and Cousin.' Was Charles' trust in him but another instance of his folly?

But that did not bear thinking of. Hastily he pulled the paper towards him, and began instead to write character sketches of the leaders of the Assembly, especially of those who had annoyed him most.

Since Argyll had declared himself, he was to be reckoned as chief of them, for the Covenanters were calling him ' a true patriot, a faithful counsellor.' He was now, in Hamilton's opinion, ' the dangerousest man in this State,' and he added, not very helpfully, " What course to advise you to take with him I cannot say; but remit it to your Majesty's serious consideration."

A personal annoyance now dug his pen into the paper as he wrote—" of them all, none is more vainly foolish than Montrose."

A pity the young man could not see that. It would teach him not to look at him, the King's representative, as if he were an unpleasant insect. Thank God there had been one man in the Assembly who dared stand up to the young rebel. And down went his approval of Southesk, the only praise that he gave undiluted by qualifications and withdrawals,—" He has beyond all expectations shown himself forwardly stout in all that has concerned your service."

* * *

It might have cheered Southesk to know that his sovereign would read such praise of him; he needed comfort, fuming and fretting in his poky Glasgow lodging. It cost ten times as much as it had any right to do, but not all the rules and restrictions could keep down the cost of living in this crowded town. He had supported the King's Commissioner by leaving the Assembly when he dissolved it; but he lingered on for some days in Glasgow, cold, crammed and uncomfortable as it was, to hear what the rascals were doing in the Cathedral.

He sent out his servants half a dozen times a day to collect the scraps of news that blew in from the draughty street corners where the retainers of great houses loitered with the latest rumours. The King had commanded that a nobleman's tail be restricted to a single page or body-servant, but in spite of that all the full tails were there, wagging furiously, flourishing their plaids about them, and glaring upon the tartans of their rival clans.

In odd contrast to these rough retainers with their haughty bearing and fierce glances and the brilliance, frequently tattered, of their plaids and saffron-yellow shirts, were the little black groups of ministers, huddling together like ruffled crows in the sea wind, their cloaks flapping and their solemn heads pecking towards each other as they discussed points of doctrine,—or, even more eagerly, the merciful dispensation of Providence which had ordained the Assembly to sit each day from ten to five, and so saved the cost of dinner.

So that it did not matter so much that the Assembly took several weeks to abolish bishops, and the new Prayer Book, and the *Book of Canons*, and salmon fishing on the Sabbath.

But this last, Lord Southesk approved, for as a good fisherman he had sworn against the practice of netting salmon often enough to be glad that it should be stopped for at least one day out of the seven.

He gave this single crumb of comfort to his wife and daughter on his despondent return to Kinnaird, and Lady Southesk attempted no answer, for once men started to talk sport there would be no end to it,—but how could her lord think it of any importance as to whether one caught fish with nets or with rod and line, when all that concerned them was that Jamie had taken clean leave of his senses, and was plunging himself and everyone else into trouble?

As wild and as ungovernable as a stag—that he should have ousted her son from the Assembly, and defied her husband—" he can never have done such things of himself. It must have been the ministers—he likes them less and less——"

But Southesk answered that the ministers were all wagging their heads over him, complaining that he was ' capricious for his own fancies,' and ' very hard to be guided.'

" ' Hard to be guided, indeed! ' " snorted the old man, " when he behaves as though he ruled all Scotland."

" And so he will," echoed in Magdalen's heart, inevitably thrilled, though all her reasonable sympathy went out to her father, who looked so much older and more tired than she had ever seen him.

But when she spoke of her husband, her father burst out that she was never to mention his name to him again. He spoke of a separation between them, and at that she went rigid, speaking her refusal only in her eyes.

Yet separation was inevitable for the time, apart from any quarrel. Southesk would not let his house harbour a rebel to the King, " for that is what he has become, however much he may dispute it,—and so have all those who dared sit on in the Assembly against the King's command. They are all drunk with their own power. You, boy,"—he pulled his elder grandson towards him—" pray against success in struggle. For whatever you strive for, if you get it, you will insist on more, and yet more. Well, don't you believe me? What are you staring at, hey? "

" Johnnie is old enough to know what success you have always had yourself, my lord," said Magdalen, who hoped to tease a smile from him, also to remind him that Johnnie was quite able to understand that his father was being blamed. But old people could never remember that a child of nearly seven was more than three.

And her father was too much engrossed to take any hint; he forgot even that he was still holding on to Johnnie's shoulder, and jerking him now away from his chair, now towards it, in accompaniment to his violent comments on the Assembly.

Her mother slid in a whisper to her to go and call for a cup of lamb's-wool, her father's favourite caudle, which she had prepared against his coming to take off the cold of his long ride,—and the roasted apple must be frothing on top of the hot ale by now, and why had none of the stupid creatures brought it?

They had brought it, and been brushed away quite unconsciously by Lord Southesk in his impatience to tell his complaint, but Magdalen was not the one to remind either parent of that.

She released her son from her father's grasp, led him out with her, and took a rushlight in its pan from a bracket outside the door; as she did so, he shook off her hand, and scampered down the passage. She stood looking after him. He had lumped her with the rest of her family, and was declaring his independence, his desire to join his father.

Her habitual reserve, imposed on her by her large and vigorous and confidently assertive family, reached breaking point; she longed to run after him, to cry, " And so do I, Johnnie, I want to go to him too,—I am his too, not theirs! "

The impulse to speak thus to a child was a thing unheard of. Her mother would have smacked him soundly for his impertinence in running away,—" well, but she would have to catch him first! " she smiled in excuse; and promised herself, " If he looks back, then I will say it."

But he did not look back; his bright hair, his stubborn little back, his sturdy legs trotted steadily on, away from her.

XIII

IT had come to war—against the bishops, people said, for not the most ardent Covenanter would admit that it was against the King.

The Earl of Montrose was made Commander General to the Covenanters' forces, an office in itself a declaration of war, and one that brought him once again into direct conflict with his father and brother-in-law, at a committee meeting in Forfar. He issued his warrant to the nobles to provide men and arms in readiness for the service of the Covenant, and Southesk replied that they were all the King's men and subject to the King's service, but no other. And he and Carnegie left the committee, and prepared measures for their defence.

Magdalen could not hope to see her husband; she must not speak of him to any of her family, not even to Johnnie, for it would encourage the child to speak defiantly of him to the others, and so call down reproof.

Her father and mother had the comfort of indignation, but that kept them silent.

A note came now and then from him, scribbled on a scrap of paper, telling her little but that he loved her.

Master Forrett was her best companion these days,—and Sir Walter Raleigh. Once she had been jealous of Jamie's pre-occupation with that history, written as it was by an adventurer, of God's strange adventure, the world. Now she felt herself nearer to Jamie, thinking his thoughts, when she sat with the great book on her knees.

" The world's tragedy and time are near at an end."

What did that sonorous prophecy foretell? Her eyes fell from the book to the smouldering sea-coal on the hearth, then raised themselves to Master Forrett, who was bending with infinite patience over Johnnie's copybook. So short a time since he had been teaching Johnnie's father, that he looked scarcely a day older himself, though perhaps his small wrinkled face was more than ever like an anxious withered apple these days.

From him she could gather news of Jamie that was not broken by angry comment nor veiled by discretion. For him, as for herself, Jamie's movements were not a matter of politics, but of intrinsic importance. He could bring back from the little town of Montrose the news that they both wanted most of their young lord.

" God help me, but I'm glad to have left his service! " he would say, puckering up his eyes in the wizened smile that made him look like a benevolent goblin. " His men complain he has wings to his horse's hoofs,—have I not known it, when I was too stiff and sore to get down from the saddle! He's dashing here, there and everywhere, raising troops and money out of nothing, subduing the whole country with his forced marches,—all before anyone can forestall him, or even guess that he's within fifty miles. He moves like a mountain torrent. Ah, his men are proud of him! Grumbling is a soldier's best way to show it. He has the sense to learn his trade too,—for all he's the Commander General, he's not too proud to take hints from little Leslie."

Magdalen had heard Rothes speak affectionately of " that rascally bastard cousin of mine," Alexander Leslie, who had served for years as a soldier of fortune under the Swedish king-captain, Gustavus Adolphus, and like many other Scottish mercenaries had hurried home to fight for the Covenant.

" What can the Covenant mean to him? " she asked in contempt; but the answer was that it meant his country, for which he had grown homesick after years of hardship and iron discipline in a foreign land. And it meant too the independence of that country from a foreign yoke.

He was a small, insignificant-looking, elderly soldier, tough and wiry as a terrier, whose rough, good-humoured authority carried weight over all his fellows. He was the practised professional where Montrose was as yet only the dashing amateur. His young Commander General had the modesty of good sense in spite of his haughty manner, and was glad to ride out by Leslie's side and breakfast with him in the open on those biting winter mornings, with their napkins on their knees and a leather black-jack of ale beside them, and hear Leslie's stories of the greatest commander that the north had ever seen, stories bitten off between huge mouthfuls of food, while they blew on their frosty blue fingers.

Gustavus Adolphus had known how to treat the Marquis of Hamilton, when His Wobbliness had fooled about as envoy to Sweden. Took Hamilton's hat from his head, he did, flung it on the floor and stamped on it, and why? Just because that was what any sensible fellow would do, who had looked long enough at Hamilton and Hamilton's hat.

And having breakfasted, they buckled up their buff coats, sounded the call to arms, and rode down into Aberdeen at the head of eleven thousand men, horse, pikemen, and musketeers, to take that recalcitrant city in the name of the Covenant. But not a blow was struck, and Magdalen hoped that Jamie was only picnicking, and that nothing very serious might happen after all.

The clouds of armies rolled up and up, the long thunder was heard of men marching, of the mustering of great horses and the hauling of cannon; and the price of peat went up, because the peat-men ran away from the Covenanters; still the war did not begin, so that people went on saying, "Something will surely happen to prevent it."

But the old country-women who came to the kitchen at Kinnaird in search of a bite and a sup, and would sit there for hours, rocking themselves to and fro, letting out an occasional croak under their black hoods, told how martial music had been heard on an ancient hill fort in Aberdeenshire, much frequented by the fairies. Drums and fifes were heard playing the marches of Scotland, England and Ireland, night after night.

For nearly a century Scottish women had possessed their homes and their men in comparative safety. Now that there was the threat of war once again, it was the more agonizing, because of that late, treacherous security.

"Will the world ever be safe?" asked Magdalen, and Master Forrett doubted that people desired it. For look at England,

so envied abroad for her mild-tempered King and her prolific
Queen, and still more for her good trade, increasing manufactures,
and the high credit of her merchants.

Yet the spirit of that country had grown stern in safety.
Prosperous conditions only gave a man more leisure to trouble
about his soul; and that, so far from sharing in the material
security, had become more and more a frightened, lonely thing.
No longer was it knit to its neighbours by the sense of unity in
national danger and victory that had inspired it in Elizabeth's
day, when pride in his country and wonder of the half-known
world were as the breath of an Englishman's nostrils. Now his
soul had to look to itself, in growing distrust with its spiritual
advisers. England was in danger of being ruled by a religious
clique, headed by the King and Archbishop. Bishops grew
increasingly unpopular. A Cambridge scholar referred to them
in an elegiac poem, called Lycidas, as ' blind mouths,' whose
congregations, like ' hungry sheep, look up and are not fed.'

The fare provided was in fact too sweet for the congregation.
They hated to hear the King's Book of Sports read to them from
the pulpit, telling them that as long as they attended divine service
on Sunday they could spend the rest of the day in field sports and
dancing round the maypole. Who was the King, any more than
the Pope, to decide these things for them?

In men's minds at different times there is a craving for restrictions, for things to be made hard. Pleasure has become too easy,
people ask, not—' will they enjoy this or that? ' but—' is this or
that necessary for salvation? '

The drab clothes of tradesmen became more conspicuous;
bright colours and music less and less respectable. Since beauty
was shunned in worship, it could scarcely be respectable anywhere
else. When the Queen danced and acted on the stage before
her subjects, men disapproved, and thought they had a right to
say so. Mr. Prynne did say so in a rude tract, calling theatres
the Devil's chapels, and had his ears cut off in the pillory in
consequence. It was no more than he suggested should be done
to all actors; and as for his *lèse-majesté*, men had lost their lives

for less in days past. But now people felt more and more that queens may not do what they like, but that men may say it.

Therefore they looked approvingly towards Scotland, where, in a Cathedral, a mixed assembly of nobles, clergy and burgesses had held what was practically a parliament, and without the King's consent.

For the last eleven years the King had ruled the country without a parliament. But here was a parliament without a King;—the notion sank in.

And just as the puritans in England had begun to grasp what the puritans in Scotland were demanding, and to feel sympathy with it, the King was forced to call on his country for supplies of money for an army against these same Scots.

Grudgingly, he was provided with as few supplies and as many objections as possible. Yet that army slowly gathered together, a mighty force, they heard in Scotland, and up came Hamilton in the spring with a fleet of ships.

But he sailed away again without even landing. His mother rode down to the shore to meet him with a brace of pistols on her saddle-bow, all ready to shoot him, should he dare come ashore at the head of an English force. He did not dare. He went back to Charles to say it was all impossible in Scotland. These family complications made everything so difficult.

Charles did not want to begin the war. He told Hamilton to refrain from fighting under any provocation; and Hamilton told Huntly, who had been made Lieutenant of the North, in command of the Royalist forces. So the Cock o' the North had got his leadership of all the provinces ' benorth the Granbeam.' And Montrose was in opposition to him as Commander General of the Covenanters.

Lord Southesk said to his small grandsons,—" Huntly's children are all tying red ribbons round their arms to show they are the King's men,—even the youngest, and that's a brat of three. Would you not like to wear the King's colours too? "

James looked at Johnnie. Johnnie looked at his grandfather, his face red enough for any royalist badge.

" I'll wear my father's colours," he said.

Southesk was as much pleased as exasperated with the boy's loyalty to his father.

He showed his sympathy with Magdalen by helping to arrange that Montrose should come to Kinnaird for one night that spring. He himself would ride to Brechin during his visit, which was to be kept as secret as possible.

" It would be wiser not to meet," he told Magdalen, and tried to make his tone sound political, not bitter. She kissed his hand with greater tenderness than she had felt for months; and he said, " There, there, it is a bad business, but don't let us exaggerate. There will be better times soon."

XIV

SHE stood at the window over the courtyard; spurts of rain and flecks of white sunshine flew over the bare sweep of country below; at last she saw three men riding at the gallop, one of them a good way ahead.

Once more she was in his arms. Broken words came tumbling out from him, unheeded by her. " I ought not to have come. It is generous of your father. Dear love, I had to come."

Ah, that last made sense. And now she too was saying things, striving to extend this present bliss into the future. " We should not be here. If I were at your own house at Kincardine, you could come as often as you like."

And leave her and their boys unguarded? No, he could not have that. What a tangle it was.

Here were Johnnie and young James, solemnly bearing a stirrup cup and jug of ale between them, for Master Forrett had divided the labour to leave no room for jealousy.

They stood close by him, one against each knee, staring at him, putting up an inquiring finger now and then to touch his sword or his sleeve of chrome leather; and occasionally he put his hand on their heads, but not in the casual, tousling way he used to rumple up their hair. He asked them questions of the ponies he had given them, Dapple and Drake, almost as though they were men; he was gentler and graver than in that home-coming from Italy only three years ago, when he had swung them to the ceiling, a boy himself, still astonished to find himself a father.

Now he was like a real father, she thought, and longed to keep him so, at her side and theirs,—and how in the world could anything matter to him more than that? Resentment was welling up again in her, the salt, bitter taste of tears through her joy in him; but she would not let them come.

They talked of one slight, happy thing after another, trying to keep other thoughts and questions at bay. She told him how

231

Johnnie would not wear red ribbons when her father wanted him to do so, like Huntly's children.

" He shall wear my colours," said his father.

" So he said. But what do you mean? " for he was unwinding a broad blue ribbon that he had been wearing across his breast like an order of knighthood. He cut off the end of it with his whinger and tore the piece in strips, fastening a bunch of them into each of the boys' bonnets.

" That was my answer to Huntly's boys. The poorest shepherd in my ranks has a bunch of blue ribbons now in his bonnet, and half the cavalry have thrown away their plumed hats and are wearing only bonnets and blue ribbons. I told you blue was your colour, Magdalen, and we should wear it. Well, Johnnie, will you be a true-blue Covenanter? "

But his gaiety dropped from him as he turned to her from the children, who were proudly strutting round the room with their new colours. He said, " Huntly wears red ribbons, and I, blue. Is that after all the only difference between us? "

" Dear heart, you are happy? Do things go well? "

But she knew as she asked how difficult it would be for him to give an answer.

His arm tightened about her, for he had felt the knowledge pass to her from himself. This it was to be married; they had been separated for months, but hope and fear had only quickened their sympathies and made them now able to share together what they had missed.

Later, she said, " You distrust Argyll,—is that what troubles you? "

Yes, there it was,—that cloud on the clear horizon of his belief in his cause,—a cloud no bigger than a man's hand, than that nervous, tenacious hand of Argyll, a lawyer's hand rather than a chieftain's, clutching at his cloak as he spoke before the Assembly in the Cathedral at Glasgow, months ago,—" showing his hand at last," as Rothes had said in satisfaction.

Argyll was now Montrose's most powerful ally, holding sway

in all the councils, and practically ruling the new civil governing body, the Committee of Estates.

" Yes, but you have the army," she said, " and they worship you. He cannot rival you there. Can you not leave it like that? "

But he was thinking how odd it was that Argyll must be his friend; while his foe was Huntly, the King's Lieutenant of the North, whose splendidly loyal answer to the Covenant had stirred an envious echo in his heart.

Huntly stood for his King, and he himself for his nation's rights—but who could say where rights began and ended? A niggard quality of senseless tyranny had already developed in the very Kirk which was fighting for freedom. When that was won, how soon would it in its turn oppress the freedom of others?

" These ministers," he burst out, " they are like carrion crows in their lust for carnage. They would have had me sack Aberdeen, which had yielded to me without a blow. But they wanted an example made of the ungodly city, and I was blamed for my ' too great discretion.' "

" Oh Jamie, for the first time then in your life! "

He laughed with her, but she could see how much graver his face had grown, and older. He would not now override her brother's election, and flout her father before all the Assembly, so she told herself—wondering if she could ever make her father see this.

Yet it gave her a pang to find that headlong boy grown into a man. He was leaner too, and weather-beaten with cold winds and hard riding; the strain of always thinking, moving, acting at higher speed than anybody else had made his muscles like wire.

A few weeks ago he had prevented Huntly and his army of twenty-five hundred from occupying the town of Turriff; had done it by dashing along the Mearns with two hundred cavalry, scarcely pausing to rest or even eat on the way; met eight hundred more, to whom he had managed to send word; and so cut off from the town a force two and a half times the size of his own.

Her pride in him now made her ask about it, but he told her disconsolately that there had been no fight,—" They had a chance to crush us, and nothing happened."

" Does that disappoint you? " she smiled.

" It disappointed Huntly, I know. He must have had his orders from Hamilton not to fight. We waited there all day, entrenched in the churchyard, our muskets guarding the dikes, expecting an attack that never came. All that they did was to parley for peace and I gave them leave to ride up through the town, and so they went away, going past us, so close under the wall of the churchyard that there was I sitting not two pikes' length from Huntly as he rode by and glared at me."

He paused, seeing again the barbaric swirl and flurry of that angry march past of the Gordons, the hereditary foes of his house. How defiantly the pipes had shrilled, and the lean rumps swung in their kilts, and the plaids and rough beards tossed past him on the wind. And then in their midst, the magnificent figure of their leader had deliberately drawn rein to stare at him in fury. Huntly would never forgive him for this shame, done to him in front of all his clan,—his family too——

"—His sons were with him,—Gordon, whom I had liked,— and young Aboyne, hot-headed enough to attack without any backing,—and even that little rascal, Lewis, a scamp of thirteen, who has run away from school, and stolen his grandmother's jewels to raise a force of his own——" His admiration rang in his voice, and his generous indignation on their behalf.

"Yes, but what has Huntly *done* for the King?" asked Magdalen.

He did not hear her; he was breathing again the keen air of that spring evening in the little churchyard. Through the stir and music of the Gordon pipes just under his ears, there had echoed the refrain that had called on Huntly's name a generation ago :

> " Oh wae betide ye, Huntly,
> And wherefore did ye sae? "

That wailing reproach might well have been uttered by Huntly's own pipers,—a cry from his own baffled friends. Yet the reproach had seemed to Montrose not to Huntly, but to himself.

Why, if Huntly and his sons so stirred his sympathy, were they on opposite sides—not merely of a low stone wall?

XV

THE 'blue bonnets' were famous in a few months.
"Montrose's whimsy," said the veterans with an indulgent
smile; "true-blue Covenanters," said the sympathetic; "Covenanting dogs," said the antipathetic, tying blue ribbons on all the curs
in Aberdeen in token of their derision; "an army of blue caps
and jockeys," said the contemptuous English, who were still more
impolite in calling their lice, Covenanters; "our panache," said
Montrose's devoted followers, for whom their leader's exploits
were already making it a crest as symbolic of daring and high
honour as the panache of Cyrano or the white plume of Navarre.
And now they were all marching to a new tune, singing :

" March, march, why the de'il dinna ye march?
    Stand to your pikes, lads, fight in good order! "

The rhyme to that in grim earnest as in the song would be when

" A' the Blue Bonnets are over the Border."

Johnnie and James were marching through the gardens at
Kinnaird, shouting it, banging on the toy drums from Holland
that their grandmother had bought for them from the pedlar, and
now cursed her ill-judgment in doing so. One could stop the
children from making that noise in the house, but not from
singing their father's marching songs in the gardens,—"and for
mercy's sake tell Daniel to keep the boys away from the library
windows." This it was to have the shadow of civil war across
the land, she groaned.

Only in the north round Aberdeen was the country loyal as
a whole to the King and his bishops,—but the new young Commander General was subduing all that part before the King came
north. What would happen then? Montrose surely would not
fight against the King himself?

"God knows what he will do next," growled Southesk.

The most disconcerting thing he did, to himself as well as

everyone else, was to bring Huntly to Aberdeen, where he was taken prisoner by the Covenanters and brought to Edinburgh. Huntly said that Montrose had promised him his safeguard,— so that either he had broken his word (" but that is fair ridiculous," said Lady Southesk) or that he had not been able to force the rest of his side to keep it.   But Magdalen was certain Jamie would never have let himself be overruled; if he gave his word and it was not regarded, he would resign his commission.

" Oh why does he not *say* what happened? " she cried, her restraint breaking for the first time.

It was her father who consoled her with his private theory that when Huntly opened negotiations with Montrose and put himself so incautiously into the hands of his enemies, he had decided that a term of imprisonment at Edinburgh was the easiest way to save his face.

He was in an intolerable position.   He got no backing from Hamilton, he was told not to fight, and he had been laughed at for marching up to Turriff with nearly three times as many men as Montrose, " hours after the young rebel had got there,—and then if you please, Montrose giving him his kind permission to ride away through the town! "

In spite of his angry tone, and his care to call his son-in-law by his title, not his family name, Southesk could not keep the ring of pride out of his voice, nor the contempt he felt for his supposed ally, the King's Lieutenant of the North.   For what had Huntly done for his King (as Magdalen had already asked) but give himself up to his enemies, with his eldest son, Lord Gordon, and now lie helpless in Edinburgh, where he proclaimed " You may take my head from my shoulders, but not my heart from my sovereign."

His sovereign had little use for either his head or his heart, as Charles showed in a distressed letter to Hamilton, complaining of Huntly as both ' feeble and false.'

That would make Huntly no better friend to the man to whom he had exposed his weakness.   In Magdalen's eyes this ' Bishops' War ' was resolving itself into a conflict solely between those who might hurt Jamie, and those who might help him. Never, so she saw from the beginning, would he get help from Huntly, whose castle, the Bog o' Gight, he was even now besieging.

And now there entered the list of his enemies the two gallant boys that Huntly had left behind to carry on his work. For Aboyne, the second son, still in his teens, joined forces with Master Lewis, and the two of them, in the name of their father, roused Aberdeen to back them under the leadership of the Provost's son, Colonel Johnstone, a fine soldier of long experience, and got together four thousand men, including six hundred of the Gordon cavalry, a few field pieces, and Colonel Gun, another old soldier.

General Leslie and his army were down near the Border, marching to meet the King's. Montrose, up in the north, was in danger of having his communications cut; he had to leave his siege of Gordon Castle and dash to Aberdeen, which he found fortified against him, with the river Dee in flood, and its narrow bridge, two miles above the town, strongly guarded by the Gordon horse and the Aberdeen musketeers.

There in the middle of June he fought the only real battle of the ' Bishops' Wars,' while down south the King's huge army lay outside Berwick, facing Leslie's army, and who knew what might be happening there at this very moment?

* * *

What was happening at that moment was that the King was signing a peace treaty. He and his army had been defeated by their discovery that the north could be so hot. The misty sunlight lay soft as a downy blanket on the hills across the Border, they quivered as one looked at them, as though they were a mirage that might at any moment disappear. It was too hot to move, too hot to argue, too hot to think, except of deep pools and long drinks. The imaginations in that army would have emptied all the cellars of England in an hour.

" My native country," said Charles in melting mood, gazing at the bloom on those hills like ripe fruit. But he presently observed that the fruit was crawling with maggots. General

Leslie knew how to take advantage of a heat wave. He had intermixed his troops with some herds of cattle so that in the haze they looked twice as many.

And then there was the expense, all those troops eating their heads off, or rather not eating their heads off, for it was impossible to get enough money out of the sullen English citizens to give them their arrears of pay; they were in bad condition; and nobody in the English army showed any quality of leadership.

And just across the Border was the disconcerting spectacle of Leslie's army in excellent condition, and spirits too, to judge by the determined sound of prayers and the singing of psalms that rose from the camp every morning and evening. This enthusiasm, encouraged by good food and splendid banners flying the legend, ' For Christ's Crown and Covenant,' was the most dangerous enemy of the King, for many in his army were so much impressed by it as to say they wished that England also would show a like sturdy independence in dealing with Archbishop Laud's fussy improvements.

All these bishops only made mischief. Now that they were up here, and could see what the Scots were at, they thought it all very reasonable, and the King had much better give in.

Besides, the lords Pembroke and Holland wanted to get back to their hunting.

So the King gave in.

*　　　*　　　*

" A lot of *cows*? Too *hot* to fight? My Lord Pembroke's *hunting*? Are soldiers really so silly? " Magdalen asked her father.

*　　　*　　　*

Many miles further up the east coast, the slanting sunlight slid over the sparkling grey and pink granite walls of Aberdeen, like water over oyster shells. Outside the town ran the river, frothing white in flood; and there, on one side of a granite bridge of seven arches, was a stationary mass of men, with men on horseback behind them. Those were the Gordon cavalry, backing the Aberdeen men and muskets.

On the other side of the river, little bands of horsemen came galloping up to the bridge, narrowing to three or four at a time as they mounted it,—and crack, crack, crack, went all the waiting muskets of the men who guarded it on the other side, while the cavalry behind made ready to charge. Puffs of smoke hung like thistledown in the still air; as they drifted away down stream, the attacking horsemen could be seen swinging round and galloping back again, followed by shouts of derisive triumph from the Aberdonians.

All that grilling June day, Montrose's forces attacked the bridge, made no impression, found their cannon balls all fall short.

"'They hold as pretty a position as ever I've seen," growled Major Middleton to his Commander General.

Montrose did not answer at once. He was observing a fresh movement of the enemy's,—a sortie from the town—"What game are they playing there?"

It proved a game more disheartening to his side than all their beaten-off attacks.

The citizens of Aberdeen,—yes, the very women,—yes, even the servant maids in their linen head-cloths and aprons,—were coming out of their granite walls to bear baskets and jugs of refreshment to their staunch defenders.

It was exasperating to see how safe they felt their position on the other side of the river, but that was nothing to the tantalizing fury of thirst and hunger aroused by the sight of those mighty black-jacks of ale and mountainous pies.

Watching the faces of his men, Montrose swore to himself to waste no time in sleep that night.

The heat of the day dragged to a thin, northern darkness. But it grew dark enough for him to bring up his heavy cannon from Dunnottar, unobserved by the enemy. And in the sultry mist of next morning he led a body of horse up the river, as if to ford it.

Then, said his men, the enemy Gun proved more useful to

them than any of their own field pieces. For the river was far too swollen after the rains for anyone to cross it except in a boat; yet Colonel Gun called off the Gordon cavalry from their defence of the bridge and sent them up the river to prevent this impossible fording, and exposed them to Montrose's new heavy artillery for little better reason than he himself gave in the correctly tough and hearty fashion of an old soldier.

" Very sound to let 'em have a peppering—harden 'em a bit— teach 'em to be cannon-proof,—that's what they need."

He was having breakfast himself at the time, but then he was too old and hardened a soldier to need peppering.

So the Highlanders riding along the river bank saw close in front of them Johnnie Seton, one of their commanders, riding by the side of Aboyne, blown to bits by a cannon ball that swept away the whole upper part of his body.

This then was 'the mother of the musket.' Her hellish roar was answered with a howl, the Highlanders broke and fled, nor could their young chieftain, in fury and then in tears, succeed in rallying them. They forced Lord Aboyne to fly with them to Huntly Castle; the citizens of Aberdeen broke from their defences; and Montrose crossed the bridge and took possession of the city.

But he encamped his men in the fields outside the town, and restrained them from any sack. His second-in-command, Major Middleton, objected on the score of professional etiquette,—a successful storming army had a right to the reward of loot. There were orders too from the Committee of Estates that if Aberdeen were taken it was to be burned and razed.

But Montrose crushed all objections with a strong hand. He had won his victory with very little loss of life on either side, and he was not going to spoil it with wholesale destruction to please " a pack of bloodthirsty old women," as he roughly called most of the Committee of Estates. They had long been urging revenge on the ' malicious disloyalty ' of Aberdeen, and hoping that " the curse was alighting upon Meroz, which came not to the help of the Lord against the mighty."

The Lord, however, came to the help of Meroz; in the middle of the angry disputes over the city's fate came news from the south that the King had signed a treaty of peace at Berwick, two days ago, at the very moment when Montrose was defeating the Gordons in the first serious battle of the war.

It was with a curious sense of anti-climax that Montrose heard of this. What had he won his victory for, since the peace had been signed at the time of its fighting; and, for that matter, for what did 'poor Johnnie Seton lie gasping on the ground'? according to the poetic licence of the minstrels' report.

It was his first taste of the futility and waste of war.

The peace gave all the advantages to his side; the King agreed to allow the Scottish Parliament to settle its civil affairs, and the General Assemblies of the Kirk to settle those of the Kirk.

But he might have done that at the beginning and saved all that trouble and expense and the admission of failure.

All Montrose's instincts as a soldier told him that Charles for his own sake should never have made this enormous gesture of mustering all the King's horses and all the King's men, merely in order to march them up to Scotland and march them down again.

XVI

" UPON the eighteenth day of June,
    A dreary day to see,
The Southern lords did pitch their camp
    Just at the Bridge of Dee."

Johnnie and James wanted to get on to the cannon ball " that
dung Pitmeddin in three."

Magdalen dandled the new baby, Rob, up and down in time
to the twanging of the harp. A fine boy he was, with large
solemn eyes that stared, rather shocked, at the ferocious faces
made by the travelling minstrel in his efforts to put fire into the
pedestrian verses; they plodded on with their report, where once
the story would have galloped into song. The ballad's palmy days
had been those of more constant and reckless adventure; the quieter
latter years had gently smothered it, as in a too comfortable bed.

Johnnie objected that if

" There's not a man in Highland dress
    Can face the cannon's fire,"

then it was because the men in Highland dress, especially those
in Gordon tartan, were cowards. James disagreed. If nobody
could face the cannon's fire without getting killed, then why
face it?

His grandmother was enchanted by his wisdom, and he not
yet six years old. It was just as she had always said, these new
inventions of great guns would make war impossible in the long
run, for everyone would run away, and then men would have to
show more sense than to go on killing each other.

But Magdalen could not believe that men would ever show sense.

When they won the war, they lost the peace; no sooner was
it signed, than Hamilton let out that King Charles had written
to him that he would " rather die than yield to these impertinent
and damnable demands "; so that now he had yielded, it could
only be to gain time.

So the Scots kept none of their promises, since they were sure the King did not mean to keep his; riots broke out in Edinburgh; and Charles demanded the presence of the Covenanting nobles for further discussion. Argyll and his friends refused to go, as they did not think it safe to trust the King,—an insult he deeply resented. Out of the fourteen nobles invited to the conference, only Montrose and Rothes went with three others.

Montrose had been greeted everywhere as a conquering hero; his victory at the Bridge of Dee was being commemorated in ballads, in compliments from all the Covenanting leaders to that " generous and noble youth," that " valorous and happy gentleman." The effect of success on a temper such as his was to make him eager to be generous to those who had not been so fortunate.

He found King Charles, who had apparently conceded everything, being bullied to concede more.

The Covenanters were certain that he meant to keep his bishops in Scotland somehow—Warriston told the King so to his face,— else why did His Majesty refuse to ratify the act against them?

Said the King, " The Devil himself could not make a more uncharitable construction."

His reddish-brown eyes were warm in anger; here was a real living man, instead of the frozen mask that Montrose had confronted at Hampton Court. Charles' expression of his anger gave the young man a pang of indignant pity. A king should not speak so to his subjects,—' uncharitable ' indeed—who the devil wanted the charity of that little cur, snapping and snarling at the King's ankles?

Warriston was revelling in the discovery that he felt no vain pride in the converse of great ones. He, the small merchant's son, who had always had to slave and struggle to keep his home together, was the only one among these nobles and ministers who refused to be pleased in any way by the King's behaviour at their interviews. He alone could see below the surface, could perceive an insult in Charles' grave courtesy, in the restraint implied in that slow, careful speech.

It was slow and careful because Charles had to overcome a natural impediment, which for his first few years had made people fear he was dumb, and, later, that he would stutter like his father. Had Warriston known it arose from an infirmity, he might have felt more kindly towards him,—but no, nothing could excuse that sad liquid gaze, which so obviously melted his comrades' wrath, —that air of bewildered dignity, as of a prince lost in a world for which he has been ill prepared. Again and again the little clerk tried to ruffle that royal, that criminal composure. When the King at last turned sharply on him and told him to hold his tongue, Warriston was delighted. The ministers could not now go on saying the King was " one of the most just, reasonable, sweet persons they had ever seen."

But nobody was reasonable,—not even Rothes, who, heavy with argument and hot-weather gout, lost his temper and told Charles that if he did not get rid of the bishops up here, he would find the Scots joining with the English puritans and attacking the English bishops as well.

It was a threat of war, of attack on the King's own country. The company stared aghast. Nobody could think what had come to Rothes, though his swollen purple veins might have told them.

Charles replied quietly that this final insult had now made it impossible for him to attend the Assembly in August as he had promised; he would return at once to London.

Montrose looked at his King; the King at Montrose. Charles saw a grave young man whom Hamilton, for one of his obscure reasons, had told him to snub when he visited him at his river palace at Hampton Court three years ago.

A lot of water had flowed under the Thames bridges since then,—so also under the Bridge of Dee. This young man had been made Commander General of his rebellious Scots subjects, had proved himself a leader of fire and resource, and had won the only considerable battle in the war, against the royalist forces.

But of all that company, both of the King's own men and the

Covenanters, his were the only eyes that met the King's in understanding, as though he saw his difficult position, and wished he were not in it.

Yet he had been leading the armies of his enemies. And it might have been prevented—one never knew.

XVII

IF the cloud on Montrose's horizon were that of Argyll's hand, the cloud on Magdalen's was that of the King.

"The hand of a dead man," Jamie had described its effect on him at his first disappointing interview three years ago. The seeds of defeat must lie buried deep in it.

And Jamie was feeling sorry for him, and angry with his own side.

"If you had seen them all strutting off from the royal interviews, so well pleased with themselves for baiting the King that they could afford to approve his manners, though they themselves had shown none!"

"Yes, for now they can say, 'As I told His Majesty to his face—and very grateful he was to me, though the rest thought me mad to say it——' "

"My sweet cynic! Your laughter is like cool water after all those hot words."

"With whom have you quarrelled, Jamie?"

"With whom have I not? And all for saying that the King should be given a fair chance."

But Magdalen, the realist, wondered what the King would do with a fair chance if he had it. For her father said he was bungling everything—and in England too. And the Covenanting leaders now said what fools they had been to trust the King's fair words,—though they had not trusted them. Their own words, for all their moral superiority of roughness, were no more trustworthy.

Charles meant to break his promise of abolishing the bishops, said they, who had already broken their own promise to disband their army,—a more dangerous body of men on the face of it.

"Why did not Charles, too, stick to his guns, rather than to the surplices?" demanded his feminine critic.

The Earl of Traquair had superseded Hamilton as Royal Commissioner, and was attacked so savagely by the mob in Edinburgh that he only just escaped with his life. But Catherine, as the new Commissioner's wife, only smiled more languidly than ever, as though the mob's howls of execration were too coarse for her to notice.

"The people?" she inquired of her younger sister. "Well, my dear Magdalen, what *are* the people? By the way, did not your Jamie address them once from a fish-tub? Or was it a beer barrel? And does he really think they matter?"

Her indifferent questions, as of a mind too fatigued ever to answer, were but the echo of Traquair's querulous self-advertisement, that now grew daily more indignant. His boys told their cousin Johnnie that their father was an important butter-pat.

He was the worst person to have chosen. But King Charles seemed to have an unerring flair for choosing the worst people,—and for doing the strong thing at the wrong moment. He repented of disbanding his army, and called back Thomas Wentworth, just created Lord Strafford, from Ireland, to pull it together again. At once Scotland was humming like a hive, collecting troops and money again in her turn, for she was not going to have Black Tom subdue her as he had done Ireland.

Surely that would prevent even Jamie being so rash as to show his growing sympathy with the King? With the deadly knowledge of psychology of a shrewd and loving woman, Magdalen now welcomed any sign of oppression on King Charles' part that would prevent her husband seeing the King in his turn as one of the oppressed.

Montrose pleaded openly in Parliament for the King's authority, against Argyll's startling innovations, which aimed at transferring the King's power "to the people," said Argyll,—but "to Argyll," said Montrose.

The answer to his fiery speeches in defence of the royal prerogative was a paper pinned to the door of his bedroom in Edinburgh, with the words, "Invictus armis, verbis vincitur."

He laughed at it, saying the anonymous writer had complimented him too much in calling him unconquered in war, with only one battle to speak of behind him. As to being conquered by the

King's words, he refuted that accusation by refusing the King's invitation to Court.

But was it refuted? People believed what they wanted; they told each other that the Earl of Montrose had been asked to Court, rather than that he had refused to go. Perhaps they guessed the reason he gave for his refusal to be far from flattering,—that " the invitation had caused such jealousy that he thought it best to stay in Scotland."

" Is it safe to use those words? "

" Dear heart, there are only three safe words in the language, and all in your keeping."

" What are they? "

" I love you," he replied, kissing her across the paper that he was rapidly folding and sealing, so that she should not plague him to write it again.

*　　　*　　　*

War broke out again after less than a year of peace, and Montrose was still the army leader of the Covenanters. To have thrown up his command would have been to do nothing,—which he could not bear; or to join the King's forces against the liberty of the Kirk, and Scotland. Such a course was still impossible to the young man who had come home burning to fight for his country.

Scottish liberty—the Covenant—the Kirk that had defied Rome and England, as Scotland had always done in the past—these were still splendid abstractions, quite distinct from the sour faces of Argyll and Warriston and captious ministers.

*　　　*　　　*

By next summer, his Blue Bonnets were over the Border. The river Tweed ran with a fierce current after heavy rains; the army had to ford it by night, and the flood looked unfathomable beneath the tossing foam. The bland, indifferent face of the August moon swam over the hosts of men gathered on the banks. Their coats of hodden grey, of the nearly white natural colour of the wool, made them ghostly and almost indistinguishable from the shore, except where here and there the moonlight gleamed on a steel buckle or a pike's head or the brass nails that studded their targes. Nearer, one saw their white, awed faces, lit by that unearthly light, all turned towards those swirling depths of waters.

It would be a hard thing to induce them to cross. Montrose volunteered and was met with furious protests. Let him be first in the fight, but not in the flood as well. Let it be done fairly, and lots cast for the choice.

They were cast, and he won,—by cheating, all his men declared. If not, then fate itself had to truckle to him.

He dashed into the torrent up to his waist, and reached the other side so quickly that he found himself there alone, for no one had dared follow. Back he went through the torrent to encourage them, and then for the third time faced the river. This time, wagons were led down into the stream to break the current, but in spite of them one of the men was swept away from their midst, and drowned. That their leader should have escaped three times over, and alone, seemed a miracle.

" He is born to be hanged," said his men proudly.

*　　　*　　　*

Leslie's forces crossed the Tyne a few days later; the river was not so alarming, but there were English troops waiting to oppose them on the southern shore. There was a brief engagement in which the English, who numbered between four and five thousand, sustained under forty casualties, and then ran away. The Scottish armies swept onwards through the north of England.

XVIII

DOWN in London, King Charles had had to call his first Parliament for eleven years, to ask for army supplies against the Scottish invasion. But Parliament refused to discuss the invasion unless their grievances were settled first.

Charles showed them letters from the Scots to the King of France. Argyll had promised to levy a regiment of Scots to send to France under his half-brother, the Earl of Irvine; in return, Cardinal Richelieu was to help finance the campaign against England. An odd alliance for those who were fighting against anything that smacked of Rome. What did Parliament think of that?

Parliament thought nothing of it. It wanted to know when that Ship Money tax would be taken off. Charles took it off. It was no use; there were other grievances.

"Things must get worse before they are better," said one of the patriot leaders.

So Charles had to dissolve his Parliament after three weeks, and Strafford had to go north without their support, and by that time the Scots, having met scarcely any resistance from the English, were in possession of Newcastle, and of all the coal supplies for London.

Charles had to patch up peace again; he also had to call another Parliament to help him do so, and a Parliament who found the Scottish invasion a great help to their politics.

"May it sit longer than the last," growled the people who were already beginning to talk of that abortive effort as the Short Parliament.

They need not have troubled, for it was guarded from the King by the Scottish army at Newcastle as securely as if every member's chair were surrounded by their pikes. It might well sit for ever in such conditions; as it was, it sat for twenty years, and for that reason came to be known as the Long Parliament.

The Scottish commissioners, chiefly ministers, went down to

London to settle the peace just as they wished, and there found, as they wrote exultantly, " a new world."

They were extraordinarily popular. The mob welcomed these respectable black-gowned worthies with loud cheers, for " whoever is not Scot is Popish " was the popular notion; and they had just been booing and hissing themselves hoarse at that painted old harridan, the King's mother-in-law, a Papist, an Italian, a Medici, who had lately dared to visit the Queen, her daughter, with a troop of thievish foreign servants. After the mud and stones they had been flinging at her, and the altar rails they had been tearing up, and the one or two army officers they had murdered on suspicion of popery, it was a change now to have someone to cheer.

The grave citizens approved of them, for they would show the King and his immorally French and Catholic Queen that his people were in earnest, and would not have white-robed Romish-looking priests moving about the Communion table in their churches.

Fashion itself went mad over them, or at least over Mr. Henderson, who suddenly found himself a society preacher. All London thronged to church to hear him tell them of their sins.

Above all, the new Parliament, in which the puritan element was very strong, proved their sympathy in the most practical way, for it agreed to pay all the Scottish army's expenses in invading England.

If only they would pay the Commissioners' hotel bills too! The London prices were exorbitant, and no amount of preaching or arguing could convince the innkeepers of the error of their bills.

" Two and forty shillings *sterling* for some dishes of little partans! Man, but it's fair impossible! Two and forty shillings *Scots*, you mean."

But the innkeeper, insolently provincial, professed never even to have heard of shillings Scots.

Still, one cannot have everything; and the new Parliament had at once put the arch-enemy Laud in the Tower, where nobody would listen to him.

" Poor Canterbury," said the Commissioners, " is now grown so contemptible."

They put Strafford in the Tower too, so there was the King's greatest soldier safely out of harm's way, and likely to be still safer, for " The Lower House will have Strafford's life," wrote Warriston exultantly. The Lower House, too, " are thinking on *moneys for us*—this in post haste—Lord encourage and direct them ! "

With the Lord encouraging and directing everything so admirably, it seemed a good time to insist on Presbyterianism being set up all over England, and so maintain " one form of Church government, in all the Churches of His Majesty's dominions."

It was just what Charles had thought, only he had thought it of the Church of England.

Substitute the Kirk of Scotland, said the Commissioners, and that would be quite different. Then there would be one great international Church of Protestants in union with that of Calvin at Geneva and in Germany, which could present an unbroken front to the international Church of Rome.

But here again, as in finance, the Scots Commissioners found the English hopelessly provincial; their Parliament not only did not care about European politics, but many of them belonged to little fussy parochial sects, scarcely to be called Protestants, since they protested against the chief protestors.

One of the new members of Parliament, a rather uncouth, ill-dressed country gentleman, but a forcible fellow, called Mr. Cromwell, went so far as to say that the State ought to tolerate them all (except of course the Catholics).

Warriston was shocked almost into a fit, while Henderson began to despair of his dream for religious unity. He had discovered the essential frivolity of fashionable congregations, and wrote of the English that they were " so bred in Riches and Plenty that they can hardly be induced to embrace any Discipline that may any wise abridge their Liberty and Pleasures."

And the English Parliament, though they promised money, did not pay it.

But worse than all these things,—while the ministers were preaching, praying, arguing and contesting for their country and religion in this benighted, heathenish, and hellishly expensive city,—they were being stabbed in the back at home, plotted against by their most brilliant and admired leader, betrayed by that cherished youth whom they had fondly called " A David chosen for the Lord."

For the Earl of Montrose had entered into communication with his King.

* * *

Montrose had been growing more and more disquieted. Argyll had been appointed as solely responsible for the whole of Scotland north of the Forth. Montrose had protested; Argyll had at once shown himself amenable, and had other names placed beside his own, including that of Montrose. But it gave no check to Argyll's real power; he did his chief work unaided by appointments.

He had refused to appear openly as a formal member of the Committee of Estates; all considered that his reason was the same as when he had been slow to declare himself on the side of the Covenanters,—that he might ' help them the better in secret.' The Committee was believed to have been his invention, and his influence was behind it. So powerful had he grown that he even relaxed a little of his accustomed caution, for he had begun to test public opinion here and there by philosophizing among his friends, as a purely abstract point, on the question whether it were in some cases permissible to depose a king.

Montrose heard of this. He boldly wrote to Charles that " your ancient and native kingdom of Scotland is in a mighty distemper,"—one which " in my opinion is contagious and may infect the rest of your Majesty's dominions."

And that the cause of this disease " is a fear and apprehension, not without some reason, of changes in religion . . . and therewith all their laws infringed and liberties invaded. Free them, sir, from this fear." . . .

He begged Charles to come himself to the next Scottish Parliament. "It is easy to you in person to settle their troubles, to disperse these mists of apprehension and mistaking,—impossible to any other. If you send down a Commissioner, whatever he be, he shall but render the disease incurable."

He warned the King not to let his subjects in Scotland dispute or meddle with his power; nor on the other hand to "aim at absoluteness,"—for "the people of the Western parts of the world could never endure it any long time, and they of Scotland less than any."

And he braced him against any possible storm,—"You are not like a tree lately planted, which oweth a fall to the first wind. Your ancestors have governed theirs, without interrupting of race, two thousand years or thereabouts, and taken such root as can never be plucked up by any but yourselves."

It was a very good letter, but when he read it to Magdalen, she said, "What is the use of writing all that to the King? He may write a good letter, but he would never read one,—he would not take it in."

"Why not?"

"Because he did not write it. He can only hear what he says himself. You showed me that."

He did not know how he had done so, but he did not pursue it; he told her abruptly that Argyll was plotting to get the Crown for himself, or if not the Crown, a Dictatorship. "He tells his friends after dinner that he is the eighth man from Robert Bruce, and his clan brag openly that they will have King Campbell, not King Stewart."

"You will never trouble with such stuff as that,—the after-dinner bragging of friends who can afford to be fools together?"

He shot a glance at her, amused, aware. Well he knew how her cool judgment could correct and counterbalance his impetu-osity, if only he could trust it ever to follow any end but that of his safety.

So he fell silent, and began to walk up and down; but then he told her.

"One of Argyll's own friends,—Lindsay of the Byres—has

told me of a scheme to make ' a particular man,' Dictator of all Scotland.   That can only mean Argyll."

She sat frozen.   She had heard of this, and had wondered what would happen when it reached Jamie.   She tried to pour cold water on it.

" Why should Lindsay tell you,—and he a friend of Argyll's? "

" He was at Saint Salvator's with me."

The answer was unanswerable.

He went on—" I am going over to Wigton's house at Cumbernauld to see what we can do about it."

" What *can* you do? "

" We are all going to meet there, and we shall form and sign a new bond, to uphold the spirit as well as the letter of the National Covenant, and to resist ' the particular and indirect practising of the few,'—that is the phrase."

" For Argyll again.   Another bond—are there not enough of them?   And you ' all '—who are they ?"

" Wigton himself, Mar, Atholl, Marischal, Kinghorn, Seaforth, Home,—oh, and others."

She noticed that none of them except Montrose were men of real power, who had much to lose in the governing of the State. They were the lesser and moderate men, who were happy to get Montrose as leader, on whom all the brunt of this enterprise would fall.

She watched him marching up and down their room, past the great carved wardrobe where the firelight flickered over the dark polished heads and wings of cherubs who gazed upwards at the twelve bearded faces of the apostles in a row above them.

In a corner was the heavy wooden cradle that had rocked him as a baby, and then each of their three young sons.   He walked so blindly that he knocked his knee against it, and it started to rock, and went on of itself, slower and lower, slower and lower, until it stood still again at last.

Into the shadow he went at the end, a shadow himself now, his face showing like a ghost's against the great door with the cross-way beams; and back he came again to her.   The firelight striped his form in bars of red and black; he was like a restless tiger, turning this way and that, seeking escape from the trap of his own thoughts.

" All this talk of plots," she began, and then stopped in despair. It was enough to engender plots of itself, just as it was believed one got the plague by being afraid of it. Whatever Argyll plotted, Jamie would never be able to prove anything against that cunning lawyer. He was the last person who should touch any intrigue,— and so was his old guardian, Napier, who had been egging him on instead of holding him back, and the two together with no more caution than a couple of schoolboys playing at a conspiracy.

There was Jamie, hot on his rage, and if Argyll were to come in this moment, he would hurl it out at him.

" I knew it from the beginning," he was saying. " He will pull down the King to set himself in his place,—not openly, but behind some committee.—What out of hell *is* a committee? Men, I suppose, like the rest of us, when apart,—but when banded together, they become a soulless monster. Why can he not come out from behind them, and show his own face? "

" Because it is such an ugly one," she cried with a little hysterical laugh. " His lady love could not bear to look at him, and that is why she ran away."

She had laughed for fear of crying. That cold spirit of Argyll's had shown how hot it could burn in revenge. He had taken no part in the fighting of these ' Bishops' Wars,' but he had made them an excuse to satisfy some private hates of his own.

He had utterly destroyed the Ogilvys' house at Airlie, though no one was there but Lady Ogilvy, who was great with child, and her household. These he had turned out of doors, then plundered and burned the house to the ground.

Montrose had written to him, telling him it had already surrendered, and was to be spared. That was more than half the reason for its destruction. Argyll was not going to take his orders from Montrose.

Now the countryside were singing a new song, the odd verses springing up here and there, no one knew by whom:

> " It fell on a day, and a bonny summer day,
>   When green grew oats and barley,
> That there fell out a great dispute
>   Between Argyll and Airlie.

> " Lady Ogilvy looks o'er her bower-window,
>   And oh but she looks warely!
> And there she spied the great Argyll
>   Come to plunder the bonny house of Airlie."

The old evil times were on them again, when laments for Border and blood feud gave rise to some of the loveliest poetry that ever sprang from unknown poets, sprang also from the blood-stained and blackened ruins of homes. The wild, lilting note was coming back to the ballad,—a danger signal that the days of security were over.

To Magdalen that note carried no echo of romance, but of grim reality, as recent as ' a bonny summer day' last July,— to be feared again, when, and by whom? She had as good reason herself to ' look warely' as had that lady, great with child, wife to the young nobleman that she herself had so nearly married.

Other words, more sinister than any in the song, linked themselves with that haunting little tune,—a sentence in a letter from Argyll to one of his clansmen, which had somehow got abroad:— " But ye need not let know that ye have directions from me to fire it."

Did Jamie know that? Not if she could help it.

" Oh, what will happen next? " she cried in so forlorn a voice that at last he perceived her distress, ran to her, begged her not to be unhappy, to fear nothing, for the truth must triumph,— " truth is not hid in corners," he told her, kissing the tears that his tenderness brought to her eyes.

And so much his old self did he seem again, so certain that all men must prefer the truth, that she began to believe it too, to believe anyway that all men must prefer this ' valorous and happy gentleman ' to Argyll.

R

XIX

BY next summer, the one man in England who could help the King had been beheaded.

The Scottish Commissioners, with their prayers and preaching, had led the London mob's howls for Strafford's blood. Parliament could not prove him guilty of any single act of treason, but it was thought that several minor acts, added together, would make a whole treason.

Finally he was condemned to death for having written that his army from Ireland would subdue 'that country.' He said that he meant Scotland by that phrase, but Parliament said he meant England.

He was led out of the Tower to his execution, and passed beneath the window of his fellow prisoner, Archbishop Laud. "Poor Canterbury, now grown so contemptible," stretched his thin hands through his prison bars to bless him as he passed, then fell back, fainting.

This then was what happened to the men who could help the King.

Charles had promised him his safeguard to London. Strafford went; and Parliament imprisoned him. Charles had sworn he would never sign his death warrant; and he had signed it.

Once again it was talk about plots that had done it. The Queen had raised money from the English Catholics against the Scottish invaders of England; that was the Papist Plot. Then she tried to raise Strafford's army to come and rescue him. That was the Army Plot. The people, terrified of a military tyranny, such as had been suffered for years in Germany, clamoured for Strafford's blood, or else the Queen's.

That was the formula that finally drove Charles to sign Strafford's death warrant—after the agonizing hours when the long-drawn howl of the mob never ceased outside Whitehall; and all night the courtiers clustered together on the stairs with their swords drawn, marking the places where they might make a stand, should that human sea outside break through the guards, and come surging up into the palace itself.

Strafford's death, or the Queen's? Charles chose Strafford's. Strafford had released his conscience, had told him he was free to do it. But had he believed that Charles would do it?

Then the King turned to Scotland. The Earl of Montrose had written to him, asking him to come there, and Charles had written back that he agreed " nothing could conduce more to a firm and solid peace " than his presence at the next Scottish Parliament. His spirits rose at the prospect of his visit. God knows, the Scots had been the prime cause of all his present troubles. Yet with that fatal facility, that evasive hold on facts, that always made him hopeful of any change, he thought that merely by going to another country he would escape the difficulties inherent in the times and in himself.

He had, however, one good cause for new hope. Montrose had been the Commander General of the Covenanters, he had shown brilliant military powers, and,—more important than his reputation or his great position (there were nobles enough in his party)—there was that about him which made the sturdiest, as-good-as-you Scot among them proud to have him on their side.

Now at last he had shown the King that he would be his friend. Charles felt that he could trust him to steer him through this tangle of apparently well-meaning men, who did their best to deprive him of every prerogative of the Crown, while promising earnest loyalty to his person.

But by August, when he got to Scotland, Montrose could do nothing for him, for he, the one man in Scotland who could help the King, had been thrown with Lord Napier into prison in the Castle of Edinburgh.

*　　*　　*

The Cumbernauld Bond, that Montrose had drawn up with his companions at Lord Wigton's house against ' the indirect practising of the few,' had naturally caused trouble. Argyll had got wind of it, and the Committee of Estates summoned all those who had signed it to appear before them. They did, owned to the Bond, and justified it. All knew that it was aimed at Argyll, the leader and support of the extreme party of the Kirk, who now clamoured for the execution of the leaders. But that was too dangerous a measure; only the Bond itself was burned, and those who had signed it were released.

This was a great advantage to Argyll, since it showed in him the leniency of a leader too strong to resent the attacks of his detractors. And his party could report whatever they liked of the contents of the Cumbernauld Bond, since they had destroyed all copies of it.

Montrose realized that his folly had played straight into Argyll's hands; furious with it, he at once committed worse, for he went back to the army in so hot a rage that he said openly in the mess, before Leslie himself, that he could prove that certain leaders in Scotland were scheming to depose the King.

Once again they all knew that the unspoken name was Argyll's, and were exceedingly uncomfortable. Montrose was an excellent soldier. It was a pity he would try to meddle with politics,— could not somebody say so to him?

Old Sandy Leslie did say so, and the young man told him one must know what one was fighting for. The former mercenary had never heard such nonsense.

Then came the blow of the discovery that Montrose had written to the King and asked him to come and attend his Parliament in Scotland. Argyll was now seriously alarmed. Just as he was getting all the reins of the Government into his hands, Montrose was contriving this against him. He could not prevent the King from coming. But he could prevent him from getting into touch with Montrose. The Committee of Estates had Montrose arrested and put in prison. The charge was treason; the only reason for it that the King could discover lay in the fact that Montrose had written to him, and he to Montrose.

He protested to Argyll that his letter was a fit and proper one, and Montrose a proper person for him to write to. He was only coming to Scotland to settle the affairs of his kingdom, as had been agreed in the articles of the last treaty.

That did no good.

On the very day that Charles arrived at Holyrood, Montrose was led out of the Castle and down to the new Parliament House, by Saint Giles', where only a year ago he had been consulting with his peers under the hugely carved roof that was then raw from the tools of the workmen. Now he had to stand at the 'delinquents' bar'; but he was glad of it, for now, after two months of prison, there was a hope that he might begin to clear himself in time to be set at liberty before the King left the country again.

But he was not even told of what exactly he was charged. The one definite statement against him was that of ' having intelligence with the enemy.'

To which he replied disconcertingly that ' the King could not be the enemy.'

With the King entering Edinburgh that very day, it was politer to drop this hastily and fall back on vague and retrogressive accusations.

He had disobeyed the Committee of Estates. He had spared Aberdeen after the battle of the Bridge of Dee. He had given quarter. He had shown no zeal, once the fight was over, in tearing out the accursed thing root and branch. He had neglected to burn the Ogilvys' house of Airlie, and Argyll had had to do his work for him. His pride had long been intolerable, and now his intentions were very doubtful.

He was led back to prison, knowing that Charles, with Hamilton in his train, would be passing through these very streets in an hour or so, and that he would not be allowed to see him; that Charles would be told of plots, against himself, against everybody, in all of which Montrose would be made to appear as the villain.

The Kirk had been the oppressed party, but now they had grown so confident that they could throw two great nobles into prison and not even bring them to trial. They were marking time, waiting ' to see what the Lord will do in England.' The

Lord had already executed Strafford; doubtless He would soon realize He should do the same by Laud.

Charles was in a bad case; if he retraced his steps in Scotland, he would lose ground inevitably in England, which had already become like a quagmire beneath his feet. The Covenanters cancelled all his suggestions for the appointment of the Ministers of the Crown. It had become an axiom that the King could do no right. He dared not try and grasp power at this juncture, and so tried to win favour. He agreed to all that he was asked, hoping that he might get it back again later.

Mr. Henderson had been made the King's chaplain, and preached a very sound and statesmanlike sermon to His Majesty on his first Sunday morning, but reproved him for not coming to hear another in the afternoon. Charles promised not to be so remiss again, and attended prayers twice a day after that.

He was shown a medal of himself, struck on his accession to the throne,—a young man with a high-cut nostril, and lovelocks flowing back from the superb sweep of the brow. What had this arrogant young man to do with him as he was now, bewildered, solitary, badgered by the ministers, bereft of his friends?

Not all he could do could procure Montrose the open trial before his peers that he was demanding. Argyll and his colleagues did not want to be harsh,—except to an insignificant relation of Traquair's, who was hanged, drawn and quartered under an old statute against ' leasing-making,' which had never been put in force before. It meant, apparently, speaking against Argyll,— and even Argyll thought the punishment a shade too severe, but Sir Thomas Hope, the Lord Advocate (who had ominously lost a tooth in the night) did not agree. And Traquair himself indignantly refused to exert any influence on behalf of his fatuously imprudent cousin,—" not a cousin at all, a mere collateral."

But the Committee could not despatch Montrose and Napier without an open trial; and they could not have a trial and yet prevent the prisoners from speaking what they knew against Argyll. Therefore the less said the better.

They tried to get Napier to leave prison without anything said at all. They pleaded with him for two hours, begging him to go quietly, but he insisted that he must first be declared innocent, —and in that case, Montrose also. He was not allowed any communication with his kinsman, or Montrose might have begged him to seize this opportunity, not to bear dignified testimony to their innocence, but to warn the King.

Charles could know nothing yet of Argyll's treachery; only Montrose could fully tell him of it; and that was why he was here. He had lost his chance to serve his King,—but had he not lost it at the beginning, by helping to start this revolt? His side had now surged beyond him; ' sides,' he discovered, are human, like the people who compose them, and subject to change. And the liberty he had fought for would soon leave liberty to no one, least of all to the King.

" The tyranny of the one," he wrote, " is preferable to that of the multitude,—the tyranny of subjects is the most insatiable and insupportable in the world."

He had writing paper and pen and ink in prison, though he was not allowed to send any letters. He had to write to himself, though he put ' Noble Sir ' at the top of the page, so as to feel that he was sharing his thoughts with a friend. His random jottings became more and more a considered treatise on Sovereign Power, and what was needed to make it succeed. Firmness, rather than patience,—" Patience in the prince is so far from being a remedy, that it forms and increases the disease."

But in the middle of his sentence, there came a pleasant surprise. A visitor from the Court was allowed to call on him, an agreeable, perky, talkative little Groom of the Bedchamber, called Will Murray, or ' Little Will,' whom Montrose had met once at Hampton Court. As this brightly coloured little man bowed and flourished his plumed hat, blowing a cloud of hyacinthine scent before him into that dark cell, the stone walls melted round Montrose, and there again were the sunlit lawns and fountains, made for a king's pleasure, the courtiers strolling back from the tennis courts, the music from the river,—a whole pleasant world that had even at the time seemed drifting, evanescent, doomed to disappear.

For an instant the vision lasted,—then the chilly place he was in echoed to the unaccustomed clatter and bustle of polite words.

Will Murray told him all the news. On the surface the King's visit was being a *succès fou*. Oh yes, they had bullied him a bit, and the length of those sermons was preposterous, but the King was winning them all over by his patience.

He agreed to everything. He was beginning to be known as the King who couldn't say no. (" My little joke—not to be taken seriously.") And so everybody liked him, thinking that he liked them, and a result of all this friendliness was that he had at last been allowed to send one of his servants to visit Montrose.

He had taken it greatly to heart that his friend should have been treated in this scandalous manner—he talked of nothing else when alone,—" ' Will,' he has said to me a dozen times a day, ' I'll not leave Scotland till my lord of Montrose is out of prison.' "

But all this popularity did not mean any increase of power, and Argyll was showing himself very ill-pleased with it. There was no one Charles could trust. As for his friend Hamilton,— " A man of straw can show the way the wind blows."

Montrose replied, " He has chosen this moment to take the Covenant. I heard that from my jailor."

" And that is not all,"—Little Will's eyes were goggling— " Hamilton is now hand in glove with Argyll. Bosom friends, always in consultation."

So Hamilton and Argyll had joined forces. Montrose had foreseen the danger when he asked Charles to come to Scotland, but had thought he could watch, and warn the King.

And now he could do nothing,—except through this glib fellow, whose rattling conversation did not inspire him with confidence.

He could write by him to the King, however—it was Will who suggested it. Was Will to be trusted? Whether he were or not, it was worth seizing on the only chance he had got.

He wrote.

Will came again with an answer from Charles, and Montrose wrote again. He pressed for even five minutes in which to tell the King of the danger that threatened his throne.

If he were powerless to secure that, then let him insist on Montrose being brought to trial, and he would make his charges against the King's secret enemies before all the world.

"We have them in a cleft stick, and you will be out of this in a week, playing golf with His Majesty on the links of Leith," cried Will, flourishing Montrose's second letter to his King as he pranced out through the prison door.

He did not come again. There was no answer to the letter. The days dropped one after the other, silted into weeks, brought no change.

Summer had passed into autumn and it grew bitter cold. The jailor's face had grown very glum, and he carried in front of him his determination to say nothing whenever he entered the room. Had some fresh plot been invented or discovered, and was Little Will the victim or the agent? Had Montrose been a fool once again to use him? Was it true what Magdalen had said to him, that he would never know one end of a plot from another?

Then without any warning one afternoon in late October, he was summoned to the King's presence at Holyrood Palace.

XX

*I*N a low, panelled room, about twenty men stood silent and expectant. At the further end sat the King in the white and rose-coloured chair that had been presented at his Coronation, his dark form as still as if it had been painted there in its gay frame.

A fire burned in the grate beside him, and in front of it stood a fire-screen, vaguely familiar to Montrose, who years ago had seen his wife and mother-in-law working for weeks on end at that crown in its centre. He walked up to the King, knelt and kissed his hand, then rose and looked into his eyes.

There he had a shock. Something cold, despairing, and certain went through him like the thrust of steel. He knew something final about Charles in that instant, something that was to determine both Charles' fate and his own.

He heard the King's slow voice greeting him, a weight of anxiety behind the formal courtesy of the words. Then he heard Argyll's lilting Highland intonation, rocking ambiguous phrases that might have come out of a lawyer's text book.

Then Warriston yapped—" A trick! Another trick! All this accursed trickery! "

Accusations burst round him like musket fire. He was confronted with his own letters to the King. Sentences were read from his last, dated October 11th, in which he had warned Charles of treachery in "a business which did concern the standing and falling of his crown."

It was Argyll who read it; as he finished, his uncertain squinting glance peered up over the letter to see how Montrose took it. Everyone was watching to see that.

It was early in the afternoon, but the sky was already growing darker outside; he could hear the wind rushing through the trees, a leaf came tap-tapping at the window pane.

" Oh God, shall I ever be on the hillside again? " he thought.

The room narrowed round him; the ring of suspicious, silent faces hemmed him in; he seemed to stand outside his body, to be looking down on it and on his King, dispassionate, removed.

Then they began to speak again, and with the buzz and crack of angry voices, time rushed back round him, and all the immediate urgency of this moment. Will Murray must have betrayed him; and his letters were being used against Charles as well as himself. The two of them, King and subject, were practically charged with plotting together to destroy Hamilton and Argyll. He could not make it out. A crowd of enemies, a web of plots and cross-purposes bound them hand and foot and tongue. He was at last face to face with his King, and they could say nothing to each other.

But could they not? What had this pack of little animals to do with them? His blood stirred quick and strong, and the under-current of his thought spun most oddly into rhyme :

> " Can little beasts with lions roar,
> And little birds with eagles soar? "

He turned to the King, knowing only that he would speak to him direct. Something that he had said elsewhere came unintended to his lips,—" Truth does not seek corners. It needs no favours."

The unexpected words put a hush upon the scene. The others looked uneasily upon him, wondering what manner of man was this, their prisoner, who had taken command of them.

But Montrose did not notice what he had done to them. He was asking the King to tell him what was this plot, in which they were both supposed to be concerned, " for I know nothing of it."

" It is this," said the King, and told it, simply and straight-forwardly, though his speech fell back once or twice into the slight stammer that he had outgrown.

On the evening of October 11th (on the morning of that day, Montrose remembered, his last letter had been taken from his prison by Will Murray) Hamilton came to the King as he was walking in the dusk of the garden at Holyrood, with some quite

unimportant petition,—and then, " in a philosophical and parabolical way, began a very strange discourse."

A faint undercurrent of amusement ran through the room at this
description, and sly glances shot in the direction of the Marquis'
self-conscious countenance.

He complained, said Charles, of calumnies against him, and
asked permission to leave the Court for a time. By next morning
his dearest friend had betrayed him to the suspicion of his enemies,
for he and Argyll had fled together to Kinneil Castle, a house of
Hamilton's about twenty miles off. Charles was then told that
they had done this because they had heard of a plot to assassinate
them in the King's own drawing-room, which the murderers were
to enter by a door from the garden.

" But not one word of this plot did my lord Hamilton tell me
in the garden," said Charles. " Once when he was accused of
treason, I took him to sleep in my bedchamber, to show I had
no doubts of him,—and this is how he repays my trust, by
suspecting me as a murderer."

Hamilton announced in a stately voice that he had always been
very active in the King's service.

" My lord Marquis," replied the King, " has been very active
in his own preservation."

There was an uncomfortable pause, while the two runaways
tried to look like the injured patriots that the crowd had applauded
on their return to Edinburgh from their flight.

While in a day all Charles' hard-won popularity had been
snatched from him; he was looked on as a man too weak to play
the tyrant, who had fallen back on the old treacherous methods
of assassination. " Never was King so insulted," remarked a dispassionate observer. Worst of all, he had begun to expect insults.

He had asked for an open inquiry, had demanded it of Parliament with threats that he could not carry out; he now begged
it of these ' examiners,' even as his grandmother, Mary Stuart,
had begged, and was refused, until the time of her execution.

Did he remember that now, as he appealed for a chance to
clear his honour?

"That chance is given to the meanest of my subjects. But you withhold it from your King, as you withhold it from his servant."

Montrose saw to his dismay that his eyes were swimming in tears. His King, who could never have quite ceased to be a child, was pleading to that company of hardened and wary men,— "I have granted you more than any king ever granted yet— and what have any of you done for me?"

It was a pitiful, an unkingly cry; only a bewildered simplicity in it prevented it from being abject. Charles was tasting that worst intoxicant, the tears of his ill-usage.

"Why do you use me thus?" he cried. Never would he see why, nor what manner of men were those with whom he had to deal.

Argyll answered him in language as 'philosophical and parabolical' as Hamilton's own. The ship of His Majesty's kingdom in Scotland had long been tossing in a tempestuous sea; it only required that he should give way to those well-wishers who would lighten her by casting out the most dangerous of her crew.

At that ominous warning, all glanced at Montrose, who seemed now to be following Strafford so closely, each step nearer to the scaffold.

But Montrose himself scarcely attended to Argyll's threat, or to the shudder that it gave even to his enemies. He had eyes only for Charles; and in them was sympathy, but also sternness, for they demanded of him that he should show himself their King.

Under that resolute gaze, something of his old high temper was restored to Charles. He turned upon Argyll, and said, "You attack this man, and deny him an open inquiry, as you deny me. We ask for the truth, but you hide it in corners. All you have given me is a private inquiry by a few of your committee,—I am not allowed to be present, and all the members are sworn to secrecy. You choose your own witnesses, you refuse even to make public what evidence you do extract. Your private inquiry is nothing but a private way to hell."

A nervous silence fell on the room; however much the King

was in their power, it was tactless of him to express it so plainly, it made all the proper formulas sound absurd.   They turned instead on Montrose, to see what admission they could wring out of him in the shock of his surprise that his private letters had been discussed by them all.   Failing to get any admission of deeds against themselves, they inquired into his intentions.

He answered slowly, and not to them.   To his King, he said, " My resolution is to carry along with me fidelity and honour to the grave."

In such strange circumstances did he make his pact with Charles. Then the one prisoner was led back to the Castle; the other remained among his Court.

XXI

S the coach bumped and jolted back up the long hill to his prison, Montrose peered out through its windows at the wild evening sky, torn into rags of cloud and pale light by the west wind; at the houses, tottering up like witches; at the octagon of the Market Cross, where he had stirred the crowd to resist the King's command. Now the Castle rose ahead of him, its outer wall blotted out the sky; his glimpse of the outside world was at an end.

Yet in it he had tasted the freedom of his mountains and woods as he had not done in all his years of enjoyment of them,—and the glimpse had been enough to set his heart singing:

"The misty mount, the smoking lake,
    The rock's resounding echo,
The whistling winds, the woods that shake,
    Shall all with me sing heigho!"

He was stringing rhymes in his head as he used to do in his schooldays; he stepped out of the coach between his guards, into the Castle courtyard, high up above the town that lay like a mist below, with that soft autumnal wind blowing all round him.

Door after door clanged behind him. He stood in the chill silence of his cell, in the smell of damp stone,—the dead smell of a church.

There were his papers, just as he had left them, scattered and untidy, when he had been summoned without any warning at a quarter past one this very afternoon. He sat down, pulled them towards him, and read what he had last written:

"And you great men—if any such be among you so blinded with ambition—who aim so high as the crown, do you think we are so far degenerate from the virtue, valour, and fidelity to our true and lawful sovereign as to suffer you with all your policy to reign over us?"

The great men who aimed so high as the crown had it now in all but name. Across his words swam the crafty, sullen face of Argyll, the doubtful face of Hamilton, the two Kings of Scotland. He looked at the door, through which little Will Murray had pranced in a reek of perfume, flourishing his letter to King Charles, and had shown it to those two men.

His mood, though now changed to despair, was still singing, still stringing rhymes; he tried to think of his newly formed theories of government, but when he began to write, his pen went over to the side of the page and dashed down in sprawling letters:

" Then break, afflicted heart, and live not in these days,
  When all prove merchants of their faith, none trusts what other
       says."

But it was not as he had heard it in his head, and there was a vile smell of tallow. The wind that blew so fresh and sweet outside the Castle walls, was whistling through the door in a shrewish draught and blowing his candle so that it guttered all down one side, forming a shroud. As he leaned forward to pinch out the supposed omen, he knew the reason of his suddenly hopeless mood, deeper than any that Argyll or Hamilton could cause.

In two pictures, seen in flashes, it came to him; the one, of Strafford lying on the scaffold, with his head severed from his body; the other, the face of King Charles that afternoon.

As he had risen from kissing his hand, and looked into the face of his King, he had seen behind the slippery and rootless optimism that had been making Charles turn this way and that, thinking to charm even such ruthless wills as Argyll's to his own purpose.

He had seen that the King's face was that of a man doomed, and knowing it. He had sent his servant, Strafford, to his death; and he would have to pay.

XXII

" **JAMES**, you are stymied."

They were at the third hole; the course was only seven, but there were about five hundred yards between each of them. Charles, partnered by Rothes, led by one, in a foursome with Argyll and Hamilton, attended by a few of his gentlemen. It was the first raw week of November, the wind had turned cold, and the King, for all his short legs, strode out briskly.

He was feeling cheerful. He was beating Argyll at his own game, for this was the only exercise that Argyll cared for; and it was the reward of virtue, since, for popularity's sake, Charles had given up a hunt in order to march in sober procession in this national and democratic sport. His popularity was coming back; everyone in time would see he was right. Henderson had grown markedly sympathetic; even Argyll had sometimes seemed convinced by his arguments; Rothes was coming round whole-heartedly to his side. It was made well worth his while to do so, for he had been promised high office in England, and marriage to the rich Countess of Devon,—and Rothes was not the man to reject these plums.

It was unfortunate that he was apoplectic; his enormous face looked quite blue as he puffed his way over the links. With a cold eye, Charles calculated the improbability of any lasting support from his chief convert. At any moment a dinner, such as he had seen him eat, or rather drink, last night, might ensure Rothes' neutrality for ever.

But in the meantime, he and Rothes were winning, and exhilaration filled his veins as he watched James Hamilton play an heroic shot well past the hole. It was now his own turn to play; it was a long putt, and the ground uneven,—a stone lay between him and the hole, and the sternly Calvinistic edict of Aberdeen had gone forth, allowing for no injustice of fate, and no remission of it: " No stones shall be removed when putting at the hole."

He chose a slender wooden spoon-faced club and was addressing himself to the ball when a man suddenly appeared at the top of the bunker. It was Traquair, who came stumbling down through the whin towards them, holding out papers to the King.

Charles swore with great fluency. " Must even the links become a council board? " he demanded through his profanity.

On Traquair's long face, heavy and inexpressive as it was, there yet showed signs of some dreadful calamity.

" Sir," he said, " there is bad news from Ireland."

Charles, who had once again raised his club, lowered it, and drew a deep breath.

" When," he asked, " has the news from Ireland not been bad? "

" Your Majesty,—it may put an end to everything. It is the most hideous—it is the Papist Irishry——"

He stumbled on with sledge-hammer obstinacy. The King should know the worst, but not until he had asked for it properly. Until at last, in spite of his exasperation, Charles did so.

He was told that in a single night the Catholics had risen and murdered their Protestant neighbours. Hundreds, perhaps thousands of the peaceful inhabitants of King Charles' possessions had been wiped out—and in the name of the religion which King Charles was believed to support in secret.

The reaction to such a crime was bound to be unreasonable. There was nothing too bad for people to say. So the King must act at once, must return to England and reassure his country. But even before acting, and even more important, he must express his horror and amazement, must sever himself utterly from the accursed thing.

This, Traquair had realized when he had tried, but with blundering tactlessness, to prepare Charles to show horror before he told its cause.

The little group of men waited, white and aghast, for Charles to speak. But Charles did not speak. He showed neither horror nor amazement.

He waited till Traquair had finished, then raised his club a third time. Traquair had done his best to put him off his game.

He would not be put off. His slow and solitary mind was telling him to shut out the damning fact, reminding him of the refuge of the child who ' has not taken it in yet.'

So he kept his eye on the ball, and with precision played his stroke; his ball just skirted the stone, and wriggled back into its course from the uneven ground on that side, then, neatly, decisively, it dropped into the hole.

He looked round on his company. They hastily sprang to attention and said it was a master stroke, as indeed it was. But he had seen their pale, abstracted faces, heard an anxious whisper or two.

Still he ignored them, said blandly to Rothes, " Two up and four to play. Your turn to drive, my Lord Rothes."

Rothes, not so imperturbable, fluffed his drive.

With determination as grim as if the game were the predestined act of God (as no doubt it was), Charles played it out to the end, dragging in his wake the three nobles who longed to be released from it to discuss this terrible disaster.

Rothes pounded after the King, inwardly cursing the swiftness of the royal stride, and gasped out how urgent it was that he should return to London at once.

Charles replied that he had given his promise to Montrose not to leave the country until he got his trial,—" if I leave him, all the world will not save his life."

Rothes gave a sudden breathless snort, either curse or contemptuous exclamation, and ran hastily on into words.

" He'll not get his trial as long as Your Majesty is here."

" That may be," said Charles stubbornly, " but it would not be to my honour if I leave before he is released."

Was he trying to make amends for Strafford, with Montrose? Rothes was shrewd enough to guess it, but he did not much care,—the whole of the leaden sky seemed to have dropped into his stomach, which heaved and surged like a stormy sea, as he thundered on,—was it the sound of his own steps that made that roaring in his ears?

" Honour," he muttered, " who has it? ' He that died o

Wednesday.' " More clearly he said, " Better go, sir. Montrose will do better without you."

The King's proud, hurt glance went past him without his even seeing it.

Principalities and powers, what were they worth now to Rothes? Not as much as a good feather bed. And who wanted a rich English countess in it, if he could get a French warming pan instead,—and sleep,—and sleep. And he had had enough to pay for that without his tithes. So what had all that bother been for?

" Pother, bother, pother, bother," he muttered as he tramped, and each foot went down into the bowels of the earth, and had to be dragged up again—and why? It was earth to earth, wasn't it? Or was that in the Prayer Book, that they had all made such a to-do against—and why? For they were good words, sound words, ' earth to earth.'

Stumbling on, not seeing where to avoid the furze bushes and the boulders, he thought of that young man he had loved, and God knows why, for he was of a high, heroic temper, which was not in his own vein, but there it was, and the young fellow could not help it that he was better than other people.

Now he was in prison and in desperate case. But " what odds? what odds? " muttered Rothes, for could any man, even in prison, be as miserable as he now was, who was to hold high office in England, and to marry the rich Countess of Devon? The young man he had loved would soon be dead, " like all the rest of us, and then all's one."

" Four up," said Charles' voice ahead of him.

" There's my requiem," said Rothes.

He went to bed, gasping and shivering; in a few days he died.

XXIII

VERY soon after his foursome on the links of Leith, Charles left Scotland. His visit, which Montrose had urged and Argyll had dreaded, had turned all to the advantage of Argyll and his party. Before he left he made him a marquis, Leslie an earl, Will Murray a Gentleman instead of a Groom of the Bedchamber, and Warriston a knight. " Rise, Sir Archibald Johnston,"—it sounded very odd to both King and knight.

When one of the loyal lords heard of the honours list he remarked that he had better go to Ireland and join the rebels there, and then there might be some chance of his getting preferment.

In his zeal to make friends with his enemies, the King suggested the appointment as Treasurer of the Earl of Morton, uncle, father-in-law, and former guardian to Argyll, whom he had brought up as his own son. But there Charles made a mistake, for Argyll declared in front of the old man's face that his uncle was unfit and decrepit; and there was another family quarrel, though Morton gave in quite meekly, showing however an increasing tendency to quote blank verse from a play called *King Lear*.

So the King left Scotland, still thinking that he could count on her as an ally; and went back to a country that was buzzing like an angry hive,—where people began to say the King must have known, may even have planned the rising of the Catholics in Ireland. And they began to say it from that bitter day in the beginning of November when he finished his game on the links of Leith.

*　　*　　*

Montrose and Napier were released. In Charles' absence they were no longer dangerous; they had been discredited, and Argyll's party was now supreme.

The prisoners came out to find their country settling down under a cloud of religious oppression.

No book was allowed to be printed until it had passed the censorship of Sir Archibald Johnston of Warriston.

Old ladies who had held to the former religion were harried into the Kirk or out of the country; spoilt young Lewis Gordon wept bitterly at having to say good-bye to his Papist grandmother, who was now chased into exile to say her last prayers beyond the seas.

Even corpses were not safe; they were refused burial if they had not subscribed to the Covenant.

To pick gooseberries during sermon time, to ' sit up drinking in company,' to indulge in ' promiscuous dancing ' or in minstrelsy which ' tends to great deboshry,' to use profane words in private speech, to greet each other on Christmas Day or even to walk up and down together, talking as though it were a holiday,— these were now criminal offences.

With so many cheerful sounds now hushed, the human mind turned sour; old women conferred in low and ghostly voices with the devil in the person of their cats; more vigorous bodies found secret pleasure in unnatural ways.

> " In such a deformed silence,
>   Witches whisper their charms."

Montrose read the words from a new London play book, illicitly smuggled into his library at Kincardine by Master Forrett, who had celebrated his lord's return with as many new books as he could buy, chiefly poetry, " for then he will be happy, no matter what happens,"—so his old tutor plotted with his wife.

The whole family was ' at home at last ' as Magdalen called it, who had longed to be at Kincardine ever since their marriage. Now it was safe for them all to be there together, and have their friends to stay with them. Lord Napier came, much older since his imprisonment, and his children, now just growing up, replacing Montrose's sisters,—for Lilias scarcely ever left Rossdhu now,— Margaret and poor pretty Dorothea were dead,—and of Kat not one word had ever been heard by any traveller from abroad.

A bitter flavour from Montrose's memory of her crept into the

wording of his deed of gift of twenty thousand marks to his
youngest sister Beatrix, provided that she should keep her body
undefiled, and not join herself in marriage against his consent.

She and David Drummond of Madertie now agreed to marry
in this lull of peace. He hoped to avoid public life and live
quietly at Innerpeffray and there build a library for all students
to use without payment, though no one had ever heard of so
odd a notion as a free library. Benevolent, scholarly, unworldly,
he was the happy complement to Beatrix's brisk efficiency.

There was another, much younger bridal couple in the house,—
Napier's eldest son, Archibald, sixteen years old, and his Elizabeth,
daughter of the Earl of Mar. She vied with her new young
Napier sisters-in-law in adoring their handsome uncle, who entertained them so royally, yet whose face looked so stern in repose.
He had a bevy of charming nieces to ride with him, laugh with
him, hang on his opinion, and wind skeins of bright silk round
their fingers to knit his stockings for him—carnation and orange
tawny—where had he last heard of that colour? An old-fashioned
name they were calling it.

He sat watching the sparks fly up the great chimney, remembered their light glinting on a necklace of orange-yellow stones,
and on Magdalen's face, seen as for the first time. She was
before him now, their boys were round them, Rob, the baby,
trotting sturdily about, while Johnnie, the eldest, nearly twelve,
was ' the living image of his father at his age,' so all the people at
Kincardine said,—and might be himself again riding back from
school in the days before the old lord died.

Now it was his nephew's wedding that filled the old castle with
winter guests, and with their favourite dogs that lounged and
yawned and rubbed against their legs and lay stretched out like
corpses before that comfortable blaze, to yap in excited dreams,
a hind leg ecstatically jerking in the air, while they lived over
again the hunting they had gone that day.

The Spanish tables were set up again in the banqueting hall;
the polished silver sconces and candlesticks gave a reflected light;
new scarlet cushions were in all the chairs. Young Archie

Napier and his cousins, Johnnie and James, carried in ivy and holly and mistletoe, and Magdalen helped the boys dress up the hall for Christmas, in spite of the Kirk's disapproval. Over one whole wall was displayed a wedding present to the Napiers from the Southesk family, of a Belgian tapestry wherein ladies and gentlemen walked with exquisite gestures into a pale landscape of pink flowers and blue fountains.

It was a blissful and dreamlike winter, and in it Magdalen gathered a new strength. Now at last, more than ever in his life, Jamie needed her. He was twenty-nine, and he had not had much time to do so before.

He was ill more than once that winter; he had not got his trial, although his legal expenses had encumbered his estates with debt. He never had a chance to clear his honour; two months after his release, he was summoned back to Edinburgh at a moment's notice, told the charges against him, and given only one clear day to prepare his answers; prepared them, including one or two apposite Latin quotations which gave him an absurd gleam of pleasure (he must tell that to old Forrett as soon as he returned),— and then after all was given no chance to deliver them.

Letters of exoneration were issued instead, clearing him and Napier, without any hearing of their case. Argyll was not going to risk a trial. He had got all he wanted; changed places with Montrose in the public eye, had put himself in the position of the high-minded patriot whose life was in danger from envious rivals, and Montrose in the position of the underhand plotter.

Montrose had fought his first duel with Argyll, and Argyll had won. But the choice of weapons had been to his enemy.

" When I cross swords with him again, it will be in actual fact on an open field," he told Magdalen.

" Dear heart, you will never have the chance. Have you not heard? Argyll has fought his first fight—a duel. The Kirk, scandalized, rushed to prevent it,—they found him, not crossing swords, but writing down his grievances! "

His burst of uproarious laughter blew Argyll out of their thoughts.

As his vigour returned, he spoke of emigration. Europe and her ceaseless bickering was played out—but there was still the New World, its very name a talisman of escape. Savages would not be as fearful as the snares of Argyll or the hesitations of the King. What she would once have dreaded, Magdalen now begged for,—but not very hard, for like him at last in this, she was living only in the present, too glad to have Jamie home to look ahead, even a month or two.

Here as in a charmed circle they were immune for the moment; no harsh silence muffled their songs or laughter or the majestic sound of words written for a player to proclaim to lords and fishmongers alike.

> " What revenge for such rigour used the gods?
> None, but suffering us to live, and know we are no gods."

" And that he will never know, nor others of him," she thought, looking across the circle of intent young faces at his proud lips shaping the words.

XXIV

THERE was a noise of scuffling in the hall. Young Archie Napier had chased Johnnie to chastise him for some impertinence to him, a grown and married man, four years his senior. There were yells and execrations,—" Let go my arm—let go I say."

" Eat your words. Say you are sorry. Say you never meant it."

" Never meant it. Never said it. It never happened."

" What never happened? "

" The King never played golf—never heard the news from Ireland—never told them not to put him off his game."

" That would be untrue," said young James gravely,—" he played better than before."

" So he would, with twenty thousand Protestants out of the the way,—yow, ow ! " yelped the victim,—and then " *Oh !* " on a sudden low note, as he found in the same instant that Archie had released his arm, but that his father's hand was on his shoulder, and swinging him round to face him. Johnnie's eyes fell before him; he wished miserably that Archie was still twisting his arm, as he heard Montrose tell him never to say that again,—" And you too, James. You are both old enough to know the harm you do your King by spreading tales against him."

" But you, my lord," stammered Johnnie, who had sworn vengeance on the King for leaving Scotland with his father still in prison, " what has he done for you? "

" And is that to be the measure of your service? Will you make merchandise of your faith and loyalty,—barter it for what it is worth? "

The two boys had never seen him so angry. They learned their lesson. It was the last time they showed resentment against the King.

James, a grave, slight child, not yet nine, who did not look nearly as old as Johnnie had done at his age, but who was apt to show a precocious wisdom, said to his mother, as he leaned against her side in the linen room, watching her sort out the sheets, " Minnie, my father will go and fight for the King now."

She stood still with the sheets on her arm, looking down at the serious face of the little boy, his " legal under lip," as she had always laughingly called it, thrust out in an earnest pout. The tiny window above his head showed a slit of dull sky turned brown by the few white flecks of snow that wandered past it. Round them in the dark room the shelves of linen gleamed white and still. She had made them herself, these pillow cases, so smooth and fine and chill to touch; she put out a hand and touched them, then let it fall to her side. Young James, standing before her, had said something that struck chill on her heart, holding it in an unnatural stillness that seemed to last for years.

" How do you know that, James? "

" Because he is sorry for him. The King could not get him out of prison. The King is the weaker side now."

" And that," she murmured, putting the sheets back on to the shelf, " is why he is so happy."

She was right, Montrose was no longer in conflict. There was no more need to clear his thought to himself in prose, only to sing it to Magdalen:

> " My dear and only love, I pray
>   That little world of thee
> Be governed by no other sway
>   Than purest monarchy.
>
> " But if committees thou erect——— "

" Jamie, you have deceived me. You promised this for me, but whoever brought the word ' committees ' into a true love song? "

" And whoever brought the thing itself into a true government? "

" At your old politics again! Shall I be jealous of Scotland? "

" It is all you need ever be jealous of."

" It is a great all."

And she shivered as he sang:

> " He either fears his fate too much,
>   Or his deserts are small,
>   That dares not put it to the touch,
>   To win or lose it all."

* * *

A vague, gracious letter, all in one long sentence, came from the King, thanking Montrose for all he had suffered, and always remaining his most assured friend, Charles R.

Its bearer, one Mungo Murray, had more to tell. Things in England were as bad as they could be. The King had tried to arrest the five most troublesome members of his Parliament. But he arrived too late; " the birds had flown," he remarked himself in the despondently fatalistic mood that always followed his abortive efforts; and the uproar that followed had forced him to leave London.

" God knows when he will return," said Southesk when he heard it. A King's man, he knew his King.

" He will destroy everyone who befriends him, and all with the best intentions," he warned Magdalen, who warned Montrose, and saw that he knew it, and that it would make no difference.

She saw the destinies that guided the two men approach each other, gradually but inevitably, like two stars that are fated to meet.

By next summer civil war had begun to roll across England and Ireland. And Charles wrote to Montrose, " You are one whom I have found most faithful and in whom I repose greatest trust," and signed himself, " Your loving friend."

XXV

THE King set up his standard at Nottingham on a cold and gusty day in August; it was blown to the ground by a gale from the north. A disheartening omen, but his wife thumped self-confidence into him with her brisk little French hands, reminded him that she was the daughter of Henry of Navarre, the strongest and wisest king France had ever had, and that she expected Charles to equal him.

With admirable foresight she laid those same hands on the Crown jewels, and carried them off into Holland to sell them there and buy munitions with the money she raised on them. It was part of the inevitable bad luck that attended her at sea that these munitions, bought at such expense, were intercepted on their way to England by the Parliament's ships, and used against instead of for the King.

She had a terrible crossing on her return, continued to be violently seasick after her landing at Bridlington Bay, and that same night was driven out of her house on the shore by a bombardment from the sea.

Raleigh was at last avenged, in the way he would least have wished. The navy had revolted against the son of the Stuart who had executed his greatest sailor.

Charles' Queen and her women had to fly out of the house in their nightclothes, while the roof tumbled about their heads, and seek shelter in the hedges and ditches. One of her ladies went mad from fright. The Queen herself showed an infuriating courage, for she remembered that her little dog had been left lying on the bed, and ran back herself into the house to rescue him.

No sooner was she safe again than she was asked to see the Earl of Montrose, who had come south from Scotland in answer to an appeal from the King. He told her of fresh dangers in Scotland; Argyll, he said, was in touch with the English Parliament, who had already found the army of the Scottish Covenant so helpful in guarding the sittings at Westminster. That army had never been disbanded, and he believed it to be Argyll's intention to sell its services to the English Parliament. He begged for authority to raise a counter army in Scotland for the King, and prevent that intention before it was carried out.

He was hopeful, indeed certain that this could be done. He told her that he knew his man,—Argyll would never fight except with a heavy majority, and at present the forces of King and Parliament were fairly evenly matched. But if Argyll were left unchecked, he would weigh down the balance against the King by joining forces to the Parliament's.

" I can bear no more of it," she sobbed, " is there no chivalry, no kindness in any corner of these accursed countries? "

And she turned for comfort to the ugly little mongrel dog she had rescued, addressing him repeatedly as " Mitte " in terms of languishing endearment. Reaction from her heroism had set in; all her courage and strength of mind were debauched in an orgy of self-pity. It was the one quality she occasionally shared with her husband, and it now wrecked their best chance to save his kingdom.

Montrose had married too young and too happily to know much about women; the grave sympathy of the young Scot was not nearly passionate enough to suit the Queen's taste. He was a fine figure of a man, it was true; his eyes had a strange, searching power; she found she could neither meet them, nor look away from them,—but, holy virgin! was it for her to have to make the advances in such a situation as this? Queen she might be, but a queen insulted, attacked, all but murdered. Surely it was a time when a handsome young man might remember that a queen was only a woman after all?

Petulantly she told him that Hamilton (who always remembered this) did not think matters near so bad in Scotland as he seemed to make out.

Within a day or two there was Hamilton to speak for himself, having followed Montrose from Scotland in a great hurry; and Hamilton leaned over her, making her feel how small she was, how helpless, how desirable.

With him, too, was Traquair, to endorse all he said of the situation in Scotland; Montrose meant well, but exaggerated; had always been a hothead, had shown himself a good soldier but a shocking bad politician. Look how he had burned his fingers with Argyll, had been accused of God knows what,—imprisoned, discredited, had lost all his following.

To raise the King's standard in Scotland would only be to stir up trouble and provoke Argyll to action. Let sleeping dogs lie.

They lay; they slept.

The common opinion at Court was that " Montrose was a generous spirit, but had not so good a headpiece as Hamilton."

Montrose sent his proposals to the King, but had no chance against Hamilton and the Queen combined. If Montrose's reports were true, then Hamilton's were false. That seemed impossible to Charles, who knew Hamilton intimately, and not at all. As for that odd business at Holyrood, Hamilton had explained everything. Charles could not uproot the convictions of years, and at a time when his inflexible mind was already jostled and over-crowded.

So Montrose was thanked for his offers and went home. Hamilton was made a duke and went back to Argyll, with whom he was more friendly than ever. Scotland, who four years ago had fired the first shots of that war that had since broken out all over England, now held aloof.

But she still had her army of Covenanters ready, raised fresh forces in it—in case they should be wanted against the Papists in Ireland, Leslie said—and was sought as an ally in turn by both King and Parliament. Argyll considered, argued, bargained, with both sides, for a Presbyterian England as reward for his services.

The King began to grow desperate, and wrote:—" Hamilton, this is a time to show what you are."

Hamilton showed it by betrothing his daughter to Argyll's son, and ignoring Argyll's negotiations with Parliament.

And Argyll, who seemed to dread the thought of Montrose as an enemy as much as Montrose had disliked having Argyll for a friend, again urged the offers he had already made, to give Montrose the highest command in the army, and to settle all his debts incurred by his imprisonment, if he would join them.

He begged Henderson to do what he could in the matter, that good and wise man who was Montrose's friend, " and, I hope, mine," said the soft Highland voice,—its hesitation giving the curious charm of diffidence to the man who held absolute power in Scotland. But diffidence lay deep in him now, a secret fear that he himself could not explain, urging him to bind to his side the young man who had done all he could to break him.

It would be hard. Montrose was too apt to despise those whom he did not love, said the master of understatement. But if he had the sole command of the army,—" Tell him that, Henderson,—and that I can acknowledge him as a better soldier than I am ever likely to be."

That much-praised modesty rang more true than Henderson had ever heard it. The man's hands were trembling as they pushed the papers on his table this way and that. Never did he look so little like a great Highland chieftain. He had taken to wearing a black skull-cap in his study, for he was subject to neuralgia. It somehow made him look like a spider; he would not have minded the comparison, he liked to think of himself as at the centre of all this intricate network of plans and politics, a man so great that he could afford to give the appearance of power to others while he himself manipulated all from the background.

So Henderson went hopefully with Argyll's offers to Montrose; and with him Sir James Rollock as an appropriate mediator, since he had been Montrose's brother-in-law, and now, after Dorothea's death, had married a sister of Argyll's. All believed that even Montrose's pride was bound to be satisfied with this offer of the highest command in the army of the Covenanters.

But he refused it.

He preferred to go back to England, where his services had already been rejected. He parted from Henderson amicably; there was no bitterness between them. But his refusal shook the minister's confidence in his own cause to its foundation. He saw that they had miscalculated the measure of this young man's pride, that it was too high to be personal. He preferred to serve, even to have his service scorned, than to command where he could not respect.

" So he has turned his coat, and gone over to the enemy," said Sir James Rollock, when they knew the result of their parley.

" No," said Henderson, " he stands fast to his grounds, and does not rise and fall with success,—that brittle square of human actions."

T

XXVI

HE joined the King's Court at Oxford.

The Queen was at Merton College, the King at Saint John's; the Court ladies walked on the lawns reserved only for Fellows; church bells rang sleepily through the soft air; the King's nephew, Prince Rupert, rode out with his troopers on forays into the countryside; the whole quiet city of dons and scholars hummed with the unaccustomed bustle of Court and camp. Like the mayflies and dragonflies skimming over the placid surface of the Cherwell and Thames, these ephemeral love affairs and intrigues, rumours and plots of war, skimmed over Oxford, to sink and drown in the steady stream of academic life.

Montrose could get no one to listen to his warnings of what was happening in Scotland, not even when he told of Argyll's offer to himself.

"One thing at a time," was the popular opinion; "Settle England first, then we can see about Scotland."

They would soon settle England, their enemies were nearly all base-born tailors and tradesmen, and as the war was costing Parliament £30,000 a week, for that reason alone it could not possibly last more than three months. So they never saw that those armies were rolling up like thunderclouds in the north, never heeded that Leslie, the new Lord Leven, had now been given their command, which Montrose had rejected. Scotland was a great way off, and the Scots were a pig-headed, self-important race, and no doubt the Earl of Montrose was just like the rest of them.

In any case, he was very unlike everybody here, quite out of it, in fact; their slick, easy manners made him seem old-fashioned, —"stately to the point of affectation," said someone who had felt his familiarity snubbed by that grave courtesy. Another impression was that he "moved as if in a romance."

So that while he felt that he alone could realize what was happening, he was looked on as a visionary. Many had never heard of his victory of the Brig o' Dee, and few felt they need even trouble to be polite to him.

But those few were of importance. That rising barrister, Mr. Edward Hyde, now tutor to Prince Charles, walked with him in the groves of Magdalen, threading their way through the heavy guns that were parked under the academic trees, and told him how he pinned all his moral faith on the Law, and all his rational belief on the necessary swing of the pendulum. Reaction, he said, was bound to come from any violent movement, such as this present. "What were your own words, my lord, for the King told them to me, and very sound I thought them—that 'the people love change, and expect from it a new heaven and a new earth,—but, being disappointed, are as desirous of a re-change to the former estate.'"

He walked on the lawns at Merton with the King, and looked out over Christ Church meadows, and saw heads, low down, drifting past along the line of the pollard willows which marked the course of the river,—heads that kept so still, one would have thought them the progression of a dream, if one did not know that they were the heads of undergraduates in their boats.

And Charles talked of his plans with a free and hopeful courtesy that should have cheered Montrose, but that they seemed to slip along, like those heads below, too easily to be quite real.

As in the grey, neutral light of dreams, where everything that occurs or is said is of equal importance, so everything was of equal importance in the grey light of Charles' mind. His young nephew, Prince Rupert, had made a fierce charge at Powick Bridge; Prince Charles showed promise at his lessons, but refused to take his medicine; the Parliamentarian leader, Lord Essex, was popular with the London citizens because he was always seen smoking a pipe; the Saint John's dons wanted to put up a statue of the King over the quadrangle, and Charles thought an equestrian one would be the most impressive—did not Montrose think so? (He knew that he looked his best on horseback,—one did not see then that his legs were rather too short.)

Never did anything so rugged as a fact or reason stand out in his talk and give Montrose a chance to catch hold of it at any point and say, " But this, and *this* is what must be done."

But he said it; and every day had less justification to do so; as his chance of raising Scotland for the King grew less and less, while Argyll prepared his forces up in the north, collecting clan after clan, family after family, to his side; and Hamilton did not stir; and Traquair coquetted on the Border, doing nothing in particular; and not a hand was raised for the King.

And down here in this sleepy place, more and more yellow leaves drifted with the green leaves downstream, as summer slid into autumn, and autumn passed, and all the leaves were brown.

On a winter's afternoon, Montrose rode out of Oxford up to Headington, and looked down on the city that lay in the misty plain like a grey cloud, carved into towers, lying in a watery sky,—a city so unsubstantial that it might at any moment float away and leave the surrounding country to its primaeval marsh. Could seven centuries of mental endeavour, raising the mind of man from that of the savage to the present furthest pitch of human learning, even now disappear, and ' leave not a rack behind '?

He was looking down on the stronghold of the King's cause,— a cause that he himself felt was losing day by day, and he powerless to prevent it, as he wandered useless as a ghost, from the future rather than the past, since he alone seemed to discern where this present time was drifting.

After green leaves, yellow leaves; after yellow, brown. After rebellion, chaos; after chaos, the rule of One,—and who would that be, and what would he do to this land?

Tradition, learning, the pride of the mind and the delight of the eye, they were enemies to this new spirit that had as yet no name nor history, that raged through England and Scotland, burning only to cast the ancient kingdoms into another mould. Once he too had been caught up by it, had burned to make the government of his country perfect, and so, in time, that of the whole world. But the spirit had led him only into a tangle of conflicting wills and personalities, all seeking their own ends; the spirit, he cried to himself, had withered and died; and it had left nothing but confusion and war.

The city below had gathered itself into the twilight and vanished.

He rode down into it, and met Prince Rupert on Magdalen Bridge. That gigantic youth reined in his horse on seeing him, and said, " My lord, there is news for you."

" Good or bad, Your Highness? "

" Both. The Parliament have agreed to Argyll's terms. Parliament has promised that if they win, England shall be a Presbyterian country. Argyll has sent Leslie with eighteen thousand foot and two thousand horse on the march against us."

" In God's name then, what is the good news after that? "

" That the King my uncle is angry with Hamilton at last, and has recalled him. He will be impeached."

It was the first friendly sign that Montrose had had from the young Prince; even now, in giving this welcome news, there was no smile in Rupert's sulky, girlish mouth and beautiful eyes. The tower of Magdalen loomed like a huge shadow behind him in the river mist, and mistily the light of the lamp on the bridge flickered up and down on his face, as he looked gravely at the stranger from Scotland.

He wore no collar, but had knotted his lace handkerchief round his throat; even his slovenliness had an air of magnificence, for the handkerchief was very becoming. His horse was fidgeting, and he bent to pat its neck; in the shadow behind his stooping form, Montrose saw that of his inseparable younger brother, Prince Maurice, only a little less in stature.

" The King asked for you," said Rupert at last, with difficulty, like a bad-tempered child who has made up his mind to be good. And as he spoke, he wheeled his horse round, and was beginning to canter away with Maurice, when Montrose called after him, " Come with me then, Your Highness."

The brothers went with him to Saint John's.

" You were right," the King told Montrose as he entered the

room; his tone made the longed-for words the most heart-rending that the young man had ever heard. At last Charles realized that the scales were turned against him.

" What then is to be done? "

It was not a question, but a statement of despair. The martyr note was creeping into his voice. It was interrupted by an unexpected answer.

" I shall not require very much from Your Majesty's hands. A small body of troops from Ireland, landed on the west coast of Scotland, a party of horse to enable me to cut my way through the Lowlands and join them,—lastly, some arms and ammunition from abroad. Your Majesty's affairs will at any rate be in no worse case than they are at present, even if I should not succeed."

" Let me go with him, and a thousand of my horse," said Rupert, " Maurice can stay here to command the rest."

The King's eyes anxiously sought those of Montrose across the little low college room. Rupert flatly refused to believe what everyone else knew, that Maurice was not near as good a soldier as himself. There was now a note of defiance in his voice; and he could give serious trouble when in one of his moods.

But Montrose steered past the difficulty. Neither of the two princes could possibly be spared from the King's side at this juncture; he would collect his horse from the Marquis of Newcastle as he went north.

All the Scots mercenaries had followed Leslie; and the Covenanters had garrisoned all the fortresses along the Border. They would have to plan where he might break through. The four men brought chairs up to the table, pulled out maps and lists of regiments. Others were called in in consultation. Some sort of supper was brought them where they sat, as informal as if they were even now on campaign.

The King told Montrose he would appoint him Lieutenant-Governor of Scotland, and Commander of all the Royalist forces there. But Montrose would have no such titles; he had learned the harm that jealousy could do; in proportion as he had won success, so had his following decreased. Let him earn his title first, he said; then, as they looked disappointed, he had an inspiration;—let Prince Maurice wear it, and he be his deputy, the King's Lieutenant in Scotland.

The suggestion pleased all of them, but most, Prince Rupert, as Montrose had known it would. He was glad to have that youth his friend.

The Prince's white poodle, Boy, strolled in and jumped up on the King's chair when he had left it for an instant, and there sat turning its long nose right and left to the company as if in imitation of His Majesty, while the two grave brothers went into absurd fits of laughter over him. They seemed on a larger and simpler scale than the rest of Charles' Court,—half foreigners, but more strange than foreign.

Rupert had earned the name of the Wizard Prince among his enemies, and not only because of his terrible cavalry charges, which none of them could withstand. It was believed that he ate children, sacrificed to Satan; that he fed Boy on the flesh of his enemies; that he took the white dog everywhere about with him because he was his familiar spirit who whispered to him the instructions that made him invincible.

A keen interest in scientific experiment and knowledge of chemistry greatly helped this evil reputation. He gave proof of them now as he touched on war material with Montrose. In his opinion, they were only at the beginning of their discoveries in gunpowder, he was certain it could be increased to ten times its present strength.

As they sat and discussed their plans, a couple of drunken undergraduates returning from some athletic supper party went reeling past under the windows, forgetful that they were the King's, groaning out a dreary comic song from a play that had lately been fashionable at Court.

> " ' But did he take the fair Lucrece by the toe, sir? '
>   ' Oh no, no, sir! '
>   ' And did he somewhat further go, sir? '
>   ' Oh no no, no no, no no, sir! ' "

" Come on, you old Orpheuses, you're both as blind as Homer! " shouted an admonishing voice, further off.

" ' But did he take the fair Lucrece by the thigh, sir ? '
     ' Oh fie, fie, sir!' "

The last echo of the supper party and the silly, sniggering little song faded gently into the damp night.

At four o'clock the King went to bed, suddenly observed Rupert's odd neck-gear on his way to the door, and reproved him for his untidy habits, yawning while he patted the poodle and pulled his ears. Affectionate, avuncular, easy, he had quite forgotten his despair earlier in the evening. Montrose was going north to win back Scotland for him; it was a pity he had not thought of letting him do it before, but how could he tell, since he had naturally thought Hamilton was to be trusted? It had not been his fault, but Hamilton's; and anyway Montrose would make everything right.

So he went, contentedly, confidently; and Montrose worked on, with Ormonde now, discussing Antrim's forces in Ireland, many of whom were the Scottish Macdonalds of the Isles who had been driven out of their homes by Argyll's clan, and would be in a fever to return and fight them.

Ormonde was very grave; he thought the enterprise a desperate one; and Montrose himself knew well that he had been entrusted with it probably six months too late, or still more probably nearly a year too late, as he remembered the high hopes with which he had rushed down to meet the Queen in Yorkshire early last spring.

But by now it was also too late to question his conditions. Had he ever intended to do so, he would never have joined the King. He must use what cards were dealt him, how and when he might.

Yawning, but well content, he went out from Saint John's into the white dawn and the sound of bells. Through the shrouding mist there showed the shapes of towers and walls of crumbling stone, that so soon acquired their look of immemorial age. The quadrangle was astir with undergraduates hurrying to chapel, their black gowns flung anyhow across their shoulders.

The air for all its penetrating damp was mild as milk, suggesting not winter but the softest days of spring. An almond tree was already in flower, its topmost branches peering over the wall of Saint John's gardens, where King Charles loved to walk and discuss the rare plants with the gardeners.

In the porch, Montrose stared sleepily at a notice that was headed with the name of his own University of Saint Andrews. It offered hospitality to any undergraduates of the Oxford and Cambridge Universities that might wish to extend their studies at Saint Andrews, in Saint Salvator's hall, the official residence of that University. A sudden homesickness for his old college swept over him; he saw his rooms round him in all their gay colours, and his trophies on the walls.

A soldier who was a poet, and might have been a scholar, he stood dreaming for a moment of the gentle interchange of hospitality and learning, that would surely outlast these wars, while an almond blossom drifted in against the grey stone, and " these are the eternal things," he said to himself.

BOOK III

ANNUS MIRABILIS

1644-1645

$\mathcal{M}$ONTROSE rode out of Oxford to raise Scotland for the King.

He rode at the head of a small body of horse. The King had solemnly blessed his cause by presenting him with the sword of his dead brother, Prince Henry; and when in lighter mood, benignly told him to ' take his chance,' in faint echo of the Duke of Buckingham's favourite phrase, which had so often sent the blood racing through young Charles' sluggish veins. His two dead heroes Charles thus invoked to the aid of his servant; they were likely to do as much for him as would his living King.

The Queen had kissed him on both cheeks and added "Dearest" to the title of Cousin. She was with child again and very ill; but her pluck was indomitable.

The grey city melted behind him; there were primroses by the roadside and the birds sang high and clear; the air grew keener as he rode north.

There was as little mortal hope for his enterprise as ever man could have; but hope is immortal. In spite of his cautious words to King Charles,—" if it fail, it will at least have done your cause no harm,"—he did not believe that he would fail. He discussed his movements with his two subordinates, Colonel Sibbald and Sir William Rollock, the brother of Sir James, and as he had long ago tactlessly told his sister, Dorothea, the only one of that family that he really liked. Odd that she should have preferred James, a smooth oily creature, when here was old William, blundering as a colt, but a real good fellow.

They were riding into a hostile and fully prepared country. It was bad enough to pass through England with so small a force in the turmoil of civil war,—but if England were divided into friends and foes, Scotland was united against him, the whole country calm in acceptance of Argyll's rule. And this he proposed to upset, single-handed, and redress the balance in favour of the King.

Unlike that King, he would not wait and see what happened; he was going to show his intentions, and so force fate as far as possible to take their colour.

He reached Durham; found the Marquis of Newcastle absorbed in some delightful old French music, and in any case incapable of giving any help in the way of men or arms—"but stay and listen to an enchanting little thing, a ' fantaisie ' . . . I'll swear this old fellow, Jacobus Clemens non Papa, is worth all your strident, affected young moderns."

They left him sitting in his satin doublet, slashed with lace, his fair, bowed head attentive to the sedate notes of the harpsichord; and rode out among the rolling curves of the hills.

They heard nothing of Antrim's Irish forces, who seemed to have earned the name of another clan, the Children of the Mist. Colonel Sibbald always referred to these promised allies as the Irish fairy tale. He was a lean, long soldier of fortune, bow-legged from much riding, who had served for years in Germany. His casual, cynical drawl of lazy indifference belied an eye as keen as a hawk's for a good inn or a pretty girl or a chance to plant a barb in the sides of their enemies. They could do nothing for the time but snatch such chances in the way of desultory fighting along the Border.

The Covenanters loudly complained that Montrose was " ravaging at his pleasure." The measure of his success could be learned by the speed with which "that generous and noble youth " became " that bloody butcher and viperous brood of Satan,"—a kind of compliment, as William Rollock remarked, on hearing that his leader had been excommunicated by the Kirk. On the same day arrived the King's patent of his new nobility, for he was made a marquis. The two things were certainly complementary.

He harried backwards and forwards, always hoping for news of the Irish, seeking his chance to cut a way for his small force through Leslie's armies. He got messengers through to his friends and relatives in the Lowlands, but none dared join him.

" If you had come a year ago," said they, " it would have been possible,—but now Argyll has his grip on the whole country."

He heard that the Queen was besieged at Exeter; then, late in June, that she had been delivered of a daughter there, but forced to rise from childbed a week or two later and abandon her new-born infant to escape from the Parliament's armies into France. "Where at least the King will be safe from her 'woman's wit,'" remarked Colonel Sibbald in approval of the news that disgusted his companions.

A piece of news that followed within a few hours of this met with all their approval, for here at last was a chance of real action. Prince Rupert had sent an urgent message to Montrose to come to his aid in relieving the siege of York.

He dashed south; but heard that Rupert had changed his mind, attacked without waiting for him, and attacked a double foe. The English Parliamentary army had been joined by Leslie at the head of the Covenanters' armies, and together, upon Marston Moor, they dealt Rupert his first and smashing defeat. He had fallen back on Richmond in Yorkshire.

There Montrose sought him, riding down through the long sultry folds of Wensleydale and Swaledale, that lay as soft as velvet in the deep sunshine of the first days of July. The tower of Richmond Castle rose grey upon the horizon from nearly forty miles away, was lost among the hills, then suddenly was above him, shadowing the city,—the castle walls overhanging the river at a height of nearly three hundred feet. But this vast monument of ancient warfare was obsolete,—as unimportant as an old suit of armour.

The town clustered round the slopes of the hill beneath it, a huddle of little climbing streets, crooked roofs and smoking chimneys. At the foot of the castle hill flowed the encircling river, broad and bland and shiningly blue in a smooth green country.

Montrose was directed to the Market Square, which was full of sullen-looking troopers and their horses, the hot sunshine glinting on their harness, the air dusty and smelling of straw and sweat,—noisy with the harsh, interrupted sounds of hoofs on cobble-stones, and men's tired voices calling directions.

In a little inn in the square, in an upstairs room that sloped unevenly down to a low window, sat Rupert,—a dazed, empty hulk of a man, unable to believe what had happened to him. The green and golden light from the window rippled upwards over his face, but that remained passive.

" Boy is dead," he said, and Montrose wondered for the first instant whom he meant. Then he added,—" he was killed in action. I left him tied up with the baggage, but he must have got loose, and he followed me into battle."

Montrose asked him outright what had happened. Rupert had had less than two-thirds of his opponents' numbers; but even so his charge had been on the point of breaking the Parliamentary horse under their new leader, Cromwell, when the Covenanter cavalry had swung in and attacked the flank of Rupert's horse, and he had got cut off from the main body of his army. And that had given Cromwell, whose troops had just begun to break, his opportunity to attack the weakest spot in the Royalist army. And how had that chance been taken!

Four thousand men lay dead on Marston Moor, most of them of the King's. Newcastle's Whitecoats had fought to the death, long after the battle was lost to their side. Newcastle himself, who had driven down into the field of battle, just before it began, in his coach and six, so that he might smoke a quiet pipe in it, had now, in far less leisurely fashion, fled overseas. All the Royalists' guns had been taken, and about fifteen hundred prisoners, many of high importance; the city of York had surrendered to the Parliament; the whole of the north of England had been lost to the King by this one blow.

As Montrose had warned, the Scottish Covenanter army had been given the chance to come in and turn the scales against the King. The Covenanters, in conjunction with this new factor, a leader " who can never have known cavalry before," broke out Rupert, " except his own nags to ride on to market, or the neighbours' horses he grazed in his fields. And now my men are calling his cavalry 'Ironsides.'" (He forgot to add that he had first given that title to his enemy.) " I tell you, it was the first thing I asked of the prisoners we took at the beginning of the battle,—' Is Cromwell there? ' "

But as that generous light died from his eyes, they wore again the vacant look Montrose had first noticed. Something more had gone from him than his unconquerable reputation, or his dog, or his hopes of the north of England.

Why had he sent for Montrose, and then not waited for him? He was badly outnumbered, yet he had attacked long before there was any possibility of Montrose arriving. He wore a look both desperate and sullen when Montrose pressed his questions—but did so because he knew the danger of leaving that mood upon him, that bitter and helpless sense of injury which if left to fester is half way to madness.

Rupert flung from him, threw open the door and called to his servant to bring them brandy. His head bumped against the beams of the low ceiling, and he stood rubbing it ruefully until the man came stumping up the wooden stair in his great boots, and set down a round black lop-sided bottle on the table with two pewter mugs beside it. Then he went out, and the latch creaked behind him. Rupert sat at the table and drank, and Montrose drank as he stood, looking down on him.

" You would have smashed Cromwell's horse at the outset," he said, " had it not been for Leslie's Scots. We must provide a counter to them, and at once. Give me a thousand of your horse and I will cut my way through the Lowlands and get Scotland for the King."

The heavy-lidded, lustrous eyes were raised to his,—the eyes of a dog, eyes of a deer, eyes like his uncle, King Charles. In them, as in his uncle's, lay the doom of his family,—childishly personal, and too much concerned with family matters.

At last he was looking the other in the face. Having got his gaze, Montrose held it, so that the young man could not look away when he next spoke.

" You have not answered me. Why did you fight? "

Rupert's face went a dark red. " I was told to," he muttered.

U

" There is only one man in England whom you would obey, and that not always. Why did you, now? "

" He charged me to fight, on my honour, however the day might turn."

" Show me the letter."

Unwillingly Rupert drew a letter from inside his doublet. He had been carrying it next his heart.

" It will be there till I die," he said, with a simplicity that robbed his words of extravagance. " I show it to you, because I see what you think of me, and I cannot bear it, though it is what all the world will think. I shall not show it again."

Montrose read King Charles' letter to his 'loving nephew,' its involved messages of affection, and then its directions, 'very philosophical and parabolical,' as he had himself once said of Hamilton's cloudy meaning.

But the purpose of this letter eventually came through, obstinate in its repetitions like the blows of a sledge-hammer. Rupert, as he valued his honour, and his uncle's cause, must fight at once and come to Charles' assistance.

Had Montrose had such a letter in Rupert's place, he would have ignored it and given his respectful reasons afterwards for doing so. It was of little use to say so to this broken-hearted boy. Rupert had quarrelled with his uncle, defied him, insulted him, but that was in their family quarrels, affairs of personal jealousy, when the King had blamed him or listened to somebody else rather than him. But when his uncle made it a matter of his own private honour that he should obey him, then he must fling away the lives of his best men, and, far worse for their cause, his own prestige.

The Parliament's armies would never again fly at the very name of Rupert. No Wizard Prince this, the friend of the devil, but the conquered foe of Cromwell, a middle-aged, middle-class country gentleman. Even his familiar spirit, that had struck terror into men's hearts, was now only a dead dog.

All this he had lost, and the best hopes of his uncle's cause because his uncle had said he would be a coward if he did not do so.

Montrose handed back the letter; Rupert folded it, and put it into his doublet. As he did so, Montrose knew that he had spoken the truth, that he would carry it there till he died, a vindication of himself that he would never show again.

II

INSTEAD of getting the thousand horse he had hoped for, Montrose gave Rupert nearly all his troops; then turned back again towards Oxford, to own that his venture had failed. So he gave out, with a cheerfulness that astonished his companions. All his plans of that spring had crumbled like a sand-castle; but other plans, secret, incredible, were forming in his mind.

Cromwell once wrote, " You never go so far as when you do not know where you are going." His greatest antagonist was now to prove the truth of this.

At Carlisle, he sent on all his men, horses and baggage to Oxford, keeping with him only Colonel Sibbald and Sir William Rollock. These were disguised as Covenanter troopers, himself as their groom, and the three of them determined to make their way alone, where an army had failed to pass, up into the heart of Scotland.

Montrose was not easy to disguise. He cut his hair shorter, but then his hands gave him away. Some walnut juice, however, worked wonders, and a judicious hacking, not paring, of the finger-nails with his whinger. But his bearing and his eyes remained untranslatable. Sibbald told him to stoop, and not to look at anybody.

On three horses, with the ' groom ' leading a fourth, and none of them too good, lest they should arouse suspicion or envy, they threaded their way north again through the network of troops, cautiously inquiring as to their position from the country people on their line of march. The main part of these were far more concerned with their coming harvest than with the progress of the war, and never troubled to know whether they were on one side of it or the other.

A sleepy summerlike indifference lay over the hot countryside. They came on its incarnation as they rounded one of the many bends in an inconsequent lane, where the mud was baked into crumbling white ruts, and the smell of meadowsweet and honeysuckle was lush and heady.

They heard him singing long before they saw him,—a raucous, lewd, and inconceivably happy voice:

> " Oh the cherry lips of Nelly,
> They are red and soft as jelly;
> *But* too well she loves her belly,
> Therefore I'll have none of Nelly—
> No, no, no, no, no, no,
> I'll have none of Nelly, no, no, no."

The singer seemed to be repudiating every female in the calendar, for bonny Betty was pretty she was sweaty,—and he could dally with Dolly or with Molly, so fair and fat and jolly, *but* one had a trick of folly, and t'other of melancholy,—and in a flax shop he spied Rachel *but* her cheeks hung like a satchel.

They turned another twist in the lane and saw him sitting in the ditch. The tall purple spears of foxgloves rose all round him; buttercups grew between his legs, each flower a disc of polished enamel, gleaming in the sun.

He was one of Newcastle's Whitecoats, though his coat was now purple with grease and wine-stains. It was unbuttoned all the way down, showing a torn dirty shirt and the fat red creases where his neck folded into his hairy chest. His red face was wrinkled into smiles; a little blue eye rolled up at them with a cock as impudent as a sparrow's, but too contented to question. He had no hat and no weapons. His hand clasped lovingly a round black demijohn.

If this meant that Newcastle's men were round here, it would be awkward for them, disguised as Leslie's troopers. Colonel Sibbald asked him where he came from, but he had no idea; asked where he was going to, but he knew still less; asked where his company was, but he had lost them, lost his way, lost his pike and his knife—" and let them all go," he cried, hiccuping, as he waved his bottle up at them. " Have a drink. I've had—plenty."

That was evident. Nothing could be got from a man so blissfully oblivious of his circumstances. They were riding on, when once again the blue eye cocked upwards, rolled from each of the Scottish troopers to the groom behind; the fat grin spread all over his face, and he said, " And there's my lord, for all he tries to look like a groom."

" You're blind drunk," said Rollock sharply.

" Drunk I am, and glad of it, but I'm not too blind to see a brand new marquis, and the best man we've got, for all he's a Scot :

<blockquote>
The—best man we've—got,
For all he's—a Scot.
</blockquote>

And here's to your Honour's very good health."

As his chin fell back and the bottle obscured his face, the three men looked quickly at each other, and Sibbald dropped his pike to a level with the man's chest. It would be the work of half a minute to run him through and leave him safely dead in the ditch, instead of alive to prattle of this encounter through the countryside.

There was not a soul to see it done; the larks shrilled overhead in the hot blue sky; the fields spread green and gold all round them; the hedges were white with the late wild roses; in all the wide, lovely scene, there was no human being but the three men on horseback and the drunkard in the ditch.

But as the trooper lowered his pike, the groom pushed his horse forward and struck it aside. The soldier hearing the scuffle, but quite incurious as to its cause, lowered his bottle and peered up over the top of it, his lips still glued to its mouth.

Right in the middle of that swaying coloured scene, between him and the sun, hung the face of the new marquis, dark against the sun. It leaned down towards him; in front of it, between my lord's outstretched fingers, was a coin as gold as a buttercup. A cool voice, that he would remember, pierced into the depths of his fuddled brain; it said:

" Let this help you find your company again. Do not speak of meeting me until a month has passed."

The soldier held out his hand, took the coin, struggled to rise, but collapsed among the foxgloves. A bumble-bee, drunk as himself, fell out of the topmost bell of one of them, and spun buzzing and booming upside down on his sleeve, with all its pollen-yellowed legs waving helplessly in the air. Its fellow boozer squinted solemnly at it in his attempt to focus his blurred vision; then, with a regal gesture, flicked it from him.

" It's in my legs," he said confidentially, smiling up at Montrose, —" I can hold my tongue. Good luck ride on with your honour."

They rode on, while behind them in fading accompaniment to the thud of their horses' hoofs on the dried mud, there trailed the voice of the fastidious moralist, rejecting yet another lady:

> " In a corner I met Biddy,
>   Her heels were light, her head was giddy ;
>   She fell down and somewhat did I,
>   *Therefore* I'll have none of Biddy—
>   No, no, no, no, no, no,
>   I'll have none of Biddy, no, no, no."

*　　　*　　　*

They rode by night after that, and over moorland, away from the highroads. The shapes of hills surged up before them, black as soot, or grey when the moonlight fell on them. Smells struck sharp on their nostrils in the night air, the honey smell of heather, the cool smell of dew, the rank smell of their horses' manes, damp with sweat, and of their tanned leather saddles, creaking under them as they rode. There was no other sound but the sighing of trees in the wind or the waking cry of a curlew, startled by their horses, winging, shrill and complaining, through the night.

Here in this silent world of black and white their adventure assumed fantastic and dreamlike proportions. They had left the world they knew behind. As if in token that they did well to do so, they heard that all their company had been captured by Fairfax, the Parliamentary leader, only two or three days after they had left them.

Of the expedition that had set out from Oxford that spring, only their leader and his two friends could now still strike a blow for Scotland.

To those friends it was a portent that they would succeed where their army had failed. They spoke too of other portents; of battles that the country people had seen waged by cloudy armies in the sky at dawn; of a dark and empty church they rode past at night, where they heard the sound of voices rising and falling in the forbidden music of the old religion.

Montrose did not need these signs and wonders; nor was he discouraged by the reports that all Scotland had accepted the new "Solemn League and Covenant," in alliance with the English Parliament; and all the nobles, with Traquair at their head, had declared themselves for Argyll. Each piece of news they got was worse than the last.

Huntly had strutted and flapped his wings for the King, "but the old Cock o' the North crows better than he pecks," said Sibbald, for his attempt was quickly smashed; Argyll had taken charge of Huntly's sons (his nephews), and the Gordons now had no leader.

Yet Montrose knew that in this step into the dark, into a country united against him, good luck would ride with his honour.

They were making their way up towards his cousin of Inchbrakie, at Tullybelton, near Perth, for Montrose was certain that if anyone could help him in this madly adventurous escapade, it would be his guide and adviser of college days, Black Pate. He would hide in Methven Wood near his cousin's place, where they had so often hunted together as boys; and could there wait for his opportunity. They were not so very far from Kinnaird, and his heart leaped at the chance to see Magdalen again, if only for a couple of hours. He sent a message to her by Colonel Sibbald, who would not be known at Kinnaird.

That night he waited for her on the little hill beyond the deer-park. In that flat country it passed as a hill, but it was scarcely more than a rise in the ground above the surrounding marsh; a few firs and thorn trees, twisted into wild shapes by the wind, rose above the scrubby bushes, looking as though they had retreated there from the bog.

As a boy, he had often paused here on his way from Old Montrose to fly his hawks over the uplands, and waved his scarf in signal in case any from Kinnaird should see it and join his party. Now he waited concealed among the bushes, for he could not go to meet her by the way they both knew through the bog; he must not show himself to any who might be abroad.

He looked down on the black jagged shape of the castle, on the gardens like a grey mist, and rising from them here and there the black spires of trees that old Southesk had planted in his youth, trees which would, he said, outlast even the castle.

Peace lay below, and the home life with his wife and children for which he ached after a year of separation. A fourth child had been born to them last spring, and he had not seen it, a daughter this time, so Magdalen had had her way at last. She had written to him in Italy hoping James would be a daughter;—young and carelessly selfish as he had then been, he had guessed why. He had left her then for three years, of his own choice, merely because it was in the usual course of education. Nothing, he now thought, even if he lived to be as old as Southesk, could ever give him again those three years when he might have been young with Magdalen. He would tell her so to-night,—and he added to it,—"We have always been going to do things together, and never have."

Above his head the trees rustled like a sigh, or a laugh,—her laugh. He could hear her answer, "What odds does it make?" They could thank heaven like the glutton that it could not take away the dinners they had eaten,—still less could it take away those they had only dreamed of.

"Yes, the wish is all," he assented in a whisper.

What fancy held him talking here to himself, no, to herself, in the dark? Was it that when he saw her, all words and thoughts would be driven out by her still presence, and all regrets, and even hopes?—for the future would signify no more than the past.

Then the first breath of that peace she brought fell on him, quieting his mind in a tense hush of expectation. The trees were quiet now above him, and all the night, like himself, seemed to hold its breath at the first whisper of her approach,—a faint swishing sound through the long grasses,—and then a grey movement rather than a form in that still grey scene. There at last she was before him, with her face like a ghost's beneath her hood, and her eyes black hollows in its shadow.

He sprang to her, and for an instant saw her as her hood fell back and the moonlight flowed over her, lighting her eyes, that shone as if with their own light. Then that white face was hidden against his; there fell over them the darkness of the trees, of their own bliss, deep, silent, and forgetful as sleep.

III

OF all the personal qualities necessary in warfare, luck is the most important. Mazarin, the Italian cardinal who was beginning to rule France, put it above any other quality, even greatness; his first question concerning any general was, " Est-il heureux? "

The fairy tales agree with that cold-blooded cynic; they acknowledge no man as hero without his magic sword and flying shoes and cap of darkness and above all the favour of old, silly and contemptible folk, whom a worldly-wise man will despise.

Montrose had had no luck so far in his venture, until he was wished it by a drunken old deserter.

Unknown to him, in the heart of Scotland another man was wandering, beset by enemies, from whom he could only escape by such luck that when it came it seemed like a miracle and a sign from heaven. This was his long-expected ally, Alasdair Macdonald, at the head of fifteen hundred of the Macdonald clan from both sides of the sea, for most of them had been driven out of Scotland by their hereditary foes, the Campbells, to islands yet further and further west, until they reached the Irish coast. These were the 'Irishes' from Antrim, whose aid Montrose had asked for from King Charles, but of whom he could hear no word during all the spring campaign.

They had landed on the west coast of Scotland at last, however, in three ships, two of them hired mercenaries from Flanders with their Flemish captains, the third, Irish, under an Irish adventurer. Alasdair collected together as many as he could of the Macdonalds on the Scottish side; but had no news of the King's Lieutenant, the Marquis of Montrose, and no notion where to find him. He too was trusting blindly to luck in flinging his army into a hostile country to look for a leader.

He was the son of Coll of Colonsay, who could fight as well with his left hand as with his right. That was the reason, it was held, that Alasdair could fight twice as hard as any ordinary man, run twice as fast, drink twice as much, and was half a head taller than other men. He was descended from Conn of the Hundred Fights, who had ruled all Ireland from the halls of Tara in the days when the Romans ruled over conquered Britain. There ran too in his veins the blood of the Vikings who had harried the islands of Scotland; and it was family tradition that a certain rusty old shirt of chain mail hanging up in one of his castles had been worn by no knight nor crusader but by one of those terrible ' summer sailors,' as the sea robbers were still called along the coast.

Legends had already sprung up about Alasdair himself. His hereditary poet, MacVurich, whose family had also come from Ireland but as late as the thirteenth century, was learned, like all who had held his post, in English and Latin; but he could show a more practical cleverness than the study of those remote languages. He knew just how to advertise Alasdair's reputation, in touches sufficiently extravagant to be popular.

Alasdair would in fact have been the perfect Highland leader of men in this expedition, if only he had known where to lead them. He promptly marched off to harry the Campbells, that being the accepted course of warfare; then found he had stirred up an army of Argyll's in pursuit of him, went back to his ships, and found that Argyll had sent two warships of the English Parliament to surprise them as they lay in the harbour. The two Dutch mercenaries had yielded at once; the Irish had fought till all were killed, and the ship fired.

So there was Alasdair with his boats burned, and all hope of retreat cut off. He marched boldly into the interior, and tried to summon the country to the service of the King. But too many of the clans had ancient grievances against the Macdonalds, and those near the Lowlands looked on these ragged, hungry, fierce-looking men, attended by their rabble of women and children, as a tribe of savages as alien to themselves as the redskins of America.

Terror heralded their approach, people fled, the city gates were closed and guarded; while stories, growing ever wilder and more horrible, were told of the atrocities in the Irish massacre nearly three years ago.

Alasdair had heard of Huntly's rising in the north, and hoped to join him, but it was squashed by Argyll's armies before he could do so. About five hundred of the Gordon clan would not submit to the Campbells, and joined the Macdonalds; otherwise they were without allies, provisions or base, in a generally hostile country. Their leader had written for instructions to the Marquis of Montrose at Carlisle, but had heard nothing beyond a fantastic rumour that he had disappeared;—he had not been with his bodyguard when it was captured by the Parliamentarians, and no man knew whether he were alive or dead.

Then came a mysterious message from him, saying he would meet Alasdair at Blair.

The Macdonalds marched on Blair and took the castle; but the surrounding clans of Atholl held aloof. They were hostile to Argyll and the Covenant, but still more to these outlandish intruders, and only waited to concentrate their forces before they should fall on them and cut them to pieces.

Alasdair had led his men into an impasse; it would be weeks before the King's Lieutenant could join them; and at any moment now the surrounding countryside might rise and annihilate them. He could do nothing but exhort his followers to patience with their sullen neighbours,—the thing most difficult in the world to himself and them.

Now his belief in the older, primitive religion of fate began to fail him; and he fell to telling his beads and praying to the saints in that despair which demands the consolations of Christianity.

"For some sign that God has not utterly forsaken me," he prayed, as he walked on the wide moor where the Macdonalds and the Gordons were gathered together in gloomy inaction.

He heard shouts in the distance; a ripple of noise and excitement was running through the Gordon troops, then a shot was fired into the air, and then a scattered volley. He hurried in that direction, thinking an attack; on all sides he saw men springing up, but their cries were of joy, not alarm. Some good news was crackling like running fire through the heather, and now it reached him——

"The King's Lieutenant has come!"

"My lord of Montrose is here himself!"

At the same moment, the whole hillside burst into a roar of welcome, a thunder of cheers, and guns fired in salute.

And now Alasdair saw, walking towards him, a slight young man in Highland dress, with trews and plaid and small round targe and short broadsword, and a bunch of oats in his blue bonnet,—attended by only one man. This then was the King's Lieutenant, who had contrived to drop from the sky into this remote place at the moment when he was most desperately needed.

But where were his bodyguard, his troops, his cavalry, and how had he contrived to fly here from Carlisle, when Alasdair could not expect him to arrive for weeks? The Macdonald poured out his questions as he embraced him and showed him to his men as their promised leader.

They made a strange pair.

The shaggy red hair and beard of the excited Irish giant towered over the King's Lieutenant. Alasdair carried the mighty two-handed sword which only he could wield. His kilt, which he wore always like his men to fight and march in, was faded and had been hastily darned, but his weather-worn coat was covered with gold scroll-work, and his plaid was fastened by an enormous round brooch of elaborately fretted gold, with a pin so long as to stick out beyond his shoulder in perpetual menace to the eyes of ordinary mortals. Ornaments of white bronze tipped the laces to his leggings of soft doeskin that had once been white.

By his side stood an Irish wolf-hound as much bigger than any other breed of hound as his master was bigger than other men. A heraldic-looking beast, narrow-waisted, deep-chested, rough-coated, with magnificent gallant head, he had to be introduced to Montrose together with his pedigree, like all the other tribal chieftains.

For "my great dog, Bran" was descended from one of the

seven Irish wolf-dogs sent out for the Roman games, when " all Rome viewed them with wonder, and thought they must have been brought thither in iron cages,"—so the Roman consul had written, in a letter which Alasdair now quoted as though it had been addressed to himself; and Bran looked up, wagging his long whippy tail, his great jaws smiling open at the familiar words.

Beside the two walked the oddly young-looking man, quiet and collected, taking it all as the most simple and natural thing in the world that he should walk twenty miles across the heather to find his army and take his place at the head of it, without any more pomp or show of power than if he had been a country gentle-man taking a friend for a stroll round his estate.

He introduced the friend, his cousin, Patrick Graham of Inchbrakie, a man with a scarred but pleasant face; and he told a strange story. Two more friends he had, he said, who were following with three horses, slowly, for one had gone dead lame,—and this was the extent of his forces.

" Howsoever you have come," said Alasdair, " you have come in answer to my prayer, when I despaired. Now I know that you will be bringing us victory."

" So I despaired," replied Montrose, " when I was hiding in Methven Wood,—and then heard of your coming."

" Tell me," said Alasdair, " for you and I are friends as well as allies from this time on."

He was looking at his new friend in a kind of awe, for surely there was something miraculous, not only in their meeting thus at last in spite of all the efforts of their enemies, but in the nature of this man. He took on himself none of the airs of command, yet Alasdair had at once felt he could accept him as his leader.

He listened to Montrose's low voice telling him how he had sat in Methven Wood, thinking of the miserable bondage and slavery brought on this country,—" and as I sat there alone I prayed to God that He would remove the curse from the land, and make me His humble instrument to do so. I looked up and saw a man running towards Perth, with a fiery cross in his hand. I went up to him and asked what this was for, and he told me that he had been sent to warn the city of Perth to raise all the country-side against the Macdonalds, who were even now in Atholl. My prayer was answered,—and now I have come in answer to yours."

If he had come at the head of all the King's horses and all the King's men, his effect could not have been more extraordinary. The King's standard was raised on the mountain side and saluted by a flourish of trumpets, a strange thing to hear in that lonely place as though at some high ceremonial.

But Montrose knew the value of ceremony. Those who would not join with wild Irishes would follow the King's Lieu-tenant and the Royal Standard; and he was soon proved right by the sound of pipes and the tramp of those very men who had only been waiting for their opportunity to attack the Macdonalds, and now marched instead to serve beside them under the Graham.

Montrose belonged to none of these Highland clans, and could command any of them. He told them of the Stuart; and men who had never seen an Englishman, burned to defend their kinsman and countryman from his treacherous English servants. Loyalty here was still a simple, almost a primaeval thing; it was a far cry from the philosophies of Oxford, and lawyer Hyde's ratiocinations on the necessity for a personal embodiment of the law. What Highlander would recognize his king by such a name?

It was a far cry from Oxford in every respect, from the most sophisticated modern culture of court and college to the leadership of this tribal host. Time, where it brings no change, stands still; and life in the Macdonald clan had been the same for at least sixteen centuries.

" Your Honour's noble great-uncle, Ranald Macdonald," so sang MacVurich to his chieftain, had taken a dislike to his fellow guests, or objected to their number, since he made the thirteenth, so had risen early one morning and slain the other twelve, then propped their bodies against the wall, where their hostess would see them from her window when she rose.

Colonel Sibbald murmured something polite about the famous

Highland respect for hospitality; but Black Pate hastily interrupted his irony.

Well might his three companions tell their young commander that he had undertaken a task as impossible as one set by the fairies, in leading this savage horde in " a proper and civilized campaign."

They would never follow one who was not of themselves. Their notion of warfare was no more than a slaughter and a cattle raid. If they won a victory, they would be off the next day—" all of 'em legging it home across the heather, with their booty slung over their shoulder."

No campaign of Highlanders could ever therefore last more than a week—and what in the name of God did the King's Lieutenant hope to accomplish in *that* time?

" A good deal," replied Montrose, and whistled a marching tune, for he was happy. He liked these people and was at home with them, easy and friendly with the wildest of the Irish kerns, who were eager to show him the honour he never claimed for himself. Nobody here could have accused him of stateliness, as in England. His companions noticed how he scorned " the keeping of state, and therefore quickly made a conquest of the hearts of all his followers, so that he could lead them in a chain to follow him with cheerfulness in all his enterprises."

IV

NOW, if ever, he must move like the wind. The Macdonald's march inland had roused all the country; north of the Grampians, all the clans were banding together against him; in the south, the Covenanters were drawing new levies every day. Perth was occupied by a large army under Lord Elcho; Aberdeen by another under Lord Burleigh, with Huntly's sons, well tutored by their uncle, Argyll, serving under him. Argyll himself was marching towards Perth at the head of his huge clan.

Montrose and his Highlanders at Atholl were in the centre of a ring of enemy forces, each of them at least three times as large. Safety might be found in the Highlands where the Lowlanders could not follow, but of what use was safety at this juncture? He must strike at his enemies before they had time to join forces. He must provide his men with war material, for they had no money, no supplies, no food, horses, nor munitions, very few weapons, and very ragged clothes. And most of all, he must do something at once to impress on them that he was born to be their leader.

"There is a fine newly-run salmon in that pool," their great chieftain, Somerled, had said to them five centuries ago, —"if I catch it, it will show that Heaven intends me to be your leader."

"There is the rich city of Perth near by," said Montrose, "we will first capture that and replenish our stores."

He was taking a far more unlikely chance than did the half-mythical Somerled.

But a drunken soldier had wished him luck, and luck came to him with crazy unlikelihood.

On the Hill of Buchanty, on their way towards Perth, they met a body of five hundred bowmen, raised in the name of the Covenant to resist Alasdair's invasion. But one of their leaders was young Lord Kilpont, who had been at Saint Salvator's with Montrose; and the other was David Drummond, the Master of

Madertie, who had married Montrose's sister Beatrix just over a couple of years ago.

They had come out to fight the Highlanders, not Montrose,—that was inconceivable. So instead of fighting they all dined together out on the heather, and agreed over their wine that the Covenant had done well to draw itself up all over again and give itself the new name of " Solemn League and Covenant," for it was nothing like the old National Covenant that Montrose had signed and fought for,—" it has ceased to be national, and is a damned sight too solemn," Kilpont declared hilariously.

Inevitably, he and David Drummond decided to leave the side of Lord Elcho's army of seven thousand infantry, between seven and eight hundred horse, and nine pieces of heavy artillery; since it was better to follow Jamie Graham to war under any conditions.

" But first you must hear those conditions," he protested.

" Why, what artillery have you? " asked Madertie.

" None."

" What cavalry? " asked Kilpont.

" Three tired horses, one lame."

" How much ammunition? "

" Enough for one round, by the front line only, if I divide the men into three lines deep."

" What weapons? "

" Some old-fashioned matchlocks, a few good claymores and Lochaber axes, some bows and arrows. And plenty of stones on the hillside."

They stared at him. Black Pate's cheerful nod convinced them that their old friend spoke the truth and was not mad.

They looked back to Montrose again, and saw him laughing,—and that silent laughter stirred through them like a wind.

" How many men in all? " gasped out Madertie.

" Two thousand two hundred," he replied.

" No! " shouted Kilpont, springing to his feet. " Two thousand seven hundred,—with our bowmen."

And so, in the spirit of one of their mad escapades at college, Montrose won his latest recruits.

Kilpont pulled forward and introduced to him a boy of about twelve years old, who had been standing just behind him and staring open-mouthed at the King's Lieutenant during those amazing answers.

Kilpont's own wife had as yet borne him no sons; this eager child, who spoke not at all, even when encouraged by his father, but was taut and quivering like a newly-placed bowstring with the excitement of this adventure, was the result of the passion Kilpont had indulged during his last year at Saint Andrews for the plumply pretty wife of an excellent French pastrycook. Montrose had always sworn that his pies had served as pander to his wife, and they proved in the end the more lasting attraction, for Kilpont had tired of her in a couple of months.

Yet here was this boy to give permanence and beauty to the commonplace affair that Kilpont would have forgotten as completely as Montrose had done, had he not been so struck with the lad that he had acknowledged him, sent him to college at Saint Andrews, and now taken him with him on this campaign.

" He's been trained a drummer boy as good as any you could find, and will rattle you into battle as fast as your pipers here can skirl you. Up now, you lazy young dog, and get your drum and squat there on the heather and show what you can do to be kept in this worshipful company, or back you'll go to school to-morrow."

With a shy grin, the boy did as he was told, sat cross-legged on the heath, and beat his tattoo.

Very light and soft it came at first, a whisper running over the ground,—then a rustle, like the wind rising in the forest trees,—then a rattle like the antlers of stags fighting in the rutting season,—then of dead bones, of skeletons dancing, faster and faster,—a dance without a tune, rhythm without melody, ticking out the march of time, throbbing through the blood in one's veins,—a pulse beating through the heart of the world— the urge of life itself, that will drive men madly towards death.

From away on the hillside, one of the Macdonald pipers answered that irresistible summons, shrilled up and called on his fellows. The pipes cried now on every side, the wide moor was whirling with battle music, and the curlews, wheeling above it, cried desolately back.

Up sprang the hereditary harpist of Macdonald and struck on his harp, his face working in passion as he sang—" I will give praise to Macdonald, for to-morrow his foes shall feed the ravens, and red shall run his path where the dead lie under his feet."

Still the boy drummed on, staring before him. The heather pricked his legs, it burned blood-red round him in the light of the setting sun, and purple away in the distance where the hills met the pale-green sky.

The bare hairy legs of men strode between him and that sky, the huge bare knees of Alasdair, like boulders of red rock. This giant (an ogre perhaps, but none the less a hero) he, Wat, would be drumming into battle to-morrow. He would be going into his first battle, while his friends, older than he, were still at school;—he would march to war at the head of this army of uncouth and terrible warriors.

But it was not they he would follow, no, not even the mighty Alasdair, who now stooped over him, blotting out the hillside, and thrust his cup between his lips as he drummed, telling him to drink of his cup and be of his board henceforward, for he was the boy for them,—"a noble boy,—you'd be travelling the world over before you met the like of that boy,—he would drum the dead out of their graves to fight for them,—there was not a corpse so cold but would rise and dance at his bidding to a merrier dance of death."

Having given the boy a sup of his raw rye whisky, he drained the flagon to its dregs. His laughter went reeling up into the clear mountain air; behind the blue of his eyes there burned the white flame that lit them in battle.

But no, not Alasdair would Wat follow, but the King's Lieutenant, for whom his father had at first sight flung away his commission from the Covenant; had told his men that they would be fighting by the side of the Highlanders to-morrow, instead of against them. And if he had not, then Wat would have gone over on his own account to this man, the Marquis of Montrose, of whom he had always been proud to remember at Saint Andrews that he was his father's friend.

Stories were still told at College of Montrose. He had ridden his horse up into Saint Salvator's Hall and given it wine to drink out of the ancient silver flagon, until it caracoled like a dancer; he had given a supper party, after winning the silver medal for archery, which had lasted until morning, and had shot his arrows over Saint Salvator's tower up against the moon, so that a new college rule had had to be made, forbidding this dangerous practice. That showed the permanence of fame to young Wat.

Now the hero of it was before him, as large as life, and not nearly as large as Alasdair. Montrose did not stir from where he sat, but his cool gaze, resting on Wat as he drummed, appraising, commending, sent a high song of triumph through the boy's heart in accompaniment to the ceaseless throbbing of his drum. For this man, who had but just spoken to him, would he drum the army into battle to-morrow; and for this man would he die to-morrow, if need be, very gladly.

His head nodded forward as he drummed; he no longer saw the fading scene around him, but still he heard the throb of the rhythm that presently he ceased to play; the sticks fell from his hands, and he knew nothing more, not even that he was happier than any boy had ever been.

V

*M*USIC and voices fell silent. The late summer light had died over the mountains; only over their rim there shone a silver edge. Above, the sky had deepened to mauve, and the faint stars shone in it here and there. The men rolled themselves in their plaids, and slept on the heather. Montrose walked over it with Kilpont, looking down on the fertile fields round Perth. Their hill was on the very edge of the Highland line, whose crags and bogs, inaccessible to any ordinary army, would have to serve Montrose as his base through the coming campaign. To-morrow he would launch his new troops on to the plain below. Now he and Kilpont discussed their disposition.

Against so large a force as their enemy's, they must stretch their battle line as wide as they could without weakening it, and must charge quickly, before the enemy had time to fire their heavy guns. Would the Highlanders stand that dreaded novelty to them, 'the mother of the musket'? These very same Gordons now in Alasdair's army had fled from it fast enough when Montrose had first encountered them under Huntly's son, Aboyne, at the Bridge of Dee.

" But then," said Kilpont simply, " you were fighting against them, and now you are leading them."

It was the kind of remark that made Montrose feel shy and grateful and afraid. He felt that he had as yet done nothing to make men trust him like this; he himself believed that they could, —but why should they believe it?

They went past Wat, fallen asleep over his drum.

" If I should be killed to-morrow," said his friend, " look after that boy. He's too good to go back to the pie crusts."

They looked down on him, at the grave and childish ecstasy that showed on his sleeping face. Montrose remembered how long it was since he had seen Johnnie and young James. If all were well by this time to-morrow, he would send for them, and old Forrett too, to bring them to Perth, that he might get a glimpse of them.

A little wind came stirring up through the heather. It had a nip of autumn in it, for this was the last day of August. Kilpont stooped and pulled the boy's plaid over him; then they passed on.

Madertie joined them with the suggestion that he should be chosen as envoy to the Covenant, for Montrose meant to carry out the rules of civilized warfare as far as possible. But he was not so sure of the honour of the Covenanters, and mentioned Beatrix and ' unnecessary risks.' Madertie was not to be dissuaded. Was he to be done out of every enterprise merely because he had had the bad luck to marry Montrose's sister? He would have no reminders of the studious life he had hoped to lead with her. He had not come out with five hundred bowmen to lead a quite life.

There lay Alasdair, deep in his drunken dreams of some Valhalla where men may fight to the death and rise to fight again. Under this exquisite sky of a northern summer, among all these sleeping, half-savage men, Montrose remembered the blue nights in Venice, and the bodies, lithe and beautiful, of men and women dancing. But the grave rapture of this night of expectation thrilled his blood with an excitement deeper than any that youth and pleasure had given.

He walked with his friends again after a long time, and knew it might well be the last time they would do so. Their lives, and his hopes for Scotland, hung on a hair's-breadth. Now at last after all these years of waiting, he would put it to the touch, ' to win or lose it all.'

His hour was upon him.

If the Fates came to any man and said, " Now for one year you shall add a cubit's height unto your stature,—you shall stretch mind and soul and body to an extent undreamed of,—you shall plan like a god and live like a hero,"—then would not any man consent to any terms for such a prize?

" It is not glory, it is not riches, neither is it honour, that we fight and contend for," wrote his Graham ancestor of three hundred years before. And it was a desire for something greater than all these that now filled Montrose, so that, like the sleeping boy and the drunken giant, he knew happiness the fullest that his heart could hold.

VI

BEATRIX DRUMMOND of Madertie was staying with her baby daughter at Kinnaird; it was safer to be there than in her own home, since her husband had gone to fight these Irish invaders. Her brown hair and broad, delightful smile were a restful pleasure; and her sturdy confidence in Jamie did much to cheer Magdalen through these weeks of waiting for any news. She had dared not tell even Beatrix of that snatched hour of summer night in which she had met Jamie on the little hill in the marsh.

He was alive, and somewhere in these parts, Daniel told her for sure, for a cannon had been heard, fired in the west, where no army was, and the sun had shone bright at midnight,—" *his* sun, as it once shone for him before, blood-red on a clear March morning, when he first fought in Scotland."

Beatrix's logic was more comforting than Daniel's superstition. " If he were dead or wounded or imprisoned, his enemies would all be shouting their heads off. You may be sure this silence is golden, and that he has gone off into the blue to hatch some mad plan of his own. Often enough he did that in the old days at Rossdhu or Kincardine."

Sir William Rollock was also missing; no doubt the two were together somewhere, and William was one of Jamie's best and wisest friends.

" Jamie's friends have a way of forgetting to be wise when they are with him," said Magdalen.

Her words were quickly proved. They heard an astonishing piece of news,—Beatrix's husband and Lord Kilpont had gone out together to fight the Irishes; and instead had joined forces with them, for at the head of the Irish they had found the Lord Montrose himself. In some incredible fashion he had taken command of that half-foreign host as naturally as if he had been their native chieftain.

He had always been more than half a Highlander,—" do you remember, Magdalen, how round Kincardine and Loch Lomond he would run barefoot over the heather and the whin prickles without even a pair of rawhide brogues,—and that when he had just come back from abroad and wearing fine foreign shoes for three years on end?" His bare feet could find by instinct the tussocks in a bog, and he could chase a stag up a hillside as fast as any wild hunter, and he could swim any torrent,—look how he alone had crossed Tweed in flood three times to encourage his men.

Now came word from Montrose himself, that they were marching on Perth.

Old Lord Southesk said they were all stark staring mad together. What in God's name were they thinking of? They could not even hope to surprise their enemy, the city was fully prepared, yet there were the young fools marching straight into the pit. His hands shook as he spoke, his voice was miserably irascible. In all the times that Jamie had given him trouble, he had never given him such pain as this. Now at last he was going to be proved in the right.

Beatrix could comfort him better than Magdalen, for whom his anxiety hurt most. She had not been strong since her last baby and only daughter, Jean, had been born last spring.

Jean lay in the deep wooden cradle, where her father and all her brothers had lain before her; nothing could be seen of her but two crumpled pink fists which occasionally appeared above the walls of her citadel, waving in the air. Beatrix's daughter, Dorothy, a sturdy eighteen-monther, would stand on the rocker of the cradle and peer down into its recesses, like a puppy into a rabbit hole.

"When Jean is older," teased Beatrix, "she can help you finish those curtains. But no, you will be sending her to a fashionable new boarding school in London like your sister Traquair's girls, and she will get so clever with her shorthand and shell work and whatever useless stuff they teach now, that there will be no holding her to her needle."

"No, I shall keep this one," said Magdalen.

She twisted the dark-green thread round her needle for the

fidgety new French knots she was working inside the sprawling leaves of her pattern. Beatrix bent a head as round and shining as a chestnut over a light-green leaf in another corner,—in darning stitch, for she had not Magdalen's patience, and her French knots always got tangled.

The curtain spread over their knees and away over the floor; on its furthest folds sat little Rob, and pulled the long black velvet ears of a solemn hound puppy. Rob was a splendid six-year-old, his father and Johnnie over again, said the unobservant, for he lacked the wild, disturbing flame that had leaped up again and again in their father, rendering him incalculable to any ordinary mind;—a flame that had begun to show, as Magdalen had watched, in Johnnie's blue eyes, at any song or tale of danger. He had been wild to go and find his father when they heard of his disappearance, and it had been necessary to keep a strict watch on him and young James, after they had ridden off early one morning on their quest, and been discovered only after hours of anxious search. James was not quite eleven, while Johnnie was just on fourteen, a great gulf at that age, and James' small fragile stature made it greater. For that very reason, he would never willingly be left out of any escapade of Johnnie's, and his brother respected his spirit.

No leaping flame in James, but a quiet and rather strange little fire, that might break out in odd ways, as only Magdalen knew, for everyone else in her family had firmly decided that James was the studious one, who should take up law, and left it at that.

But it was Rob, with the steady brown gaze and the gentle, clumsy movements, rather like a hound puppy himself, who, said Beatrix, would pull the house of Graham together again in the future, when all these silly wars were over; and she would feel her small daughter perfectly safe if only Magdalen would consent to marry them—or did she not approve of the marriage of first cousins?

The two women laughed and chattered over their work; it did not strike them as either odd or courageous to do so, when even now the ravens might be feasting on their husbands' bodies.

VII

MONTROSE and his men slept only for a few hours on the moor on that last night of August. As next morning dawned, they marched down the Sma' Glen away from the line of the Highlands, and on to Tippermuir, about three miles out of Perth. There they saw Lord Elcho's army drawn up in battle array to meet them,—seven thousand foot, extended to a width that seemed certain to outflank the small force opposed to them, and at either end of it a body of between three and four hundred horse; the right wing under Elcho, the left under Sir James Scott, their best professional soldier. The nine pieces of artillery were in front of the army.

With such odds on their side, a fair proportion of the citizens and ministers of Perth had thought it a good Sabbatical exercise to turn out and see their foes cut down on a Sunday morning. For " the better the day the better the deed," they said, when Montrose courteously sent Madertie as envoy under a flag of truce, to ask, first, if they would not respect the King's commission and lay down their arms; second, if they would prefer postponing the battle to a more suitable and less sacred day.

Their better deed was to imprison the envoy and send him on to Perth, to be hanged as soon as his friends were slaughtered.

" Jesus and no quarter," they chose as an appropriate battle-cry, for God had spoken through His ministers,—" and if ever God spoke truth out of my mouth," said one of them, " I promise you in His name a certain victory this day." His promise was backed by numbers, horse, guns and ammunition; who were all to meet nothing but " a pack of naked runagates, not three horse among them, few either swords or muskets."

But they were also, for the first time in history, to meet a Highland charge, led by a man who was not a Highlander.

Montrose saw his flag of truce abused, and Madertie taken prisoner. There was nothing for it now but instant battle. He could not draw up his men in the usual six-line formation, or they would instantly be outflanked. So he placed them three deep, with the Irish in the centre under Macdonald; Kilpont and his bowmen on the left; and himself on foot in trews and plaid, together with Black Pate, at the head of the Atholl men, to confront the trained soldier, Sir James Scott. Montrose wore a helmet, carried a targe on his left arm, and in his right hand a light pike, ' the queen of weapons.' He ordered his front rank to kneel, his second to stoop, his third to stand, and use their pikes or throw their stones over the shoulders of their comrades. The little ammunition they had, he advised keeping till they were in the thick of the enemy.

Some of Elcho's horse made a skirmish, hoping to draw the impetuous Highlanders from their order. But Montrose held them in restraint, and detached only a small force to meet the horse, which they drove back with their pikes on to their own ranks in confusion.

Then was the moment to attack the centre; the Highlanders swept forward, smashing through the infantry and the cannon fire as though they had never feared its roar,—while the shrieking of their battle-cries rose high above it. " *Lamh dearg aboo!* " (" The Red Hand to Victory! "), yelled the Macdonalds.

They made their stones far more effective weapons than the gunners, clumsy with terror, could make their guns; and now, getting at close grips with the enemy, those who had muskets discharged them in their faces, then used them as clubs. The centre broke, and fled back to Perth.

Sir James Scott and his left wing made a rush for higher ground on a ridge that would give him a point of vantage, but Montrose outstripped him with his Atholl men. His mountain training stood him in good stead now, for still he was at the head of his Highlanders as they surged up on to the ridge, where the bees buzzed unconcernedly in the heat of the morning sunshine, and the larks sang overhead.

Soon they brushed the dew from that hillside. With a fierce shout of triumph, he swung them round on to the slower Lowlanders below, and had an instant's vision of their red, gasping faces, as he led the charge down on them. In a few minutes Sir James and his picked levies from Fife had been driven from the ridge, and into the general rout.

The battle had turned to a spate of screaming men and horses, blind with panic; behind them, so that the blood burst their veins with terror, came a red trail of carnage, the yells and terrible laughter of the Highlanders, wilder even than the skirling of their pipes,—closer and closer behind them came those naked red legs, leaping in great strides that no man and not even the horses could outrun. Above the heads of his Highlanders the long red hair of Alasdair blazed in the wind of his own speed, like a flaming banner to lead them to victory. His eyes gleamed white with the lust of killing; men were mowed down round him; like a wolf he leaped up and with one hand snatched a man from his horse, and scarcely paused to kill him as he thrust on.

The city flung open her gates in surrender; the torrent rushed through; but now came the check.

Their commander would have no sack, no looting even. He had prevented the enemies' guns from being turned on their late owners in pursuit; and the Highlanders in their hurry had not much objected.

But to take a town, and then not to be allowed to sack it; it was against all common sense, all fairness; what in God's name were they fighting for? and they half-starved, and the rags falling off their backs, so that for very decency their first duty should be to strip every over-dressed citizen they met, and burn them out of their cellars where they hid,—and yet there the cowards were allowed to stay, snug as rabbits in their burrows,—while this quiet young man who had walked so casually over the hills to them and told them the King had sent him to be their leader, as if indeed that King had been God Himself, and he but just dropped down from the sky,—this elegant young man, who mixed his wine with water instead of drinking himself mad and shouting drunk, like their great leader Alasdair,—this slight young man, whom their Alasdair could have crushed to death between his huge arms as a bear might crush a stag, yet whose commands he followed with quick obedience and delight, and indeed they were never given as commands, but as the common fruit of their two inspirations,—this unaccountable young man in fact was everywhere at once among them, ordering them off the justly earned fruits of their victory,—and for some reason that no one could understand, nor even remember to question till afterwards, no one thought of disobeying.

He even ordered the town's sheriff-clerk to write " a general protection for the inhabitants of the town of Perth." Compensation was to be given to his soldiers; the citizens were to pay fifty pounds to Alasdair, and large contributions of cloth to make new clothes for them all.

Poor fun that. And to-night no doubt there would be feasting and rolling in drink among the leaders, and Alasdair would sway and stagger like a falling tree as he bragged of the numbers he had slain that day, with his cup held high, and the torchlight glinting on his rolling eyes,—and who knew what ungodly cause for mirth and pleasure they would find to finish the feast?

But—" What shall we do with those dirty scoundrels, the ministers, who did their best to call down God's wrath upon us? " said Alasdair.

" We will ask them to dinner," said Montrose.

It was his favourite way of commemorating a victory with his enemies. So the ministers were ' urged ' to come, and dared not refuse, and one of them, Mr. George Halyburton, hastened to remind his host of his family connection with him through William Halyburton of Pitcur, who had been first husband to Montrose's wife's sister, Lady Marjory Carnegie, now the Viscountess of Arbuthnott. And having established this, Mr. George Halyburton said grace.

For that he was sternly reprimanded afterwards by the Covenant. Forced to eat with these rebels against God he may have been, but to have blasphemed by uttering God's holy words over the meat that they had stolen from His children—but here Mr. Halyburton lost his temper and his sense of decency combined, and with a red, angry face replied that he would like to have seen any of the dignitaries of the Kirk who in his place would have refused to do whatever the Marquis bade him—even if it were to kiss the Marquis's— but before he could soil his lips with an image that might have proceeded from the mouth of the coarsest trooper rather than that of a minister of grace, the scandalized congregation of his judges hushed him down.

But no shadow of his future disgrace now fell upon Mr. Halyburton as he sat, proud, though a trifle bewildered, at the board of this Marquis who turned out to be a surprisingly modest young man, and who capped Mr. Halyburton's Latin quotations with a witty ease that made the minister feel what a social success he was himself, and how much better fitted to be the chaplain of marquises (and possibly, whispered his secret heart, even of kings) than the unappreciated minister of a dull commercial city like Perth.

Beside the Marquis sat David Drummond of Madertie, who was to have been hanged that evening, if all had gone as Mr. Halyburton had promised that God had promised, instead of the world turning topsy-turvy. He sat between his friends, Kilpont and Montrose; they clinked glasses with him, and laughed and looked long at each other in their incredulous relief; and, said Montrose to him, leaning across the corner of the table and singing:

> " Now, Davie, my billie, quoth a' the three,
> The day is come thou wast to dee,
> But thou'rt as well at thy dinner here
> Sitting I think 'twixt thee and me."

Here they were back in the old great days, of sudden death suddenly reprieved, and the unexpected, unbelieved re-union of old friends.

But Alasdair was not so happy. Well he knew that " Wherever Macdonald is sitting, that will be the head of the table," as his ancestor had explained on his visit to Queen Elizabeth. And Montrose, while treating him with the same courteous freedom as his old friends, did him all honour. Yet these formal introductions of himself as ' the Major General of His Majesty's

Irishes' made him uncongenially aware of foreign standards; and all this polite talk with ministers, throwing in quotations and college stories, made him shy of drinking or even boasting too much, and exposing himself to the smiles of the Sassenach.

Mr. Halyburton was discussing theology with Madertie, who had shown a very pretty taste in divinity at college. The Macdonald turned a lofty glance upon the white-faced whipper-snapper of a minister, who now inquired of him in a tentative voice as to the religious difficulties in Ireland.

"There are no religious difficulties in my country," replied Alasdair majestically. "There would be no trouble there at all, if it were not for the bloody Protestants."

So grand a retort at his disposal made him glad of his restraint in drink.

But he felt it grossly unfair, for why should a man let himself go in battle, and deal red death in hundreds with his own hand,—and then forgo all the joys of carnage at his leisure and rape and loot; but sit up at table as good a scholar with his tutors, and be paid £50 in due course of time as though it were a lawyer's fee?

He did not know how Montrose had got his Highlanders off their legitimate prey as he had done; it was some sheer power of devilry in the young man,—it was magnificent, but it was not war.

"You cannot keep it up, my lord," he told his commander. "You have put the comether on them, and they are all thronging each other to be eating out of your hand. But you will have to give them their heads next time. A rich fat city like this, and are we to get never a purse nor a woman out of it?"

"Have you not women enough and too many in your train? We cannot feed the half of them."

"The woman of the stranger," said Alasdair gravely, "is ever the one desired."

And in disapproval he listened to his commander's prosaic category of guns and horses and ammunition and clothes stripped off those slain in battle. These were but the winnings in fair fight,

Y

outside the city walls. The city itself should be the prize. And he could not answer for his own men much longer.

They were indeed grumbling furiously at these new-fangled notions of conducting war as though it were a bargain, and one in which the conquered came off best, for half the cloth meted out to them was moth-eaten, and Alasdair's hereditary purse-bearer, MacSporran, complained that he never got his full fifty pounds.

VIII

MONTROSE had his share of the spoil. As he had promised himself, he sent for Master Forrett to bring him
his two elder sons, that he might have a glimpse of them during
the three days which were all that he could stay in Perth.

They hardly believed their ears when they heard the message.
Kinnaird rang with their racing footsteps, their shouted scraps of
news, as they rushed to tell everybody all about it.

" Oh Minnie, have you heard there was a drummer-boy
there, younger than I ? " cried Johnnie, " and they say he's Lord
Kilpont's bastard, and Kilpont means to take him all through
the campaign."

" And have you heard," chimed in James, " that ten of the
fat burghers who went out with the army burst from running
back again to Perth ? just burst,—like bladder footballs,—I wish
I had seen it."

" Our uncle Madertie was envoy and they said they would
string him up,—but, Minnie dear, he's out again now and none
the worse, so don't look troubled,—and yes, he *is* younger, he is
only twelve and I am fourteen,—and oh *where* are my riding
boots,—not the new ones, they pinch, but the old pair that has
just been mended ? "

In half an hour they were to start and find everything they
wanted to take or show to their father. James had written a
poem and could not remember where he had put it—in a box
with three marbles, an elf bolt, and some shells, he *thought,*—
on the other hand it might be in any drawer in any cabinet, or
possibly in one of his shoes, which he persisted in regarding as
a place of safety. His aunt Beatrix told him his father had
always written his poems in the margins of his school books, to
be sure of not losing them,—an unfair reproach, for James had
been rebuked when he did so.

Rob wanted to send the hound puppy to his father, a magnani-
mous instinct, for he had gone about crying dismally when he

339

found that he was not to go with his brothers, and hugging the puppy for consolation, who had supplied it by licking the pleasantly salt-tasting tears from his cheeks.

Johnnie wanted to take so many things that Magdalen knew he hoped to stay on, and when, unwise in her anxiety, she asked him, he flared up and said, why should he not? when Kilpont's bastard had drummed all those yelling Irish into battle, " while I was sitting here, swatting with old Forrett. I tell you, Minnie," (for he had never been able to give up their old baby name for her) " if my father sends me back, or to Saint Andrews, I shall run away from school as Lewis Gordon did when *he* was only thirteen,—and I shall join him wherever he is, and so I shall tell him. None of you have any right to keep me as a child now, when the King needs men."

Though he said the King, it was plain whose royalty and whose need were burning in his eyes. She would not be able to keep him from his father, Magdalen knew that.

> " And therefore for nae venison, Johnnie,
>   I pray ye, gang frae hame."

Venison, or fighting with his father in the thick of it,—no, she could not hope to keep this one.

She wrote an answer to Jamie's note to her and sent it with Master Forrett, for Johnnie might forget it, and she sent a plaid that she had woven from goat's hair as it kept out the damp better than wool, and would be useful when he was sleeping out on the heather again. And she looked out the couple of books he had asked for, and some boots; and ran down into the kitchens for some of her mother's famous short paste and the old Burgundy, since he was entertaining the enemy ministers, and it was well to make friends with the mammon of righteousness; and sewed a button on to Johnnie's coat as he sat already mounted on Red Rowan, for of course he had never noticed it was all but off,— and now as she sewed, she wished he had not noticed it at all, for was it not unlucky to sew anything on a person?—but if so it was too late now, and she must think instead of all the things he was to be sure and remember to tell his father, which she had forgotten to put in her letter.

Red Rowan champed at the bit, and tossed his head, and was in a fever to be off, no less than the boy who sat him, looking down on his mother, with the sunlight and a smiling eagerness on his rainbow-lidded eyes, that only saw her in flashes here and there as he blinked them against the sun, for behind her upturned face that yearned towards him he was seeing a picture of his father on horseback, magnificent, terrible, in the midst of a battlefield strewn with his dead enemies; and of himself riding up to him, and being given the command of half his army.

" Yes, Minnie," and " Indeed I will," and " My dear Minnie, I am not a baby now," and he was gone.

A clatter of hoofs, a cloud of dust, and then the hot sunlight lay as still upon the plain as though those two had not just ridden across it, and vanished.

*   *   *

" Old Forrett will take good care of them," said Beatrix, " he said he would bring them in on the north side of the town, for they say that on the other side you can walk to it from Tippermuir on the dead, and they might engender plague in this heat."

" I wonder why any of us are alive," said Magdalen, looking round the courtyard that had grown so empty.

" To carry on the world," said her sister-in-law, putting her arm round her shoulder and leading her into the house.

She had heard how nearly her husband had met a felon's death through joining this mad adventure of her brother's; yet she was as calmly cheerful and practical as ever.

" She is the woman men need in wars—and women too," thought Magdalen, as Beatrix said to her, " Look, here is poor old Rob left behind, and the boys promised to make him a toy coracle hours ago, and it has never been finished. Have you found some more hazel twigs for it, Rob? Good, then I will get the canvas—we need not oil it till afterwards."

" No, they cannot take Rob yet," thought Magdalen, " but how soon will it be? "

A year, a day, an hour,—time folded in on her, making her its prisoner. She longed to beat against its bars, to bewail her fate, to cry that women should not stand it, that women must rise and refuse to obey their lords ever again, until their lords should obey them in all that really mattered.

" Why, Magdalen, what a long face," said her old father, meeting her in the hall, " the lads have only gone for a couple of days."

IX

THEIR father was not in the battlefield; they did not even come through the battlefield, and bitterly they complained of Master Forrett's old-womanly fussing; they rode into the town, with their cousins of Braco and Orchill in charge of them, and it was all quite tidy, with no sign of the fighting anywhere; the only difference from the Perth they knew so well was in the number of Highlanders that stood about and stared into the shops, some in their worn-out tartan, and some in the oddest variety of dress, snatched from the dead soldiers and citizens that lay outside the gates of the town.

One gaunt fellow wore an alderman's chain across his hairy chest, which his ragged shirt barely covered,—and the flat black velvet cap of magistracy on his floating yellow elf-locks. Another swaggered in a dark-green velvet coat, " very neat and respectable," as he was saying himself in the Gaelic, but his scrawny knees stuck out beneath it, very surprisingly, from under a tattered saffron kilt. A groan, a shriek, a blood-curdling yell made the boys leap in their saddles in hopeful anticipation,—but it was only a piper tuning up at a street corner.

All these lounging strangers stared with a hungry, angry, baffled gaze upon the two boys, their fine horses and silver-mounted harness and rich cloaks.

" The Lord Graham and the Lord James, sons of my lord Marquis of Montrose, the King's Lieutenant," announced Master Forrett hastily and loudly to everyone of whom he asked the way. He was directed to the house of Margaret Donaldson where the Marquis lodged; and there, everyone in the town seemed to be going at once, some at furious speed, captains, and messengers, and burgesses with ledgers under their arms. They went into the high hall of a fine house; it was filled with men coming in and out, and the sound of subdued, respectful voices. They saw their uncle Madertie talking cheerfully to a town councillor; he did not look at all like a man who had just escaped hanging.

343

There, high above them in a gallery at the end of the hall, sat their father at a table, writing. Men in Highland dress stood about him; people came up to him and bowed and murmured questions, and went hastily away again. It gave Johnnie a little shock to see him sitting there so still amongst all the bustle, his head bent over the papers. He looked just the same as when he had read Virgil with them a year ago, and not at all as though he had been wading through blood for three miles.

He saw them and waved a hand to them, and Major William Rollock, whom they had often met at home, came up to them and led them up the wooden stair into the gallery. Their father was before them, they kneeled, and he gave them his blessing, then raised them and kissed them on the cheek and asked how they had left their mother, and was pleased to hear their aunt Beatrix was with her, and wanted to know a crowd of silly little things, even that they had begun to make a toy coracle—" for Rob "—interposed Johnnie hastily, " but we left it to the women to finish."

He was not at all anxious for young James to drag out these childish irrelevances, just when he wanted to impress his father with the obvious fact that he was now a man. It was a pity really that young James had had to come too, it made people class them together, when of course James was ridiculously babyish even for his years. There he was gaping up in the most unabashed manner at a gigantic Highlander who had just come into the gallery with a dog as high as an ass beside him,—and, in a flush of excitement, Johnnie suddenly realized that he was in the presence of that terror to his countryside, already half legendary as hero and villain, Alasdair Macdonald himself.

The Major-General was introduced to the Lord Graham, and won his heart by at once commiserating with him for not having arrived in time for the battle; he asked how many dead he had counted on the way here.

Alas, Johnnie had not had the chance to count any, owing to Master Forrett's ' nursemaid care '; and was for once thankful when James piped up, asking if it were true that Alasdair had killed as many as eight hundred with his right hand alone, and if so, how many had he killed with his left?—"for you are left-handed, are you not, my lord?" asked the literal James.

To which Alasdair replied gravely that he let not his left hand know what his right hand doeth.

With a formality that much flattered James, Alasdair introduced him to all the hereditary officers of his household,—the MacBeth, his physician, who knew the properties of every herb in the world; the MacKinnon, his marshal; the Macduffie, his recorder; the MacLaverty, his speaker; the MacArthur, his piper; the Mac-Sporran, his purse-bearer; the MacVurich, his poet; the MacRury, his smith and armourer.

James wanted to know what happened if the hereditary poet of the day were no good at poetry,—or the purse-bearer no good at accounts—or the harpist had no ear for music. Could they change over?

But the Macdonald had never known of such a case. Driven into a corner by James' relentless logic, he protested that one might just as well ask what happened if a hereditary king were no good at kingship.

James thought for a moment, then answered, "War."

He was an argumentative and persistent youngster. But in any serious matter the Irishman's reasons were such as to appeal to him. When Alasdair in his good nature escorted them to their rooms across the road, they heard a fluttering and banging against the rafters, and found that a robin had flown in at the open window. Alasdair put up his huge hand and caught it, then placed it very gently between James' hands; and the boy, feeling the soft, warm creature, its heart beating so fast against his fingers, demanded a cage, that he might keep it always.

But Alasdair told him he must never imprison nor harm a robin, who has borne the blood of Christ on his breast ever since he sat on the Cross and sang to comfort the dying Christ,— "and if we had but the understanding of birds' language, we should hear that it is the Mass he is singing to this day."

"Are you a Papist?" asked James in a shocked voice, putting

Johnnie on tenterhooks. He felt it was his mother's fault for encouraging James; he hoped that Alasdair would make excuses for his youth, as he could not guess that the boy though so small, was nearly eleven,—far too old to be hoisted up on to Alasdair's shoulder, even though it were done in compensation when James confided to him his fear that he would never be as tall as Johnnie.

" You are tall enough now, then," said the Irishman, and told him of a giant in his own country, who was so tall that he had to go up a ladder to brush his own hair.

At the banquet that evening, the boys sat on either side of him, and heard, as the giant drank deeper, how the first Donald of his race had cut off his own hand, and flung it from his boat on to the island shore, that he might be the first to touch and own it, and that was why they had the Bleeding Hand on their coat of arms; as well as the galley that the three princes had sailed in from Ireland to Scotland,—but the Campbells stole that for the galley of Lorne in their coat of arms—" as they steal everything."

Johnnie leaned forward with a provocative gleam in his eye. " I heard," he said, " that the Campbells sailed in that galley in the Flood, because they were too proud to go with Noah in his Ark."

" They were not," shouted Alasdair,—" they were too mean to pay the ferry fee. And what did they get by it in the end? for their galley was rotten for lack of a ha'porth of tar, the way they were all sunk."

" Then how is it there are Campbells to this day? " inquired James.

" Because the sea spewed 'em up again, knowing they were born to be hanged."

And his laughter engulfed all the other voices round the table.

Madertie, always a considerate man, saw to it that the two boys got enough of the sweetmeats and not too much of the wine.

Montrose watched with pride and amusement while James echoed his mother's deliberate little air, and Johnnie, like an adventurous but well-mannered pup, enjoyed tackling Alasdair. The boy was shaping well—a fine head and carriage of his shoulders, and taller than he himself had been at his age.

As he looked at his son's shining and sleepy eyes, he felt as though he were living his life over again,—a life just such as he had wished when, at the same age as Johnnie was now, he had sat nodding at his father's funeral feast. Round him then had been all his relatives, and here were many of them again,—the old familiar names, though in scarcely any instance the same faces as had borne them then,—the Grahams of Fintry and of Orchill, the Grahams of Braco, of Balgowan, of Nether-Cairnie, of Inchbrakie. In the past, they or their fathers had prosed to him their good advice on agriculture, while he had wished that the days of adventure were not over.

They were not over, they were here again, and himself directing them. A few months ago he had been a hanger-on at the English Court, unable to get an audience. Now he was a Highland chieftain; his second-in-command and Major-General, that ogre in war, who was solemnly telling his small boy how he had once seen the black soul of Judas look out of the eyes of a seal on the Irish shore.

The two worlds that made his life were strangely mingled at that moment. Magdalen's letter lay inside his shirt, and now and again he touched the plaid she had woven for him, " since you are a Highlander now, Jamie, and when shall I see you again? "

He could stroke her handiwork, into which had gone so many waiting thoughts, and not the softness of her hair.

* * *

Like a stone thrown into a hive, setting the enemy all astir, came the news of Tippermuir. One of them wrote, " Lothian and his regiment are to guard Stirling Bridge. Argyll is marching. Calender, Lindsay, Montgomerie, Dalhousie, Lawers are posting from Newcastle with their regiments of horse and foot."

It was exactly what Montrose had wanted. He was taking the weight off the siege of Newcastle, and relieving the King's forces in England. But he must deal another lightning blow before any more of his new troops drifted away. The Atholl men all found it worth while to take their plunder home, and so did most of the rest of the Scots Highlanders, little as they said they had got.

After a couple of days, practically only the Irish remained,—" and I," said Johnnie, " for you need every man and horse you can keep with you now, and if old Forrett stays, why should I not stay too? "

Old Forrett had said he was not so old but that he could still be my lord's secretary and purse-master; and well he had proved it within a few hours of his arrival at Perth, in counting out the contributions levied on the town, and showing where they fell short.

" I followed your lordship's journeyings," he said, " when you were less than the age of Lord Graham here."

" And did you not then say that I used to play spillikins with your bones, jolting you backwards and forwards over the Grampians? "

" If I did, it's no consolation to sit on a cushion, and know that nobody takes count every time the roughness of the road costs your lordship's nags another shoe."

His former pupil smiled down on the crumpled old face, eager as a schoolboy's. " So you too will be a Highlander? " he said.

He would, he won his point, and then Lord Graham began on his. He would not go home again, nor to school with young James at Old Montrose. Wherever he was sent, he would not stay, and if he did, ten to one their enemies would swoop on him, and carry him off, so what would be the odds? It was his strongest argument. Magdalen was still unmolested, but then she was with her father and he too old now to fight, and still not too much on one side or the other,—" but with me there, of fighting age, the balance would just topple over," cried Johnnie, flushed with this urgent exercise of his wits, pressing against his father's shoulder as he sat in his chair, as he wondered, considered, longed to do as the boy suggested, and take him with him on his mad career.

It was true that of all people his just-grown son, the young

Lord Graham, would not now be safe away from him. So said his logic and reason, trying to sound unbiassed; but behind them his longing heart urged that since he had left and must leave his home behind, he should take this much of it with him, should see his boy grow into manhood, in a wild, mountaineering campaign that was more like a boy's dream of soldiering than the prosaic reality of modern mechanical warfare.

So he consented, and wrote many reasons for it to Magdalen; but the thought of her left without either of them would catch him suddenly as he slept, tired out as he was, so that he would start awake, crying, " We will come back to you! Do not be so afraid ! "

" A soldier should not marry, still less than a monk," he told Forrett, who seemed to doubt the advisability of any man following such a practice. He sent young James, who was very sorrowful, back to Kinnaird, while Johnnie rode gaily on with him and Alasdair and Madertie and Kilpont and young Wat, with whom he made great friends, in spite of his own seniority, and tried to play his drum, but could never learn to manage the sticks properly, and asked him if he had really walked to Perth on the bodies of slain foes.

Wat was disappointingly uncertain. He thought he had seen a dead man, but could not be sure, there had been no time to notice anything. His fingers were still cramped from drumming, and that was all he could really tell about the fight. Anyone who had had a glimpse of him marching sturdily through that devil's throng, hands whirring his frenzied tattoo, head up, seeing nothing, hearing nothing but the rhythm of his drum, could have told Johnnie that what the boy had walked on then had been air.

X

IT was a much smaller force Montrose now led to the attack of Lord Burleigh's army at Aberdeen, which he must smash in a few days, or get caught between it and Argyll's. He hoped, too, to recruit cavalry in the north, and was joined by old Lord Airlie and his two sons, Sir David and Sir Thomas Ogilvy, with forty-five horsemen. An adventurous kinsman of Huntly's, Nathaniel Gordon, ex-pirate and ex-brigand, who had lately fought in that abortive rising of the head of his house, also joined him with thirty horse.

But he had no more luck than Alasdair had had in wooing Huntly himself, who stayed sulking at the Bog of Gight,—" And well is it named," cried Alasdair bitterly, " since all who place their hopes on the Gay Gordons walk on uncertain and marshy ground."

Huntly had sworn that if the King should fall, he cared not if himself and his house were buried beneath the rubbish. He seemed now to prefer that condition, to serving beside the young man who years ago had forestalled all his lumbering movements with his lightning marches, and made him, the Cock o' the North, look a fool before his men, as they rode past the churchyard wall of Turriff. That sour reflection—' it is your own doing '—was all Montrose had for comfort, as he looked in vain for help from the Gordons.

His first, almost inexplicable success shook him as it will shake a man who has been forced to wait too long in inactivity before trying his luck. That first success might so easily prove the only one. All round him he heard news of his lands being confiscated and his friends imprisoned. His need to hurry urged him day and night. He would lie awake, wondering what he must do the moment he got up, and then found he had barely slept an hour.

Early one morning, little Wat, who had been sleeping out on the heather, came crying to him with the terrible news that he had found his father lying murdered in his tent.

350

Kilpont had shared his tent with his lieutenant, a Highlander, James Stewart, who had stabbed him in the night, and escaped to Argyll. There, as they soon heard, he was welcomed with a free pardon, and, it was supposed, a reward. For Argyll now offered a reward of £1600 sterling to whomsoever would murder Montrose. The murderer of Kilpont then may have been an agent in a plot against higher game, had been discovered by Kilpont, and so stabbed him. Only one thing was certain from this crime, that the Covenant had decided to observe none of the rules of war. Assassination, and the hanging of envoys, were encouraged as praiseworthy weapons in God's work.

" And these are the foes," said Alasdair, " to whom you will be kind at the expense of your friends. If I had that man here who stabbed Kilpont, a Stewart as he was, but a cur with the heart of a Campbell,—then I would pluck that heart from his living breast, and glad I would be to do this small thing for your friend. But you no doubt would be trying him with a court of law and allow him every justice. My lord, in times like these, justice must run in a red torrent or not at all."

" Wait," Montrose told him.

His face was dark and compressed these days. Johnnie did not care to stay by him. He sought out young Wat, who was suffering passionately for the death of his father. Little enough he had seen of that gay, handsome and witty young man, but he had come into his humdrum life at the pastrycook's at Saint Andrews like a young god out of the sky, had put him into college, had had him taught the gorgeous art of drumming, and then started him on this impossibly exciting adventure. But now his father was killed, and the adventure would soon be over for himself.

Johnnie hotly declared that his own father would look after Wat, as he had promised Kilpont; and himself and Wat would fight out the campaign together. " It will be up in the mountains next, you know, to beard Argyll in his own lair. We shall have such a winter as no soldiers have ever seen before. My father says we must travel light, without tents. We can make fires in the woods perhaps, and toast venison on the points of our dirks, and hear the wolves howl, while we lie snug in the heather."

In the shimmering dusk of an early September, the prospect seemed one of fairyland. They had been out in the wood with catapults and stones, such as the street boys were using as real weapons now in Paris, to see if they could not get a rabbit or two without wasting any ammunition. It would all be good practice.

Now they made a fire of bracken and dead wood and flung themselves before it; they lay on their elbows in the thick leaf mould, their shoulders hunched in curves like a puppy's, their legs stretched out in lithe repose. Johnnie had made a whistle out of an elder stem, and was playing one of the piper's tunes upon it; for once he was the musician while Wat lay and criticized and drummed an accompaniment with one stick against the trunk of a tree.

A wild cat ran along a branch a little way off, and crouched, glaring at them, its globed eyes magnified into green lamps in the firelight. Wat drew out his catapult, but before he could take aim, the great round head and its Chinese devil's stare had vanished.

The woods grew thick and dark; a stream lisped and rippled unseen below; a tiny crescent moon hung low down, caught in the branches of a tree.

"Turn the silver in your pockets," said Johnnie, but Wat had none.

"We will wish instead," he said, and they wished, but not aloud, for to tell would destroy the power of their wishes. Yet they must have been much the same, to judge by the talk that followed. They made plans for the future; they would continue to have adventures together, and by the side of Montrose. They would never go home until the three of them had conquered Scotland for the King, and Johnnie had killed Argyll; and Wat, the slayer of his father.

At that, sorrow fell on him again, that he should have forgotten his father while he had hunted and talked and laughed with his friend. But Johnnie flung his arm round his shoulder and would not let him blame himself—" Your father liked you to be happy and us to be friends, as he was with my father—and so we will be, always."

Soon Wat was chuckling as he told Johnnie how he had cajoled the man who had been chosen as envoy to Aberdeen to-morrow, to let him go with him.

" You might have asked for me too."

" My lord would never hear of your going."

" Nor you either."

" Ah, but he need not hear of me."

" Well, he shall then."

Wat sat bolt upright in the firelight; his eyes, that had been wet for his father, now bright with anger.

" Is my Lord Graham a sneak? "

" He is not. You make me talk like the Macdonald. Sit down and stop being a fool. But I think perhaps I may be one —or worse, a coward,—if I do not tell him. Look how they would have hanged my uncle Madertie."

" *After* their victory. And that they'll never get. My lord of Montrose wears victory on his face."

" He has not lately," muttered Johnnie, but so low that Wat did not catch the words, and took them for a growl of dissent to his project.

" In any case they would never trouble to hang or imprison a drummer-boy," he pursued, " and it gives an envoy importance to have one with him. Say what you like, it is the drummer-boys who give an air to the army."

" What is there to be gained by it? "

" Why, I shall see the town, at peace, before we all come hurtling into it, and I shall see the fat magistrates' faces go purple when they read my lord's letter, and I shall get a drink, and perhaps a silver coin to turn in my pockets at the next new moon."

" You'll never keep it till then! "

They laughed and rolled over and talked of other things, contentedly at peace in that eternal summer evening that is only known in boyhood.

z

XI

ONTROSE sent his envoy to the citizens of Aberdeen to command their surrender. Should they defy him, he warned them to remove all old people, women and children to a distance outside the city walls, since the flight of their armies would be directly through the streets of the town, and those who remained could expect no quarter.

The envoy returned safely but in a white fury; he told his commander that those inhuman butchers had killed a child under a flag of truce.

Montrose's face went grey in a sudden horrible fear.

"Not my Lord Graham. He is safe, sir. It was only a little drummer-boy who would come with me, the poor little rascal, he was so eager, I hadn't the heart to refuse him,—and the magistrates were kind to him and gave him a silver coin, but then, as we came away, someone shot the boy dead,—for the sake of the coin, I daresay. We had to leave the poor lad unavenged."

Young Wat had won his silver coin and lost it,—murdered within a week of his father's same fate.

Had it indeed been Lord Graham who now lay dead in that treacherous town, Montrose would have sent the city up in smoke to avenge him. Should he do less for this boy, whom he had already loved, as he had loved his father,—who had been needlessly, brutally smashed to death for the sake of a silver coin?

A hot red mist swam before his eyes; there was the smell of blood in his nostrils. For the only time in his life he knew that vampire rage that can make a man long to tear his enemy to pieces, with teeth as well as hands. He turned to Alasdair, and the chieftain flinched before the look on his face. But his speech was calm.

"If we win, your men shall have the sack of this city," was all he said.

The magistrates had written that they understood no quarter

354

was to be given, "except to old persons, women and children." That was not what he had written. He had told them to remove all old persons, women and children, or they could expect no quarter. They had not obeyed him; they should have no quarter.

They had understood well enough, their heads were the hardest in Scotland,—a city of granite heads, granite hearts, of a skinflint meanness that counted a coin above a boy's life,—in his rage he felt that he had always hated Aberdeen,—that when he had squandered the wine in her streets for the beggars to drink, it was because he had wished to see them running red with the blood of her parsimonious citizens.

Johnnie came running to him, crying for the death of his friend, and for vengeance,—" Kill them, sir, kill them all, the brutes, the devils,—but, oh sir, I knew he was going, and I did not tell you because he would have called me a sneak,—and I let him go without me."

" Be still," said his father, " he shall have vengeance."

So quiet was his voice that Johnnie's grief and rage froze together. He stared at his father's face, and fell silent.

Montrose gave the order to march.

* * *

He avoided the fortified Bridge of Dee, which he had taken five years before, but at the cost of so much trouble. This time he had crossed the river higher up, and led his army down the north bank to where Lord Burleigh's marched to meet him, with over two thousand infantry and five hundred horse. This was about two miles from the town. Montrose's infantry had dwindled to fifteen hundred, but he now had far more weapons and ammunition, about seventy-five horsemen, and the nine guns he had taken at Tippermuir,—these considerably smaller and lighter than Burleigh's artillery.

He divided his cavalry into two bodies to guard each wing of his infantry, with Nathaniel Gordon commanding the left, and Sir William Rollock the right. He and all his men, to avoid confusion with the enemy, had stuck a bunch of oats in their bonnets, plucked from the ripe cornfields near by. He was now on horseback, with his son and Lord Airlie and the younger Ogilvys by his side, and Alasdair commanding his Irish in the centre.

The first move was to the Covenanters; under cover of their heavier artillery fire, they took some cottages and garden walls that had the ill luck to lie between the two armies, but were soon driven out from this point of vantage by Alasdair and his men, who got ahead of the rest of the army.

Young Lewis Gordon rode out from the Covenanters at the head of his eighteen horsemen on a little charge of his own, in the grand manner, all firing their pistols, then wheeling round and retiring at the caracole. It made no more impression than if it had been, as it looked, an exercise at a cavalry school; and other isolated charges followed with as little result.

But under cover of these flourishes against Montrose's right wing, a hundred of Burleigh's horse and four hundred foot worked their way round to the rear of his left flank, and would have demolished it, had not Montrose got wind of their manœuvre in time, and ordered Sir William Rollock to swing his cavalry on the right wing round to the aid of Nathaniel Gordon's.

This left the right wing defenceless, and now from Burleigh's army came Forbes of Craigievar and his troopers, in no elegant caracole, but in a fierce charge to mow down the Irish infantry. They were not mown down. By order of Alasdair, who was as cool now in this desperate moment as he had been laughing mad at Tippermuir, the Irish fell back on either side and let the troops crash through, then closed on them from behind, so that now it seemed that it was the cavalry that were being mowed down. Saddle after saddle was seen to be riderless, emptied by musket fire or the thrust of the pike, or clutch of the Highlanders, who held on with one hand while they stabbed with the other. The troop was swallowed up, and scarcely one returned from that charge.

Montrose had now had several hours of hard, uncertain fighting, with none of the sheer animal excitement and astonishment of Tippermuir, but with his brain strung taut and cold with the necessity to watch every corner at once of this confused battle-field.   He had been backwards and forwards from one end of his troops to the other, now dividing, now consolidating his cavalry.

Not till that small force was all but exhausted did he see his first real opportunity that day.   The enemy's cannon were doing heavy damage, but the Irish had learned to disprove that

> " There's not a man in Highland dress
> Can face the cannon's roar."

Said one of them, winking up at his Commander-General, as he helped finish the ghastly work of a cannon ball by cutting the skin that still attached him to his severed leg,—" I am sure your Honour will be mounting me in the cavalry, now I can no longer fight in the foot."

" I will be mounting you this moment," Montrose answered him, and ordered one of his few horsemen to get him out of the thick of the fight; then, in the same breath, swerved, galloped down the ranks, shouting to his men to club their muskets, bring out their claymores and get to close quarters with their enemy. He swept his whole battle line forward into the centre of the Covenanters' army, broke through, and drove it back to Aberdeen. Hundreds were slaughtered before the city was reached; through the streets of the city the pursuit and butchery continued.   Now Alasdair's men had their way, and were allowed to work their will on the conquered town, unchecked.

Montrose left the town for his camp.   Master Forrett came and pleaded with him; the wise and kindly Madertie thought it a mistake to alienate the city, which had been loyal in the past, and was Covenant probably only by compulsion.

But Montrose would listen to neither reasoning nor pity.   His ears were deafened with a loud singing noise like many waters. The hard-won contest had only intensified the red mist that swam before his eyes.   For hours he had seen blood, smelled it, drawn blood spurting from men's veins, tasted it from his own lips, which he had bitten as he fought.

He did not stay in the town, not only because he would not

call off his men, nor see what they were doing, but because he did not know what he himself might do if he were there.

There may come a time in a man's life when it is torn up by the roots, and reversed. Such a time had come to Montrose. All that he had cared and worked for before, justice and pity and the defence of the defenceless, were now torn up from his mind, leaving it raw and bleeding. Of what use was it to think that he could struggle on against the stream, that he could uphold what his enemies had determined to destroy?

The price of assassination lay on his head; they had tried to murder Madertie; they had murdered Kilpont and his son. This was the world as he must now know it. The stream of life ran dark, its courses evil—bloodshed and tyranny and treachery and the cruel greed of money—these things made up the life of man.

He had thought he could make it a splendid and a shining thing; he was wrong. Let Alasdair's men rob and rape and tear the clothes from their victims before they killed, so that they should not be stained with blood. What did it matter how many people died, now that hope was dead, and the young lovely courage that had once leaped in the heart of a boy, mad with excitement in his first adventure, whose fair body now lay rotting in the midst of a screaming city.

*   *   *

Johnnie had plunged into his tent, and there stood swaying, his eyes bloodshot and staring. His father moved heavily towards him, asked if he were hurt.

He answered thickly, " Alasdair took me to see it. I thought it would be sport. I saw a woman——" he stopped, turned a liverish brown, and collapsed at the door of the tent, where he was violently sick.

Montrose lifted him and put him on his bed, where he moaned a little, turning his head away from his father. His eyes still wore that glazed look of horror. They would lose it, but they would never again look as they had done yesterday. Always at the back of them there would now lie the knowledge of what evil could be seen in the world.

Looking down upon his face, Montrose knew that he had killed something in this boy, as surely as that the other had been murdered.

He called Forrett to attend to his son, and rode out into the streets. For a few moments he sat his horse, dully looking on at what he saw.

What had these shrieking victims to do with his dark mood, or with the death of his drummer-boy? What did it help that another scene of horror was added to the world, and by him? Was murder to beget murder for ever, until at the latter end the world was wiped out in blood? Then all he had fought for was in vain, was now made vain by him.

He looked round him on the death, not of his enemies, but his hopes.

A man rushed out from a doorway, through a little crowd that was being horribly busy, and flung himself on his horse for protection. In his bonnet he had stuck a wisp of oats, Montrose's own badge, in the vain hope it might prove a safeguard. Two Irish Highlanders were pursuing him, and would have dragged him back into his house to torture him to reveal his treasure, but Montrose drew his sword and laid it across the man's shoulders towards his pursuers.

" You will leave this man to the King's Lieutenant," he said.

The Highlanders stared up at the figure on the horse for the first time, then wheeled round to leave their victim, in search of other quarry. But Montrose called them back, and commanded them to stay by him and help stop the sack. " We must be out of this town at once," he said, " and at Kintore ten miles away."

He found Alasdair and told him his decision; he did not even think to notice what effect it had on him. He had made up his mind what should be done, and nobody and nothing should turn him from it.

The men had got out of hand, and it was hard work to tear them off their prey. He ordered trumpets to sound and a proclamation to be given to get them out of the town. They thought Argyll was upon them, and this helped the more clear-headed to obey. Those who were more than half drunk, or maddened with lust and bloodshed, were dragged off by their fellows. In time they were all outside the city, reeling and stumbling into the line of march.

Then came the toll of the city's dead. Somewhere from a hundred and thirty to a hundred and sixty was the loose estimate, —nothing to be compared with the sacks in the German and Swedish wars, said the old campaigners. Nor were the names of any women among those registered as murdered. On the other hand, a number of these now followed the army among the horde of Irish women and children.

The list of the horrors might well have been worse. But the exact number of those killed was as immaterial as when Montrose had seen the whole world swim in blood because of ' the death of ane.' Was not the death of Christ but ' the death of ane '?

He had allowed a sack, and a sack of what was in the main a loyal city. Worse, he had handed on the old hideous tradition of revenge that had wrecked Scotland again and again, and was wrecking it now. He had done this although he had seen it so clearly; and therefore his blood-guiltiness was blacker than Alasdair's.

The first thing he did when they got to Kintore was to call his son to him, tell him that the sack had been stopped, and would never be allowed again.

" Looting there may be," he said, " but for any outrage or murder the punishment will be hanging, and so I will let them know, as soon as they are sober enough to take it in."

The boy stood red and sullen. He felt he had shown himself a weakling; he tried to mutter something about not caring what happened to a lot of greasy citizens. His father put his hand on his shoulder, and swung him round that he might look him in the face.

" That is a lie," he said. " You know, as I do, that what I have done to this city is a foul and horrible thing, that it will be a lasting blot on my name. I ask you to help me see to it that there shall never be another."

Johnnie looked at him in helpless devotion. He felt, as many men had felt and would feel, how gladly he would die if it could prevent any harm or dishonour coming to this man.

He had lost his childish confidence in the goodness of the world, but in its stead he now won, though all unknowingly, a deeper knowledge of good and evil,—that they might exist in the same person, even to extremes,—but that the good would last when the evil had crumbled off and become merely an ill-famous story, inexplicable and unattached, throwing no light on the main character, so that in time,

> " like tales
> Ill told and unbelieved, they pass away,
> And go to dust forgotten."

But all that the boy saw of this knowledge was that already he could not believe his father had really given the order to sack Aberdeen.

" It was not you," he mumbled shamefacedly.

XII

AFTER they had left Aberdeen, Montrose watched his son carefully, fearing some breakdown, But it was he himself and not Lord Graham who fell ill, and that so seriously that his life was despaired of, and his enemies eagerly gave out the news of his death. It was a collapse after severe fatigue and strain. Exactly a month ago he had left Carlisle, disguised as a groom, to work his way up north, and since then he had done and dared so much that all his nerves of mind and body had been tautened to snapping point.

In his delirium he spoke often of Aberdeen, worried that if he did not sit still, his portrait would never be done in time for his wedding,—called to Lady Pitsligo, nodding like a cockatoo in the gallery at three black crows below,—complained that they had broached barrels of blood in the street for the beggars to drink, and one cried, " Take, drink, this is my wine ! " And at that his ravings grew worse; he seemed to confuse his son with the murdered drummer-boy, and to regard himself as the slayer.

As though his unconscious mind now paid the penalty, his delirium helped to efface the memory of the sack from his son's. The boy's frantic anxiety lest his father would die or go mad, left him no room for images of past horror.

When he heard that their enemies had ordained a day of public thanksgiving to God for the supposed death of the King's Lieutenant, he sobbed in helpless fury; and that was the moment when Montrose, recovering consciousness for the first time, asked to see his son, noticed his red eyes, and put one or two faint but penetrating questions to him. Johnnie hated to croak the ill-omened news, but there was no cheating those eyes, even now that they were dulled by fever.

" They are giving thanksgiving services that they are delivered from ' this ravening lion of Montrose.' "

To his intense relief, a smile stole over his father's wasted face.

" Find me my Aesop," he whispered.

Johnnie found the battered copy that Montrose had had at Saint Andrews; then with a sudden, delighted guess at his father's meaning, he turned to the fable of the lion who shammed dead, and then arose to astound his enemies.

" Here it is—and yourself, my lord," he said, showing it to him. The weak head on the pillow gave a nod, the eyes closed at the same moment, and Montrose had his first natural sleep since his illness.

In a very few days he was up again and declaring that he was as strong as ever. It was Lord Graham's good news, he said, showing how well he had put the fear of God into his enemies, that had hastened his recovery.

Other news hastened it still more rapidly. Alasdair had determined to go west and see how his own castles there were faring, and to raise recruits among the Clan Donald by telling them of the victories he had won, together with the mighty Montrose. Hereditary bard and harpist and piper and speaker and recorder were all hard at work commemorating those victories, with so exclusive an eye to their effect on the Clan Donald that there was scarcely any room left to mention the mighty Montrose.

So their leader was left for the present with only five hundred men, and no chance as yet of getting in the third smashing victory which he had hoped would bring in the whole of eastern Scotland to the King's banner. So far from that, recruiting in these parts had been set back by the sack of Aberdeen. It might be the ordinary method of civil war on the Continent, but no true Scot was going to serve with a Commander who expected him to sack his native cities. Put like that, it proved a most effective piece of propaganda.

Argyll's activities were not so well advertised. Without the provocation of any fight, he was putting to fire and sword the houses and lands of everyone suspected of even sympathy with the King's cause. His army overran and devastated most of Huntly's domains; and he kept by his side his two nephews, George, Lord Gordon, and Lord Lewis, in helpless witness of the destruction of their father's property. Their uncle held them in a grip stronger than armed force; it was their father's endless debts to him that made them his prisoners. With nearly all the Huntly estates mortgaged to him, Argyll was virtually the head of the house, and now took the Bog of Gight itself for his head-quarters.

He had with him over two thousand five hundred foot and fifteen hundred cavalry, yet complained that his army was too small; so that fresh levies had to be sent to him from Leslie's armies in the north of England. He had been careful not to reach either Perth or Aberdeen too quickly after the battles; in each case he marched into the city only when Montrose's little army had marched out of it several days before. Scotland was beginning to complain that their uncrowned King Campbell was not a sound man to have at the head of military affairs.

And no secretary could put on paper the complaints of old Leslie, now Lord Leven, at parting with his much-needed regiments in England, to a commander who had already more than three times the number of his opponents.

Montrose had written a despatch to the King and sent it by Sir William Rollock from Kintore, soon after his victory at Aberdeen, and was humanly glad that he had done so while the news could be so good. He would now have little to give beyond that of some few recruits, among them about a hundred and fifty Gordon cavalry from Strathbogie.

With an army whose total was not a thousand, he proceeded to bait Argyll's huge force, burned the lands of Covenanters in answer to its laying waste of loyalist country, and led it a dance all round the Gordon and Angus country,—' a strange coursing,' Argyll's now doubtful admirers began to call it.

Here, there, and everywhere at once moved Montrose's army, keeping close to the friendly foot-hills that fringed the Central Highlands, and darting from them whenever he saw his opportunity to harry the Covenanter armies that marched ponderously through the Lowlands along the east coast. The small band of wanderers was now as tough and wiry as a winter herd of deer, and travelling nearly as light, for they had buried in the bog the cannon they had won at Tippermuir and Aberdeen; and all the women and children had gone west with Alasdair.

And after these mountaineers, all round the north-east of Scotland, and round and round again, there lumbered, at a distance of a week's march, Argyll's army of four thousand, with its pipers proudly announcing that 'the Campbells were coming, hurrah, hurrah!'

In the centre of it, more important, and certainly a deal more active than all his horses and men, was the pocket committee that he took everywhere with him to represent the Government, so that through it he could issue his commands to the nation. The seat of Government had become a floating company, which, with discussion and doubt and question, argued and debated and hampered and hindered every movement that its generals wished to make, so that it was invariably made a week late.

Until suddenly, through a piece of bad intelligence work on the part of his usually excellent scouts, Montrose found his army almost within firing range of Argyll's, which he had thought as far away as the Grampians.

He was in as bad a trap as any enemy could hope to drive him. He was at Fyvie Castle, on the Ythan, a house surrounded on three sides by bog. His hundred and fifty Gordon horse had just deserted in the almost inadvertent manner peculiar to the Highland regiments, whose home affairs were liable to assume inconvenient prominence in the middle of a campaign. He had no more than fifty horse and eight hundred foot in all; and, what was worse, he had run clean out of ammunition.

Argyll's intelligence work had been better than his enemy's, for he knew of all these facts, and for once, with the odds at rather more than five to one, felt bold enough to attack. On the one side of the house that was not a bog, lay a rough ridge of low hills unusually well-wooded for that part of the country, and these Montrose seized upon as his only possible point of vantage. But as he hurried there, he saw that a regiment of Argyll's foot had already occupied the dikes and low stone walls to about half-way up the hill.

Below, was the vast body of the main army,—a thousand of the Campbell clan, fifteen hundred militia, seven troops of cavalry under Lothian, Argyll's master of horse, and fourteen more under the Earl Marischal. The infantry who had already taken possession of the lower slopes of the hill were picked marksmen with their muskets,—and Montrose's men had neither powder nor shot.

He turned to a young Irish officer in command of one of Alasdair's regiments, whose pluck and dash he had already noticed.

" Come, O'Cahan, let us get our powder and shot out of these fellows."

Manus O'Cahan grinned back at him. This would be something to tell in Ballymena. At the head of his company he crashed down through the scrub; their pikes and claymores gleamed like a torrent through the brown autumn trees; then came the yell of their battle-cry—*Lamh dearg aboo!*—as they launched themselves on their entrenched foes, and soon cleared that formidable position of the enemy. Manus O'Cahan trudged up the hill again with some of his men, and proudly laid several bags of powder at the feet of their commander.

Said one of them softly, " We'll have to be going back again for the bullets. The stingy hucksters have left us none with the powder."

" You will have to run fast to catch up with your enemy," said Montrose,—and they could see the flying musketeers already joining the main army down below. Movement was now visible all through it; were they going to attack in whole force? No, they were beginning to retire across the Ythan,—it could only be for the moment, Montrose was certain of that. Even if Argyll wished to abandon the attack after the failure of a single regiment, Lothian and Marischal could never permit such a disgrace.

" So they have gone off to hold a committee," cried young Lord Graham, dancing up and down in his excitement, " and they will dispute the next move in the battle, 'and fifthly, my brethren, and sixthly, and seventhly——' " He found that if he stood still he was shivering all over, which was most unfair, for he was not at all afraid.

But he had no chance to stand still, nor had anyone else, for his father was commanding them to lay their hands on every pewter plate and vessel in the castle and melt them down as fast as they could, " and we'll have shot to go with this powder by the time those sluggards have crawled back again."

All over the castle they rushed, looking for pewter and lead, dragging down the beautifully-wrought leaden cisterns and gutter-pipes from the roof. High up behind the battlements of warm red stone, there had been added in Queen Mary's day an extra floor of sloping roofed rooms. Johnnie Graham peered in at an attic window, uttered a whoop which he quickly checked, looked round to see that no one should share his spoil, and then crawled into the attic.

A few minutes later, he came clanking and hurtling down the stairs like a troop of knights in mediaeval armour, and plunged up to the bread-baking furnace in the huge kitchen. There, directing the boiling down of the lead into bullets, was Manus, son of the Giolla Dubh MacCahan that was foster-brother to the Earl of Antrim,—a lean long young man who softly whistled a tune, while his steady slits of eyes never flickered from the seething cauldron.

" Where have you been, my fine hero? " he shouted to his General's son,—" Come and serve scullion under me, for it's head cook I am here."

" Not a scullion,—I'm a chambermaid," gasped out Johnnie, flinging his spoil down at O'Cahan's feet.

It proved to be a quite irrational number of pewter chamber-pots that had been stored in the attic,—and shouts of laughter attended their conversion into shot.

The word came that five hundred of the Covenanter cavalry, with Lothian himself at their head, were moving out to the attack. Down charged the Irish musketeers, holding on to the looped leather stirrups of Montrose's fifty horsemen; and delivered their volley, so well placed and so utterly unexpected, that Lothian's attack was turned into a rout, which might easily have been a massacre had the cavalry been allowed to get still deeper into the wood. But the musketeers were too eager to start their 'Charge of the Chamber-pots,' as this was called ever after.

As it was, the five hundred troopers who fled back to the main army spread such terrifying reports of men who had been ammunitionless a few hours before, and had now been supplied by the devil himself, that any skirmishing that followed lost all its effect before it started. The Earl Marischal's brother, the best of the Covenanting officers, was killed, and Argyll, utterly disheartened by his first personal attempt in the field, moved his army once again across the Ythan.

He told Marischal that he had been unlucky to him and to his poor brother, and said something under his breath about the Lord having always loved to chasten him. But Marischal refused to play up to his appointed rôle as bereaved brother; he muttered venomously that any one would love to chasten a man who insisted on putting water between him and his enemy.

Quarrels and complaints seethed round Argyll as he slowly withdrew his army, having found that during their second retirement, Montrose and his men had slipped away under cover of the night. He felt that his own clan avoided his eyes,—and all because he hated to waste their lives in unnecessary risks. He could see so clearly how great would be the loss, how slight the advantage; he was the wisest statesman in Scotland, who had guided his country clear of English and royal interference, and put them into a fair way to rule themselves through the spiritual democracy of the Kirk. Yet all this counted for nothing, because he could not swagger and spill blood and say the right word on the spur of the moment in the heat of battle, like that swashbuckler, Montrose. It was unfair. He had not been brought up as a soldier, nor as a Highland chieftain. He had studied at Saint Andrews, and gone in for archery and golf.

So had Montrose, was the exasperating answer.

Then Argyll proved himself the statesman. He offered free passes to all Montrose's officers (who numbered nearly half his army since Alasdair's departure) and the surety of his protection, should they wish to go home and see to their estates, now that the winter was coming on them, and no sensible man could think of going on fighting until the spring came again.

Montrose, now in the Gordon country at Strathbogie again, hoping that after his three victories, Huntly would surely join him, hoping too that Alasdair and his men might arrive at any moment, held a council of war.

At this council one after the other of his officers pointed out that the days were drawing in, and the snow was creeping down the mountains, that fighting was a summer's job, and a mountain campaign in winter might kill them all, certainly those of Lowland upbringing,—that they had homes to see to, wives to visit, cattle to put under shelter from the bitter winds,—that it had been a glorious autumn and they would all meet again in the spring and make that still more glorious, but in the meantime, as Montrose must understand——

Yes, he understood.

Off they rode as fast as the leaves fell down, for all sensible fellows must go home before the snows fell. Even Colonel Sibbald went, and that gay adventurer, Nathaniel Gordon, slipped off without any leave taken. Forbes of Craigievar, who had been his prisoner on parole since Aberdeen, broke his parole and ran away. Montrose turned to his other distinguished prisoner, Forbes of Largie.

" Do you mean to steal away too? " he asked.

" I would rather die than do so," he answered.

" Then you may go,—on your parole, to return when I want you."

It looked like the end of the campaign. November had settled down on them, thick with mist and rain,—snow in the hills. Lothian's horse had gone into winter quarters. Argyll was in Atholl, doing propaganda work among the loyalists. Montrose led his few remaining men across the Grampians.

With him was Lord Airlie and his two sons, Sir David and Sir Thomas Ogilvy. Old as he was, and ' valetudinarian ' as he was called, he had flatly refused to consider what effect the cold and fatigue of winter marches across pathless mountains might

2 A

have on his constitution. Nor did he flinch now, when Montrose in a single night covered twenty-four miles of rocks and snow-drifts, flooded streams, and bogs more dangerous on a wild night than any army, and plunged down upon Dunkeld.

He was within sixteen miles when Argyll heard of the approach of his enemy.

Argyll had dismissed all his cavalry—but the odds were still four to one in his favour—but then they had been five to one in the last battle, and yet he had not won,—but then here was his chance to redeem his position in the eyes of his clan and the nation,—but no, no, not just when he had sent away the cavalry.

He fled to the garrison at Perth, told his Campbells to go home, and the rest of the army to shift for themselves, then went with Lothian to Edinburgh, quarrelling all the way. At Edinburgh, the Committee of Estates inquired with the utmost respect what he had done beyond tiring out his soldiers and Lothian's by coursing three times over round about Spey and Atholl; and in answer, he complained that through envy or emulation or negligence or inability, or all of them, he had not been properly supported.

A rude voice called out, "What's wrong with three thousand foot and fifteen hundred horse?" but was promptly quenched. With now exaggerated politeness, the Estates thanked him for his invaluable services, and commended him for having shed so little blood.

But Argyll, still 'much grieved,' surrendered his commission as General-in-chief of the Covenanters. It was offered to Lothian, who refused to touch it 'for any request,' and so did one general after the other until General Baillie, who had proved himself one of Leven's best soldiers in England, reluctantly consented.

Argyll thanked God that he had washed his hands of it. He too went home, to spend Christmas in his castle at Inveraray,—not in vain jesting and merriment as his enemy had done at Kincardine three years ago, when Argyll had in his misguided clemency released him from prison,—but in study and philosophical discussion, and family prayers for two hours every morning and evening, and sermons by distinguished preachers.

The little seaport town of Inveraray, with its new schools and shops, was a centre of the modern theology and of education and of commerce, as befitted the capital of the Campbell kingdom. An impregnable kingdom it was, isolated out there on the western coast, yet far inland at the end of Loch Fyne, and as its kings had often boasted, secured from attack by the sea on the one hand, and on the other by high mountains, to whose few and dangerous passes only the Campbell scouts held the key. Argyll himself had often said he would rather lose a hundred thousand florins (no mean test) than that any mortal but a Campbell should know those mountain passes to his country. It was easier to reach it from France and Spain than from inland Scotland, so that for generations it had been at peace, and could devote itself to commerce with Europe. The Clan Campbell was therefore more civilized as well as more prosperous than its neighbours. Could anything be happier than this godly household, the centre of its little world, living in perfect peace and security? So its head demanded of his family, and his devoted wife agreed with all her wonted tender reassurance.

But his son, Archibald, young Lord Lorne, complained bitterly to his mother at finding that he was to be given an English Bible and the *Practice of Piety* for Christmas presents (though it was only owing to her long hours of intervention that he was to be allowed any at all), and threatened to run away before Christmas to escape the six long sermons that would commemorate that former festival as a fast day.

Argyll suspected another motive for this threat; Archibald had been tiresomely persistent with his questions about Lord Graham, his junior, who was fighting by the side of his father,—and Argyll told his wife that his own son wished to desert him for the side of that malignant destroyer, Montrose. Poor Margaret wept, and tried to assure her husband of her son's love for him; but he found more consolation in writing down his reflections. Some day he would compile them into a book of letters to his son; then even that ungrateful lad would see how much wisdom and experience his father could lay at his disposal, if only he would ever use it.

But rather oddly, with all his brains, he had no ease in writing;—his jottings on Religion and Study and Courage struck him as cramped and inexpressive. It must be because he did things, rather than wrote them, he told himself,—a man of action, that was it,—and there again was confronted with the thought of Montrose, who wrote both prose and poetry of as clear and ringing a quality as his words in battle.

Was he to be for ever worsted by his rival? At least he could show how little value there was in these showy and facile qualities.

So he wrote, " Courage loses its merited honour, if wilfulness and overguided petulancy overbear it; a well-grounded reason, without prejudice to a man's honour, may justly countermand a rash and inconsiderate resolution."

This gave him pleasure, until at last the pen took charge, as it will do at times with even the unreadiest writer, and some impulse of sincerity, unintentional and most unwelcome, made him add,—" It is better to trust in valour than in policy."

XIII

ALASDAIR had come out of the west again at last, and well did he justify his absence, for he brought with him five hundred more of the Scottish Macdonalds of the Isles and Clanranald and Glengarry and Glencoe, also recruits from other clans such as the Stewarts and Macleans and the Camerons of Lochaber.

He met his Commander on their old trysting ground of Atholl, and great was the rejoicing and the feasting that they held at Blair Castle, which Montrose had managed to keep as a permanent base to his operations throughout the autumn. So many more heroes had to be introduced, so much had to be told, to be drunk to and congratulated on, that the late November night was scarcely long enough for it all.

Alasdair had heard of Fyvie, slapped O'Cahan on the back and called him the General's powder-monkey, and insisted on Lord Graham telling him about his raid on the chamber-pots. In Alasdair's opinion the miserable softness and degeneracy of most of the Lowland lords was due to just that effeminate invention, as if a man dared not put his nose or anything else out of doors on a brisk night.

And now to business. What were the plans for the winter? One of the chief objectives of that autumn had been carried,— Argyll's army had been kept away from the operations of the war in England, and not only prevented from joining up with Leven's army there, but had had to demand reinforcements from it; the Seat of Government had been kept perpetually on the run, and small prestige was left to it.

Montrose had hoped to sweep down on the Border, where Leven's army had retired from England to its winter quarters, but the only moment when this had been possible had been just that when his Lowland gentry were all availing themselves of Argyll's obliging offer of free passes to their homes.

Now it was the Highlanders' turn to reject the plan because they had no interest in its objective. King and Covenant were as yet new-fangled and artificial interests compared with the age-old motives of their warfare. All these clans and septs were now banded together by one common impulse, their hatred of the encroaching power of their great rival; and one prayer at least they could all most religiously utter in unison:

> " From the greed of the Campbells,
> Good Lord, deliver us! "

Montrose could give his army no pay, he was as dependent on their goodwill as if they were boys who had chosen to play a game together. He must play their game, if he were ever to get them to play his. His hope was to get them to the Border and finally to join the King's armies in England; but he could not do that until he had smashed utterly the King's enemies in Scotland.

The chief of those enemies now reposed safely in the inaccessible fortress of Inveraray.

" The fox is snug in his lair," said Alasdair, " and no enemy has ever yet won through into the heart of the Campbell country, even in summer."

" Can the mountain passes be crossed at all in midwinter? " asked Montrose, " and what hope is there of our stumbling on them? And what cities and food should we find across the mountains? "

Said Angus MacAlain Duibh, a Macdonald of Glencoe, " I know every farm belonging to MacCaillan Mhor, and you need never want for tight houses, fat cattle and clear water."

" So be it," said Montrose, " the fox is snug in his lair, and we will ferret him out."

But he would not let his old tutor endure such another march as that which he had just led him across the Grampians down on to Atholl. He told Master Forrett that he would have no accounts now to draw up between the wolves and the eagles in Badenoch; he must return to Kinnaird.

Forrett refused at first to obey.

" Would I ever let your Lordship play truant when you were

my pupil, and do you now command your tutor to do so? It is against all law and order."

But Montrose laughed back at him that it was in accordance with the old Irish law, as he had learned from Alasdair—" To help him against poverty, and to support him in old age, these are due from the pupil to the tutor." How could he support Master Forrett's old age against the poverty of the mountains better than by driving him out of them?

Just as he was saying good-bye to him, and Johnnie was giving message after message to young James about the care of Ruddy, his red setter, and his hawks, and all the stories about the campaign that he was to be sure and tell him,—Montrose had a sudden impulse to go too, with his son, and both pay a flying visit to their home for a few hours before they started on this mad enterprise into the mountains.

They rode by night, sent on a messenger to warn Lord Southesk on the morning of their arrival, which must be kept as secret as possible, and snatched two clear days and one night at home.

And Master Forrett sat blinking like a little contented owl at the sound roof above his head, and the blazing fire before his feet, and asked James questions in Latin to see how much he had fallen off since he had ceased to tutor him, but was too happy to pay much attention to the answers.

There was some question as to whether Johnnie could not stay now as well as Forrett, and avoid the terrible rigours of the coming winter campaign. But even Southesk thought it more dangerous for him to stay than to go, since the Covenant were bent on 'making examples,' and what better one could there be than young Lord Graham, who had moreover now taken up arms against the Covenant?

"So he must go on with you," said Magdalen, " ' since you've left him no other guide.' "

The line from the song slid out inadvertently, the only touch of bitterness in their snatched bliss. Never had it been so exquisite, nor so precarious. His visit might endanger the house he loved so well, yet he could not reproach himself for it, since to Magdalen it was now worth any danger.

There was no fear left in her love. She had won clear of it. Both their minds were still; body and spirit had transcended them. Three safe years with Jamie had once been not long enough to quiet her anxious heart; now a few dangerous and breathless hours made it lie at rest. She had learned that security was not at any-one's command; bounded by time and chance, it might fail the most peaceable and far-sighted. But safety lay in love, in accept-ance, in eternity.

And laughter touched their fellowship again, like the wheeling flight of a swallow, swooping on the most unlikely occasions for it,—as when they spoke of the Covenanters' destruction of one of Montrose's beautiful castles, that had never yet been sung, as had the fate of the Bonny House of Airlie,—and Magdalen demanded what poet, however rude and local, could find rhyme or poetic reason for lament in such a name as the Bonny House of Mugdock?

It was now the dead of the year, cold, tempestuous and stormy, in the early days of December, dark with cloud, when the flat fields lay sad and sodden below Kinnaird, and the seagulls cried harshly over the wet purple of ploughed lands after rain, and the wind hurled through the thin orchards, and apples were stacked in rosy pyramids in the barns, and Lady Southesk said, " We must make some apple cheese for Lady Anne Cunningham, for her teeth are all going, and she can eat nothing solid, and detests such slops as porridge and bread-and-milk."

" Though I'd never trust Annie not to bite," said Lord Southesk, and the two old people had laughed with friendly malice, as Magdalen now laughed with Jamie.

She was jealous, she said, of a certain Captain Francis Dalziel who had enlisted a small company of horse in Carnwath's troop under Montrose that spring, with a black banner at their head that showed a naked man hanging on a gibbet, and the motto, " I dare." Captain Dalziel's real name was Mrs. Pierson, and nobody knew why she had thus appeared, dressed, and fought as a man.

" You have a very tame wife, Jamie. Why cannot I too
follow you to the wars, armed to the teeth? "

" Mrs. Pierson's teeth were part of her armour—they stuck
out."

" How thoughtful to tell me that! And you will love me
although I do not fight by your side? "

" I love you all the more that you do not care on which side
I fight nor who wins, as long as those you love are safe."

It was true, for he needed that very contrast to the wild flights
of his adventures, and the emotions that he aroused in others.
His hero-worshipping nieces could not give him the repose that
he craved in Magdalen. Her adoration of him, devoid of the
wild glamour that it had for others, was like a cooling drink after
so much wine of adulation. His greatest comfort lay in the faint,
sceptical touch of her voice, in her deliberately ordinary attitude
to life, when he was in the midst of leading his Homeric allies
through a campaign as preposterous as their own sagas, a campaign
that a boy like his son might well wish would last his lifetime.
But he himself was not a boy, not even primarily a romantic.

That was the secret of his hold on the heroes and ruffians he
led, whose pride it was to rush blindly into fight,—that he himself
never lost the coolness of his judgment, that it was his reason that
flamed white-hot in action, prompted his most daring commands,
turned disaster into victory by a rapid calculation, a deliberate
word flung at the critical moment into the fight, which acted
like wine and fire.

Johnnie told his mother of his new friends' berserk deeds,
unhindered by their wounds; and she was only reminded that his
father had been ill and had cheated her, for she had not been there
to nurse him.

" He cheated his enemies worse, then," cried Johnnie, and told
proudly how his ' good news ' had stung his father to recovery,
" so that he sprang up and frightened them much more than he
had done before."

She looked from her husband to her son, grown so much taller
even since she had last seen him. Their bodies were hardened,

supple as steel, not an ounce of them but played its part as a perfect fighting weapon. Three months had metamorphosed Johnnie from a schoolboy to a splendid young cavalier, brown and lean and full of terrible stories,—yet still the child peeped out in his pride in the jokes he had with the Irish soldiers, who delighted to make half a plaything, half an idol of their Commander's son.

*　　*　　*

It was the child in him that tore her heart as he left her again; it was the grown cavalier (at fourteen) that tantalized young James with cruel envy, as Johnnie rode off beside his father, with a swaggering air and a wave of his hand in gay farewell to the women and children and the old grandfather and tutor, all standing on the steps of the castle to watch that little group of dark figures riding over the plain towards a torn rift of fire and white light in the stormy evening sky.

The streak of sunset showed the distant hills. Magdalen had seen Jamie ride off into them ever since she had been a child; never had she done so without wondering when she would see him come back. He belonged to the hills, and she to the plains.

Her mother and father were trying to distract her attention with little kind comforting remarks. But she did not answer them; she turned to Master Forrett, and said, " Did you not say the mountains were once as flat as this plain? "

" Before God raised them," he replied.

" Yes, the God in their hearts, the fire that burned there and would not let them rest."

" Come indoors, my lamb," said her mother, " one cannot see them any more now."

" Where is James? " she asked.

James had gone indoors already. He could not bear it, he would wave his handkerchief no longer, but crept away from the little group on the castle steps, and was discovered later by Magdalen in the cubby-hole under the stairs, where they kept his and Johnnie's guns and rods and fishing tackle.

She looked in with a rushlight in her hand, and there he sat sniffing in the dark, because he had ridden away with Johnnie last time, and why could he not do so now?

"You will ride away too in your time," Magdalen told him. "Stay with me now for a little."

He put up a sticky, rather damp hand, for he had been rubbing his eyes, and touched her cheek.

"You are crying," he said, as accusingly as though he were innocent of it. "Don't do that. Sit down, and I will tell you a story."

The hanging game-bags and landing-nets made an uninviting harbour. James seemed to have a liking for such impersonal places. Once he had told her something she knew, but dreaded to hear, among the shelves of white sheets in the linen room at Kincardine, while the snow had fallen slowly outside the little window. Something about King Charles—and about Jamie— but she did not want to remember.

"Come up to my room, and tell me the story there," she said.

They went upstairs and sat by the fire and toasted their hands and noses while their heels and backs remained chilly. They watched the logs crackling and sparkling across the red-hot sods of peat that smouldered into furry ash, grey-white as the fur of the little mountain foxes in winter.

Up in the huge chimney, a wind moaned and whistled and caught the wood-smoke; now blew it back with showers of ash into their laps and faces, making their eyes smart; now whirled it upwards with a sputter of red sparks.

It would be bitter cold on the moor to-night. Montrose and his men travelled now so light, they encumbered themselves with tents no more than cannon. When they stole marches over the mountains, they dared light no fires.

Johnnie had said he slept as snug as a bug in a rug, rolled deep in the heather in a nest of men lying close for warmth, with their wide plaids unwound and swaddled round them.

But how would they keep alive when the great gales tore

across the bare mountain side and swept the snow into the hollows, in drifts deep and wide enough to bury the men as they lay asleep?

How should Johnnie keep alive in weather fit to perish the crows?

" You are not listening to my story," said James.

XIV

CHRISTMASTIDE at Inveraray was not merry, but it was comfortable. French wines from the Port of Saint Malo, figs and raisins from Corsica, cane sugar and tobacco from America, were all to be got more easily and cheaply in those little shops than in Edinburgh. Lady Argyll herself could look in at their windows and wish someone would give her a Christmas present from them—a dozen yards of real Spanish taffeta for a new dress, or that pair of scented leather gloves.

Her eldest son bought a green parroquet on his own account, and swore he would teach it sentences out of the *Practice of Piety* with blasphemous words attached; the only drawback was that the parroquet turned out to be of a kind that did not speak.

Long meals, longer sermons, an oppressed liver and general sense of dissatisfaction, was young Lord Lorne's impression of Christmas.

" If only anything would happen," he said to himself as he kicked his toes together during the fourth sermon that day, to prevent his cold feet going to sleep, as he only wished he himself could do, but if he even blinked, his father was certain to notice it—and prod him awake? Not he. Young Lorne would welcome the diversion, but his father would be afraid lest the congregation should observe it. He would lecture his son afterwards instead and for as long as another sermon; he might even insist on his praying with him.

He glanced sideways at his father's now heavily pendulous nose, his compressed mouth and narrow eyes—would he himself look like that when he was his age? He was tortured by a longing to yawn, he began to yawn, he must yawn if something did not happen to prevent him.

Something happened—a shout in the street outside—the church door was flung open—a shaggy red-bearded man in a sheepskin coat stood there aghast, staring at the congregation—so young Lorne saw him for one instant as he was getting his breath,—then there was a mighty scraping of stools as the congregation surged upwards to their feet, a volley of questions, a woman's shriek, a child's frightened whine, and above it all the man's high shout in Gaelic (and for the first time Lorne was thankful that his father had insisted on his learning the Gaelic as a child)—" They are on us! They are over the mountains! They are burning and killing as they come! "

In the midst of the hubbub one old man, who was stone deaf and very nearly blind, imagined that the congregation had risen because the sermon was at an end, and burst forth with a toneless shout into the psalm he knew to be appointed—

> " Behold, how good a thing it is,
>   And how becoming well,
> Together such as brethren are
>   In unity to dwell ! "

" The Macdonalds are upon us! " shrieked the congregation.

" Montrose and his men are on the hill! "

" They are not two miles off."

" They will shut us into this church and burn us all alive."

But very soon there was nobody left in the church except the old deaf man, who did not know why they were all in such a hurry. He would not be hustled, and continued the service in his own voice, that he could not hear.

A few minutes later, a handful of men who had outstripped the advance guard of Montrose's army looked in at the open door, and saw a tall old man in his shepherd's coat and plaid, with his sheep-dog by his side, standing alone in the middle of the church, proclaiming a metrical version of one of the psalms in a wandering, oceanic voice, like the rumblings and echoes in some deep sea-cave.

Awed, rather frightened, they crept out again.

Argyll had been improving the defences of his castle of Inveraray in case the impossible should happen, and he had begun to gather his clansmen together to provide reinforcements, should they be needed later against Montrose inland.

They were needed here and now.

But not at this instant's notice, not with the enemy in sight,—how could one do anything in a few minutes? It was useless to resist—it was all hopeless—hopeless—but alas it was not hopeless, that was the agony of it; it was possible, even easy to escape; a fishing boat lay all ready manned in the loch, and the wind was in the right quarter; he and his family could be aboard in two minutes and speeding down before the wind to Roseneath.

Oh the torture of decision, when every flying minute meant that those savages were nearer to him, nearer and nearer,—"within two miles," they had said, and surely that was now a quarter of an hour ago,—or no, was it really only three minutes? Why could he not think? His brains were rattling in his head—or was it his teeth chattering? Something must be done at once, and he had done nothing.

In any case, get her Ladyship on board at once, and Lord Lorne, no matter how he resisted,—if the boy struggled, pinion his arms, commanded his father, his teeth shutting down on his lower lip,—and was it his fault that he had been caught like a rat in a trap?

He saw his family go or be dragged on board; his wife was flustering him by her tears and cries to him to come too; before he knew what he had decided, he was following them up the plank.

The sails were hauled up, rattling; they flapped and filled with the wind as the boat was pushed off from the shore across the little slapping waves that gleamed pale in the wintry sunshine. It was done now, they could not turn back, they were scudding before the wind. And borne on the wind, now faint, now unmistakable, mocking, pursuing, horribly merry, came the first wild dance of the Macdonald pipes.

"We must fall back on Roseneath," said Argyll, seeking, he knew in vain, to propitiate with that military word the huddled heap of shame and misery that was his son.

"I wish I were dead—dead," the boy sobbed in answer.

Suddenly his father snarled back on him—"Do *I* not wish it?" He knew it to be true—it would be easy for him to die—if only there were no choice, no hope of escape, nothing to be decided in a hurry. "But of what use would my death be?—there is no other man who can guide the state. At Roseneath I can plan my campaign, I can consult with Baillie how to smash our enemies. To stay now would be to acknowledge defeat."

The seagulls screamed in answer. His son gave none. Again came those pealing, triumphant notes of the Macdonald march, now descending on the little city. And the words that he himself had written fitted themselves to that gay music of death and destruction—' It is better to trust to valour than to policy.'

XV

GENERAL WILLIAM BAILLIE was sent for to Rose-neath to consult with Argyll as to the next move against Montrose. He found that 'to consult' meant 'to be commanded.' Not because Argyll was the leader of the Government and the pillar of the Kirk, but because he was MacCaillan Mhor, and none but he should command the vengeance of his clan. Baillie's shrewd eyes flicked open in an ironic glance at this warlike attitude in the chieftain who had fled before he even saw his enemy's claymores.

What he saw made him wish he had not betrayed his amusement. The Marquis wore his skull-cap and long black furred cloak as usual indoors; his arm had been injured in a fall from his horse since his arrival at Roseneath, so that he wore it in a sling. A peaceable, inactive man, with a stoop and a probably rheumatic arm, was the first impression of his appearance. But behind those little red angry eyes there lurked the misery of the animal that knows itself wounded to death, whose only hope is that it too may destroy.

He was insisting on his sole right to avenge his clan, because he had deserted it. Not the most loyal Campbell of them all but must curse him in his heart as the Chieftain who thought first of saving his own skin, while now through the length and breadth of his kingdom rose the smoking fires of his people's homes.

The Macdonalds, the Camerons and the Stewarts were harrying the Campbells, as so lately the Campbells had been harrying them. They had left their mark on the impregnable walls of Inveraray, they were feasting on Argyll's cattle, laying waste his lands, destroying his strongholds. And only their utter annihilation by the Clan Campbell, led by its chief, could wipe out their shame and his.

So he took a high hand, told Baillie that he was to make over his picked troops of Scottish militia to himself, and then retire to

Perth and keep in touch with Seaforth's army of Covenanters at Inverness.

And Baillie told him that he had served under Gustavus Adolphus; that he had done the best part of the Covenanters' job at Marston Moor, while old Sandy Leslie, my noble Lord of Leven, was riding hell for leather from the field, asking the quickest way back to the Tweed;—that he had been begged and persuaded and all but forced to accept the supreme military command in Scotland, and that he was—well, surprised—if he had now to take his orders from the man who had voluntarily surrendered that command.

" For, damn it, am I in command or not, that is what I want to know? "

" The Committee of Estates is of the opinion——"

The General interrupted with his own opinion that it was impossible to control a military campaign by a God-damned debating society.

" If I live," said a low, a very gentle voice, " you shall have cause to remember this day."

After that, Baillie thought it wiser to choke his profanity, agree to whatever was proposed, and approve of whatever had been done.

Sir Duncan Campbell of Auchinbreck, an excellent general, " though sadly given to vice and deboshry," complained his chief, had been summoned from Ireland to lead the clan in battle, as Argyll's injured arm might prevent his taking an active part in the fighting (he insisted on explaining this in full, where Baillie was anxious to slur it over in his embarrassment).

The Campbells, with Baillie's reinforcements, would advance from the south, driving Montrose's army up towards Seaforth's in the north; Baillie's at Perth would guard any retreat to the east; on the west was the sea coast. Montrose's little force would certainly be caught in a trap between the three great armies.

" If we get not the life of these worms chirted out of them," said Baillie, rubbing his hands, " the reproach will stick on us for ever."

He glanced hopefully at Argyll, but his genial encouragement had shed no warmth on the atmosphere. A chill, dead eye looked back at him. Perhaps the word ' reproach ' had been a mistake.

*   *   *

Montrose's men were full-fed now on the best of red butcher-meat, cattle to kill and cattle to drive off and keep; they had white wheat bread and French wines to feast on.

Alasdair rescued a father and two brothers called Angus and Archibald,—all three nearly as large as himself—from the dungeons of one of the Campbell castles. There was a great family reunion. The father was hailed by his clan as Colkitto, the famous Coll Macdonald of Colonsay, who could fight as well with his left hand as with his right,—an old man whose beard was snow-white, and his face too, as were the faces of his sons, from their long imprisonment in the dark.

' The winter foxes,' those three were called by all the other ruddy, weather-beaten men. They showed no other traces of their imprisonment, were as hale and hearty as Alasdair himself, and able to drink as deep after their fare of bread and water, and by no means always that.

Once after a long fast, they had been served with some very salt meat, and thought their enemies intended to drive them mad with thirst as long ago they had done to Hugh Macdonald, who gnawed his pewter dish into strips before he died, raving. This they told now as a merry tale of the fate that they had escaped.

Their eyes gleamed ice-blue in their white faces; Lord Graham, who had been feeling so stern and full-grown a man, was pulled back into the tales of his childhood, of trolls who drive the Snow Queen's sledge down from her glittering home in the north. Here he was carousing with these strange giants, hearing their stories, singing their songs; and now, as the campaign began again, marching by their side.

For two days they marched in a sou'wester gale that threatened to blow them off the sides of the mountains. Sometimes the whole army had to file through a pass so steep and narrow that half a dozen men could have held it at bay.

One old woman did hold it at bay for a few minutes, a gaunt figure with grey hair streeling through the blinding sleet, and a great scythe that she swung in circles round her, so that the first of the invaders fell to the ground, and there lay dying.

" Kill the witch! " they shouted, and quickly overmastered her, but Montrose would not have her killed.

" Is that because I am a woman? " she flung at him in scorn through her bared teeth. No kindness had she known on that score, driven out by the herd to live alone on the mountains, because she was a woman, old, lonely, with a red-lidded, quivering eye—and who knew but she might be a witch?

" It is because you are a brave enemy," he answered; and they left her at the door of her hovel of stones and turf, still grumbling defiance at them, the mountain looming up over her indomitable old head.

They came down on to Loch Etive; the gale had died down, the sun shone on calm waters, but there were no boats to cross in.

Old Colkitto marched round the end of the loch with his three sons to call on the Campbell of Ardchattan, who owned those lands, and came back to say that it had all been arranged satisfactorily,—they were not to touch Ardchattan's cattle, and he would provide them with ferry boats. Great wonder was expressed at this easy bargain, and many compliments on the address of the ambassadors, until Colkitto admitted with a little smile that showed his yellow teeth in the depths of his white beard,—" the man may be prejudiced. His mother was a Macdonald."

So owing to the family feeling of Colkitto's eighth cousin once removed, they all crossed the loch; made short work of a sloop of Argyll's that had been sent to attack them from the sea, and captured all its fine brass guns; welcomed a band of recruits from Appin, and were welcomed by the men of Glencoe; stayed a night at Inverlochy, where lay the mighty castle at the foot of Ben Nevis; and so reached the head of Loch Ness by the end of January.

By that time the army's numbers were down to fifteen hundred again. A Highland victory always lessened the victorious as much as a defeat; the cattle of the Campbells had been more effective than their claymores in driving back half Montrose's soldiers to their homes with them. The rest were tired out with their mountain march; and an army of five thousand lay ahead of them at Inverness under Seaforth.

It was at this moment that a messenger came over the mountains with bad news. This was one of the Macdonald's hereditary bards, Ian Lom of Keppoch, and his message was that Argyll had mustered an army three thousand strong, under the command of the trained and valiant soldier, Sir Duncan Campbell of Auchinbreck, that it was moving in pursuit of Montrose and had got as far as Inverlochy, where it had pitched its camp just about thirty miles south of his present position.

Montrose was therefore about half-way between the Campbells and Seaforth's forces; further inland lay Baillie's; on the west was the sea coast. Between three armies and the sea,—it was as good a trap as Baillie had promised, and ' if they had not the life chirted out of them,' what was to prevent it?

Johnnie Graham stared at his father, who sat at his table, writing. It might have been a letter home, so fluently and readily did his pen move over the paper. What plan had he that could be helped by letter, what further allies to call on in this desert?

" What is the date? " asked Montrose.

He was told, Wednesday the twenty-ninth, and Johnnie saw him write—" the penult dayes of January, the year of God one thousand, six hundredth, fourtie fyve years."

Then he signed it in big letters and asked his son if he would come and sign now too, or wait till he had heard what it was. Without a word, Johnnie came forward and took the pen from his hand, and signed, close beneath his father's name.

The paper was a bond, uniting all who signed it in an oath to fight to the death for their King against his enemies. It was a curious moment for Montrose to state his principles, why he was fighting, and for whom.

Johnnie, with a preternatural clarity of vision that came to him now and then in the excitement of this campaign in the ice-clear mountain air, wondered if it were his father's provision against his death,—to show that whoever were his allies or his opponents, he was not fighting in an obscure feud of Grahams and Macdonalds against the Campbells, but that he was the King's Lieutenant in Scotland first and last.

Whatever the impulse of his action may have been, the effect was excellent. Men were calmed and made easy by the fact that on top of this news of enemies hemming them in on every side, their commander-general could devote the whole of that day and the next to the signing of this bond by all the names—or marks—of their chiefs—and there almost were as many chiefs as men-at-arms.

It had the mysterious significance to the simple and unlettered of all things written and signed. (Had not the Clan Campbell won even more power by their charters than by their claymores?) It lifted their campaign from the age-old familiarity of raid and feud between clans, to the strange and holy purpose of a crusade.

XVI

THE 'penult dayes of Januarie' had passed; very early on the morning of the ultimate, the army was on the move again. Said its leader, "We will smash the strongest first."

Seaforth's army in the north was the larger, but it was made up chiefly of townsmen and raw recruits. Argyll's army was under Sir Duncan Campbell, a first-rate general, and it had Baillie's picked troops added to the whole fighting power of the Campbell clan,—a magnificent body of men, trained in war, well equipped, and burning to wipe out the shame that had been put on them by their hereditary foes, the Macdonalds. So that though they numbered three thousand, and Seaforth's five thousand, they were by far the most formidable.

Montrose had led his army up the Great Glen of Albin by the shores of Loch Lochy to Loch Ness. Now they must go back on their tracks, but by another route, for their only chance lay in a surprise attack; and Argyll's and Seaforth's scouts would be scanning the Great Glen for a sight of them. No canal nor road ran there then, but it was held to be the only possible route between Inverlochy and the head of Loch Ness by which any army could travel, certainly any army with horses, and in mid-winter.

Montrose thought otherwise. With the help of Ian Lom who had come by the hill road of Glen Roy, and of stray cowherds, he was sure of finding a way across the mountains for his men, and even for the little bodyguard of horse under Lord Airlie, which carried the clarions to salute the King's standard.

His men had been rested for two or three days and well fed, and so he told them, as he advised them to buckle in their belts and not hope for any food but the oatmeal they could carry, for that, mixed with water, was all the food they could have till they won back to Inverlochy,—and no later, he promised them, than to-morrow evening. He himself had no more, nor had Willie Wallace three and a half centuries ago, when he and his handful of men had set out on their shaggy ponies to conquer the huge chivalry of England.

His way through the mountains was a rough one; it started in the river bed of the Tarff, which led them for some miles up into the hills. The winter's morning was still black as they plunged into that icy shallow running water, and began to splash their way up among the rocks. The few horses had to be led.

Johnnie felt as though his feet were being sawn off, then all feeling left them, so that he did not know how he moved,—he stumbled, slipped,—shouted with laughter, as old Colkitto, his beard glimmering in the darkness, gripped him by the shoulder and saved him from falling full length in one of the pools that lay like black pits among the tumbling white foam.

The hills towered over them, grey monsters, scarcely to be distinguished from the sky; but that was every minute growing paler, and then came a shaft of red through the blackest clouds, and suddenly the whole vast scene took shape and colour round them. There they were, struggling out of the course of the stream in the growing light, to see the dawn come up behind the Monadhliath mountains.

The raw wind came down their sides, and cut at Johnnie's wet legs, but little he cared with them roughened already to a surface like leather. Rawhide brogues, cut from the fresh untanned skin of cattle with all its hair on, bound with leather thongs and pierced with holes to let the water run through, those were the shoes for this journeying. He wore a kilted plaid like the meanest of Alasdair's kerns, and a sheepskin coat with the wool turned inside for warmth and so protected by its natural grease that in the heaviest rain or snow his shoulders remained dry inside it. In no other clothes could one move so freely over mountains that any Lowlander would have called impassable.

He could not ride, for not only did the cold then strike more deadly, moving as slowly as all had to do, but it was the most difficult part of the work to get the horses over those precipitous slopes, all slippery with ice; and more than once it was thought they would have to be left behind. The springing ease of Alasdair's great wolf-hound, leaping and trotting his happy way over the most difficult ground, was an insult to the clumsy, panting efforts of every other beast, with four legs or two.

The wide surfaces of rock were no harder nor smoother than the bare stretches of bent, shining white with frost. The alternative was generally to wade knee-deep through snow;—and they were lucky it was not worse. A snowstorm or thick mist might have wiped out the little army altogether, driving it blindfold into some vast drift. But the hillside lay clear in the faint sunlight of the easterly wind that turned all colours pale and grey. Across a further slope went, in a long, lolloping trot, the dark shapes of some beasts that they knew to be wolves.

They could not stop to rest that night, nor could they make a fire that might warn some possible distant scout of their whereabouts.

Down by a frozen stream in a deep hollow, they passed through a strip of scrub and stunted trees; their topmost branches made a pattern like the hands of skeletons against the frosty evening sky; a few dead leaves still clung below, making a dry, rustling, hushing noise as they passed through,—a noise so faint that it made Johnnie suddenly aware of the silence all round them.

One of the men killed a roe buck with an arrow from his long bow; in an instant, a hurried, hungry cluster of men had gathered round it, cut and colloped it asunder, and fallen on its raw flesh.

" Here's a juicy bit for my young Lord Graham." Johnnie tried to share his bleeding morsel with his father, who refused to lessen the rations; and the boy, sick at first taste of the warm tough flesh, without salt, soon devoured it all greedily.

The raw meat gave him new strength; he stumbled on through the growing darkness, saw the full moon swim out above the mountains, giving light enough to the tried mountainy men to distinguish among the varying blacknesses of the moor.

He heard the long howl of a wolf rise lamentably through the night at sight of such strangers as had never before ventured into these wastes. He saw the army before and behind him, streeling out in a black dotted line across the glistening icy slope of the mountain.

Each breath he drew was so cold that it hurt; he seemed to have no breath left; he staggered forward and would have fallen, but for his father's hand.

" The lad is nearly spent," Montrose said in a troubled voice to Alasdair as he came up to them; and for answer Alasdair hoisted Lord Graham upon his back, winding his plaid tight round and round them both, so as to warm him and hold him fast.

It was no use for Johnnie to protest that at fourteen he was a grown man, and ' quite as tall as some of our men.' He was carried in turn by Alasdair's biggest Highlanders, their warmth against his keeping him snug, where he would have frozen on horseback.

" This is I, Johnnie Graham," he told himself incredulously, as the warmth stole into his numbed brain and made it for a few minutes unnaturally aware. Less than six months ago he had been doing lessons at Kinnaird and Old Montrose with his little brother under Master Forrett; and now he was riding on the backs of giants, to follow his father's campaign through country where no armed men had ever dared pass before.

No one but his father could make them do it;—he saw him moving, now forward, now back, among all that endlessly straggling column, walking beside them, cheering them on by telling them that in less than twenty-four hours now they would have reached their goal,—and then they would smash the sons of Diarmaid once more, this time for ever. Johnnie could see the men stepping out with more pride and courage when his father had spoken to them.

And then Montrose came back to where his son rode on the back of one of Alasdair's kerns, and put his hand on Johnnie's arm, and told him that he had kept up with them magnificently, and that in less than two days he should be taking his ease in a castle. The boy looked sideways at him, his face, drawn with fatigue, pressed against the broad shoulder in front of him.

" I don't want to rest in a castle," he said, " I wish we could go on like this for ever."

Montrose looked at him in anxiety; he thought his son's eyes very bright in the moonlight,—was that only the moonlight, or a touch of fever?

Cold and white as a corpse, the second dawn came over that desert place, and now it was the first of February. They were at Roy Bridge, not more than nine miles from Inverlochy, if they could have gone direct, but they had to keep hidden among the hills.

They were now on the slopes of the mountains round Ben Nevis, the highest in Britain. The Campbells had sent out no scouts over the wilderness they had been crossing, no commander could have thought that necessary,—but now there was a constant danger that they might meet some advanced patrol. And so they did, not long after fording the Spean, a swollen, roaring torrent that reached their middles,—when they clashed full into a foraying party of Argyll's.

" Be it so! From that foray they never returned! " sang Ian Lom Macdonald, as they proceeded on their way. For not one man of that band did they leave alive to run and tell Argyll that he had seen the whole of the King's army in Scotland,—a scattered column amounting to no more than fifteen hundred, struggling across the frozen mountains with the footsore, stumbling tread of desperately weary men—gaunt, shaggy, ' raw-footed ' men in sheepskins and rough plaids that had been drenched in the Spean—their eyes ravenous, and red with lack of sleep—a pack of hungry wolves in the stinking garb of wet sheep.

On they clambered their way among the hills, until, as the evening sky reddened in frost again, they came up over the lower slope of Ben Nevis that looks down upon Inverlochy. Montrose was in the advance guard; it was not till eight o'clock that the rest of his exhausted army had come up with him.

Down below lay the Castle of Inverlochy, and round about it the camp of the Campbells, three thousand strong. They must have seen some of the column come over the shoulder of the lower slope, but they can have had no idea that it was anything more than a foraying party of raiders from some hostile clan, who would not dare attack the full force of the Clan Campbell.

Montrose knew that his men were finished for the time being; they must have sleep before they attacked. Supper they could not have, except the last few grains of their oatmeal, mixed with water into a paste, and eaten on the points of their knives for lack of spoons. This he too ate, walking among them as he did so, and telling them of the good red beef and wheaten bread that would break their fast to-morrow down in that plain below, when they had beaten their enemies.

They looked down on that plain, clear in the moonlight, and laughed at sight of the huge camp, as active and stirring as a disturbed ant-heap, with tiny black figures scurrying here and there.

Beyond the dark towers of the Castle, in the narrow strip of moonlit water that was Loch Eil, lay a galley, with lights on board, and now more lights were seen being carried by figures that came down from the Castle and went on board. The men above wondered and joked as to what this might be.

" Is it the Galley of Lorne? " Johnnie hazarded. " It is well for Argyll he has it on his coat of arms,—there he is sailing away from the battle again! "

Whatever it were, the enemy were evidently taking no chances but were busying themselves with preparations, whoever the rash intruders above might be.

" They will know soon enough to-morrow morning," said Montrose, " when they hear the clarions salute the King's Standard."

A childish love of ceremony and vain show, so Montrose's detractors argued, for starving men to plant that standard on a desert slope, and blow trumpets before it, as if on parade before a king.

' Montrose's whimsies '—banners and clarions and blue bonnets and even wisps of oats flaunted as a panache—he had a boyish gusto in doing these things with a high, gallant air. He never lost all such instincts of a child; and there was a value in this youth and gay courage—and not only to such wild and simple men as he was leading. It had been well worth it to drag those trumpets across the mountains on the backs of his frightened horses, as they slid and stumbled across the slopes, and plunged and splashed through the torrents,—worth it for the effect they would have, not only on his own men, but on his enemies.

He sent out pickets and gave the order for rest. The men fell in heaps on the frosted heather, lying as close as a litter of puppies, with their plaids wound tightly round them; and were asleep as they fell. He himself felt as yet no inclination to sleep. He had just achieved one of the most amazing flank marches in all history. He had led fifteen hundred men and a body of horse, without food and without rest, for thirty-six hours, and scaled the inaccessible mountains of Lochaber in midwinter.

No need now for rhymes to come into his head. At last he was living his poems, as even he had not dared dream them. There is a drunkenness of emptiness as well as of fulness. Exhaustion, cold, and extreme hunger, when mingled with achievement and hope, can go to the head like iced wine; and on this wine Montrose was drunk, as he stood on Ben Nevis, unconscious of the pain of his aching body.

XVII

JOHNNIE'S joke had been truth; the torches carried by men going towards the galley had flickered on a tall, stooping figure in the centre of a little group, who hesitated now and then in his rather halting walk, as though uncertain of his course. Their ruddy light leaped from side to side while the light of the moon shone steadily down on the pale, doubtful face of the Marquis of Argyll. Sometimes he stopped altogether, and seemed about to turn back; but when he did this, his companions closed round him, arguing and urging him on, and one or other would take his arm (the sound one, for the other was still in a sling) and almost drag him along with them.

These men were the present representatives of Argyll's travelling committee from the Committee of Estates—Mr. Mungo Law, an Edinburgh minister, an Edinburgh bailie, the Laird of Niddrie, and Sir James Rollock, his brother-in-law, who had once been that to Montrose. Said these men to their uncertain and unhappy chief:

" There will be no battle—if anything, it will be only a skirmish with a horde of cattle raiders,—and would you perhaps throw away your life in such a wretched business? "

" Your lordship cannot fight with an arm in a sling."

" I can command," said a faint voice.

" You can send Auchinbreck your commands from the galley. He is a tried soldier, and he is in command."

" Your lordship is the chief support of the Covenant. Your life is invaluable, we will not allow you to risk it."

But something propelled him on board the *Dubhlinnseach* (the " Black-sailed "), stronger than all their words, stronger even than their blessedly comforting actions, which made him believe that he was being forced unwillingly to go, in spite of his resistance. And that was a prophecy made by the ' old fox,' Alan Macildowie of Lochaber, the man most gifted with the second-sight in all the Clan Campbell, who had seen that a battle would be lost at Inverlochy ' by them that came first to such battle.'

Argyll, for all his legal and theological training, had his natural share of Highland superstition. It had been for that reason that he had chosen a marquisate as his honour on the King's last visit to Scotland, for it had been foretold that a squinting and red-haired Campbell would be the last Earl of Argyll,—and here was a cunning way to circumvent the inexorable workings of fate. Now there was no way to circumvent them except by escape. If a battle were to be lost at Inverlochy by his clan, at least let it not include the loss of its chief.

They should never have chosen the black-sailed galley to bring him here up Loch Linnhe—he had thought she looked like a bird of ill-omen. They should never have risked stopping here at all; he had told Auchinbreck so, and now told him so again in half a dozen messages from his galley.

He must strike camp first thing in the morning, and push on north through the Great Glen, and join forces with Seaforth as soon as possible, and smash Montrose between them. And would he send back a written message in his own hand to tell what he had discovered of that mysterious force of men seen on the slopes of Ben Nevis?

Auchinbreck, pestered and inclined to be sullen, had discovered nothing of them. He had sent out scouts, and there had been some slight skirmishes with their outposts, in which his men were certain they had killed at least one of the intruders, but nothing more could be discovered of their nature but that they were Highlanders. It was impossible to attack in any large force up the sheer side of the mountain in the middle of the night, and they must wait till the morning.

So they waited till the dawn, and now it was Candlemas, the 2nd of February, the day for taking down one's Christmas decorations. Argyll unwillingly remembered the heathenish old customs in his father's house, as he came shivering up into the raw air on deck. He had not slept all night, so anxious had be been to see what the morning would disclose.

Loch Eil showed first that the morning had come,—the glimmer and then the white gleam of the narrow water, lying like a drawn sword beneath the mountains. They gradually reared their black shapes among the black clouds. The white sword was drawn across the sky, followed by a bar of flame. The clouds rolled past in the wind of the upper air, catching the fury of the sunrise, and now showed the topmost peaks, turned to fire.

As the waters of the loch began to burn red, there rose from the side of Ben Nevis the ringing call of a clarion. This was no battle music of raiding kerns, but the trumpets of the King's army, saluting the King's Standard. From the highest mountain in the three kingdoms, they pealed forth their royal salute into the white and scarlet air.

" Sons of dogs, come, and I will give you flesh."

Not even that barbaric pibroch from the Cameron pipers on the mountain side, now tingling and dancing down the wind, could strike such terror into the hearts of their foes as did that formal blast of trumpets.

" Montrose himself is up there———"

" Montrose is upon us———"

Like flame through a cornfield, and as destructive, the word rushed through the camp in the plain.

Their chieftain, in his galley of the mourning sails, knew for certain at the first blast what he had dreaded all that night— his arch enemy was upon him.

How should he ever look his son in the face again, if he fled from this fight too? A bitter envy fell on him of Montrose, whose son fought by his side.

The certainty of his fears drove him beyond panic into despair; he besought his committee to let him go on shore again, and lead his clan to defeat and death,—" since that is all that God will ever allow me to do."

But his committee would not allow him to do any such thing. Instead, they ordered the seamen to stand by in readiness, and the moment they saw any signs of the battle going against them, they were instantly to haul up the anchor and the black sails of the *Dubhlinnseach*, and make down the loch for the sea.

"We expect defeat, and therefore we get it," groaned Argyll.

Oh for one impulse as clear and burning as the peal of a clarion, that should call his tortured soul out of its prison and set it free to know what it wished, and to do it!

2 C

XVIII

Inverlochy in Lochaber,
February 3rd, 1645.

MAY it please your Sacred Majesty:
The last despatch I sent your Majesty was by my worthy
friend and your Majesty's brave servant, Sir William Rollock,
from Kintore near Aberdeen, dated the 14th of September last.
Since Sir William Rollock went, I have traversed all the north
of Scotland up to Argyll's country; who durst not stay my coming,
or I should have given your Majesty a good account of him ere
now. But at last I have met with him, yesterday, to his cost; of
which your gracious Majesty be pleased to receive the following
particulars.

After I had laid waste the whole country of Argyll, and brought
off provisions for my army of what could be found, I received
information that Argyll was got together with a considerable army,
made up chiefly of his own clan and vassals and tenants, with
others of the rebels that joined him, and that he was at Inverlochy.

Upon this intelligence, I departed out of Argyllshire, and
marched through Lorn, Glencoe, and Aber, till I came to Loch-
ness, my design being to fall upon Argyll before Seaforth and
the Frasers could join him.

My march was through inaccessible mountains, where I could
have no guides but cow-herds, and they scarce acquainted with a
place but six miles from their own habitations.

I was willing to let the world see that Argyll was not the
man his highland men believed him to be, and that it was possible
to beat him in his own Highlands.

The difficultest march of all was over the Lochaber mountains;
which we at last surmounted, and came upon the back of the enemy
when they least expected us, having cut off some scouts we met
about four miles from Inverlochy. Our van came within view of
them about five o'clock in the afternoon, and we made a halt till
our rear was got up, which could not be done till eight at night.

The rebels took the alarm and stood to their arms as well as we, all night, which was moonlight and very clear.

There were some few skirmishes between the rebels and us all the night, and with no loss on our side but one man. By break of day I ordered my men to be ready to fall on, upon the first signal; and I understand since, by the prisoners, the rebels did the same.

A little after the sun was up, both armies met, and the rebels fought for some time with great bravery, the prime of the Campbells giving the first onset, as men that deserved to fight in a better cause. Our men, having a nobler cause, did wonders, and came immediately to push of pike and dint of sword, after their first firing. The rebels could not stand it, but after some resistance at first, began to run; whom we pursued for nine miles together, making a great slaughter, which I would have hindered if possible, that I might save your Majesty's misled subjects.

For well I know your Majesty does not delight in their blood, but in their returning to their duty.

There were at least fifteen hundred killed in the battle and the pursuit; among whom there are a great many of the most considerable gentlemen of the name of Campbell, and some of them nearly related to the Marquis.

I have saved and taken prisoners several of them that have acknowledged to me their fault, and lay all the blame on their chief.

Some gentlemen of the Lowlands, that had behaved themselves bravely in the battle, when they saw all lost, fled into the old castle, and upon their surrender I have treated them honourably, and taken their parole never to bear arms against your Majesty.

We have of your Majesty's army about two hundred wounded, but I hope few of them dangerously. I can hear of but four killed, and one whom I cannot name to your Majesty but with grief of mind, Sir Thomas Ogilvy, a son of the Earl of Airlie, of whom I writ to your Majesty in my last. He is not yet dead, but they say he cannot possibly live, and we give him over for dead. Your Majesty had never a truer servant, nor there never was a braver honester gentleman.

For the rest of the particulars of this action, I refer myself to the bearer, Mr. Hay, whom your Majesty knows already, and therefore I need not recommend him.

. . . As to the state of affairs in this Kingdom, the bearer will fully inform your Majesty in every particular. And give me leave, with all humility, to assure your Majesty that, through God's blessing, I am in the fairest hopes of reducing this Kingdom to your Majesty's obedience.

And if the measures I have concerted with your other loyal subjects fail me not, which they hardly can, I doubt not before the end of this summer I shall be able to come to your Majesty's assistance with a brave army, which, backed with the justice of your Majesty's cause, will make the rebels in England, as well as in Scotland, feel the just rewards of rebellion. Only, give me leave, after I have reduced this country to your Majesty's obedience, and conquered from Dan to Beersheba, to say to your Majesty then, as David's General said to his master, " Come thou thyself lest this country be called by my name."

For in all my actions I aim only at your Majesty's honours and interest, as becomes one that is to his last breath, may it please your Sacred Majesty,

> Your Majesty's most humble, most faithful, and
> most obedient Subject and Servant,
>
> MONTROSE.

*   *   *

This despatch was written at top speed, like all that Montrose wrote, and with the battle still reeling to and fro in his brain. Tired out from it, he had had his first meal for nearly forty-eight hours, had at once fallen into the dead sleep of utter exhaustion; and as soon as he was up next morning, wrote to King Charles.

Yet only one half of his letter was concerned with the victory he had just won, which had destroyed for ever the fighting strength of the most powerful clan in Scotland. In the other half, he went very thoroughly and carefully into King Charles' present affairs,—considering the reports he had heard of a suggested peace treaty, whose terms 'might make your Majesty a King of straw.'

This made him anxious to show with all his force how confident he now was that he should be able to provide King Charles with a secure base and reserve in Scotland. " Come thou thyself "— it was always his appeal to the King. The bulk of the rebels in Scotland would, he knew, be shocked at the thought of any personal disloyalty to the King; they followed Argyll's policy only because Argyll had had the whole country in his grip.

Now Montrose had loosened that grip, and utterly smashed its military power. Fifteen hundred of Argyll's clan lay dead, together with their general, Auchinbreck. Along nine miles of the plain they lay in their green tartan, and in the waters of Loch Eil, that were reddened long after sunrise. Many had rushed into those waters, in their desperation to try and escape the slaughter by swimming out to the galley of their chief.

But with her anchor weighed and her black sails filled, the *Dubhlinnseach*, that bird of ill omen, had drawn away from the shore, and was slipping fast over the sparkling water towards the open sea.

Montrose had omitted, perhaps even forgotten to mention that ignominious cruise of the galley of Lorne. The cowardice of his enemies was no concern of his.

Nor was that of his friends, if cowardice it were, or only common-sense, that had made the bard, Ian Lom Macdonald, refuse his invitation to join in the battle, with the objection that he would do more useful work by sitting up on the hillside to see how it went, and composing a personal account of the battle by an eye-witness.

And the report of the non-combatant (untranslatable in English) was far less cool and dispassionate than that given by the leader in the fight. Ben Nevis had trembled, the earth had shaken, as his clan swept down like a whirlwind from Loch Ness to Loch Eil, and the Campbells rushed to meet them like the waves of the sea. But like waves they were broken into spray, and no more seen. No harp would mourn for the false race of Diarmaid, but the birds of Loch Eil would cry rejoicing as they wheeled to their feast.

Snug homes the Macdonalds had had, now a heap of cold ruins, fair had grown the braes of Lochaber, now a bare desert,—white bones of the Macdonalds marked the path where the Campbells had slain and burned and driven their foes beyond the seas. Now it was the turn of the Macdonalds to put the Campbells to a colder exile, to drive their enemy at the point of the sword into the salt waves.

Death in fact was a game of tit for tat,—and life only slightly more glorious and exciting than death.

XIX

NOW that the clan of Diarmaid were finished as a fighting unit, most of the Macdonalds could not see what they were carrying on the campaign for. Montrose had to remind Alasdair that there was still a war on in England, and that it was his eventual object to join in it. It all seemed very far-fetched to Colkitto and his other two sons, Angus and Archibald. They would not go east with Montrose into the Gordon country. But they could not persuade Alasdair to remain with them.

" I have fought too long with my lord of Montrose," he said, " to hope for any better sport than he can give me."

Cavalry must be recruited from the Gordons; he could not go south through the Lowlands without it, and he only had the little bodyguard of horse under Lord Airlie and his surviving son, Sir David Ogilvy.

Even those few horses he had were scarecrows after all they had gone through,—" the Beggarman's Line down their haunches is so deep you could dig potatoes in it," their Irish grooms complained.

But of cattle and weapons and all manner of good clothes the troops were now well plenished. The Major-General of His Majesty's Irishes could go as finely dressed as any courtier, with a plumed hat and a silver-laced cloak and a pair of gauntleted Spanish leather gloves,—and a special gillie to carry the lot, since, as Alasdair remarked, it was all very well to have such things about one, as long as they were not in the way.

They marched up to Inverness and then east to Elgin, where Seaforth was holding a committee meeting with other Covenanting lords. Never was there so quick a way to break up a committee as when the news reached it that Montrose was marching on the town. It dispersed on the moment; as Seaforth's army of five thousand at Inverness seemed to have already done.

Previous Covenanters now tumbled over each other in their haste to serve under the royal standard; in a few days Seaforth himself marched up to sign the bond that Montrose had drawn up against him and his other enemies, when the King's Lieutenant had been all but caught between them at Loch Ness. Down went Seaforth's small signature, cramped by having to squeeze in after the names in large text of Montrose and Graham and Airlie, amid the surrounding rabble of scrawls and flourishes and marks that branched off in all directions from the little group of leaders.

And soon room had to be found for another, the most welcome name of all. On one of the blustering last days of February, three riders on fine horses came clattering down the cobbled street in a mighty hurry, followed by a body of men. Johnnie at the window turned and called to his father, " They are wearing trews of the Gordon tartan."

Montrose was out on the steps of the house by the time they were dismounting,—and was greeting his old friend, Colonel Nathaniel Gordon, who had so unaccountably deserted last November, and with him, Huntly's heir, George, Lord Gordon, and his younger brother, Lewis.

Now Nathaniel Gordon's conduct was made clear. He had been following a plan he would not speak of till it was accomplished, for fear of disappointment or betrayal,—he had pretended conversion to the Covenanters, and so was able to get in touch with young Lord Gordon, whom he had found virtually a prisoner in his own domains. But now the power of Argyll was broken, and Gordon was free in his home at the Bog of Gight to fly the Royal Standard from its tower.

No sooner had he heard that Montrose was at Elgin, so near to him, than he and his brother and their cousin Nathaniel leaped on their horses, hastily mustered a body of two hundred troopers, and dashed off to him. They had even persuaded Lord Huntly himself to come with them, or rather Nathaniel had—" If you had heard him ! " interrupted Lewis; " a missionary is his true trade,—he actually converted my father."

" But where is my lord Marquis? " asked Montrose.

Alas, where indeed? Huntly's conversion had carried him so

far as his horse. Once mounted, he glared into the distance, turned his horse's head, muttered something that sounded like—" Two King's Lieutenants cannot take the field together,"—and without a word more to any of them, summoned a small body of the horsemen round him, and rode off in the opposite direction—" who knows where? "

It sounded an insane example of jealousy and vanity; Lord Gordon tried to soften it by saying he would pass out of that mood,—" I have seen it drop from him like a cloak that he has been hugging about him."

" And then he will fling another about him, and see how he looks in that," laughed Lewis.

My lord of Huntly was evidently a family tradition, his fantastic egoism a cause for amusement and even pride, since he was so splendid to look at, so imposing to listen to, so generous and extravagant and careless of consequences. He had run through fortune after fortune, he had begot an enormous family, and scarcely noticed they were there, he had determined to fight for the King, but only when to do so would put him into the position of sole glory.

And his sons not only resembled him, but longed to do so,—all except the eldest, and, thank Heaven, the most important, thought Montrose, as he looked at Lord Gordon, and found the young man's eyes fixed on himself.

" It is seven years, my lord," said Gordon quietly, " since you rode up to our house, and I said I wished I could join you."

Since then he had been by his father's side in that ' glaring match ' against Montrose at Turriff; he and his father had been led captive by him to Edinburgh; he had as much reason as his father to resent fighting by the side of their former opponent.

Yet he now thought only how he had at last fulfilled that wish of seven years ago, when into his crowded household, as hot with moods and jealousies and self-assertions as a rich cake is with spices, there had come the man who had made him feel what freedom it would be to serve something beyond one's own ends or caprices.

He had not known much freedom. His uncle Argyll had dragged him by his side while he laid waste the Gordon lands, burning and destroying all that his army could not consume. To all Gordon's expostulations Argyll replied in a calm and gentle manner that there was no present remedy, but that he must have patience and keep fair accounts of his losses, and the Estates would pay it all back to him. And his uncle crowned this absurdity by embracing him and praying him to believe that he cared for him as his own son.

His nephew broke out that Argyll must wish rather to ruin the Gordons than catch up with his enemy. Whereupon his uncle closed the argument in his favourite fashion by walking out of the room in the middle of what Gordon was saying, and shutting the door after him.

" It was prison," Gordon now said; and like a man escaped from prison did he seem now, as he listened to all that Montrose said, with a delight that gave his ordinarily quiet and pleasant demeanour a shining vigour. Here at last he sat by the side of the man whom his heart had instinctively acknowledged as his commander. They talked and laughed together and drank toasts, with the ease of old friends.

But Lewis, his flamboyant young brother, was never quite at ease. He was as finely built as a highly inbred racehorse, with all the pluck and dash and go in the world,—but in which direction would he go? No one could ever be sure. As Montrose watched him he realized how steady and gentle a hand would be needed to keep this young colt from galloping off on some course more perverse even and contradictory than his father's.

Lewis' vain, glancing eye shot all round his company in challenge to them not to find him amusing, as he rushed into a vivid picture of " the Ruling Elder," or " the Merchant," as his irreverent nephews called Argyll, who had made the Civil War itself seem a trivial thing compared with their endless money worries.

" And the Merchant has given my sisters generous dowries—but how? By mortgaging every penny of them on the estate. Jean says it is my father's fault—she swears she hates him, but women are always saying that, and never do."

A child's face that suddenly sharpened into that of a vixen,—a clamorous demand for seven-and-sixpence for some rather odd purpose,—that early impression of the Lady Jean Gordon flashed back after years into Montrose's mind.

Lewis' laughing voice was racing on, tumbling over itself in his excitement. " You should hear his own son on him, and how short he is kept. Young Lorne is not a bad fellow, but his father——"

Alasdair Macdonald was growing bored with so much crowing from the young cockerel.

" Ah, your uncle is a gay lad," he said, " and here's a toast I would be proud to drink to him—less power to his elbow, if that be possible, and more power to the sling that holds it. I hear he was still wearing it when he turned up at Edinburgh just now, as if he had been at a bones-breaking, and much sympathy he got for his poor arm."

" He can still wield a pen, though," said Nathaniel Gordon, " that is mightier than the sword in his hands."

" What has he been writing now? "

" The death warrant of my lord of Montrose, that he shall be hanged, drawn and quartered whenever he shall fall into the hands of the Committee of Estates. And the offer of a prize of twenty thousand crowns to the hands that catch him, alive or dead."

" Well, now," said Alasdair, " isn't it a pity the hands can only walk fast enough to catch my lord Marquis when they are running away from him? "

A roar of laughter round the table greeted the latest measure of revenge on the part of their defeated foes.

" You are very quiet," said Alasdair to Lord Graham, in what he imagined to be a low tone; " were you discouraged by all my fine hero's talk? "

His glance at Lewis made the half-heard sarcasm clear enough to that sensitive youth, and at once his handsome face was aflame with indignation. Were recruits from the noblest family in the north to be treated with mockery—and to a spoilt whipper-snapper who had no business to be there, sitting up among all the warrior chieftains when he ought to be at school?

Already had Lewis discovered the younger generation.

*　　*　　*

" And if you think I'm going to stay here to be taught my business by a brat of a boy who thinks he's an old campaigner just because he's been carried across the mountains on the backs of the Macdonalds,—do you know what he said to me,—' I should have thought any fool nowadays would know better in a battle than to retire his horse at the caracole as if he were in a riding school.' "

" What had you said to him? " asked George Gordon.

But the initial stages of a quarrel did not interest Lewis; he had been insulted,—that was enough. He might possibly have told Lord Graham that he was a pampered puppy and an unlicked cub—" and what the devil are you smiling at? "

Said his elder brother, " It's so short a time since you complained that people had called you that. Well, now you have passed it on to Lord Graham, you should be satisfied."

Lewis hunched his shoulders and thrust a face white with fury almost under George Gordon's chin. " Satisfied? Yes, I'll get satisfaction. It's doing him too much honour when he ought to have his head smacked, but I have consented to cross swords with him."

It was Lewis who very nearly had his head smacked, but Gordon was just able to restrain himself. Not only must this preposterous duel with his Commander's son be stopped, but Lewis must be prevented from flying off in a huff, and half the Gordon Highlanders with him. But Lewis would only consent to make up the quarrel if Lord Graham apologized. After a long pause, he added—" In writing."

" Had you not better write out a list of your grievances, like our uncle Argyll before his duel? " suggested Gordon.

Lewis laughed involuntarily at the memory, and then found he could not get back to his pedestal of offended dignity. Gordon drew a breath of relief that he need not after all trouble his hero with these schoolboy quarrels. But there was in any case no need, for Lord Graham had fallen ill.

XX

*T*HEY had all moved on to the Bog of Gight, where Gordon glowed with pride to do the honours of his home, now a fortified royalist camp again, as it had been when Huntly had made his isolated and therefore frustrated campaign on the King's behalf last spring. It was now the first blustering days of March, and Montrose was thankful to have his son in the comfort of Gordon Castle, for he had been worn out by the terrific strain of the mountain campaign that winter.

Now he lay deep and snug in a goosefeather bed, with curtains round him of white and scarlet silk from China, and need not care how deep the snow fell. He could hear the fretful cry of new-born lambs through the gusts of east wind, and the cawing of rooks as they built their nests in the high trees that Huntly's magnificent father had planted when he was a young man.

There were women enough in the Bog of Gight to nurse him, but they were all driven out by the Irish wife of one of Macdonald's captains, who had great knowledge of medicine and was nick-named Bebinn after a famous lady doctor in her country.

The women who followed the Macdonalds were of all kinds, from the wives and concubines of the kerns who were as wild and fierce as their men, to this quietly adventurous lady who took it for granted that she should follow her lord to the wars and place her powers of nursing and the dressing of wounds at the service of his comrades.

And when it came to his commander's son,—would it be herself that would leave him to be stifled and bled to death by the barbarous doctors of this uncivilized country? For would they believe it, there was no such thing as a sweating-house in the whole land, or she might have got the rheumatic aches and the fever together out of the poor lad in a vapour bath, the way she need not bleed him, for that she would not risk, his heart had not the strength for it.

She smashed those panes of the little windows that were not

made to open, and told the Gordons' scandalized family doctor that in any hospital at home in the good old days, the patient would have had four doors open to the four winds of heaven, and a stream running through the centre of the house, but that she supposed there was no more knowledge of hygiene here than there was of anything else.

" If she is so proud of her home, why does she not stay in it ? " grumbled the physician, once he was safely outside the sick-room. " It is my belief the Irish only come here for the sake of telling us how superior they are."

Bebinn could not have stayed in her home, for she had been driven out of it on to the hills with all her family when she was a girl, and her father's house and lands given as one of the new ' plantations ' to a Glasgow trader. Her mother had died of the effects of exposure, one of her sisters from starvation, so that she had had good opportunity to practise her early acquired art of doctoring.

She was tall and plump, with pleasant, laughing features, a white skin, thick ropes of black hair round her head, and hands of which she took great care, lamenting to Johnnie that it was no longer fashionable to dye the nails crimson as in the days of the heroes, when every good house and the guest-house of every monastery had a bath, and all the men bathed after hunting and carefully combed their long hair before sitting down to dinner.

He lay luxuriously contented with the low sound of her voice as she moved about his bed. The candlelight gleamed on the necklet, shaped like a crescent moon, that fitted round her firm white neck; it was of gold so finely wrought that no jeweller to-day knew how it was done; it had been made by the Sidh, she said, magicians, skilled in science and metal-work, who once ruled all Ireland, but now live under the earth in the elf-mounds, where they have built palaces that are ablaze with light and jewels.

The beauty and learning and noble living of ' the old ancient days,'—he had caught glimpses of them in the talk of even the roughest of the Irish kerns,—and now they shone about the sick boy as he lay in bed, dreaming of what he would do when he was full grown.

When he and his father had put the King on his throne again, he would ask in reward that he should be given the old title of the Lord of Ireland, and he would rule her with the wisdom of the Norman lords who had made themselves a part of the country, unlike the later colonists who had ruined Ireland by exploiting her for their own commercial ends; for the last hundred years they had settled in thousands like locusts on the land, driving the people out of their houses and fields to wander homeless and starving among the hills, until they had been reduced to utter savagery of spirit as well as of body.

" When you are Duke of Ireland," Bebinn told him, " we will raise an army for you out of Ulster as fine as that in the Tain, where every man had a cloak of a different colour, some orange, some white, some blue, some yellow, and in their midst a young red-freckled lad in a crimson cloak, and who should that be but your Honour's self? "

" No, for I'll be a man then."

" You will indeed, and you shall make me chief doctor and give me a laboratory for students to be making all sorts of experiments."

" And what shall I make O'Cahan? "

" Tamer in chief to your Honour's pets," said Bebinn, with a glance across the bed at the great Manus, who was imperturbably engaged in feeding a baby squirrel with milk from his mouth, squirting it drop by drop down a dandelion stalk.

There were no animals that O'Cahan could not tame; he had had as pets, but not, he explained, all at the same time, a crane, a crow, a badger, a wolf, a deer, and two sparrows that he had taught to fly at two darts, one red and one blue, which he would shoot from a blowpipe at a tree, and the one sparrow would fly after the red, and the other after the blue, and bring them back and put them into his mouth.

He would stay in for hours on those bright spring days to be with the boy when Bebinn allowed it, carving chessmen for him to have for his own to play with when he was better, or playing on a little flute the tunes of his famous cousin, Rory Dall O'Cahan, " which you thieving Scots try to claim as your own, and just because he did you the great honour to come over on a visit with a large retinue, and died here."

Manus O'Cahan was famous enough himself by now, and infamous to his enemies for the courage and the cruelty that he had shown in the wars; but like many Irishmen he was prouder of the deeds of his illustrious kinsmen, even of those so peaceable as an old blind musician's.

Alasdair came in too with his great dog Bran, and in his hand the magic green stone that the Macdonalds had kept for over a thousand years, ever since their chaplain, Saint Maelias, had brought it into the family. It had the power, said Alasdair, to remove stitches from the sides of sick persons, and if the patient were not going to recover then it would of its own accord get out of the bed and roll away.

" It looks like a green goose's egg," murmured Johnnie,—and Bebinn murmured still lower some further comparison, not flattering to its owner. He and his stone and dog were soon swept out again by her; and she came back into the room, quoting her ancient medical authority that " Dogs, fools and talkative people are to be kept away from the patient."

Johnnie's illness was very short. He had seemed at first only over-exhausted, but there came high fever, and two or three days of tossing in that great bed, where faces hovered over him. There was one like a moon, set in black hair above a ring of gold, that swam before him and disappeared but always stayed somewhere near him, for he had only to call and she came again.

Until he no longer wanted her, for there was his father's face, keen and high like a hawk's, with the clear eyes that could always pierce through the mist that now surrounded him; and his father's voice could always be heard, low and ringing, when the others could only move their mouths at him and say nothing. And his father's hand came down on his shoulder and made him know that all was well, when nothing else in that room remained, and

2 D

the curtains of his bed had turned into the white and scarlet sky beyond the mountains, where he had stood beside his father and heard the trumpets salute the King's Standard at dawn.

That hand was still on his shoulder, though its touch grew lighter and lighter yet,—but now he did not need its touch to tell him that his wish had come true, that he and his father would go on like this for ever.

* * *

Montrose saw his son die. Years ago, at the same age as that son, he had seen his father die. A world of peaceful family life, of security and leisure, had rolled away since that great gathering of his family had met together for weeks to do honour to the old Earl. Now his heir was buried in haste at the little church of Bellie, in the country of a rival clan,—"And long will the Gordons be proud of it," said George Gordon.

The Irish wanted to give him a wake as long as that of Saint Patrick or Brian Boru, with a King torch of the thickness of a man's body to burn before the house; but there was no time for that, nor to collect any of his family.

But Lord Graham had mourners enough. Four chiefs bore his coffin on their shoulders. The Macdonalds of Antrim from over the sea, the Macdonalds of Glengarry and Clanranald, of Keppoch and the Isles, the Camerons of Lochaber, the Macleans from Morvern and Mull, the Farquharsons from Braemar, the Gordons, the Grants and the Stewarts, the men from Skye and Orkney, from Uist and Kintyre, from Atholl and Nairn and Moray, all the different clans in turn marched over the bleak, dun-coloured heather, each with their pipers playing their immemorial lament for the dead, their inconsolable music sobbing and wailing like the lament of lost spirits borne on the cold air.

When all the clans were gathered together, then the women rushed forward, a rabble of mourning furies, and with frantic gestures threw themselves upon the coffin, beating their hands upon it, then flinging them above their heads,—beating their breasts, tearing their hair, while the wail of the keeners rose and fell in long dying cadence, and one voice after another cried out, in verse made up on the instant, the love and honour that all the Highlanders, Scots and Irish, had had for the dead boy.

He had been their prince and their playfellow, their hope, and the tenderest object of their protection. Like his father he had been made free of their charmed circle, and before he was in his grave had passed into their other world of legend and song. Like a song he was remembered, a gay hunting song on the notes of the horns, that is heard only in the freshness of the morning.

And with him went the last moment when Montrose had felt himself that boy.

XXI

WITHIN a week of Johnnie's death, young James, who did not yet know that he was now Lord Graham and his father's heir, was riding down the street of Montrose, four miles from Kinnaird, accompanied by Master Forrett, to buy some new fishing tackle. Just as they had stopped before the little shop, there came a troop of cavalry clattering round the corner of the street, and at their head a tall, lean, horsey-looking gentleman, with a long scar on his cheek, and beside him, rather oddly, a ragged boy of the town, who hung on to his stirrup as he ran.

"There he is!" yelled the boy's shrill voice. "That's my lord James!"

"And that's your shilling, my boy," replied the gentleman, smiling at James in a way that precisian felt to be extremely familiar on so informal an introduction,—"And now, my young sir, you will have to go with us."

James thought at first he was still addressing the ragamuffin, and was wondering why he looked so cheerful, when the gentleman rode up closer to him, put his hand on his pony's bridle and began turning his head round.

"Who are you?" asked James.

"You'll soon know," said the genial but bad-mannered stranger.

For one wild leaping moment, James thought he might be a messenger from his father, come to take him to him. But he was Sir John Hurry, a Covenanting soldier, returning from a raid on some of Montrose's men; he was now taking James and his tutor prisoner, to be sent on to Edinburgh Castle. He had good reason to be cheerful over this lucky windfall, and his raid had also been most successful.

Montrose was now in camp at Kintore near Aberdeen, which the Covenanters had evacuated, and had given his word that the Irishes should not come within eight miles of the city. But the gay Nat Gordon organized a pleasure party of about eighty companions to ride into the town and enjoy a really good dinner, for

420

some of the inns had excellent cooking and wines. Sir John Hurry, who happened to be near by with about eight score horse, got word of this, and charged through the town, cutting down all the dismounted men who happened to be standing about, utterly unprepared in the streets; and drove off their horses. Nat Gordon, deeply closeted with the chief innkeeper in the cellar, dashed out to find that some of their best captains had been killed and among them Donald Farquharson, one of the finest men Montrose had. A miserable remnant of the pleasure party rode back to Kintore, as empty as when they rode out. Nat Gordon had to force himself to tell his commander of the carelessness that had cost them so dear.

For the first time since the campaign had begun, Montrose gave way to fury with his own men. The blind, needless stupidity of such a chance enraged him, and the wanton destruction of necessary men,—but more than all, the loss in Donald Farquharson of a friend who never lost courage or hope or his temper, or the joyful alacrity he showed in all he did.

Everything seemed to be drifting from him at once. Old Lord Airlie was another victim of the winter campaign ; he had fallen dangerously ill, and now the army was on the march again he had to be sent to Huntly Castle at Strathbogie to be nursed, with a guard of several hundred of his horse. The Atholl men had begun to go home; the Gordons under Lord Lewis showed every sign of doing the same. Seaforth, who had been sent to his own country to fortify it against the Covenant, had taken the opportunity to change sides again.

Montrose's men were again short of food and ammunition, and their clothes in rags, for the plunder of Inverlochy had had plenty of wear and tear. His recruiting had to be carried on by threat of fire and sword, but the Covenanting lords preferred to see the threats carried out rather than join the Royal Standard in company with Western Highlanders and Irish.

There were strong fortresses for them to retire to ; in one of them, the Earl Marischal, whose brother had fallen at Fyvie, shut himself up with sixteen ministers, among them Montrose's old travelling companion to Aberdeen, Mr. Cant, who told Marischal that the smoke of his burning barns was " a sweet-smelling incense in the nostrils of the Lord." What Marischal replied was not recorded. He sent no answer to Montrose's repeated warnings, and refused all parley with him.

Montrose had still had no answer to his letter to the King, despatched nearly two months ago; and without any promise of help from the King he could not now march on the Lowlands. His army was rapidly dwindling, and General Baillie blocked the road to the south with three thousand men, most of them picked regulars.

He must do something quickly to hold the remnant of his men together, and counteract the Gordon grumblings, spread by their junior leader, who complained they had had no profit nor excitement since they had joined the Standard.

So he sent the weaker portion of his army on to Brechin with the baggage; and with the rest marched all night down on to Dundee, the most important Covenanting town in Angus. He summoned the magistrates to surrender, and on receiving no answer, stormed the walls, captured the guns on the little mound of Corbie Hill, turned them against the defenders, and entered the town. The citizens hurried to arrange a formal surrender with Lord Gordon, while the Highlanders burst into the shops, flung lengths of cloth over their shoulders, stuffed money from the till, raisins, dried figs, and even, in the agitation of the moment, split white peas, into their knapsacks.

Soon they found what they were really seeking,—loaves and cakes and meat pies at the pastrycooks, smoked herrings, and, above all, barrels of wine and ale. They had not halted in the march all night, nor been full-fed for many days,—now many of them drank till they fell. At ten o'clock that morning, the 4th of April, the assault had begun. By early evening a remarkable peace prevailed in the stormed town, and their commander looked down on it from Corbie Hill with a somewhat grim amusement.

To Black Pate of Inchbrakie, who was standing beside him, he said, " They have got their pay."

Black Pate gave a glance at the worn face of his commander and knew well enough what he was thinking.

Down in England, two months ago, Cromwell's New Model army had been formed, twelve regiments of foot, eleven of horse, under the strictest new training,—and, what was far more important, every man in it received regular pay.

" You have made your New Model army," he told Montrose, " and out of such stuff as Cromwell and every other man, alive or dead, has never been able to handle. The Highland armies of the past had the courage of the wild cat, but it was never any good against a Lowland army. All their great fights against us were heroic defeats. But look what new war material you have made of them! "

Montrose looked at the little market square below and the four streets leading out of it, full of the drunken forms of ragamuffins, staggering with their spoil, or clutching it to them even as they sprawled in slumber on the ground.

" Your last remark was unfortunate," he said; and their eyes met in one of the old friendly grins that had united them since boyhood. There was no need for Montrose to say what he was thinking; but this last month had beaten down a good many of his defences, and he said it.

" I can transform my material," he said, " I cannot alter its conditions. One of the King's English generals said he feared unpaid soldiers worse than the Covenanters,—or the devil himself. If I could pay my men, I should not have to provision them from the countryside,—semi-starvation on a little oatmeal and water, or else a couple of hundred cattle! If I could give them regular pay, they would not have to leg it home across the heather, as you once warned me, driving the cattle before them, with their booty slung over their shoulders, to wives and families that would starve if they did not go. Every man who did that, I would shoot as a deserter—if I could give them regular pay to send home. I cannot,—and so my army here is now barely six hundred foot and a hundred and fifty horse—less than a quarter the size it was two months ago. I cannot,—and so I have to promise them loot as encouragement, and give them their heads as I am doing now, curse it!"

Black Pate laid his hand on his arm. "They've done the town no real harm," he said, "a house or two has been fired, that is all. They're so leg weary that the drink has taken them quietly."

"Let them burn it to hell," broke out his commander, "it's not that I care for now. Think of the advantage that fellow in England has over me! Cromwell is a born leader of men and cavalry trainer, I'll grant you. But would that get him where he is now, if it were not that his side have the money? The Parliament holds London and the richest trading towns,—they have all the finances of the city and the Jew moneylenders behind them. Up here, Argyll owns the money. They can afford their little luxuries,—their regular pay, the price of twenty thousand crowns on my head. We cannot afford them—and that's the real odds against us."

He felt nearer to despair than ever in his life.

Johnnie lay dead in Bellie kirkyard, young James was imprisoned in Edinburgh Castle. He could not let himself think of these two, nor of Magdalen's grief,—to do so would be to tear himself in pieces.

Deliberately he set his mind to the problem of his position. He knew well that this war material of Highland regiments, that he had improvised, would outlast his time, and might become famous in history again and again. But he could not use it as later leaders would do,—his hands were tied by the lack of money.

And he remembered a summer evening nine long years ago, when he had come home to his country, and sat with Napier in the fading daylight of his study, and heard him talk with such grave disquiet of the power of money.

That power might well conquer all other forces in the end.

He could not say so, for not even to Black Pate, the solid standby and consoler of his schooldays, might his commander let go so far of his despondency. So heavy and unbearable had it grown that he now looked down upon the drunkards below with envy, and wondered whether he should not seek their means of oblivion.

" I have a good mind to get drunk," he said, and Pate nodded in approval, for he thought his cousin was probably near breaking-point.

" I can take charge," he said. His cheerful good-humour remained imperturbable. His father was in prison at Edinburgh; his mother, in the Tower of Tullybelton which still stood intact, was persecuted by the Covenanters; the family's principal castle of Inchbrakie had lately been burned and battered down.

They turned to come down from the mound, when they saw a man galloping furiously towards them. He shouted as he got within earshot, so breathlessly that they could not at first catch what he said. But they did the next instant,—it was one of their own scouts, and he was crying that Hurry and Baillie had joined forces, and with an army of three thousand foot and eight hundred horse were now marching on the town,—were within a mile of the West Port.

XXII

*T*HE best part of the men were drunk, many of them already sunk in slumber, the others settling down steadily to the business of drinking. In this state, even if they could be induced to move, it would be all but impossible to get them to abandon the plunder they had collected.

Others had heard that shouted news. As the scout reached Montrose, they ran up from all directions, and at once he was the centre of a group of officers, all giving frantic and contrary advice, though all of despair. Alasdair was not drunk, but had drink taken,—the white flame of battle blazed in his eyes as he ran towards them, laughing loud, and shouted, " Let us make a last charge as they come in at the West Port, and see how many we can drag with us to our death."

" Will you throw away the King's cause? " cried Black Pate to Montrose. " Save yourself, and get another army."

" It is only the loss of a few hundreds," urged Sibbald.

" Go,—and we can shift somehow," came Pate's voice again,— and there against it was a boy's voice, shrilling above the men's,— " Listen to the Lowlanders! Let them run! I shall get my men to fire the town, and we'll all burn up to heaven together."

Montrose's hand gripped Lord Lewis' shoulder, and shook it.

" Get your men together and out at the East Port," he said. " Pick out the sober and get them to prod the others off the ground with their pikes if need be. And if you see a bucket of cold water, cool your head in it as you go past,—that will make you fighting drunk instead of despairing drunk."

" Fighting? But we have to run away? "

" You'll get fighting too," Montrose promised him.

His voice was more cheerful than it had sounded all this last month. He brushed aside the clatter of suggestions all round him with—" Do your duty, gentlemen,—leave the management to me,—the event to God."

As he gave his orders, urgent but unhurried, his eyes sought those of each man in turn, and saw to it that they would be carried out.

Black Pate, who had a minute or two ago seen him on the verge of utter failure of courage, could scarcely believe it when in this desperate moment he saw on the face of his commander that old grave smile that used to curl up the corners of his mouth into the shape of a half moon.

He now set himself to get every man out of the town in the space of a few minutes. His cavalry officers rode up from the market square through the four main streets, driving all the men in them like sheep towards the East Port and the Seagate. They shouted their orders, and used the point of a sword or pike if the men showed any reluctance to drop their weightier booty. But the news that the enemy was upon them was the best weapon. It had run like wildfire through the crowds of looters, and none of them were as yet dead drunk, for they were tough and had only just begun to get down to it seriously.

But even those who helped Montrose do it, did not know how it was done. Alasdair set his dog Bran to rout out the sleepiest, and the great wolf-hound did good work. Cursing, grumbling, calling to their comrades, the men huddled and bustled each other out somehow through the gates of the East Port and the Seagate. One of the Irish still hung on to the rare treasure of a large clock, complaining that it was terrible heavy, and had it knocked off his back. The cavalry came last; as Montrose rode out with the rearguard through the Seagate, they heard a shot behind them.

" There's Hurry's van coming in at the West Port," he said to Black Pate, and his voice was as quiet as ever.

The confused mass of men were flinging themselves somehow or other into the line of march. Their commander rode forwards and backwards, straightening and sorting it out, until he had got four hundred of his foot in front, with those most drunk to the fore, and the more sober driving them on behind. Then followed the two hundred musketeers, with the hundred and fifty cavalry,— the strongest part of the army in the rear, in case they were overtaken.

They were, soon enough, for Hurry's horse charged them when they were only a few miles from Dundee. But Hurry could not bring up all his cavalry at once, and Montrose's musketeers beat off the pursuit, "picking them off their saddles as fast as they came up, as neat and pretty as you could wish," so Manus O'Cahan reported to his flustered infantry in front.

It was getting dark by now as the royal army drove furiously on along the sea-coast, up towards Arbroath. Rain fell in heavy spurts, making the night thick and black, drenching the men to the skin, and turning their road to a slippery morass. Then the wet blindness rolled away, they saw the stars and the shimmer of the sea in the clear night of a northern spring.

Somewhere about midnight their course was changed; they had been marching north-east along the coast, but now they turned inland, and were marching almost due south-west as far as they could make out. It seemed mad to the soberest,—might they not crash at any moment into Baillie's army, who could hardly be all following along behind Hurry's horse, with their noses to each other's tails? Baillie must know that their one hope of escape was westward in the hills, and be guarding the passes there.

But they did not crash into Baillie, and well before dawn they were marching north again. Morning showed them the hills, their refuge, only three miles off, and Careston Castle, one of the Carnegie houses on the South Esk, near by them.

Stupefied with sleep, some of them were just able to grasp what had happened. Baillie had tried to cut them off from the hills by pushing on before them to Arbroath by the shorter route across inland, instead of following the curve of the sea-coast, as Montrose had begun by doing. Thus he meant to catch the little army between his and Hurry's forces, and the sea.

Montrose had guessed that his enemy would follow this strategy, and had acted on it, by going out of his northerly course, turning on his tracks, and then turning north again, and so managed in the darkness to get past behind Baillie's army. They were now clear of it, and their safety in sight. His men were dead beat, falling out by the wayside, and he ordered a halt. They fell to the ground, asleep before they fell.

Montrose sent out cavalry vedettes to guard them from any surprise attack, for as soon as it grew light, Baillie and Hurry would discover how he had slipped between them, and be turning in fresh pursuit. It was a grave risk to give his men an hour or two of respite, but it was a risk that had to be taken.

They had marched nearly sixty miles in this last night and the night before—in the intervening day they had stormed and looted a town, and then, tired and famished, got blind drunk,—then reeled into the line of march again, at double speed now, flying from the enemy, and having to turn and fight running engagements with their pursuers again and again. All this they had done for thirty-six hours on end without a pause.

They had had about a couple of hours' rest when his scouts brought news that Hurry's cavalry were hot on their trail, and the business of beating up the men began again. But this time it was far more serious. Many of them had been asleep even as they marched, and now they could hardly be induced to wake even at the 'push of pike.' Panic itself could do nothing for them, now that they were half dead with weariness, and only wished to be entirely so. Three miles off stood the hills, but could they now reach them before they were all cut down?

Montrose and his officers just managed to get up a fair amount of musketeers to support the cavalry by the time Hurry's vanguard was upon them. The clash and firing of a battle soon brought the rest to their senses. Blindly they groped and staggered on to their bruised and bleeding feet, heard orders somehow, or were pushed into following them, did something, they scarcely knew what. Again Hurry's horse were driven back, and the little army stumbled on towards the hills from whence came their help.

Once there, among the bogs and rocks, no large body of cavalry could follow them. Once there, they would soon meet with the men whom Montrose had sent on to Brechin with the baggage, and who had taken to the hills, their accustomed base, at the first news of what had happened at Dundee. Once there, they could fall on the heather and sleep as though they would never wake again. By midday they were there.

Yet again Montrose had given his men their pay. No other commander, they knew, could do what he had done. This retreat was to make him more famous even than his victories, with the masters of war in England, Germany and France. Yet not for that glory, any more than for gain, did his Highlanders and Irish follow him, but because, like the magic heroes of their own stories, he enlarged the stature of their lives to the uttermost, and made it something more than human.

This monstrous fuddled nightmare in which they had been made to lurch along at top speed, bewildered with the wind and rain splashing on their faces, while their feet dragged swollen and heavy as hot lead, plunging on through the blind darkness and unknown danger, moving now north-east, now west, now north again, in answer to curt words of command that had to be repeated and urged before they could be understood,—this surging nightmare had still its interior glow, its blissful indifference as to what might happen next, even while the drink died out of it, for behind it was a sense that they were in good hands, that their commander would see to it that all was well, that now, even more than in a victorious charge, they were heroes following a god.

*　　*　　*

Montrose too had his pay. A beggar, tramping his way across the Grampians, came on the camp of the wandering army, and asked to be taken to its leader. Montrose knew him instantly. He was no beggar, but James Small, son of the laird of Fotherance, who held a minor post at the English Court, and had undertaken this desperate mission of finding his way up through the enemy country in disguise, in order to deliver a letter from the King, in answer to the despatch Montrose had written to him after his victory at Inverlochy.

King Charles had not got that despatch until a month later, in March, and by then he had already refused the peace treaty of Uxbridge, on which Montrose had offered his advice. One of the King's chief reasons for refusing it was that the ' oblivion ' or pardon demanded for his enemies, was not to be extended to his friends. Montrose in particular was to be exempt from it,— the sentence of execution passed on him by the Committee of Estates was to be carried out as one of the pledges of the peace.

Montrose had not known of this condition until now, when James Small told him of it as the main cause of the King's refusal. Not again, if he could help it, would Charles betray a friend to his death.

His cause had been going badly in England ever since last July and the defeat at Marston Moor, but now he was elated by Montrose's victories, and wrote to tell him that he was sending him five hundred horse under Sir Philip Musgrave, and that he would himself come with his army to Scotland, as fast as he could move it, and join forces with Montrose.

XXIII

*L*IKE a heath fire, the army of Montrose fluctuated, changed its shape and course and purpose, so that no man could tell its numbers or its chances against the enemy or when or where it would appear next.

But the results of his battles were clear enough. After Inverlochy, old Leslie, Lord Leven, had to send some of his best regiments to Baillie; and himself, thus weakened, stuck firmly at Carlisle, refusing to go and help the Parliament's armies further south, as they demanded. This made trouble between the allies. Leven openly expressed his desire to cut all the Parliamentarians in pieces; and Cromwell said he ' could as soon draw his sword against the Covenanters as against any in the King's army.'

He was now the coming man on his own side, and it was plain that if it proved successful he would never let the Parliament keep their promise to the Covenanters of making England a Presbyterian country by law. In vain the Covenanters tried to break his power, and pressed to have ' the firebrand ' removed from the Parliament's armies. He was far too useful. It was the Parliament's promises of Presbyterianism that would be broken, like so much pie-crust.

" No King, no Scot, no Presbyterian government! " shouted Cromwell's army whenever they saw their Scots allies.

The Covenanters, who had thought it was only the King that broke promises, were being ingenuously disillusioned.

There was another result of Montrose's victories, terrible to his own side; the Kirk now clamoured ferociously for reprisals on all those of royalist sympathies who were in their power. Mr. Cant and Mr. David Dickson were praised for their ' zeal and piety ' in heading a deputation to the Scottish Parliament to demand the execution of some of Montrose's friends. But Parliament thought it better not to be too drastic while Montrose was victorious; they only imposed a large fine on Napier, who was over seventy, and confined him and all the members of his family, including the women and young girls, as state prisoners.

Montrose's nieces were closely interrogated as to their treasonable action in wearing mourning for their young cousin, Lord Graham; they were allowed no communication with their father or each other, and might only take the air from the castle tower once, or at most twice a day, in the presence of the constable of the Castle.

Lord Southesk had done all he could to keep Magdalen's home together, but now only the two youngest of her children remained with her. How long would they or she herself be safe?

It was an agonizing position for the household at Kinnaird, glorying in the news of Montrose's triumphs, but knowing how each fresh triumph might further endanger his family.

Then a bombshell fell on the Covenanters. The King's secret messenger, James Small, was taken and executed on his way back from Montrose to England. The papers found on him showed Argyll that the King intended to come north. Once again his worst terror was upon him—the King in conjunction with Montrose,—it would mean the end of himself. He did all he could to stir up his generals, and only increased the violent irritation between them after the flight from Dundee.

Leven was furious at having sent his best troops to Baillie for a wild-goose chase that achieved nothing; Baillie accused Hurry of treachery in never attacking the retreating army with all the full force of his cavalry at once; Hurry said that Baillie had no more strategy than a hen. Hurry was sent north to raise new levies, Baillie was settled once more near Perth, and it was hoped that Montrose would eventually be caught and crushed between the two forces.

Lord Southesk, who brought the news to his home, had also heard popular accounts of the utter destruction of Montrose's army on the flight from Dundee; but the new urgent efforts on the part of the Covenanters gave him a shrewd guess that these reports were merely Argyll's propaganda.

To the countryside at large, Montrose had become a terror

incalculable as the forces of nature. If a few goats were seen on the tops of the hills in the twilight, they were thought to be the Macdonald men, and people fled.

But the fear of the Solemn League and Covenant was the creeping dread of a daily personal tyranny in tiny matters, prying into the most intimate details of a man's private speech and behaviour, crippling all hope and power to change. And with it went the still deadlier fear of the torments of hell, which were confidently promised to all those who did not support the Covenant. Now came another fear.

While Montrose and his men wandered on the mountains and laughed at their enemies' threats of execution by hanging, drawing and quartering, plague crept through the towns on the bodies of rats. It met a weakened power of resistance from the human community, who had had the sunshine squeezed out of its life by the iron determination of the Kirk towards " the maintenance of a serious style of manners," and " the uprooting of superstition."

A cavalier poet in England showed sound medical sense in his prescription—

> " My wife will dance and I will sing,
> For sure it is the very best thing
> To drive the plague away."

But in Scotland at this time dancing and singing were legal offences,—and so was it to make a pilgrimage to a holy well or the neglected shrines of local saints, as people had done in the old days in time of pestilence, to give themselves hope for life, and comfort for those who had died.

To do so now was superstition. God had written what He had written, and nothing that the people could do, nor any heathenish saint, would alter it by a hair's-breadth,—while as for those already dead, the overwhelming majority was known to be damned. The creed of predestination may show courage; but it is the courage of despair.

Holidays that only made the grey streets vacant and silent,—

the fear of hellfire as the only permissible superstition,—these now helped to feed the plague.

It was creeping towards Edinburgh, and there in the Castle above the town was James, who was now Lord Graham, with his tutor, Master Forrett, in prison.

Still Magdalen could not believe these things. If James were there, she might believe that Johnnie was dead, but now there was nothing through the house but a great silence. People said things to her and sobbed; and she scarcely heard them. Rob looked at her with round, frightened eyes, knowing that both his brothers had gone, and he must now be the man of the family; but she never noticed his efforts. Little Jean cried, and she hushed her as mechanically as if she were a noise, and no more.

She wrote letters to James, and answered his questions about his dogs and hawks and favourite pony. She sent him all the things she could; she looked through the shelves for books to send to him and Master Forrett. Here were the play books the little tutor had bought for Jamie when he had come out of prison in Edinburgh Castle. She opened one of them at random, a modern one called *The Broken Heart*, and stood staring dully at three lines whose sound came back to her in her own voice—

> " But I have signed a Covenant with sadness
> And entered into bonds without condition
> To bear these tempests calmly."

Her resignation was of stone; it seemed that nothing could break it, because her heart was broken.

But those who sign a Covenant with sadness give more hostages to fortune than their children. Her husband came back and reminded her of that.

*   *   *

Like a thunderstorm his army had been circling round and round their home, sometimes even marching through the streets of Montrose, not five miles off. Every day came fresh tales of his exploits; they surrounded him like the flames of his burning progress, so that she could not see through them the face she used to know.

Now at last she saw it again, not dimly in her mind, through the fiery smoke of battles, ever more remote from her,—but before her, close to her, looking down on her from horseback in their courtyard. His eyes looked through her, knew all that had stood frozen in her heart, knew that it was not frozen, for still it beat, for him; she put her two hands over it to still it, but it would not be quieted. He was down from his horse, beside her, he had lifted her up in his arms, and once again she saw his eyes, then saw nothing, felt nothing; and it was he now who put his hand in terror on her heart, for she had fainted.

He carried her into the house, up into their room. She opened her eyes on to his face, as he leaned over her. He had laid her on their bed with the green curtains.

" Was it unlucky to choose green? " she asked, " it is the fairies' colour."

It was strange to be speaking like this at random, not knowing what would come next. All these weeks it had been—

> " Oh still she stood, and bitter she stood,
> And never she shed one tear."

And now the first glimpse of him had released that icy ' bond without condition.' Her heart was not broken, for he was still there to break it. That was in no one else's power, not even Johnnie's, nor young James'.

" You will not do it, will you? "

He did not know what she was imploring him. He took her hands in his; they had grown very small, it seemed, but then they were always thin,—and cold, too cold,—he put them into his breast to warm them, and they could feel his heart there, beating in strong, steady strokes, how unlike her own.

" Little cold claws," he said, and then suddenly he slipped from the bed to its side, kneeling there beside her, and put his head down upon her breast, and let it lie there, for he was tired.

He had stood with his son beside him on the top of the world, and seen his enemy fly from before him; and now his son was dead, and his enemy was preparing ever fresh armies against him. His second son had been snatched from them. His estates were forfeited, his houses lay burned to the ground, his fields laid waste.

He had come home to his wife, and felt how frail a hold he had left her on life,—only her hopes for him.

For he knew now in the deep silence of their peace together that what she had been imploring him just now was not to break her utterly by his own death;—and how could he assure that, when sentence of death by the law of the land had gone out against him, and twenty thousand crowns was the price offered for his murder?

"Dear heart," he said, "you know me here with you, whenever I am from you. Will you not know it still, if I were dead?"

"It would be a great peace for you," she said.

For her too perhaps. She did not face that. But peace lay round them, here and now. Their hearts ceased from straining into the future. They had even courage presently to speak of the past, of Johnnie. She asked who had nursed him. He told her.

"One of the Irishwomen!" she exclaimed in horror, and it was as though she had said a cannibal savage. Did he not know it well already, Montrose could see in his wife's eyes the popular notion of his allies, and the major reason of his difficulties in finding recruits to fight alongside of them.

"As fine a race of men as any soldier could hope to lead"— it was what a General might say of black troops from Africa. The Lowland Scots could not believe the Irish had had more civilization than that. What they and the English settlers had made of that civilization, was too recent in their memories.

Magdalen had to drag her mind from pictures of hovels shared with swine, of the filth and ignorance of homeless outcasts, of the barbarities of long-deferred vengeance, as he told her of Bebinn, whom he had left in charge of an improvised field hospital at Blair Castle.

"The last thing I did before coming here was to write a pass for a sick soldier to go there,—Donochy of Celly, a very good fellow."

She knew she had no need to ask if Johnnie had missed her when he was ill. There had been no time for that, no room left for her; she knew that no boy ever lived or died more happy. His adventure with his father had continued through the very gates of death; and she could not grudge that to his father's son.

* * *

Her husband and her father discussed together how she could make her peace with the Covenant through her father, and so safeguard the remnant of her children.

Was she then to swear allegiance to the very men who had set a price on her husband's head?

Her father advised it; so did her husband.

" Your nieces are in prison for honouring you," she said, " the Napiers are punished because they are your friends. Shall your wife be the one to compound with your enemies? "

" Yes, for it is my wife's duty to preserve what she can from my enemies. Will it be any satisfaction to me to know you are in a dungeon for my sake, or to have Kinnaird a burnt-out ruin like my own homes of Mugdock and Kincardine? "

" He speaks sound sense—especially about Kinnaird," said old Southesk, thinking to persuade his daughter, and never seeing the quiet delight it gave her to hear Montrose advocate this unheroic and practical course.

Her father sat himself heavily at the library table, where so often in her childhood he had spread the painted charter of King James before her; and set himself to write the letter that was to comply so tamely with their enemies. She turned towards her husband where they stood together in the deep embrasure of the window.

" So," said she, " I am to keep in with your enemies,—and then when you have won all England as well as all Scotland for the King, you can beg his pardon for your recreant and disloyal wife."

Suddenly she knew for the first time how jealous she had been of Johnnie riding off into the mountains by his side, and even of those adoring nieces in prison for their love of him. Timid and delicate, she had always sought refuge in unromantic irony from the longing to share his adventure and his fate.

" Do you remember," she said, " how Queen Mary ' repented nothing but that she was not a man, to know what life it was to lie all night in the fields, or to walk upon the causeway with a knapsack, a Glasgow buckler, and a broadsword '?—But no, all the glory is yours, and I stay here."

He put his hands on her shoulders and looked into her eyes.

" Your own glory needs no other," he said, in so grave and tender a tone that she no longer wished she were a man.

Men enough he had to follow him to the death. Here was the hope of his life, and hers, as they sat beside each other in this window seat, looking out to where the wild April sunshine blew across those familiar pastures,—a peaceful landscape under the torn silver lights,—a country like herself, he told her,—and other things too, precious, small and carelessly uttered, as though he had forgotten he was speaking.

" My dear and only love," he whispered.

The old man at the table, who sat writing with his back towards them, complained that their half-heard murmurings drove his words out of his head.

" Shall I read this sentence to you? " he asked, to stop them; and came towards them with the paper in his hand, saying, " I will take it with my grandson to Edinburgh, and show him to the Committee, and answer for my daughter's obedience to them."

He read aloud, " That the Committee of the Estates may ordain and allow the Earl of Southesk to deliver Robert Graham, son to the late Marquis of Montrose, to Magdalen Carnegie, his Mother, to be kept and entertained by her."

" The *late* Marquis of Montrose? " repeated Magdalen.

" It is the formula," said her father pettishly, as he handed the paper to Montrose, wishing that women did not always fasten on such trifles to fuss over.—" Your husband is dead by law."

XXIV

HE rode away to conjure another army out of the heather, to send Macdonald into the west, and Black Pate into Atholl, and George Gordon to Strathbogie, all for more troops. Young Lewis had decamped with his men, either in answer to his father's summons, or because he was in a temper, or because he had already fallen in love, and married, without waiting for his father's consent.

But in his place there appeared another brother, Aboyne, who had escaped from Carlisle, with his arm in a sling, for he had put out his shoulder—"out of pure sympathy with my uncle of Argyll, to see how much it need cramp one's movements."

How much, he showed by a surprise cavalry attack on Aberdeen, and the capture of a score of barrels of gunpowder from two vessels which he boarded in the harbour.

Like his brothers, he was at his happiest when in danger; indeed for Aboyne it was the only time when he was really happy. A few years older than Lewis, he was not so wild a flibbertigibbet as that inconsequent youth, but his vanity was of the darker and more deadly strain of his father's. His courage could face death gaily; but it could never find life sufficiently rapturous.

He came back with his twenty barrels of gunpowder, glowing with his exploit and the anticipation of telling it to his commander, in such haste that he reached him that same evening,—and then when he arrived, there was Montrose at supper with two new-comers, lads younger than Aboyne.

They were Archie Napier and another nephew who had just joined their uncle, having escaped together from their Covenanter jailors,—among them Archie's Covenanting uncle of Bowhopple, who had already complained of the boys' 'preposterous love' for their uncle of Montrose.

" Could they have found no other evening on which to come? " muttered Aboyne, in disgust at the unnecessary amount of pleasure

440

that showed already on the face of his commander, before he himself had had a chance to put it there.

But then Montrose sprang up to greet him in delight at his safe return, whether successful or no,—and then heard what loot Aboyne had brought back with him, and came out to look at the barrels, and praised their rare old vintage, and told him how thirsty he had been for it, for they had run clean out of ammunition,— and so great was the laughter and the admiration, and so often did Aboyne have to tell how he had won the prize, that he found himself the most glorious member of the family party before he had time to notice and resent that he was being drawn into it.

His straight brows, drawn low and level over his keen eyes, relaxed their strained air of ill-temper, always on the watch for occasions to feed it. His brother, George Gordon, had never seen him so calm.

And Aboyne in his turn saw the rather worried elder brother he had always known, preoccupied with his family responsibilities, transformed by his grave and confident happiness. A stab of deeper envy than any he had felt shot through his confused spirit, as he saw that Gordon's was now free.

*   *   *

When Nat Gordon brought his young cousins to serve under the Royal Standard, he introduced the most disturbing factor in Montrose's campaigns. A civilization of as fine a culture as that of this once wealthy and extravagant old family, with all its fierce religion of personal prowess and personal rivalries, had bred a highly complicated stock, as fine in its ideals as a Chevalier Bayard, as petty in its quarrels as a nervous woman.

Until now, all Montrose's movements had been affected by his need to work in conjunction with the Gordons, the greatest potential royalist force in Scotland.

From now on, his career was to be directly influenced by the impulses, magnificent or puerile, of this incalculable family.

Lewis had given him warning of its dangers by flinging off with his men for no reason that his own brother, George Gordon, could explain—unless, as he confided to Nat Gordon with a shrug, the boy had never got over his envy of Lord Graham's Highland funeral,—" though I told him he made me willing enough to give him the chance of one myself."

Then it was the turn of the gold side of the medal to show itself, in Aboyne's dash on Aberdeen, while still suffering from a wounded shoulder.

And now George Gordon himself came to the fore.

In that difficult battle at Auldearn, that best showed Montrose's genius,—when he had for the first time to act on the defensive instead of attacking, and had also for the first time a chance to use modern methods with his cavalry—it was George Gordon's magnificent charge that finally won the day.

Montrose went to Gordon's help on his recruiting campaign, for his small force of cavalry was being beset by Hurry's horse. A wounded boy, called James Gordon of Rhynie, had to be left behind in one of the cottages, and two of Hurry's lieutenants murdered him brutally as he lay in bed.

Montrose and Gordon joined forces again and were pursuing Hurry's army out of the Gordon country towards Inverness,—so they imagined, for Montrose did not realize Hurry's strategy, until his enemy turned his army in the night, and swung back upon him.

It was before dawn on a thick, raining night early in May, when Alasdair's scouts, who had the ears of the wild deer, heard shots about five miles off, and Montrose guessed at once that they must be those of Hurry's men, firing off the damp powder in their muskets to clear them. That meant that Hurry had taken a leaf out of his own book, had lured him out of the friendly Gordon country, where he would get intelligence from the people round about him, and had turned to make a surprise attack at dawn. If it had not been for Hurry's wet powder, and the long ears of the mountainy men, Montrose's army would have been badly caught.

As it was, he had less than an hour of drenched, faintly dawning daylight in which to draw up his battle line. There was just time and light enough to choose his ground,—the straggling village of Auldearn on a ridge above a curved stream and swamp, that would give Hurry some difficulty to cross, and less chance to deploy his much larger force all at once.

Then he set himself to outwit the enemy who had stolen the first march on him. He put a screen of a few musketeers in front of the village, and ordered them to keep firing continuously so as to give the appearance of holding it in force. Gordon's cavalry he kept concealed behind the ridge at the south end of it; Alasdair and his men were placed at the north end, to stand the first brunt of the attack, and with them he placed the Royal Standard, to make Hurry think that he himself was there.

He had thus no centre to his front, and no big guns, for he had never had a chance to dig up those he had captured and buried in the bog during his autumn campaign. He had to trust for defence to a Highland infantry that he had never led to anything but attack.

Alasdair was in a very good position for defence, on high and comparatively dry ground, with the stone walls of kailyards, orchards and farmyards to serve for entrenchments. He needed every bit of his advantage, for he had only five hundred men; and Hurry's infantry, that now marched across the stream to the attack, were three thousand strong, and supported by a thousand horse. But a worse danger than these numbers awaited Alasdair, and that was that the regiment who led the force across the bog was that of the Campbells of Lawers, one of the two finest regiments in Scotland, and the only considerable body of the clan Campbell that had not been wiped out at Inverlochy.

And as these Campbells splashed and squattered their way through the marsh of this dark and drizzling morning, announcing their accustomed intelligence that the Campbells were coming, they looked up at their ancient enemies, the Macdonalds, snugly entrenched behind garden and farmyard walls, and shouted insults at those dirty cowards who could not face a foe in the open, but waited in the pigsties until they were routed out.

It was too much for Alasdair.

" What is it the Campbells are calling us? " he said softly to Ranald Og Macdonald of Mull.

" Pigs, your Honour," was the equally soft answer.

" That is very bad manners," said Alasdair, " we had best give them a lesson."

Without waiting to give any signal to his men, he dashed out of the enclosure and down upon the enemy in the bad boggy ground. No signal was needed but the sight of that redhead, leaping like a flame through the murky air, and the call of his battle cry. With an answering yell, the Macdonalds came scrambling and hurtling over the walls of the yards and orchards to follow their chief. They too had heard the insults of their ancestral foes, and were burning to get to grips with them. But the sheer weight of numbers slowly pressed them back, and soon there was the danger of being outflanked and totally surrounded. Step by step, disputing every inch of the way, they were forced back to the position they had been so mad as to forgo.

But now Alasdair made up for that folly to the best of his power, which became more than human. He had been first to charge down, he was last to go back, guarding his men's approach to the farmyards with the mighty sweeps of his sword. The pike-men were upon him, but he caught their long pikes on his wooden targe. An ordinary man would have been borne to the earth by them, but round went Alasdair's sword again, cutting them through at one stroke, leaving his shield bristling with their heads.

Now he himself with his brother-in-law, Davidson of Ardnacross, and Ranald Og Macdonald, had reached the archway in through the farmyard wall. They wished him to go in first, but he would not till they were safely in, and they were struggling with a thick surrounding group of men, who swayed back as Alasdair struck, and struck again, then stopped short, for that huge sword, that scarcely a man but himself could lift, had snapped in his hand.

Davidson of Ardnacross handed him his own, and in that same unguarded instant was struck to his death. In the confusion, the enemy had got in through the archway, and Alasdair dashed in to clear it of them.

Ranald, just outside, was keeping a dozen pikemen at bay; ' he turned his face to the enemy, his sword was at his breast, his shield on his left hand, and a hand-gun in his right hand.' So said one who saw him, ' and the pikemen who were after him halted.' But at that moment some bowmen, running past, shot their arrows at him, and one went a fist's length through both his cheeks. He threw away his gun, and laid hold of his sword,— tugged at it, but it would not come,—tried again, and the hilt twisted round in his hand; he had to lower his shield-hand to take hold of the sheath, and this time drew it,—but in that instant when he had to drop his left arm with the targe on it, he received five pike wounds in his unguarded breast.

Yet he reached the gate of the yard, and was backing through it,—but as he did so, one of the enemy, following closely to get in first and cut off his retreat, ducked his head under the arch in the wall. Alasdair cut it off with one sweep of Davidson's claymore, and it bounced against Ranald's shanks, while the body fell in the gateway. Ranald picked up the head and looked behind him at the door, ' it was then he saw his companion.' Alasdair pulled him back through the doorway, cut off the head of the arrow that stuck through Ranald's two cheeks, and drew it out.

But many stragglers had not won back, and again and again Alasdair rushed out of the enclosure to attack the foes that beset them, and help them enter. That was the battle of giants in a saga, but only in a saga can even giants fight with the odds eight to one against them, and win.

Montrose heard from a messenger that the Irishes were being badly worsted, but he kept that quiet;—the Gordon horse were mostly untried recruits and needed encouragement. He rode down their ranks, shouting to their leaders, " Macdonald is winning the victory single-handed! Are there to be no laurels for the house of Huntly? "

In the dismal rain, where the new levies sat their horses with hunched backs, and shivered, waiting for the word of command that was to put them to the test, this gay shout burned and tingled through their veins, making them certain of victory and of themselves. Their young leader, George Gordon, caught the fire, and called to them, " Remember Donald Farquharson and James Gordon of Rhynie! Let each man of you avenge those two to-day." The two names were their battle-cry.

Montrose swung the Gordons round on to the enemy's centre, and thundered in among them. It was the first time he had enough cavalry to use in shock tactics, as he had always longed to do, and as Rupert and Cromwell had shown it could be used. Now, instead of a mere support to musketeers, he led the charge home, right into the midst of Hurry's flank guard of cavalry.

It was led by Drummond, who had only just got across the bog with difficulty, and had thought Montrose was with the Royal Standard and Alasdair in that losing battle in the kailyards.

In the flurry of this utterly unexpected cavalry attack, led by Montrose himself, Drummond shouted out the command to his horse to wheel to the left, when he meant to the right, and so overrode some of his own infantry, turning the confusion into panic. Montrose, Gordon and Aboyne drove the cavalry before them, and plunged up to the help of Alasdair against Hurry's infantry.

But Alasdair, determined to the last to show that odds of eight to one were nothing to him, had already rallied all his remaining men together, and now charged out once again upon the enemy's shaken centre. It was all that was still needed to break it utterly; the whole Covenant army became a reeling, flying mass of men, and after them for fourteen miles sped their pursuers, the Gordons and the Macdonalds.

Mungo Campbell of Lawers, the last fighting chief of the clan of Diarmaid, lay dead on the field, with nearly all his splendid regiment, and with the Border regiments, and the best of the Lowland officers. Seaforth, finding he had again backed the wrong horse, escaped to Inverness, and Hurry with a hundred horse to Baillie. But Hurry's army no longer existed, for two thousand at least lay dead. Their ammunition, baggage, money, and sixteen colours of their regiments, were all in their enemies' hands.

" And which of us did the most slaughter, do you think? " asked Alasdair with modest coyness at the end of the day.

Bard, recorder and harpist were all eager to express the same opinion. But it was the eye of his commander that he sought, and then looked hastily away again, not wishing to ask too plainly.

" The greatest slaughter and the greatest feats of arms I have ever even heard of among living men," said Montrose, " were done this day by my Lord Alasdair Macdonald, and Ranald Og Macdonald, and Lord Gordon,—and three others."

He had seen Gordon's eye flicker anxiously at his brother even as he glowed at his own praise; and now, however much they clamoured for the names of those three others, he would not give them, for they gave a chance to everyone, from Aboyne to any obscure kern in Alasdair's forces, to think he may have been one of the three that his commander had noticed.

As they sat eating and drinking, and the rain fell softly on the roof of the house where they had lodged themselves for the night, they went over each move of the battle, and Montrose had to admit to Gordon that he had believed the Macdonalds all but finished, when he gave that cheering news of their winning the victory,—" but what help would the truth have been to your raw recruits? And you yourself, my lord—would you have fought singing, as I heard you, if you had believed the day lost? "

" I might," said Gordon, " for loss or victory would make little odds as long as I fought with you, my lord. If all your plans should fail, and you had to wander as an outlaw on the mountains, I would be happier to share that with you than any fortune with another."

" Now would you say as much to me? " asked Alasdair of Ranald Og Macdonald, whose chest wounds were all swaddled in bandages, but who had flatly refused to forgo the banquet,— " or can you indeed say anything at all, since that arrow made a hole in your two cheeks? "

Said Ranald, grinning painfully, " I can say the name of my preserver—Alasdair Mac Cholla-chiotach Mhic Ghiollesbuig Mhic Alasdair Mhic Eoin Cathanich."

And that, as they were agreed, was no bad test.

XXV

THE Gordons were now in full glory, and none gayer than the Lords Gordon and Aboyne. But Aboyne had put out his shoulder again in the battle; he was given sick leave to go home and rest, and departed full of confidence that he would return, bringing his father with him and the clan in full force. Alasdair had lost many of his best officers, and most of the remainder were wounded; these now went off, "to lick their wounds," as their chief put it, feeling they had earned a respite. Hurry's army had been wiped out, but there was still Baillie's to reckon with,—two thousand infantry and several hundred horse; and now, as a reserve to Baillie's, Lord Lindsay of the Byres was raising troops from Angus and Perth.

Montrose had seen nothing of Lindsay of the Byres since the old disastrous days of the Cumbernauld Bond, when he had first tried to grapple with Argyll in diplomacy, and had taken so bad a fall. Lindsay had been a college friend of his, he had been eager to talk against Argyll and his insufferable ambitions, and so Montrose had thought he would be willing to support himself, and later the King. That showed his simplicity.

Lindsay was still on Argyll's side politically, and still talking against him personally. A vain busybody under his air of good-fellowship, he was never happy unless he was criticizing, and naturally his friends provided better scope than his enemies.

Now it was Argyll's military incapacity that gave him so much to talk about; over and over again he showed on the dining table, with salt-cellars, mugs, and bread pellets, exactly what he would have done had he been Argyll at Fyvie, Inveraray and Inverlochy. And if he had been Elcho at Perth, and Burleigh at Aberdeen, and Hurry and Baillie now everywhere. He talked his way into the confidence of Parliament, and was soon regarded as the coming military man.

Montrose and George Gordon, left alone for the moment with only the Irishes and the Gordon horse, decided that while they were waiting to recover their full strength again, they would nip this new hope of the Covenanters in the bud. Baillie stood in the way of the south, but they lured him on north and west in chase of them until, exhausted of provisions, he had to withdraw to Inverness; and Montrose could seize his chance to dash south to meet Lindsay in Atholl.

" Nothing I desire better," said Lindsay, when he first got the news that Baillie had left the road to the Lowlands open for Montrose, and that he himself would soon have a chance to prove on the battlefields, as well as among the cruets, how superior was his generalship to all others in Scotland.

But when he heard that Montrose had reached Glen Muick, he thought he had better be nearer his base, and fell back on Newtyle in Angus as fast as his enemy himself could have moved.

Once again Montrose crossed the South Esk, he reached the river Isla, he was within seven miles of Lindsay,—but there came the check.

Lord Aboyne arrived overnight, with no reinforcements beyond a small bodyguard for himself, and in a ferociously sullen temper. His father had sent him in hot haste to demand the return of all the Gordon horse to Huntly Castle at Strathbogie. He blurted this out to Montrose and George Gordon together.

" What reason did my Lord Huntly give? " asked Montrose.

" What reason should he give? " cried George Gordon, " but the same one, that has been behind all his actions always,—that he is jealous of your glory, my lord, and will do all he can to dull it. He has been waiting for a chance to pay off old scores,—now he thinks he has got it."

" He has got it," said Aboyne gloomily, " we are finished."

Gordon swung round upon his unfortunate younger brother and cursed him.

A dark flush went over Aboyne's already injured and angry face. " Is it my fault ?"—he began, but Gordon cut across him,—

" Yes, it is your fault, you fool. Don't I know how you worked him up, showing him how proud you were to serve with my lord of Montrose, when a grain of sense would have kept your mouth shut. Here we are within two hours of falling on Lindsay, —and my father's lunacy wrecks all our plans. But you shall not give his orders."

"All the men with me know of them, and are now telling the rest."

"Then I will go out now and tell them this—if a Gordon deserts from the Standard while I am in command here, I will have him shot,—yes, though it be yourself."

"My Lord Gordon," said Montrose's grave voice, "you cannot shoot your clan for obeying their chief, nor your brother for obeying his father."

Gordon looked at him, his dark eyes helpless with misery. "What am I to do?" he said. "Are we never to win clear of this chuckle-headed peacock?" None smiled at the unfilial description.

Gordon himself was all but sobbing in the bitterness of his shame and disappointment.

"Steady, boy," said his commander, low to him. He had done a moment's hard thinking while the brothers raged. "Lord Huntly may have had good reason to recall his clan. Baillie is uncomfortably close to his country. We may as well return and get our recruiting over before attending to Lindsay."

"And be baulked of all our plans at the last moment!" exclaimed Gordon.

"You will have to be that again and again in a campaign like this. It would only cripple us if we tried to keep to a cut-and-dried plan with such material as we have. I have one final object, —to get to the Lowlands and there join with the King's armies, and I have been baulked in doing that every time I had a hope of it. But every victory we win in the north brings it nearer. If we smash Baillie's army as we have smashed Hurry's, Lindsay's reinforcements will go for nothing. We have already given a bad jar to his recruiting. Let him think it over for the time."

Gordon knew it was special pleading, that his commander was making the best of a bad job. Yet so serene did he appear that almost against his will the young man felt cheered, believed that the maddening caprices of his family might not after all mean the ruin of their high purpose. He discussed the change of plan for some time with Montrose until he had himself well in control again; then turned to his brother, whom Montrose had already tried to bring into the discussion, and said, with that smile that showed the essential sweetness of his temper under its sudden fires,—" I was angry with our father, not you."

Aboyne had responded as shortly as possible when Montrose had spoken to him. He now avoided Gordon's eye, and said to a spot somewhere in the ceiling, " You threatened me as a deserter."

" Oh God damn your eyes," replied his brother wearily.

* * *

Montrose was not the only commander to suffer contradictions. The ' Committee of Defeated Generals,' as some were calling the Committee of Estates, since Argyll, Burleigh and Elcho were its most influential members, had tired of sending fresh orders each day to Baillie, and now appointed a small branch committee to remain permanently attached to him, and give him the benefit of their advice, as advised previously by the head committee.

While Montrose sent Alasdair to call back the Clan Donald in force, and George Gordon, with his inseparable friend and cousin, Nathaniel, to recruit their troopers all over again, and Black Pate once more into Atholl for his men,—Lindsay was ravaging Atholl for no particular purpose, and Baillie, having done the same in the Gordon country, began to besiege the Bog of Gight.

Montrose joined with Gordon again, and marched up to the great castle, where they tried to draw off the besiegers. Skirmishes made no impression on them. Montrose then tried sending a trumpeter with his compliments to ask the honour of an encounter with Baillie's army on the level ground in equal combat.

But Baillie was not the man to start that Froissart stuff at his time of life. He sent back a grumpy answer to the chivalrous challenge, that he was not going to take his marching orders from the enemy.

Montrose struck camp and retired south towards the Lowlands.

Baillie saw that it was fairly hopeless to think of taking Gordon Castle, which was being well guarded by Gordon of Buckie, and a hundred watchmen every night. His Committee were anxious about the Lowlands and their precious white hope, Lindsay of the Byres. His men had heard that Alasdair and most of the Macdonalds were absent from Montrose's army, and clamoured for the chance to get in a blow at it while that terrible ' red-armed knight ' and his Red Hands from Ulster were away.

So Baillie, sick of doddering about the Gordon country, sick of the repeated signs of mutiny among even his best regiments, sick above all of his committee, who flatly refused either to leave him alone or to accept his resignation, set off in pursuit, and the hope that he might perhaps have a stroke of luck this time.

He reached the boggy banks of the river Don by the 2nd day of July, and saw that his enemy had halted on the other side, on the rising ground called Gallows Hill, near to the village of Alford. It looked a very small force, but Baillie hesitated, for might not Montrose be concealing some of his army behind that hill, as he had heard from Hurry he had done at Auldearn? In any case he would not be such a fool as to risk a direct attack uphill, but would march round and outflank him on the right. He got all his army across the river; and then observed that Montrose had changed his line of front, and that his troops were now drawn up to face north-east as if to anticipate Baillie's flank move.

It gave the general a horrible fear that Montrose himself had planned that flank move for him, and had tempted him into making it, so as to lead him into a trap. He did not know the ground, and might have to go through more swamp before reaching his enemy; and if he were defeated he would certainly have a bog and a river behind him to check his retreat. He declared that he did not like the look of things, and gave the order to halt.

At once his committee were all round him, giving him their opinions. Argyll himself had joined it two days ago, in order to see that it was carrying out his instructions properly. He could now therefore give them in person, and he thought it would be a grievous error to retire now, and would have the worst possible effect on the minds of the troops.

" Dare-devil! " growled the General, just not loud enough for Argyll to hear; but at his sarcastic look, a very ugly glance passed from the sunk yellow face of the political chief to the beefy but equally worried countenance of the Commander-in-Chief.

Balcarres, his master of horse, eagerly seconded Argyll. He had five hundred fine cavalry and was longing to try them. The enemy could not at the most have more than half that number, even if some of them were being hidden.

" And the Macdonalds are not there," he added, tactfully expressing the chief reason for attack which MacCaillan Mhor, the chieftain of the rival clan, might feel shy in uttering.

" And fourthly," argued that chieftain, " the enemy opposed to us are in the habit of making the first attack; do not allow them that advantage to-day;—engage them instantly."

He spoke with resolution, licking his parched lips. This was the true courage, as he had some reason to tell himself, to speak thus while his heart rolled over and lay cold as a stone in his breast.

But while they were disputing, Montrose was already taking Argyll's advice, and had sent George and Nathaniel Gordon to the first attack.

Once again, his battle line was completely different in arrangement from his last. He had his cavalry on either wing, the left under Aboyne, backed by some Irish musketeers under O'Cahan; the right under Gordon, with Nathaniel in command of the infantry in support. He himself was in the centre with a mixed lot of Lowlanders and Badenoch Highlanders; and his nephew, Archie, the young Master of Napier, was in charge of reserves of infantry, concealed behind Gallows Hill, as Baillie had shrewdly suspected, but just too late.

George Gordon on Gallows Hill looked down on the advancing enemy and saw, behind the army, in enclosures, guarded by two companies of infantry, all the cattle that Baillie had driven off from Strathbogie to feed his travelling troops. Their lowing now rose loud and mournful behind all the clash and shouts of their jailors,—and " Do you hear that? " cried Lord Gordon, " there is the lowing of *our* cattle, which that dirty thief has lifted from our lands! "

His face was black with passion. The gentle, thoughtful youth, the flower of the most modern civilization among his extraordinary jumble of comrades, was transformed into the primaeval Highland chief, to whom cattle meant not only food for his clan, but wealth and power,—a symbol of it older and more direct than money.

" A lot of *cows*? " Magdalen had asked, wondering. The cows had conquered again and again, as Montrose had found to his cost in Highland warfare. It was to take their cows home that the Macdonalds were now absent, and Alasdair in search of them. And cows now propelled the fury of the Gordon cavalry charge, stronger than any chivalrous motive in the passionate breast of their leader.

Like a thunderbolt he came down at the head of them on to Balcarres' horse, and for a moment it seemed that the whole of the Covenant left wing would be broken. But Balcarres, a good cavalry leader, rallied his horse, bringing up another squadron to meet the attack; and there was soon a dense and struggling mass of men and horses, into which the musketeers could not shoot without hitting their own side.

George and Nathaniel Gordon were the first to carve a way out with their swords; and then Nathaniel shouted the order to his musketeers to throw down their muskets, draw their swords and stab or hamstring the enemy's horses.

His young friend turned a horrified glance on him, but, scoffed that practical pirate as he wheeled round, " Is a horse's belly more sacred than a man's? " And they rallied all the men they could disentangle from the mass, and charged again.

Aboyne now plunged down on Baillie's right wing, with O'Cahan and the Irish foot close behind him. The two wings of Gordon cavalry closed in from either side on the Covenant army. Montrose advanced his centre, and unleashed his hidden reserves under young Napier. Their sudden appearance from behind the crest of the hill was the last move to unnerve the enemy, which had already begun to give way all along the line. Now Baillie's best regiments were overborne, and the defeat became a stampede.

All along the side of the river, Montrose's army pursued, down even to the camp-boys, who leaped on to the baggage ponies and came yelling after the chase, so that their terror-stricken foes imagined yet another body of cavalry had been loosed upon them. The leaders had made a bolt for it, along with the remnants of their cavalry, and were being furiously hard pressed. Glengarry all but caught Argyll, but he got away, after changing his horse a second time for one yet faster.

Balcarres too was galloping in a neck-to-neck with Baillie, in a way to win the Cupar races, cried George Gordon, mad with excitement. He and his cavalry had won the last battle; now it had won this.

His joy was beyond reason, the rushing air in his nostrils was heady as wine, his horse felt the rapture in his bridle hand, in the press of his knees, and answered with a long snort of pride and delight.

"We'll not let all the rascals escape us," called his rider to his men,—"I'll bring back Baillie as prisoner if I have to drag him by the throat out of the midst of his bodyguard."

They answered with a cheer, set spurs to their horses, thundered nearer and nearer to that flying body of cavalry.

Baillie heard their shouts hot in his ears, but still dared not turn his head as he drove his horse madly on. Now he saw Gordons fighting with his troopers on his right and on his left, but still he was not surrounded, and dug his heels into his horse's bleeding flanks as he leaned his heavy body forward along its neck, his breath sobbing in short painful gasps.

He was wrenched back, his horse plunged, while another bumped against it. Someone had caught hold of his sword-belt, he looked up into the laughing face of a young man who was shouting to him to yield himself prisoner.

Baillie was hastening to do so, when the hold on his belt was suddenly slackened, the wild laughter fled from the face beside him, the gleam went out of it.

Baillie stayed to see no more, he urged his horse on yet once again, and soon found he had left all pursuit behind.

The pursuit was stopping in all directions. Everywhere the word was running,—" Lord Gordon has been shot. Lord Gordon is dead."

He had been shot from behind, no one knew how,—a stray shot in all probability.

Aboyne stopped his chase of Balcarres, his clan forgot their hopes of plunder.

Victory and gladness died in their hearts, they hurried to where their young chief lay, and stood silent round him, looking down upon him. The face that a moment since had shone like a torch, to lead them to conquest, was now a still carving, the dark lashes lying grave upon the cheeks, the flashing eyes and laughing mouth shut fast in death.

At the sight of his beauty and his stillness, at the knowledge that he was indeed dead, and would never again lead them into the battle that gave him the delight of a lover, their silence broke out into wild cries of lamentation; they flung themselves down beside his body, kissed his face and hands, and praised his beauty, his courage, his nobility, and his youth that now would never leave him.

Aboyne stood among the simpler griefs of his followers; his was sharpened by envy. Before his aching eyes, the wild geraniums and the broom spread patches of purple and gold; the young spikes of bracken danced light as feathers over the hillside, and caught the sunlight in a shimmer of green. George Gordon had taken the easier path; he had died young, glorious and happy, and left Aboyne to carry on alone.

" And he is *my* brother, and *I* loved him, and he never knew how much," came in wave after wave of increasing bitterness,—for he and Gordon had quarrelled ever since Aboyne's return with his father's disastrous commands nearly a month ago, and Aboyne had meant to make it up and somehow had not done so, and now he never could,—and there was his commander, whom Gordon had loved more than him, more than anyone in the world, kneeling by Gordon's body, in a passion of grief that Aboyne himself would give anything in the world to share, but could not, for his heart was pent up in iron bands.

Montrose's best hope for his cause lay dead upon the trampled earth, but that was not now his grief.

' Never did two of such short acquaintance love more dearly,' said one who knew those friends.

XXVI

BAILLIE went and laid his resignation before the Government, and had it handed back to him, with speeches of thanks for his services, and polite regrets for the heavy defeat just dealt him 'by the late Marquis of Montrose.' There was no escaping his impossible position, for the Government recognized him as the best leader they could find, and refused to lose him. They were indeed desperate, and determined to make an united effort from every part of Scotland that they could control. They passed an Act of Parliament, levying a new army of ten thousand foot and five hundred horse, most of which were to assemble at Perth by the end of July. Regiments were mustered from Fife; the lords of Cassilis, Glencairn and Eglinton raised troops from the west; Hamilton's brother, Lanark, collected a thousand foot and five hundred horse from Hamilton's tenants.

Nor were these the only reinforcements. Baillie's advisory committee was increased to sixteen, and now included all the leaders who had been defeated by Montrose, as well as Lindsay of the Byres, who had not waited to be defeated.

These awful warnings all round him proved anything but encouraging to Baillie. Most of all he was upset by the presence of Argyll, who had now set himself to be Dictator of the Committee, as he was of Parliament, in a spirit of fanatical resolve that was oddly disturbing to a plain man.

For Argyll believed blindly in his own propaganda, was doggedly insistent, to his colleagues as well as in his public proclamations, that the Lord of Hosts was with him, and the God of Jacob was his refuge, and evidently believed himself a chosen instrument for the Lord's work.

His tireless and intricate brain, his power and wealth, even the ancient enmity of his race with that of the Graham, were all dedicated to this one purpose, the destruction of his enemy, Montrose. He could be content to die, he sincerely said, did he but know that he had brought about Montrose's death.

Such fixed yet frantic hatred did not, as Baillie knew, make for good soldiering qualities. He was to conduct the coming campaign with Argyll like a millstone round his neck. And it would be Baillie who would get the blame. Poor Drummond had been executed after Auldearn for giving the wrong word of command in the flurry of that utterly unexpected cavalry attack from the Gordons. It was another awful warning.

Then that clerical busybody, his cousin, the Reverend Robert Baillie, one of the Covenanting committee in England, was writing to all his leaders in Scotland to suggest that ' those six thousand foot we hear of should be sent down into England to help the work of the Parliament there, and with them some gracious ministers,'—(General Baillie was quite willing to concede him those)—because, in Cousin Robert's precious opinion, ' Montrose will be cheaper and more easily defeated here in England than he can be there in Scotland.'

This demand was all the more unreasonable because the Parliament's armies had a month ago won their greatest victory over the King's, at Naseby in the Midlands. In this, Cromwell, the coming man, had definitely and mightily arrived. Since he hated the Covenant, the Presbyterian Church, and the whole Scottish nation, this defeat by him of their enemies was not likely to prove an unmixed blessing to the Covenanters.

But at least it should prevent the King from coming north to join with Montrose, or from sending reinforcements to him, according to those alarming plans discovered in the spring. And old Leven now felt it safe to leave the Westmorland border, where he had been hovering all this time to prevent that move, and marched south into England.

But in one respect Naseby had made the professional soldier, such as himself and Baillie, very uneasy. The Parliamentarians had shown their gratitude to the Lord for their victory by slaughtering all the Irishwomen among the camp followers of the royal army and slashing the faces of all the Englishwomen.

The ministers might talk of a just vengeance on vice and ' deboshry '; but no soldier was going to be so partial as to imagine that all the women who followed the King's armies were painted harlots, and all those who followed the Parliament's and Covenant's were respectable matrons with their marriage lines in their pockets. The plain fact of the matter was that in a war like this the families of the common soldiers on either side were bound to be following their men.

Four thousand Scotswomen and children came straggling after Leven's army as he slowly marched south. And now that the hosts of the Lord had started the business of slaughtering and mutilating women, the idea of reprisals might well enter the heads of their ungodly enemies. So that the hardened mercenaries who had served under ' that thundering scourge, that terror of Germany, Gustavus of Sweden,' now cursed the clergy who had communicated their blood lusts to the soldiery.

It was a hot, stifling summer, very helpful in the breeding of rats and lice. The plague had crept to Edinburgh, and the Parliament moved to Stirling. The plague crept to Stirling, and Parliament moved to Perth, where the levies were being mustered under Baillie.

Nobody knew where Montrose was, nor how strong his force, until suddenly it was said that his army was within a few miles of the city, that a large force of cavalry had been seen on the hills. Instantly the city's gates were closed, the guards were doubled, Hurry's new bodies of horse were kept shut within its walls, and the temporary capital was put practically into a state of siege.

Each day in the high summer weather, Parliament met in the dark old hall and debated the measures for its defence, every member in terror lest at any moment he should hear the uproar that would mean the thunderbolt had fallen, and his last hour on earth had come. Yet they wasted hours in discussing how they should root out the house of Huntly from the face of the earth, as they considered they had done with that of Montrose, by ordering all Gordons as well as Grahams who stood for the Covenant, to change their name. The cramping fear that paralysed the whole city seemed to have crippled their wits.

But after several days some more enterprising scouts discovered that Montrose's cavalry consisted chiefly of baggage ponies, mounted by musketeers, a screen that had succeeded in shutting up his enemies.

Hurry made some sorties with his cavalry after that,—lost a good few, who were picked off their saddles by Montrose's musketeers, but had the satisfaction of making the enemy retire from their camp in Methven Wood towards the hills, and so rapidly that some of the Irishwomen straggled behind, were taken and butchered.

Baillie swore furiously at Hurry for this, telling him he had missed his chance to cut off Montrose's retreat, by waiting to kill off a lot of women. First Naseby, now Methven. They were running up a long bill for their enemy to pay.

Said Argyll, " The Lord will not give His enemy the chance to pay."

" Your Lordship knows best," retorted Baillie,—" but my reverend cousin now admits that he does not know the Lord's mind, nor what He means by humbling His servants against the expectation of the most clear-sighted."

Argyll showed no such ignorance. The Lord meant to humble, not His servants but His enemies, by lifting them up that their fall might be the greater.

Some arguments are unanswerable. Baillie's reply was to send in his resignation again; the Committee's was to refuse it.

Montrose's army was moving first south and then westward of Perth; it looked as though he intended to cut off Lanark's new army, which was marching from Glasgow, before it could join with Baillie's.

The Committee were agreed on one point at last, that the enemy army must be cut off before it accomplished this. It was believed to be of far greater strength than it had ever mustered before,—but then so were the armies of the Covenant, which had just been reinforced by three new regiments from Fife, and the remnant of Argyll's Highlanders.

Both sides had realized that the next battle must be the decisive one, and were putting every ounce of their weight into it; nor, it was obvious, would Montrose strike this time before he was fully prepared. So Baillie went after him as fast as he could along the Allan Water, but there again he fell out with his Committee, or rather its Dictator.

For Argyll had just heard how one of his possessions, Castle Campbell, had been sacked and burned by the enemy; still worse insult, his young ward, Ewen Cameron of Lochiel, a black-eyed rascal of a schoolboy, had been in the castle, and instead of longing to avenge the action, had tried to join the rebels and fight against his guardian. It seemed that Montrose held enchantment for every boy in the country, while Argyll's face sagged more and more heavily in an age that was not of years.

He insisted on reprisals, and waited to burn the house of Airthrey, belonging to the Graham of Braco, and Lord Stirling's house of Menstrie, though Baillie was driven nearly mad by the delay.

" Are we to waste time in little revenges like a mob of angry women? " he fumed,—" for God's sake let us stick to the main object."

By the sun-baked evening of August 14th he was at Hollinbush, and his scouts brought him word that Montrose was at Kilsyth, only two and a half miles off, and had been joined by the 'valetudinary' Lord Airlie, whom everyone had expected to die decently in his bed of fatigue. But there was the undefeated old gentleman back again, with his son, and young Alexander Ogilvy of Inverquharity, a boy fresh from college.

" All infants and dotards," muttered Argyll, but his practical sense had to admit the news that eighty horsemen of the Ogilvy family had accompanied the infant and dotard.

Aboyne was there too, they heard, with the Gordon horse, so Montrose must have collected all the cavalry he could hope for.

Lanark and his new army was by now just twelve miles off from Baillie, who decided that it would be madness not to wait for them; they would be with him in a few hours; this was to be their greatest chance of smashing the enemy; and why take any unnecessary risks?

So he appointed pickets and went to bed.

At dawn on the 15th, the misty milky dawn that promised a grilling August day, he was woken by his scouts, who brought him news of the enemy as ordered.

Almost on their heels, Argyll appeared in the doorway of his tent, his stooping form dark against the white morning light.

"Whereabouts are the rebels?" he asked curtly.

"Still at Kilsyth," replied Baillie.

"Might we not advance nearer them?" rejoined the other.

"We are near enough already, if we do not intend to fight,— and we do not intend it until Lanark comes up. Your Lordship knows well how rough and uneasy a way lies between them and us."

"But," said Argyll, "we need not keep the highway; we may march upon them in a direct line through the cornfields and over the braes."

With silent obstinacy, he had ignored the reference to Lanark. His face was so sunken with lack of sleep that the pale skin seemed to hang in folds and pouches. Baillie's round rubicund countenance, cheerful, in spite of his apprehensions, by reason of a few hours' deep sleep and the sound working of his digestion, onaoperated Argyll as much as his own did Baillie.

Nothing, the General considered, would keep this man quiet till he had had a sleeping-draught and a dose of rhubarb. Aloud, on a sigh that touched the patience of despair, he said, "Very well. Let Lord Lindsay and the rest of the Committee be called in from the next tent."

They were called in, and Argyll drove them before him like sheep. He had been tossing and turning in his brain all night all the moves possible on their side and the enemy's. And he had convinced himself that Montrose meant to slip through their fingers and escape to the hills. If they delayed a few hours to wait for Lanark's reinforcements, they would lose their prey altogether.

But if they attacked instantly they would have Montrose in a trap, for his army lay in a hollow with the river Forth to the north of him, cutting off his retreat to the Highlands,—and by

" Nor your Lordship above Newtyle," retorted Burleigh.

" My lords,—" expostulated Baillie, and then—" What the devil are they yelling back at him? I believe he has given them the choice whether to retreat or attack,—those savage battle cries are their answer."

" Why are they undressing? " asked Lindsay, but knew the answer, which none of them gave—' So that they can charge uphill in the coming heat, quicker than our heavily accoutred infantry can charge down.'

They saw the Highlanders, in answer to Montrose's order, unwind and throw down their plaids, and knot up the long tails of their saffron shirts between their legs to keep them out of the way. At almost the same instant the three generals saw a number of these men running up as fast as wild cats through the bushes and undergrowth at the head of the glen, towards some cottages and garden walls which might prove a useful vantage ground to either side.

Baillie had hoped to keep his flank movement hidden from the enemy, and had instructed his men to keep behind the ridge of the hill along which they marched. But to his horror he now saw one of his officers, Major Haldane, break off from the centre of the main march, and lead a body of his musketeers down the hill to attack this position of the cottages, pulling after him four regiments of infantry (one of them Argyll's) towards the edge of the ridge.

This unauthorized move of his would expose the whole plan to Montrose. It was in vain for Baillie to gallop back and try to recall Haldane. He had already been driven back on to the other regiments by the Highlanders;—and a mere repulse to an attack was never enough for them.

Alasdair at once sent a counter-attack from the Maclean clan. As they charged uphill, the Macdonalds of Clanranald, not to be outdone by their ancient rivals, charged also towards the dikes on top of the ridge. The distant fire of the enemy only excited them the more; but this was not so much an attack on the foe as a race for precedence between the clans.

The Clanranalds overtook the Macleans, and broke right through their ranks, jostling and pushing them aside in their determination to be foremost. Young Donald of Moidart won, and was the first to leap the dyke, but Lachlan of Duart was just behind him, and so were the MacGregors, all mixed up with the Macleans and the men of Duart.

Up over the dikes on top of the hill there came leaping all those long red shanks under their yellow shirts, their targes held high on their left arms, their heads bent low under them for protection, and in their right hands their gleaming claymores.

The four regiments that Haldane's move had led to the edge of the ridge, tried to make a stand against the savage onrush, but soon broke and fled. The Covenanting army was cut right through its centre, and its forces in the rear were left squirming and disorganized like a decapitated caterpillar.

Yet this wild and independent action was as likely to upset Montrose's plan of battle as Haldane's had upset Baillie's. For when the clans charged uphill in that frantic helter-skelter, they exposed themselves to the chance of a heavy cavalry attack on the flank.

So Montrose said to Lord Airlie, as they watched from their eminence in the middle of the valley.

The old man, recovered after weeks of fever, and now sitting his horse again beside his commander, swore volubly at those mad rascals' antics. They did not deserve the success they seemed to be getting,—and what was Balcarres and all his horse doing that he did not cut them in pieces?

" He must be somewhere up there," said Montrose, and then—" Look! What is that the sun is flashing on—there on the left? "

It looked as though it were on the windows of a house among the rocks and scrub on the hill, but the windows were moving.

As he had spoken, he had guessed that it was the steel cuirasses of Balcarres' cavalry that had caught the sun. They had already crossed the gap at the head of the glen, and were making up to the hill on Montrose's left. This would give them a very strong position for attack by a charge downhill. To forestall them, he sent a body of Gordon infantry to hold the hill against them. He dared not use his cavalry till he saw how Alasdair's men were faring.

Balcarres had done better than Haldane in keeping the main part of his troops concealed behind the ridge. But now more and more of these came forward to meet the Gordon infantry, who were soon driven backwards towards the edge of the hill, and were in great danger of being overwhelmed.

Aboyne was one of the little group of commanders who sat their horses, watching the course of the battle. Montrose had insisted that he should not expose himself needlessly to danger, but remain in the rear with a bodyguard of horse and give his orders from there. He was fidgeting furiously at this restraint, which he knew to be reasonable since his brother's death, and his father's now frantic efforts to recall him from the campaign.

But that put him in no better temper; he had said no word while the two other commanders discussed the next move; and now, looking up to the hill on their left, he saw that his men were holding the crest with the greatest difficulty and were gradually being driven back over the edge of it.

There must be a heavy weight of cavalry against them. Plunging horses could be seen silhouetted here and there on the sky line, and the confused bobbing of heads. His clan had marched into what looked like a death trap. He could bear it no longer, but rose in his stirrups and with a shout to his men led the Gordon horse in a charge to their help, galloping up the slope in his haste and getting his horses badly winded before the encounter.

Those gleaming cuirassiers made charge after charge from over the top of the hill; the Gordons were pushed steadily backwards and soon were in danger of being surrounded. It looked as though Balcarres must have the whole bulk of his cavalry up there over the ridge. But it was fairly clear by now that Alasdair's race of the clans must be successful. Montrose determined to afford all his cavalry for the battle with Balcarres.

"Now, my Lord Airlie," he said, "will you show seventeen what seventy can do?"

And while his son mustered the rest of the Ogilvy horse, the old man and the boy, Alexander of Inverquharity, went off at a steady trot at the head of their men. The Gordons, unable to extricate themselves from Balcarres' cuirassiers, who seemed to be coming on interminably over the ridge, felt the shock of the Ogilvy horse as it plunged through them against the enemy, and were able to get clear, and charge again.

And again and again, as Nathaniel Gordon now came to their help with the last of the cavalry. That meant that Alasdair was being victorious in his part of the battle, and the knowledge put new heart into them. Airlie, bare-headed by now, and his white hair flying in the wind of his own speed, pulled his men out of the mêlée, got Aboyne to do the same, and all plunged back again in a final charge of such fury that the cuirassiers were driven back over the ridge and on to their own infantry.

On came the Gordons and Ogilvys, but even they did not do more damage than Balcarres' terrified horse, plunging and trampling the crowded ranks of their own musketry. Their huge numbers only added to the hideous confusion. Both cavalry and infantry broke and fled.

Baillie, utterly distracted, had been galloping over the field of action, sending warnings to Argyll and his staff to retire, ordering officers to their posts, hearing on every side the maddening question of his subordinates, " What am I to do now? "

What indeed? He tried to disentangle the screaming confusion of flying horse and infantry, but they overbore him in their blind flight. He dashed to the rear, hoping to bring up the Fife reserves, but by the time he got there, the Fife reserves had decided that there was no sense in waiting to be killed, and were making for home. All the rest of the Covenanting army decided the same, but most were too late.

Montrose's trumpets were sounding the general advance; his main army came up to the top of the hill, and looked down all round them on thousands of flying foes.

The pursuit and slaughter lasted for a dozen miles. When it was over, they found three cannon at the first position of Baillie's army, which might have been the greatest help in covering his flank march. But they had been forgotten.

" He must have been badly flustered," said Montrose sympathetically.

Only a few hundreds of that army escaped, but among them were all the chief leaders. Baillie, Balcarres and Burleigh shut themselves up in Stirling Castle. Lanark, thankful that he had been too late for the fight, fled to Berwick; Lindsay of the Byres as far as England; Cassilis and Glencairn further still, to Ireland. Only the sea seemed safe enough to Argyll. He rode twenty miles to Queensferry, dashed on board a ship that was lying at anchor in the Roads of Leith, and insisted on the Captain hoisting sail and taking him down the coast to Newcastle, well across the Border.

The common soldiers on foot or on inferior horses paid the price of the Irishwomen ordered to be killed in cold blood at Naseby and Methven Wood.

" Man, it was a grand day," said one of Alasdair's men at the end of it.—" At every stroke of my sword I slit an ell of breeks."

XXVII

THERE was no Covenanting army left in Scotland. Its leaders were all in exile or in hiding. Montrose was everywhere recognized as the representative of the King, and the ruler of Scotland.

The year of miracles had come full cycle. It was August 1645. In the last days of August a year ago, Montrose and his cousin had walked twenty miles across the heather to pick up a little army of half-starving men. Within three days he had led them to his first victory over the ruling government of the Covenant, which held the whole country in subjection. Within one year, and in six crushing battles, he had beaten army after army of that government, until after its final defeat it no longer existed.

The chief towns of Scotland, and foremost among them Edinburgh, Glasgow and Linlithgow, hastened to send him their loyal submission. The shires of Renfrew and Ayr sent deputations to placate him, laying all their former disloyalty at the door of the Covenanting clergy and the spiritual tyranny exercised by them. Sir John Hurry, who had been a loyalist before he was a Covenanter, now changed his coat again, and left the enemy camp to join Montrose.

The objections that 'all decent folk' had declared against a general who could use Irish troops in Scotland now suddenly vanished. All the nobles and great families were either hurrying in person or sending representatives or repeated letters, urging their loyalty and longing to help the King's cause both with their purses and with every man on their estates. The Earl of Traquair, who had wobbled so long in his stately fashion, now showed the way the wind was blowing by sending his eldest son and heir, young Lord Linton, to pay his court to the conqueror, with the present of a troop of horse, and promises of more.

Most powerful and important of all these, and well aware of it, as of the ridiculous aspect of all these proud lords tumbling over each other in their anxiety to acclaim the winner, was the Marquis of Douglas, who had shown the sights of Rome to his young compatriot a dozen years before. He had been Lord Angus then, an amused and amusing youth, whose cheerful sophistication had since developed into a shrewd cynicism. If he felt at all abashed at having waited till now to declare himself, he was not going to show it.

He was no knight-errant, as he had always known Montrose to be,—" Knew it even that night we dined at the English College, do you remember, and that pleasant golden Roman wine? It does not travel well, that's the pity. No, I cannot say the Bloody Heart still beats very strongly in the Douglas race, but then it's three hundred years since my ancestor thought fit to take the heart of the Bruce to the Holy Land. One does not do those things now. But my lands of Dumfries and Clydesdale are wide, and full of recruits, and your Lordship's success has convinced me I can employ them in no better cause than that of your army."

It was the opinion of all, though generally less frankly expressed. Montrose's camp had become a Court, attended by the chief nobles of Scotland. The Earls of Annandale and Linlithgow and Hartfell, the Lords Fleming and Erskine and Seton, Towers of Inverleith, Charteris of Amisfield, Stewart of Rosyth, all crowded round him, eager to pay homage.

Alasdair was sent to repress any of the new Covenanting levies that had so lately been formed in the West; and found none. Everywhere he was greeted with cheers and protestations of loyalty, and nowhere so eagerly as at Loudoun Castle, the house of that fierce Covenanter, the Lord Chancellor of Scotland, who was most conveniently not at home. But he left his wife, Lady Loudoun, to do the honours, which she did most heartily, as well as sending her major-domo, John Halden, to Montrose, ' to present her humble service to the King's greatest servant.'

Alasdair sang her praises on his return in florid burlesque of their interview,—" And isn't that the grand old lady—took me in both arms, she did, and gave us all a feast that would have made Lucullus hang out his tongue, ' and my old buck,' says she, or some other such words, signifying approval,—' it's a great thing you've done for Scotland,' says she, ' for we're all of us sick to death of this God-damned Solemn League and Covenant,' says she, ' and to hell with the bloody ministers,' says she,—and I'll swear to you if I'd have given the time to stay another day to convert her, it's ' Up with the Pope ' she'd be spouting now over her glass."

There was no holding Alasdair these days. But Montrose was determined to keep his army in restraint. After only two days at Kilsyth, he had marched upon Glasgow, thinking to meet Lanark's new army coming from there. But Lanark's new army had all dispersed, and their leader fled out of the country.

Montrose warned Glasgow of his approach, to make ready provision for his army, and to keep the citizens within doors. The town council promised him £500 sterling for his soldiers, if the city were left undisturbed; and he made clear to the High-landers and Irish that any attempt at sack or loot would be punished instantly by death.

They could not believe he really meant it, and they victorious over all their enemies, and the fair city of Glasgow the richest booty that ever they had set eyes on, with shops and booths and market places displaying everything that the most extravagant wish of man could desire.

But he showed that he meant it. One or two houses were looted and burned, and he had the offenders promptly hanged.

" He can afford to slight his old followers, now he has got these fine Lowland lords to eat out of his hand," said the grumblers.

But now he was Governor of Scotland, and would have to govern. He moved the army out of temptation's way by making his camp up the river at Bothwell, half a dozen miles from the city, leaving his praises to be sung in a spate of Latin verse by the local poets.

From that armed court he wrote to the old Scots poet, William Drummond, arranging for the publication of his last poems and pamphlets, which had failed to win the approval of Warriston, that rigid literary censor.

" I am glad to be in time for that, for he is very old," he said, as he sent Colonel Nathaniel Gordon eastward on this pacific message; Drummond's familiar lines were in his mind, urging him to make good use of what was left to them of life's wasting day.

> " Thy day posts westward, passéd is thy morn,
> And twice it is not given thee to be born."

The old friend of Shakespeare and Ben Jonson wrote his majestic congratulations to the Viceroy of Scotland, that His Majesty's crown was re-established, the many-headed monster of rebellion all but quelled, and " by the Mercy of God on Your Excellency's victorious arms, the Golden Age is returned."

A golden age it was, in the valley of the Clyde, with the sea-gulls wheeling white against the dark woods on its banks, in that high August sunshine. It lasted until the end of August.

By the 1st of September, Nathaniel Gordon had returned from his mission, and from another, which he had had first to carry out, and that was the releasing of the royalist prisoners in Edinburgh. The Tolbooth had been crowded with them in hideous conditions of semi-starvation, rats and disease. Those in the Castle were mostly in far better case, but the Castle, outside the city, had not yet surrendered itself to the new government, and Montrose would not take his army anywhere near it, for the plague was now raging in Edinburgh. So he had told Colonel Gordon to exchange his prisoners for those in the Castle.

But one prisoner flatly refused to be exchanged, and that was young James, now Lord Graham. Fully realizing his importance, he objected that his release would mean his father having to forgo, from among his prisoners, " a more valuable officer than myself."

The forethought and unselfishness of such a decision from a boy not yet twelve years old was cited in amazement,—the heroism, devoid of glamour and excitement, of preferring to remain in prison in time of plague, seemed positively unnatural.

But James always knew what he wanted. He was very comfortable where he was, thank you, he told Colonel Gordon, and at last had time for all he wanted to do, which he had never had before. The Governor was a very interesting man, and knew all about ship-building, which was James' particular hobby at the moment. He did not want to be a sailor or explorer or anything like that, but just to plan ships and watch them being made ; in the meantime, while waiting for a dockyard, he was making models of them with the Governor.

As for the plague, he argued with good reason that it made very little odds what one did about it. Two girls of gentle birth called Bessie Bell and Mary Gray had gone away from the city that summer and lived up on the hillside in a hut made of branches and bracken, so as to escape from all danger of infection. They were heard singing as they rambled through the woods ; then the singing was heard no longer ; someone went and peeped into their nest, and there they lay dead in each other's arms ; now the woman who washed James's clothes sang a song about it.

Short of such a retreat as their 'bower on yon hillside,' Edinburgh Castle suited James as well as anything.

But through his hermit-crab detachment, his determination was giving him a happy pride and confidence. He, who had always longed to be as brave and strong and tall as Johnnie, who had so envied his brother that glorious brief winter of his life beside his father, was now getting his own chance. In his passive way, the way which best suited him, James could now also be a hero ; and not even the prospect of seeing his old friend Alasdair again could tempt him from it.

So Nathaniel Gordon came back without him on that golden first day of September, when he rode into the camp on the river side with his hundred and thirty rescued captives,—haggard, pallid men, bearing the marks of rats' teeth on their bodies, who stared bewildered at the sunshine and the unfamiliar faces of men, and moved strangely among the liberties of this victorious army.

Another visitor rode into the camp that day, and was greeted with great acclamation and ceremony. This was old Sir Robert Spottiswoode, the King's Secretary of State for Scotland, bearing letters from the King, and a patent that created the Marquis of

Montrose Lieutenant-Governor of Scotland. Montrose was now invested with all the powers and privileges which had been formally bestowed on Prince Maurice. He had the power to summon Parliaments, and at once prepared a proclamation to be issued to the chief towns, summoning a Parliament to be held in Glasgow in October.

"And this is the very day, God be with it," said Alasdair, "that we first smashed the rascals at Tippermuir a year ago. Can your Lordship believe it?"

Nobody could quite believe anything. Like the released prisoners, they went about dazzled with their glory. Only Montrose took it for granted that he had won, that all the other nobles of Scotland were glad of it, and eager to join him.

Colonel Nathaniel Gordon wished he did not take it so much for granted. He knew the temper of those men better than did Montrose, who was too ready to judge others by himself. He still hoped for Huntly's alliance, never seeing, as did even Huntly's friends, that he ' could not endure to be a slave to his equal ' ; nor that this was the normal attitude of the nobles, whenever one of their number was raised up over them.

Nor could he believe that Alasdair should really hanker after the loot of Glasgow ; that Aboyne should really be jealous of the praise given to the Ogilvys. They could not be thinking of those things, now that the kingdom had been won for the King.

But where was the King?

Montrose had fulfilled his promise to him, made six months ago at Inverlochy. ' I doubt not before the end of this summer I shall be able to come to your Majesty's assistance with a brave army.'

But the King had never kept his to Montrose, made last April, that he would send cavalry under Sir Philip Musgrave, and would himself join him with all the speed he could. He and his secretary, Lord Digby, had planned this together; but since then the battle of Naseby had been fought and lost, and the King's army had had no chance to come north. All this last year he had been losing ground in England, as fast as Montrose had been gaining it for him in Scotland.

But now Digby's hopes, dashed by Naseby, had been revived by Kilsyth. Now could all the disasters and muddles in the south be retrieved, and he felt more assurance than he had done since the war began, of ' God's carrying us through with His own immediate hand, for '—so Digby wrote privately to a friend and in no compliment—' all this work of Montrose is above what can be attributed to mankind.'

Such praises Sir Robert Spottiswoode now repeated to his new master, the Governor of Scotland, while he handed him the letters that contained the King's thanks, though indeed Charles ' would not so injure words as to put upon them what they are not capable of.' He had less difficulty in giving his instructions that Montrose should march south to the Border, and there join forces with the Border earls. The most important of these, Home and Roxburghe, had already written several times urging Montrose to come to Tweedside, telling him the numbers of men they would add to his Standard.

So he wrote to the King, telling him he hoped in a few days to cross Tweed with at least twenty thousand men for His Majesty's service,—and where should they meet with His Majesty? He asked this of Spottiswoode, who could not answer.

For Charles was paying a visit to the Marquis of Worcester, who entertained him sumptuously at Ragland with banquets and hunting parties. There he wrote graceful apologies to Montrose for his own misfortunes, which were the cause, he said, ' though it is the more for your glory, that " shall be " is as yet all my song to you.'

It was Charles' chief misfortune that ' shall be ' was all his song through life. Never was his loathing of the here and now, that goading need to decide and act on the moment, so deep as at this present. All his fortunes in England had slipped from him, and his only hope to reclaim them lay in another country.

Yet he lingered at Ragland, craving only for the sad drugging of his soul in furiously active inaction. On horseback he was King indeed, and had won at an early age to that kingdom against odds that would have defeated most men. To lead the chase, to forget in the throb and rhythm of his horse, in his confident and daring guidance of it, in the keen rush of the air against his cheek, in the baying of the hounds, and the whole wild flying scene beneath the indifferent sky, that he had lost one kingdom, and might, while hunting here, be losing another,—this was his way to prove himself a King.

So, ' in melancholy feasting and hunting,' he let time slip past him,—and more than time slipped past.

The Covenanting army in England, led by David Leslie, a greater soldier by far than his family connection, old Sandy Leslie of Leven, had had news from Argyll at Newcastle, as fast as he could send it, of the defeat of the Covenant at Kilsyth, together with commands and entreaties that Leslie should hurry back and defend its cause in their own country, rather than go on fighting the battles of the insolent and ungrateful English Parliament.

So Leslie threw up the siege of Hereford to march north against Montrose, and with him went five thousand cavalry, the bulk and best of the Covenanting army in England. He intended to pick up about a thousand and more from the garrisons of Berwick and Newcastle, and there also to join with Argyll.

Had the King been on the watch, he could have intercepted this army and prevented it ever reaching the Border,—indeed, as David Leslie himself admitted later, there was a moment when Charles' armies could have utterly smashed him.

But that moment was the present.

Charles missed it, and Leslie went past him on the road that he had left clear to Scotland.

XXVIII

TWO days after Sir Robert Spottiswoode's arrival, Montrose called a grand review of all his troops in Bothwellhaugh. There, in that flat marshy meadow by the river, beneath the scarlet of the Standard, he was presented with his royal commission as Viceroy. As the first act of his sovereignty, he knighted Alasdair before all the army, proclaiming him Captain of the clans in the service of the King, and gave a speech in his praise that made the Macdonalds burn to prove themselves greater heroes than ever.

But Alasdair had decided that the best way to do that was to march back to the Highlands, to a campaign where booty was the rightful reward of victory, and no man would be hanged for taking it. His highest motives also impelled him; his father had summoned him; the homes of his clan were being harried; and, he told Montrose, he would be no true Highlander if even the King's cause came before that of his own blood.

Montrose could not urge commands or threats to the ally he had just knighted, who looked on himself as the representative of a foreign power. All he could do was to take the departure of his allies with the most charming grace he could command, so as to encourage their swift return. That, Alasdair devoutly promised, when he returned thanks for his new honours in a speech expressing passionate friendship for his commander. His promise convinced himself, but not Montrose.

As he saw that red-headed giant march up round the bend of the river and into the north at the head of his clan, with all his pipers playing the march of the Macdonald men, and a bodyguard surrounding him picked from the finest of the Irish troops, Montrose did not think he would ever see him again; and he did not.

The most marvellous year of Alasdair's life, as of many others, was over.

Away he marched with his men towards the distant shapes of the mountains; their kilts and the tails of their plaids swung with a jaunty criss-cross movement; the shrill skirl of their pipes came ever thinner and more faintly mocking through the bright, late summer air.

Away they went from history, and the march of great events. Colkitto of the snow-white beard and glittering eyes had beckoned them back into that older, other world to which they belonged; a world of legend; a world of personal loyalties and enmities as simple as in childhood, and as free and irresponsible; a world of personal combats, hand to hand, as in those days when there were giants on the earth; of hunts that lasted for days, while at night the hunters slept in the forest; of feasts where heroes in their cups and in the songs of their minstrels could see themselves as gods.

Their plaids melted into the heather, their music into silence; the clouds came rolling down from the hills like a heavy curtain, closing on that world which was to last them for just another century,—until, exactly a hundred years later, the great-grandson of the King they had been fighting for in that annus mirabilis, 1645, would arrive alone in Scotland, as Montrose had done, and once again would band the Highlands together to fight for him, and once again would lead them into history, this time to their destruction. Then would they pay the penalty for refusing to march with the times; the roads and bridges, that they had refused as effeminate luxuries, were made by others, the Highlanders destroyed as a nation, and only then made part of the changing outer world.

For one year Montrose had been able to absorb them into his larger purpose, and make history of the stuff of fairy tale. But he too had to pay the penalty, when with their help he attained a position that no man would have thought possible a year ago. With their help he reached the foot of the rainbow; but the fairy gold that lies there was melting between his hands.

*　　*　　*

Manus O'Cahan would not follow the rest of his clan. He and five hundred of his Irish were determined not to leave their general,—"for now that your Lordship has so many fine new friends," he told him, " it is possible you may still need a few old ones to keep the balance."

Those new friends caused a deal of dissension. The inflammatory Aboyne, even the quiet and casual O'Cahan, who was apt to flick his light eyelashes open at a stranger without speaking, in a manner very disconcerting, were with difficulty restrained from telling Montrose's new followers that they had waited till the war was won before they would come into it.

Aboyne indeed regarded the newcomers as a personal insult to himself, inasmuch as his commander's easy and friendly welcome of them made him certain that they were being preferred before him. To feed his discontent there came every day some fresh messenger with letters from Huntly, peevishly reproaching his son for adhering to the man who had always loved to slight their family pride,—that form of worship which Aboyne had been taught to regard as the noblest sentiment in the world.

Tortured by indecision, Aboyne told Montrose of his father's demands that he should instantly return home. He tried to make his application for leave with stiff formality, but the keen eyes before him would not permit it.

" Come, boy, this is not the crux of the matter. What is it? "

Out tumbled all his complaints in an untidy, unimpressive heap. Each of them shrank and withered as he exposed it to that cool and kindly gaze, so that it did not seem worth the telling.

Montrose had sent him back twice over for more cavalry before Kilsyth, because he had not brought enough the first time,—and his brutally frank cousin, Nat Gordon, had told him he was a feeble recruiting sergeant. That was what it boiled down to in words, but it had been twice as large while it tossed and tumbled in Aboyne's uneasily ambitious brain.

And then a pamphlet had been written on the campaign, giving all the praise for the victory of Kilsyth to the Ogilvys, " when everyone knows it was the Gordons who won Kilsyth as well as Alford "— but at thought of Alford and his brother's death, and the deep friendship that had existed between him and Montrose, something seemed to turn and twist in Aboyne's heart.

Montrose had been very careful of him at the later battle, had tried to keep him in the rear, and had insisted on his recall when he was pursuing the flying enemy, lest he should meet the same fate as his brother. All this only fed his obscure resentment. Not for love, but conscience, did Montrose so guard his life. To Gordon, who was like his own brother, he had allowed the recklessness that he would permit himself. Aboyne longed to win a like friendship with this man before him—to force him to acknowledge him his equal.

He broke out, " I wish I were dead like my brother Gordon. He was the only one of us who was not under a curse."

" Will you lay one on yourself of your own making? " asked his commander sternly.

The young man's fiery and uncertain glance fell before his eyes.

He heard Montrose say to him, " Your uncle Argyll is behind all this. It is he who prompts your father's demands. You know well enough how all his threats and promises to your house have been aimed at its ruin. Will you let him ruin even its honour? "

" No man shall say that of us! " flared up Aboyne.

" They will say it if you help Argyll's purpose to destroy your King. You can do it in no better way than by removing your cavalry from the only victorious army the King now has."

There was a few seconds' pause. Aboyne was wrestling with his confused emotions rather than with these statements, which he knew to be true. As Montrose had said, they were not the crux of the matter, and he had suffered a vague disappointment while they were despatched. But he dared not speak again of his complaints, they had sounded so silly.

Montrose put his hand on his shoulder. " If I have done you injustice," he said, " I did not know it. But, Gordon, will you let it destroy this that we are fighting for? "

He had called him by his brother's name, which Aboyne would now have borne but for his own title. His face reddened in a painful pleasure and quickened towards denial of the question.

But Montrose did not wish any protestations. Instead he shared with him his plans of meeting new forces on Tweedside.

It was rumoured that David Leslie had raised the siege of Hereford and turned his army to march north to Scotland, but King Charles' armies should intercept him before he reached the Border. If they did not, " God may rain Leslies from Heaven if He choose. We have shown that we can fight them."

In the high air of these impersonal ambitions, Aboyne's sense of injury dropped from him like the chains of a prison; his spirit rushed out to meet the sun at last, and he eagerly flung himself into his commander's plans. This it was to be free; he had no time even to notice it until he went to bed, and was suddenly aware that he had not been so happy for weeks.

But happiness could not stay with him. He woke at two in the morning with an attack of indigestion; he had drunk too much whisky with Manus O'Cahan last night, for his unwonted elation had made him want to increase it, and the whisky was raw and heady stuff, and O'Cahan an imperturbable drinker, difficult to keep pace with.

In the cold hours before dawn, Aboyne remembered all the people to whom he had already complained bitterly of Montrose's treatment of him, and to whom he would now have to show that he was of a meeker temper. He had already given orders to his cavalry to come back with him to the Gordon country. Was he to tell them he had changed his mind? Perhaps he had better go, after all, for a time, and then when he returned he would be all the more appreciated.

And at once in a row, like goblins, swelling ever larger and larger, there stood again all the wrongs that had been done him, and the determination of all Montrose's army not to acknowledge where their victory was due to his house.

*   *   *

Montrose had received the King's Secretary of State on the 1st of September; had held his review of the troops and his own investiture as Viceroy on the 3rd, seeing off Alasdair's men on that day.

In the evening of it, he talked with Aboyne, and thought him settled; on the next day, the 4th, he broke up his camp at Bothwell, and began to march south to Tweed.

On the 5th, Aboyne left him with all his cavalry.

" Do you mean to steal away too? " he asked of Nathaniel Gordon.

" I would rather die than do so," he replied.

" May you not be taken at your word, then! "

" Why should I, my Lord? Because Leslie is on the march against us? They say he has already passed Newcastle and picked up Argyll there. He may be over Tweed by now."

" Then Home and Roxburghe would send us word of it while they are dealing with him."

Nat Gordon was scowling, and did not answer. Manus O'Cahan had already that day asked him, " What news of those fine heroes? "

Nat had none beyond his own vague distrust, which he had seen shadowed in the keen light eyes of the Irishman.

Lord Erskine came in with fresh news. Leslie's army had been picking up troops near Berwick; it could not be less than six thousand by now, and of these more than five thousand were cavalry. His advance guard was commanded by Colonel Middleton, who had served under Montrose at the battle of the Brig o' Dee, when they had taken Aberdeen for the Covenanters. He and his men were certainly across the Border,—report said that all the army were.

Erskine advised a retreat to the Highland line. " Your Lordship has only Lord Airlie's horsemen now, and that is less than a hundred. You cannot meet Leslie's with that number."

Back to the hills again,—that was the course they were all urging. His help had come from the hills again and again. And now yet again he had to conjure up another army before he could meet his enemy,—and " Raise the clans again," said his advisers round him, for that was the way he had always done it.

To do so now would mean a long delay, while leaving Leslie an open field in Scotland to win back again all that the Covenant had lost.

But more than this, Montrose had learned to his cost how little stomach for fighting the Highlanders had when they came too far south of the Highland line. If he were to lead his army into England, as he had promised his King, it would not be an army of the Highland clans.

He must now look to the Lowlands and the Border counties for his troops. Douglas had been despatched some time ago to raise cavalry from Clydesdale and Nithsdale, and he was to meet him next day at Torwoodlee. In two days more he would be meeting the Border earls at Kelso, and their forces would be at least twice as many as those of Douglas, so that he would be able to keep his promise to the King.

His hopeful assurance infected his friends. Everything would probably work out according to plan after all.

And there were surely other armies as well as Leslie's coming north. Where were those troops of horse promised by Digby, whose praises of Montrose's victories showed a positively religious fervour?

The Secretary for Scotland, old Sir Robert Spottiswoode, wrote with urgent frankness to the King's secretary, Lord Digby. There they were moving towards Tweedside according to the King's plan, having carried out all their part of the programme, and 'dispersed all the King's enemies within this kingdom. We had no open enemy more to deal with, if you had kept David Leslie there, and not suffered him to come in here, to make head against us anew. It is thought strange here that at least you have sent no party after him. . . . If you would but perform that which you lately promised——'

He stopped; how could he at this distance make Digby understand that here was King Charles's last chance to win back his throne? Yet not even on that could he concentrate his thoughts.

They were filled with the image of his new master, and the quiet courage with which he had met blow after blow. He told Digby how the Viceroy had been 'forced to let his Highlanders go for a season,' how, no sooner had they gone, than 'Aboyne took a caprice' and carried away the greater part of the cavalry.

' All these were great disheartenings to any other but to him, whom nothing of this kind can amaze.'

Would Digby understand from that what manner of man was this, whom the greatest of men should be proud to serve?

It was Montrose's cause he was urging now, rather than Charles', as he wrote, ' You little imagine the difficulties with which my lord Marquis has here to wrestle with. The overcoming of the enemy is the least of them; he has more to do with his seeming friends.'

Those seeming, sliding, shadow friends included the King. Highlanders who must go home after every battle,—boys, touchy and quarrelsome as hysteric women,—lords of the same rank as himself, and therefore furiously jealous of his superiority,—soldiers without pay,—all these he had contended with, and won.

But now came the ultimate factor. He had conquered Scotland for the King; whose song to him was all of ' shall be.'

When Montrose had vowed his service to the King in Holyrood Palace, he had known that he was doing it to a man who was conscious that he had betrayed his servant, Strafford,—conscious that he had earned his own doom, which would involve that of others.

XXIX

CONTRARY to the fears of the most sceptical, Lord Douglas was at Torwoodlee with a large body of horse. But he gave a brutally frank account of them. " I doubt if the half of them can stick on a horse at the gallop," he said, " they have all grown flabby on peace and oatmeal. Their grandfathers drove off the English cattle, and grew strong and red-blooded on it, but now they all sit at home and grow oats. Half a century of union between Scotland and England has turned all our moss troopers into old women."

It was true enough, as Montrose had regretted in his boyhood, little knowing what it would come to cost him; the days of the Border raiders were over, their deeds an old song; the farmer of to-day, who had never seen his fields in flames, nor driven his cattle into his peel tower, was not going to be in any hurry to bring back the bad old times.

As they rode down Gala Water towards Kelso, another re-cruiting sergeant joined them, and that was Magdalen's nephew, young Lord Linton, who had also gone home to raise mounted troops from Peebles. His father, the Earl of Traquair, accom-panied him, for his house was near by, and he could not resist this opportunity, he said, of paying his respects to His Majesty's gallant Viceroy.

He looked much older than when Montrose had last seen him; there was something incredibly ancient, white and secretive about that long sheep's-face, framed in its venerable locks. His praises of Montrose's military genius were fulsome, his reminders of their family connection frequent and obsequious; and all the time that he talked and talked, his glances flickered out from under his heavy white eyelids and went wandering over the troops, until Douglas bluntly asked him if he were finding the numbers too small.

Down shut the eyelids again very quickly, and Traquair, in a voice at once injured and courtly, explained both that nothing was further from his thoughts, and that the small numbers of the Viceroy's army only added to his glory, for he had shown that he could win against any odds.

He bade a tender farewell to his son, who looked as though he would be sick when his father kissed him, and reminded Linton of many injunctions, since in all probability they would not meet again for many weeks.

" Mouldering corruption! " breathed Douglas to Montrose as they watched him ride off. " I believe he came for no other purpose than to spy out the nakedness of the land. He never asked of the Macdonalds or the Gordons—that shows he had already found out that they had gone."

" He has left his son and his troopers as hostages," said Montrose, " so he can intend no harm for the present at any rate."

" If he hates Linton as much as Linton hates him, that can be no good hostage. But yes, I suppose as long as he and his troop are here, we are safe. There goes one of the Border earls. Let us see what the other two will have to show for themselves at Kelso."

They rode into Kelso on the 8th, and went clattering over the cobble-stones in the great market square. But the market square lay bare in the September sunshine until their coming, and the tall grey houses round it looked blankly down on them. There was no sign of any troops, nor of the ' other two ' of the Border earls. There was no news of them.

For twenty-four uneasy, anxious hours, Montrose waited for them. What could have happened? They had had their instructions from the King. More than that, they had written to Montrose on their own account, over and over again, urging him to come to the Border and join forces with them.

Douglas was certain that Traquair was at the bottom of this,— he had let them know how weak Montrose's army was now, and they had shirked joining him until it was stronger. It was a vicious circle, for if everyone waited for security, it never would grow strong enough to provide it. But the majority of the Scots nobles were too long accustomed to playing their own game to consider any other.

After waiting a day and a night, startling news came suddenly to Kelso. Home and Roxburghe were with Leslie, had been taken prisoner by Middleton's advance guard, was the official report. Nobody believed it. The two lords had had good warning of Leslie's coming, and there had not been the shadow of a fight. Instead, they had gone twenty miles out of their way to surrender to his army.

They had joined Montrose while he was the winning side, but when his army dwindled so rapidly, and his enemy's, six thousand strong, rushed up from England, it was plain that they had been too hasty; and this was the best way to back out while there was still time.

Now seemed to be the right moment for Douglas to prove his cynical philosophy, and back out too. But he did not. He suggested turning west, and believed that the ancient power of his name would have more effect in recruiting there.

But he was wrong, for the power of the ministers had overborne tradition; everywhere was the new belief that nobles and kings were but ' God's silly vassals ' like everyone else, coupled with a belief of infinitely greater magic,—that what the Covenant bound on earth, God would bind in heaven. The man who fought against it not only risked ruin and death in this world, but earned a certainty of hell fire to all eternity.

So they went on a fruitless journey to Jedburgh, and there stayed the night, and Montrose slept in a bed which they said was the one Queen Mary had slept in when, ill as she was, she had ridden eighty miles to Bothwell's bedside where he lay wounded. She had nearly died after that; they had opened the windows in this room, as she lay delirious, that her soul might go out into the free air.

" Would to God that I had died in Jedburgh," she said later.

Perhaps the bed was haunted by her unhappy spirit, for those words seemed to echo in it all the night. " Would to God that I had died that time in Jedburgh."

Death, defeat, despair, raised their heads and looked him in the face for the first time since he had lain in prison at Edinburgh

Castle. Death seemed infinitely kindly. Many more people spoke well now of Queen Mary than they had done in her lifetime, for all that she had stood for the old faith. Still better did they speak of the poet king who had tried to bring justice to this land, and had been murdered for it, more than a century before her time.

Scotland was a country that did not value its heroes and heroines until they had been dead a long while.

* * *

In the morning the sun shone bright over the old Abbey that Henry VIII had done his best to destroy, but that still bore witness to the dead Queen Mary's faith; and as they rode, there in the distance, in the midst of a sea-blue plain, up sprang the Eildon Hills, where King Arthur and his knights lie sleeping till Scotland shall again have need of them.

Montrose forgot that he had ever, even for an hour in the haunted night, lost hope and confidence. Yet the chief of this country, the ' bold Buccleuch,' whose name had rung along the Border, was with Leslie; and scarcely any of the people round would come to the Royal Standard.

" It is your confounded Irishes that are keeping them off," Douglas told Montrose,—" they may have forgotten everything else, but they will never forget how stout King Harry sent Irish troops against them because the English Borderers had grown too soft. And for that matter, I have not heard that your Irish to-day take many prisoners."

" Nor did the English Parliament at Naseby," said Montrose curtly.

" Tut, tut, man, where is your sense of proportion? That was Irishwomen they murdered, and quite another matter from anything belonging to a kindly Scot. As for the faces of their fellow-countrywomen, it was sheer charity to slash them open for the better preservation of their virtue."

" They did it," said O'Cahan, coming unexpectedly towards them on that silent, lounging stride of his, " because of the great fear and hatred they have of anything that may bring pleasure to the heart of man."

Their talk made Montrose wish more strongly than he had ever done before that there were not three hundred Irishwomen with their children following his army. Bebinn was with them again, having come to see her husband honoured among the other captains at the Viceroy's grand review at Bothwellhaugh. Since then she had refused to leave his side again, and was very merry about it, giving as her reasons, first that she was jealous of him with the other women, and then that she would not leave the army until they had marched to London, and pulled out the Stone of Scone that Edward I had put under his coronation chair, and taken it back, not to Scone, but to Ireland, where it used to be the throne of the High Kings of Tara until the thievish Scots stole it, eight hundred years before King Edward stole it from them.

" And why not back to Jericho? " asked O'Cahan, " for wasn't it Jeremiah himself who brought it from there to Ireland? "

Their laughter lightened the heavy air of suspense,—all the more because Bebinn was believed to have glimpses of second sight, so that she could hardly be so gay if any disaster were impending.

The summer was still preposterously fine. A misty September heat lay over the blood-red heather like the bloom on a plum. It could not last, everyone said. The summer was like a ripe fruit, heavy and ready to fall. The morning and evening fogs grew denser. There was no wind. A dreamlike hush and stillness was over all the land. The huge spaces of the Border country had rolled up into hills as they marched west.

Montrose must then seek his refuge in them once again, until they were reinforced,—when and by whom? There was still no news from Digby of the fifteen hundred horse he had last promised; and Sir Robert Spottiswoode had had no chance as yet to send any messenger with the letter he had written him. Montrose decided to write himself with it to the King; it would be a long and difficult letter and one that he hated to write, but it would have to be done and as soon as possible. He would have to admit his project had failed; he could not now lead an army across the Border.

A confused sense of urgency beset him with regard to this letter; he kept thinking of the arguments that he must use in his demand for troops, and then forgetting them; he felt that until it was off his mind he would have no room nor freedom to think of anything else.

" I will not go to sleep to-night till I have written it," he said to Spottiswoode when they reached Selkirk on the evening of the 12th, " we will despatch a messenger at daybreak with it and yours together."

He also ordered a general muster of the army at daybreak, so that they should at once march on to the hills. The rendezvous was to be held in a meadow below the little town, where the streams of Yarrow and Ettrick meet. He left his men encamped there, in a good position, guarded by the hills on the north, and the two streams. The guns they took at Kilsyth were parked in the rear. On one of them was the name ' Prince Robert,' chalked on it by the Covenanters who had taken it from Rupert at Marston Moor.

Montrose sent out a mounted patrol under one of the Ogilvys, and left the further appointing of his sentinels and scouts to his officers. It was the first time he had done this, but the advance guard and flankers that he had sent out during the march had reported that the whole countryside was quiet; they had learned from the country people that Leslie's army was far away on the Forth. Montrose went across the stream to Selkirk, to a house in the West Port where he had decided to lodge for the night, so that he might discuss his plans with one or two of his cavalry leaders in peace and quiet, and get that letter off his chest.

He kept saying to himself, " I cannot keep my promise to your Majesty. It is now impossible to bring an army across the Border. To-morrow I must lead a retreat into the hills." The words filled his mind with bitterness and agitation, but he did not show it.

They dined off a boiled sheep's-head, and their commander told his company with much amusement how he had passed the open door of the kitchen while the woman of the house was cooking it, and heard her say over the pot that she wished it were Montrose's head, for then she would be careful to hold down the lid. They demanded indignantly what he had said or done, but he had not troubled to reveal himself,—" it might have embarrassed her," he added, smiling.

The countryside of Selkirk was strongly Covenant, and this was but another instance of it.

Dinner was cleared away; a smell of mutton and tallow remained in the misty air. A thick autumnal fog drowned all the night. In its dripping intensity, sounds were muffled, soaked in darkness. Inside the poky little room, where Montrose sat at a table with Douglas and Spottiswoode and Airlie and young Napier, the fog filled all the corners, and fought against the feeble light of the badly made candles.

As he watched the worn face of his commander, which to-night looked a deal older than his thirty-three years, Spottiswoode considered whether he could not make his letter to Digby any more urgent. He pulled it out of his pocket, where it had been for two days and had got a trifle rubbed at the edges and stained with tobacco shreds, and looked it through. Scattered sentences here and there caught his eye,—' Traquair has been with him, and promised more than he has yet performed.'

If he told all that he felt about Traquair, he might indeed put that more strongly, but it would not be wise, with his son in their camp as their ally.

—' Only a little encouragement from you (as much to let it be seen that they are not neglected as for anything else) would crown the work speedily.' What premonition had made him write that, two days ago, when Montrose had still been full of confidence?

But now that confidence seemed to have turned into the false security of acceptance that comes from exhaustion and weariness of spirit,—the wish to leave things to chance, and just wait for what happens. There was no doubt that he was deadly weary. His eyes, usually so clear, were heavy and inert; Spottiswoode wondered how much he had slept during the last couple of nights.

At about eleven o'clock, he urged his commander in a low voice to go and sleep, but "Not till I have written that letter," he said, though he admitted that it would take him twice as long to-night as at any other time.

" I have heard that your Lordship wrote your long letter describing Inverlochy in less than half an hour," said Spottiswoode.

" Ah, but that was a victory," Montrose answered. "We must get another one shortly if you are to see me as a quick correspondent." (' I cannot keep my promise to your Majesty. To-morrow I lead a retreat into the hills.' Once he had written that, would it cease to mock his brain?)

The others withdrew to another room, leaving him alone. A bed had been made up in a corner of the room, and he would go to rest the moment he had finished. He gave orders that he was not to be disturbed except for any really serious reason,—a necessary injunction if he wished to get some unbroken sleep, for the last few nights had been full of rumours and false alarms breaking in on his rest. This general nervousness was a natural result of so many disappointments and reversals of hopes. It was partly due also to the fact that they were in hostile country.

The captains in the West Port had cause to remind themselves of this again that night, for just before midnight, as they were getting to sleep, one of the outposts, Charteris of Amisfield, staggered in, declaring that he and his men had been attacked in Sunderland village about three miles off, and that most of them must have been killed, for only he and two others had escaped. His account was so confused as to be almost incoherent, and though he had been sobered by the fright he had had, it was plain that he had been drinking heavily. Neither he nor his two companions had been able to distinguish anything of their assailants, but then, as they protested, the night was as dark as inside the belly of a black dog.

Airlie and Douglas agreed that this attack must mean a raid by some of the country people, who had seized the chance of a foggy and moonless night to surprise the little band of outposts. They debated whether to wake the General, but decided he could do no more than they would now, which was to send sergeants over to the army camped in the field, with orders to send out more mounted patrols, and report results to headquarters as soon as they came in.

Douglas did not go to bed, so as to be instantly ready in case of any further accidents; but the scouts, who returned at the first glimmer of daybreak, all heartily damned themselves if there were an enemy within ten miles of them. They had been led through the thick night by men who knew the country; it occurred to Douglas to wonder if these were Traquair's tenants,—but Traquair could not be laying a trap for his son and his troopers.

It might be well, though, to question Linton. Douglas sent a messenger to him to come at once and speak with him.

By this time it was after five o'clock and just daylight, though thick and grey; while a heavy blanket of fog hung over the valley between the streams. The people of the house in the West Port had been stirring some time; now the woman of the house, with the grimmest of tight-shut mouths between her sharp nose and chin, was bringing in bread and ale.

Montrose came out of his room, dressed and cheerful, stretching himself and demanding, " Breakfast, breakfast."

He stood arranging his collar of fine Dutch linen over his steel cuirass, holding up a pewter plate as mirror.

" Fop! " whispered Douglas in his ear, as he passed him to fetch some ale. Montrose cut off a crust from the loaf, and the stale bread crumbled like sawdust.

" That shows what they think of us here," he said as he dipped it in his ale and laughed in his old easy way, which had won so many and various men to follow him.

Standing there, silhouetted against the raw and feeble light, he looked his old self again. As always he was surprisingly well groomed, his curled hair smooth and shining, his cuirass bright, his high boots of soft leather brushed to a silvery light and shade. Except for the small moustache and pointed tuft of hair beneath his lip, he looked much the same in this light to Douglas as when he had met him in Rome,—a youth then, shy, and rather stiff, and only a little slighter than now.

But now the whole man had eased out into a careless generosity of genius, among men who were utterly unlike him and each other, but whom he had made of his own kind, because he had filled them with his own purpose, never thinking how he did it, ' like wealthy men who care not how they give.'

" I always knew he had it in him," thought Douglas, flattering himself as men do who have known great men in their youth; and then, modifying his prevision,—" But not that he would mix with all men like this."

For there was Montrose talking to Spottiswoode with just that touch of courtly deference which gratifies an old man,—as happily at his ease with him as he had been when carousing with Alasdair and O'Cahan,—savages, Douglas considered, whom he could never have expected to find as the companions of that proud and reserved youth in Rome. But his pride had diminished, as his reason for it had increased.

To Spottiswoode's anxious inquiries as to whether he had had any sleep, he answered, " An hour or two,—but I have done that letter! " then pulled it out to add the date, as he asked what it was. They told him, the 13th of September.

He did not write it immediately, he stood with his pen in his hand, his face oddly shut against the present scene. His companions remembered this later, and thought it must have been some foreboding of the future that then visited him. But it was the past he was seeing.

On September 13th, exactly a year ago, he had stormed Aberdeen, and allowed the sack of the city. That was no good day to him.

He shook himself from his thought, put the date on his letter, and said to Douglas, " You seemed to be having some scuffle in the night while I was writing. Was it anything? " Douglas' jaw dropped. So their commander had been awake and sitting up writing when Charteris had tumbled in on them, and he might just

as well have been told of it at once.   Not that it would have made
any real difference.

"Nothing of any importance," he answered, and began to
tell him about Charteris.   He had only said a few words, when the
messenger he had sent to Linton came into the room, and said,
"My Lord Linton has left the army during the night, and all
his troop with him."

XXX

THROUGH the window came the clanking, champing sounds of the officers' horses, brought up as commanded to the house, and snuffing and sneezing the misty air out of their nostrils.

The sounds were very clear in that little dark room, where the leaders stared upon each other at this news. They had watched as for a sign of foul weather when Traquair's son should leave them ; that he should steal away like this in the night with no word to anyone, must show that a heavy storm was imminent.

Before anyone could speak, it broke upon them.

Montrose's scout-master, Captain Blackadder, burst into the room, his face so wild and staring that his frantic words were scarcely needed to tell his news.

" They are on us! " he gasped,—" Cavalry! All cavalry! Thousands of them. Our scouts are all driven back,—they are on the army by now."

Montrose dashed past him, out of the house, on to his horse, and with Douglas, Airlie, and young Napier close behind him, galloped madly down to the meadow in the plain they called Philiphaugh.

Chaos was there. Not an officer was in his place. The men had been cooking their breakfast, slack and easy in the false security that their commander had given them, because for the first time he had not appointed his pickets himself, but had left the camp that he might write undisturbed to King Charles. There could be no possibility of danger, if their general could leave them to write letters.

So they cooked their breakfast at leisure, with the officers scattered and casual, when through the white mist there came the thunder of Leslie's horse,—black clouds of cavalry surging up out of the fog,—vague, enormous, plunging down on to them, yelling with excitement, scattering the cooking pots and the men grouped round them.

O'Cahan and his five hundred Irish infantry rushed to the shallow trenches they had dug overnight, and at once put up a fight. But Douglas' new levies ran from the field without waiting to fire a shot.

Douglas met some of them as he galloped up, and tried desperately to rally them, but their blank unseeing faces gaped at him like dying codfish, and they merely swerved from his sword and went straight on past him. Cursing, he rode on alone, and soon found that of all the southern forces and nobility he alone had stayed.

He joined Montrose, who had got together a hundred horse, and now charged the enemy with such frenzy that for a brief moment they actually checked the whole vast body of attacking cavalry.

But another attack was being made by Leslie's musketry from beyond the Ettrick stream, firing at random in the mist, but the fire was thick enough to be fast picking off the men on the royalist right flank. And soon these musketeers had crossed the stream and were attacking from the rear. Leslie must have divided his army into two parts; and Montrose's army, now only six hundred, was being surrounded.

His few horse cut roads deep into the enemy, but the on-surging waves of cavalry rose out of the fog, crashed against them, and came on again as interminably as the sea. Through the misty confusion and turmoil, Montrose saw his men being cut down right and left,—saw foot soldiers, or those who had never managed to get their mounts, flying from the pursuing cavalry,—had a momentary vision of a terrified cur that scampered between his horse's hoofs, yelping in a high scream.

As far as he could tell in the fog, he soon made out that he must have lost the half of his cavalry.

The Irish were beating back the horsemen again and again,— but again they came, till the trenches were so full of dead they could no longer hold them, and they were driven out to take up another position round Philiphaugh farm. More than four hundred of them were killed by now; and the others had no thought except to sell their lives as dearly as they could. The Covenanting troopers, who had learned this to their cost, now held up the fight, and promised quarter to every man if they would surrender.

The game was up. There had been no battle, but a surprise and a massacre, and now that the Irish were down to a hundred men, surrounded on all sides by Leslie's thousands, and offered quarter, there was nothing to make it worth while to go on being killed. They threw down their arms and surrendered themselves as prisoners.

Montrose had no thought of escape. He was showing the gay and frantic fight of a man who does not expect to live.

He had put his fate to the touch, and had first won and now lost it all. He was clear of fate, and fought with a careless freedom that felt like happiness.

It was Douglas who tore it from him, pushed his sweating and snorting horse up to him, and cried,—" They have got wind of the baggage and are grabbing it as fast as they can. We might even now cut a way through them."

Montrose laughed, wiping his face, which was bleeding from a cut.

" To what end? " he asked. " We have lost all that was left of the army."

" You have lost a few hundred men. Save yourself, and you can get another army."

" You are worth more to Scotland than any army." It was his nephew, young Napier, speaking now, in a sobbing gasp of fatigue and excitement—and then came old Lord Airlie, on the deep note of authority,—" Get out of this, my Lord, and raise another army for the King. He is lost if you do not."

He hated their urging. Why should he go on raising armies for the King, who would not send a man to help him ? This was the best way to end it all. His men had died round him in hundreds; and now that death had come to himself, swift and inevitable, let him not reject it, to meet it in other and worse ways.

His men said he bore a charmed life, that neither bullet nor sword was forged that could kill him; years ago, when he had crossed Tweed in flood three times over and was not drowned, they said he must be born to be hanged. These things he had neither noticed nor remembered, yet now they gave zest to his determination to share the fate of his men.

" Do you cut a way through, my Lord," he cried to Douglas, " and carry on the work. I have shot my bolt,—it is your turn now."

Douglas seized his General's bridle rein, turning his horse's head.

" Will you give up? " he flung at him, " and us with you? "

They were close round him now, about thirty of his friends, and all determined either to die or live with him.

He threw up his head, looking round on them, and his face set. He had answered their purpose.

They charged again in a desperate onrush, drove and hacked their way through, found presently that they were no longer surrounded, and that the road to the west was free. They rode up the vale of Yarrow, and here and there before them, as the mist drifted and swirled upwards, there came the cloudy shapes of the hills, into whose safety he had meant to lead his army this day.

At thought of that, his despair, no longer gay, since he was no longer greeting the death that would so quickly end it, overwhelmed him, and he slackened his horse's gallop, and looked back.

His nephew, young Archie Napier, guessed his thought; in an agony he pressed nearer to his side and stammered out,—

" Sir,—if you cannot think of us—remember—there is your wife."

The boy's passionate care for him shamed him; through it, he had an odd glimpse of Magdalen, as though he had looked in through a window, and seen her lay down her sewing and bend her head, listening for the sound of his horse's hoofs,—as perhaps she was doing at this moment. That quiet scene took from him the false courage that accepts death and defeat. She, who was never brave, so she said, gave him the courage for life. He knew he could not give up, not yet, nor ever.

He smiled at his nephew, denying his impulse, for now he could give good reason for his movement.—" There are some of Leslie's horse coming after us," he said.

They turned and charged their pursuers, routing them completely, and taking prisoner the captain and two cornets, each bearing a standard, who were in charge of the troop.

Then they rode on, until they reached the house of Traquair. There they demanded admittance, and speech with Lord Traquair or Lord Linton. But the gates were closed and guarded against them, and the men-at-arms on guard said that their lords had refused either to admit them or to speak with them.

Wet cobwebs were spun all over the gate-posts, covering them with a mesh of shining threads. The old grey stone building stood stark behind them; its blank walls, its narrow slits of windows, its three watchful turrets, stared grimly back at the little group of tired horsemen. It was like a dead face, seen through the now faintly sunny mist, the face of a house doomed to be haunted. Built for security a long time ago, it would stand for a very long time yet; but few would care to live in that ' desolate house,' as Catherine Traquair herself was to call it a few years later.

The sharp conical hills rose behind it; the clouds were rolling up over the silver stretches of bent. The horsemen rode on into the hills.

Hours later, another and much larger body of horse rode up to the house. This time the gates were flung open, and Lord Traquair himself hurried out between his servants, bowing and rubbing his hands; stood there a moment with the sunlight sparkling on his grey locks while he congratulated the conquerors, then led General Leslie and Lord Argyll in to dinner.

XXXI

"IS it therefore infallibly agreeable to the Word of God, all that you say?"

So Cromwell asked once of the ruling ministers and elders of the Kirk of Scotland, and then told them,—"I beseech you in the bowels of Christ, think it possible that you may be mistaken. There may be a Covenant made with Death and Hell."

That Covenant they now proceeded to keep.

Judaism rather than Christianity, and the Judaism of the captive tribes in ancient Egypt, had become the national religion.

But a yet older and more horrible religion had been stirred up in the turmoil caused by the destruction of old authority, and this was the belief in devil worship, with its attendant rites of human sacrifice. Fear of God, fear of the devil, the two were merged, and all the haunted land suffered from it. The Mother of God had been the mother of all men, but God the Father, on whom all eyes now turned, to the exclusion of His Son, was no father, but an enemy exulting in destruction. Placate Him with burnt and blood sacrifices, show yourself on His side, or you were utterly destroyed.

Just a month after its downfall at Kilsyth, the leaders of the Kirk suddenly found themselves all powerful again. Now was their chance to show the real nature of the God they worshipped. General Leslie was guilty of admiring his foe; he had openly said, " I never fought with better horsemen, and against more resolute foot." And his soldiers had promised quarter to the hundred Irish who had surrendered at Philiphaugh. But when the 'gracious ministers' who, as Mr. Robert Baillie had requested, accompanied the Covenanting army, heard of this, they declared that it was 'an act of most sinful impiety to spare them.' These Irish, they truly said, had given no quarter themselves; when they had won a battle, they had hewn down the flying foe, and taken no prisoners.

Said the Covenanting generals in answer, "Yes, but these men

503

were selling their lives too dearly by killing our men as they died, and so we thought it cheaper to buy them with a promise of quarter, which cannot now be broken without dishonour."

The ministers could not see the point. Blood for blood was the necessity, and it was only a soldier's quibble to make a distinction between the blood of fighters shed in battle, and that of prisoners butchered in cold blood. But since the lay mind must have its legal-sounding quibbles instead of leaving all to God's good pleasure, the ministers did their best to satisfy it by explaining that the quarter had only been given to the leaders, and not to their men.

O'Cahan and his adjutant, Stewart, and Lachlan of Duart, who had headed his men in that uphill race of the clans at Kilsyth, were therefore taken to Edinburgh, to be hanged over the Castle wall, without trial, as their share of the quarter promised them; and the army was let loose on the prisoners, to cut them in pieces, drive them into the river and guard the banks with their pikes, or make what other sport they chose of them. Two hundred cook boys and horse boys were also butchered, and the three hundred women and all their children. Some had escaped through the countryside, but the hunt for them continued for many days after the battle, and all were killed in time. The countryside bore record to them ever after. The Dead Wife and Slain-Man's-Lea were now local names for hill and valley.

To the women, many of whom were great with child, the soldiers showed a perversion of instinct such as had made the ancient world account Nero a monster; but in this year of grace, 1645, their mode of slaughter was sanctified as a religious rite. Everywhere the ministers were preaching on such texts as— ' They shall fall by the sword ; their infants shall be dashed in pieces, and their women with child shall be ript up.'

The soldiers themselves could not stand as much of the horrors as did the clergy who urged them on. A nephew of the Reverend Mr. Cant's, also in the ministry, was asked later, " Mr. John, have you not once got your fill of blood? "

There was one who could not get his fill of it. Archibald

Johnston, now Lord Warriston, though drunk with vicarious delight in the butchery, was still more agonized lest there should not be enough of it. All the nobles taken prisoner on promise of quarter after Philiphaugh were brought to Saint Andrews to stand a trial. The lay members of Parliament, meeting at Saint Andrews, were not eager to put them to death. The formal execution of prisoners of war, especially when they had been promised their lives, was without due precedent.

But such worldly reasoning was swept away by Warriston. What were 'honour' and 'precedent' in the sight of God? God was angry. He had shown it by sending ' His two great servants against us, the sword and pestilence.' He was angry because His people had been too merciful to delinquents and malignants; let them show no delay now therefore in revenge, or God would again visit them with His displeasure. He entreated Parliament to ' unity amongst themselves,' but did not encourage that unity by comparing the House to ' Noah's ark, which had in it both foul and clean creatures.'

He was backed by petitions from the Kirk in one parish after another;—the ministers of Jedburgh besought the Parliament to 'cut off the horns of the wicked'; the assembly of the Kirk in Fife entreated that the ' zealous purpose of executing justice upon the bloody men' should 'speedily be put in execution'; while in Galloway ' the watchmen of the Kirk ' took Warriston's view that the chief cause of the suffering of Scotland from plague and sword was the former ' sparing of malignants.'

So the old gods conquered, Christianity died, and in its name devil worship, born of fear and encouraged by the lust of cruelty, ran rife through Scotland.

Colonel Nathaniel Gordon, Sir William Rollock, Alexander Ogilvy of Inverquharity, not yet eighteen, ' a lovely young youth,' as his prison bailie called him, and another boy in his teens, were among those who surrendered after Philiphaugh and were executed.

" The work goes on bonnily," said one of the ministers, and the homely words of satisfaction passed into a proverb.

The case most bewildering to the ordinary lay mind was that of Sir Robert Spottiswoode, an old man and a non-combatant, lawyer and scholar, who had been Lord President of the Court of Session in Scotland for many years. He had succeeded Lanark as the King's Secretary for State in Scotland, and this was the only crime that could be urged against him by a Government that still declared its loyalty to the King's person. Moreover he had surrendered to Lanark and been promised quarter. It was feared for a moment that this particular victim would have to be let off; but the letter he had written to Lord Digby and had never had an opportunity to send, was found in his pocket, and that proved his death warrant.

He was not allowed to speak to the people on the scaffold, for he had shown that he knew the Bible as well as his judges, and had quoted the answer of the Prophet Elisha to the King of Israel, concerning the treatment of his captives,—' Thou shalt not smite them: wouldest thou smite those whom thou hast taken captive with thy sword and with thy bow? '

So Mr. Robert Blair spoke instead on the scaffold; and Sir Robert told him quietly that he spoke blasphemies, abominable to God. He then prayed to the God he himself worshipped; " Merciful Jesus, gather my soul unto Thy saints and martyrs, who have run before me in this race."

The night before his death he wrote to Montrose, begging him that ' as you have always done hitherto, so you will continue by fair and gentle carriage to win the people's affection for their prince, rather than to imitate the barbarous inhumanity of your adversaries.'

The request was granted. There were Covenant prisoners in the Castle of Blair; there were many who cried and clamoured to Montrose for reprisals. But he refused to try and rival his enemies in deeds of cruelty, and told his troops that if quarter had been offered by any one of them, even if it were by the meanest corporal in his army, that promise should be kept.

He had already got troops to himself again. He was in Atholl, and there four hundred men left their harvest (no mean test) to follow him, and were presently joined by the Farquharsons and some horse.

With these he threatened the towns, in desperate attempts to stop the execution of his friends, and in some cases succeeded in suspending them for a time.

At last the King kept his promise to him, and sent Digby with fifteen hundred horse across the Border, a month too late. Leslie's armies were now between him and Montrose; Digby had to retreat to England, his men fled into the hills in Cumberland, himself to the Isle of Man. Montrose heard of this at the same time as of the first executions by the Covenant.

He heard how his best cavalry leader, Nat Gordon, was beheaded; and Manus O'Cahan hung without a trial, 'to show how much they despised his nation.' Bebinn lay hacked to death; her golden collar, of workmanship so fine that in this degenerate age it had seemed the work of magicians, was melted down into a shapeless lump of metal.

The Golden Age of William Drummond's congratulations had lasted less than three weeks. The age of blood and iron had returned.

It broke the heart of old Lord Napier, who died that autumn; and of the Kirk's finest servant, who had worked and prayed all his life for it, and could not bear the manner of its triumph. Alexander Henderson, who now fell ill and died within a year, wrote his prayers 'to remove God's heavy judgments from this miserable land,' from which he so longed to depart that 'never was a schoolboy more desirous to have the play than he was to have leave of this world.'

Yet still Montrose did not lose hope. Disaster and tragedy stung his spirit with the determination to surmount them. There was still an English royalist army south of Tweed; still Huntly to be won to his side; still a chance that Alasdair and his Macdonalds might return. Black Pate, whom he had feared dead at Philiphaugh, had also escaped, and won through to his side again; and once again the two comrades in arms were raising horse and claymores.

All news was fugitive, casual and uncertain. Among the reports of deaths of one friend after another, there came news of one utterly unexpected, shattering the belief that he would not despair. The Lady of Montrose, it was said, had died,—or if not yet, was dying.

XXXII

MIDDLETON'S dragoons were all over the country near Kinnaird. But with a few horsemen (the fewer for speed if not for safety) Montrose made a dash across country. He must see Magdalen, alive or dead.

So once again he rode eastward towards the sea, down through the hills. The wind raced over their slopes, through the running silver of the bent. All round him was the scrubby brownish purple surface of the heather, and breaking through it the gaunt bones of the ineradicable rock. The speed of his riding made the wind sting in his nostrils; his heart was a hammer, urging his horse along. The flying scene swung past him, yet every fleck and shift of light and shade upon it stamped itself upon his desperate mind. Now and again he caught glimpses of the plains below, of sheep dotted here and there in them as still as haycocks, of seagulls flying low and white against the curve of the further hills, and beyond them the carved white clouds, stationary in the blue distance, that had always made him think of Magdalen.

As so often before, he was riding back to her through the hills; it had been a ritual repeated through the course of his life; now he was doing it for the last time. Those other rides, unnumbered, unremembered, linked together, made a chain that reached back into his schooldays at Glasgow, when he came riding eastward on his holidays to Kincardine and Old Montrose. When it was broken, the side of his life would be withdrawn that linked him to his home and his childhood.

But he did not think of this as he stared before him at the rain that now came dipping and trailing its long grey skirts over the plain until it fell plump on his face. Sunshine, rain, the stump of a rainbow that sailors call a wind-dog,—he stared at the scene that had been the background of his life.

His thoughts of Magdalen were dull and confused. Behind them, there slowly swam into his memory, piece by piece, a little scene that had happened long ago in Italy, and that he had quite forgotten until now. His meeting with Douglas may have brought it back to him, for Douglas, then Lord Angus, had been there, and one or two English youths from the English College at Rome, when they had gone for a joke to consult a sturdy peasant woman who could tell fortunes.

Suddenly she stood as clear again in his mind as when she had stood before him, all those years ago, turning her heavy body from one to other of those laughing, fair, foreign lads, as a bear at bay will turn to the dogs that are baiting it,—and flung answers to their questions casually, contemptuously, then fell silent, and stared at Montrose, who had asked none. When she spoke next, it was in a hurry, mumbled so fast and low he could hardly catch the words, which had been remembered and wondered over for a little, then lain buried until now.

" Your life is a bright morning in a northern country," she had said, " you ride out, the sun shines, the streams shine on the hills. You ride alone, but men come down from the mountains and across the seas to follow you. They follow you to glory. They follow you to the death. There is the sound of trumpets high up in a lonely place. Good luck will ride with your honour. You will conquer your enemies. But those who love you will betray you. The sky goes black, the sound of trumpets in the mountains has turned to thunder. Rain falls, rain and tears, tears and blood. The blood of women runs in the rivers, the rivers are red with blood. All you have done is overthrown.

—" Again you ride alone, but in the midst of a multitude, and they are silent; they stare at you, who are their conqueror."

Her gabbling had ceased on that, her massive head sank forward on her chest; she would not speak again.

" It all ends well, then," Douglas had said as they came out together into the hard sunlight, that never gave the look of fleeting splendour, too brilliant to endure, that Montrose now saw before him.

" It ends well," Douglas had said, but he had said it only to cheer them, Montrose had known that, for no multitude will greet worldly triumph in silence.

And now he knew that the latter scene was what Magdalen had always dreaded for him.

" I have brought her more pain than joy," he thought, as he rode down into the peaceful plains, and saw the trees and towers of Kinnaird rise dark above the marshland.

Here was the hill where he had met her in the still white night only a little over a year ago, when his desperate enterprise was untried, and he had not yet put it to the touch to win and lose it all.

The country people were beginning to call it the Marquis' hill, she had lately told him, though they knew no reason to do so. Perhaps their memories were reaching back to the days of his boyhood, when he used to ride out from Old Montrose to fly his hawks on the uplands above the marsh, and would stop his impatient horse on that hill, and wave his scarf in signal to any from Kinnaird who might join his party.

He came to the deer-park, the orchards, the garden below the house, where he had often sat and talked with the head gardener, Daniel, and watched his keen, triangular old eyes scan the clouds that raced by above the massive garden walls.

He rode into the courtyard, and there left his horse, and looked up at the great silent house that had always been in a bustle at his coming. He could not speak to the servants; but in the hall he saw Lord Southesk coming towards him, so slowly that his questions died on his lips. But the old man was merciful, and spoke quickly.

" She is not yet dead," he said, and then a moment later, " I knew you would do it."

In his eyes, as well as anguish for his daughter, was anxiety for the man he loved as his own son. Middleton's dragoons were patrolling all this part of the country, but he had known that the boy would win his way through them. And he had known that Magdalen would not die until he came.

Now he led the way to her room, telling Montrose in jerky, dropped words, every few steps, as to the nature of her illness. The doctors could not explain it, but she had not been strong since the birth of her last child; in the last two weeks she had had severe pains, fever, then become unconscious, as far as they could tell. In the last few days it had been certain that she could not live.

Her husband stood by her bed once again; he saw her now only as she would be when dead,—the thin features sharply cut, the mouth a compressed line, the eyelashes shut upon her cheeks, their two half-moons darker than he had ever seen them, against that white, grey-shadowed skin. She was fast escaping him; his touch could not recall her.

They thought those close-shut eyes would not open again; but before her death they did, and saw him by her.

In the now cloudy blue of those eyes he knew so well, he could discern a hovering smile, as though to the end her love was capable of mockery. She triumphed, because, in spite of all the hazards and fearful odds against him, she was dying first. Peace had come to her, not with his death, as once she had fearfully foreseen, but with hers.

Their married life had been led under the shadow of tragedy. It was in the nature of the unquiet times, and Jamie's headlong spirit, that together they must wreck their home. Yet her love and her courage had grown in proportion to that necessity. Of late years she had learned to ask nothing more of life than their love, knowing that that was of a measure such as few are accorded. She had not hoped, not because she despaired, but because to hope is to fear.

And now, not in despair, but in joy, she could at last relinquish him, and be glad that in so doing he would be free of her,—released by losing the thing he held most dear. Whatever of disaster or tragedy came to him now, he would not have the agony of giving it to her.

Her life slipped from her with that smile, more easily than she had ever parted with any of her possessions.

He found himself, an hour later, still standing by the empty shell of that once sad and then gallant spirit. Nothing he could do would ever hurt her more. He had lost his dear and only love, the thing

most precious in all the world.   It would not matter to him now
what happened; it would hurt only himself.

> " They have most power to hurt us whom we love;
> We lay our sleeping lives within their arms."

He had tortured her sleeping life with the long nightmare of
her fears for him.   Now she was safe from him; and he was free
of her, as of all the world,—as the saint or seer or absolute artist
is free, to dedicate himself utterly to his cause.   Her death, suddenly
as it had fallen upon him, seemed now a thing fated and inevitable,
so deeply was it in accord with the unspoken wish that he had
known in her ever since their love began.

EPILOGUE
THE ETERNAL THINGS
1651

EPILOGUE

JAMES, second Marquis of Montrose, looked out of his window, and saw a courtyard paved with red and white flags that glistened as smoothly as if the sunlight on it were an extra polish added by the industrious housemaids. The sunlight poured into a covered alley, and was sliced off by a transverse section of shadow from the arched roof. At the other end of this tunnel was a glimpse of another courtyard, where the sunlight was broken by an occasional glancing movement from a child in a white apron playing with a white-and-brown spaniel. There was a splash of red from a flower in a tub; the walls that rose round these neat, minute scenes were of warm red bricks, arranged in patterns that had been remembered since the Romans.

"I like this place," said James to himself, as he turned from the large windows that went right up to the grooved wooden ceiling, to the room where their light fell so clear and pleasantly. The floor was of white and black marble tiles, clean as a scrubbed plate. Even the fine Persian rug was not permitted to encumber it, but was spread over the table. A spinet stood in a convenient light. On the cool grey walls hung a mirror and one good picture. The chimney-piece had two pillars in front of it and curtains drawn across it like a puppet stage; there was a little carved head over the arched doorway; and all round the base of those demurely plain walls was a row of blue and white Delft tiles, with a miniature picture on each.

James' books stood so that he could see at a glance which one he wanted; only one corner was untidy; his golf clubs (he had found he would never use them in Holland) were jumbled behind his bow, which had seen a good deal of service at the archery meetings of ladies competing with the gentlemen in polite society. Here the weapons of early warfare were tamed to a social function as pleasant as the music parties, where men and women played their chamber music together, their primitive interest in each other transformed, absorbed, into the harmony of their art.

James found himself at home in this clean bright world, where the men showed so much practical common-sense and kindly humour under their high black hats, and the placid women, with smooth plump faces and solid knobs of fair hair, busied themselves so contentedly with the arts of making a home. Never had he seen so much washing and rubbing and polishing as in Holland, such insistence on the importance of all the little details of daily life, from the perfect pastry and rich vegetable soups cooked by the maids in their tight white caps, to the well-brushed little spaniels who flounced about after their mistresses' silken skirts through the shining rooms, and never behaved there in the distressingly natural fashion that had so frequently occurred in Scotland.

When that name came into James' head, in however trivial or casual a fashion, something in him stiffened and braced itself as if to prepare him against another shock. His present quiet existence would shiver into unreality beside the wild memories of his childhood—that glittering chain of his father's victories, and the shadow of his mother's silent fears—his father's lightning visits to his home—his own visit to his father in his barbaric camp of heroes—the long months he had spent in prison in the Castle of Edinburgh, and then at last his release from it to find his mother dead, his triumphant father defeated, and his guardians' only hope of safety for himself in sending him to be educated abroad.

So quietly had his mother lived and died, that three years later, owing to the confused state of all public business in her chaotic country, the rent-roll of her estates referred to her as though still alive,—a grotesque contrary reply to the frequent public mention of her husband in his lifetime as " the late Marquis of Montrose."

But now that anomaly was removed. Five years after his defeat at Philiphaugh, James Graham, first Marquis of Montrose, had been hanged, drawn and quartered in Edinburgh.

And since all images or thoughts of Scotland, however casual or trivial, led towards that grim scene wherein his father had been hacked in pieces before the public gaze, young James, second Marquis of Montrose, now turned hastily to his spinet, opened it, looked for an instant at the pale scene of trees and clouds painted inside its lid, sat himself on a broad, comfortable chair with a square of blue velvet fastened by gilt nails on to its seat, and began to play a charming fantaisie by Jacobus Clemens non Papa, which pleased his purist ear better than any of these strident, assertive moderns.

Here he was secure from tragedy, among these tripping, perfect notes, in this room like a blue-and-white porcelain plate. The smooth enamel of its walls, of all those trim walls outside, enclosed him. Yet so insecure a thing is solid material, so penetrating and intrusive is the imagination, that not all James' five senses could keep him where he sat on the velvet seat of his broad and comfortable chair. Through walls, and notes of music, and sunlight on the patterned tiles, there showed a scene that he had not witnessed, of those tall crazy houses in Edinburgh, rising higher and higher, tottering over each other's shoulders, alive with the single intention of all the watchers that craned from their doors and windows, to see the Great Marquis go by to a felon's death.

It was of no use to go on playing against that dark scene. He got up, walked round the room, twirled his globe on its axis till America was uppermost, then Europe again, said aloud in the cool dispassionate voice that his mother had always laughed at, calling it his legal judgment voice,—" My country is a sow that eats her own farrow "; and then in a sudden fury, very rare to him, beating his hands against the revolving world, " Why was I not at Kinnaird instead of young Rob and Jean—a couple of children; they could do nothing—*I* might have helped him to escape! "

It was more than a year since his father had been led as a prisoner through the country on his way to death, and had been allowed to see his younger children and his father-in-law as he passed by Kinnaird. James was then as now abroad. But now, as then, he could not remain so. The last six years were in his head more often than the present moment.

This was what had happened in those years.

In the winter that followed his defeat at Philiphaugh and the death of his wife, Montrose set to work to raise another army. No sooner had he begun to win to this, than the King sent to tell him that the best way he could serve his cause was to lay down his arms, dismiss his soldiers, and exile himself from his country,—for the King had decided to give himself up to his enemies.

Montrose left Scotland, and went from Court to Court of Europe to try and get help for his King abroad. Charles rode into the Covenanters' camp on their promise of safeguard. Argyll handed him over to Cromwell's army, on the day that he received their cartloads of deferred pay from the English Parliament.

Two years later, Charles was beheaded by order of Cromwell and the Parliament.

Huntly and Hamilton were executed within two months of their King, whose cause they had damaged as badly as any enemy had done, by their selfish and spasmodic attempts to combine it with their own personal motives. Huntly, who would only win glory if he did not have to share it with Montrose, now died more nobly but no more usefully than he had lived. Hamilton, who had risen too late to try and save his King, now fulfilled the uncertain prophecy that had clouded his life; he succeeded to Charles's crown, as had been predicted, but the crown was a martyr's, not a King's.

The King's execution caused a revulsion of feeling in Scotland. Argyll and the Covenanters had Charles II proclaimed King in Edinburgh, and sent commissioners to him at The Hague. They could give him the support of the Covenant; Montrose could give him that of a soldier who " never had passion upon earth so strong as to do the King your father service." Charles II thought he could use both; so that people in Scotland did not know if he were chiefly backing Montrose or the Covenanters.

The year after Charles I's execution, Montrose landed in the north of Scotland, once more to raise it for the King, who all the time was negotiating with his enemies. At the outset of his campaign, his minute army, delayed by false hopes of reinforcements, was surprised and routed; Montrose had his horse killed under him; escaped into hills he did not know, and after three days of wandering, lost and starving, gave himself up to a man he had thought friendly to him. But the Laird of Assynt sold him to his enemies; he was taken by them to Edinburgh, to be hanged, drawn and quartered.

Argyll hurried on the execution, without a trial, making use of the sentence that had been passed years ago upon his victorious enemy, who had then wandered free on the mountains and laughed at his threats. There was need of haste; a storm of protest and petitions against his death came from the different countries in Europe. They came too late.

Within a few weeks of Montrose's death, Charles II went to Scotland to join the Covenanters, and was as much in Argyll's power as if he had been a prisoner. But Cromwell returned from his destruction of Ireland, invaded Scotland with the whole force of his army, and smashed the Covenanters, first in their own country and then in his. Young Charles had again to fly into exile. Scotland was reduced to the state of a conquered province.

Old Lord Southesk, the moderate, was heavily fined ' for wishing well to King and monarchy.' The Earl of Traquair, who had wobbled so anxiously in his efforts to be with the winners, was finally condemned as a loser, imprisoned, but set at liberty by Cromwell in ' a kind of pity,' more cruel than any death sentence; he was deprived of all his estates, his son refused to help him, and he even begged for bread in the streets of Edinburgh.

The consequential Traquairs had become the most abject of poor relations. James' letters from home were full of the trouble caused by their importunities; his grandfather and his uncle Carnegie refused to accord them even a pretence of sympathy.

"They are like to go mad," wrote his young brother, Rob, whenever another begging letter came from their poor bewildered aunt, Catherine Traquair, who could not understand the cruelty of her father and brother, since she had flatly refused to believe in her husband's treachery to Montrose. She had to ask her husband not to write any more to her father, since whatever he wrote was misinterpreted, and " let me say what I can to the contrary, it avails nothing."

Sordid family quarrels which left an old man, who had been Lord Treasurer for Scotland, crawling in semi-starvation, like a

winter fly about the streets he had known in his days of state,—
James could not bear the picture. He had longed to avenge his
father on Traquair after Philiphaugh, but revenge should come
swift and terrible, not through such slow degradation.

He was out of pocket as usual, his allowance had had to be cut
very short since his father's estates were destroyed and forfeit,
and now there was this crippling fine on those of his mother's
family. But he began to look round on his possessions, which like
his mother he treasured with such tender and precise care. His big
globe, which already made him feel a traveller; his bow and spinet,
equal links between him and the society of his friends; his books,
essential to his pleasures as well as to his studies,—it was agonizing
to decide which of them all he could bear to part with. He had best
do it by casting lots and then pretending that the object so chosen
had been stolen, as though he had had no choice in the matter.

He was already pretending that his money would not help
Traquair, but his aunt Catherine, whom he had always thought
an objectionable woman, but she had once given him a tip and it
was only fair now to pay it back. But how should he cast lots?
He could think of no better way than standing in the middle of the
room and pointing at everything in it while he said the old infantile
counting game—

> " One-ery, two-ery, Diggory Davey,
> Allabone, Crackabone, Henery Knavery,
> Pin, Pan, Muskedan—"

It looked as though the spinet were going to be the one for
' out goes he '; he had rather the picture went than that,—he
hurried it on breathlessly—

> " Twiddledy, Twaddledy, Twenty-one—"

There was the sound of flat, dragging steps; someone was coming
down the passage through the open doorways. James' voice
dropped to a whisper, suddenly aware that he had been shouting,
and his finger was still outstretched at arm's length as he twirled
it past the globe, and on to the chairs at

> " O U T spells *out*, and—"

A heavy slouching figure stood in the doorway.

There was still the Persian rug before the spinet. James dropped his finger, he uttered no further sound, but a smile of deep thankfulness did in place of the words ' out goes he.'

Then he turned towards his visitor. He had never seen the man before, lumpish and shaggy,—' a mangy bear ' were the words that shot into James' mind. He held a parcel between his hands with the same clumsy care that a bear might hold a cake,— an untidy parcel done up with knotted string and a torn copy of the French *Gazette*, while he peered at the youth before him under thick reddish-grey tufts of eyebrows. He said in a voice surprisingly musical and resonant like the deep melodious twang of a violoncello,—" Are you my lord Marquis of Montrose? You are not like him."

James felt himself flushing, and furious that he should do so. Why should he mind the testimony of this rude stranger with the face of a grotesque dummy? But he did mind, had always minded, that he was not like his father, as Johnnie had been. The man was too intent on some purpose of his own to notice his effect,—he was pushing the parcel towards James, and his voice, now almost muttering, was saying,—" Take it—it is yours." His fingers pulled at the string, tore off the sheet of newspaper, and then a piece of rag, and James saw a pretty casket of fretted gold, and wondered where it was he had seen it before.

As the man thrust it into his hands, he knew that he had held it like this in his childhood again and again, and had opened it hopefully, only to discover each time a broken seal ring and a coin with a hole in it. It was the casket that used to stand in Queen Mary's room at Merchiston, the casket that had been given long ago by the Doge of Venice to young Archie Napier's grandfather, " the logarithms ruffian, confound him! " his irreverent descendants were now saying over their mathematical lessons.

" Open it, my Lord, open it," said the man in gruff impatience,— " it now holds your father's heart."

There was a steel egg-shaped case inside; it had been made

out of his father's sword, the man was now saying. James heard his voice surging through a loud singing noise in his ears. He said to himself, "This cannot be happening. I shall wake up." His father's sword, his father's heart, in the hands of this gross stranger! But the stranger was looking at him; James had the painful feeling that he had spoken aloud without knowing it.

"It was in the hands of his enemies," said the man.—"They hacked his body to bits, to show them in all the chief towns of Scotland. What did he care for that?

'Let them bestow on every airth a limb'—

"That poem he wrote in prison the last night of his life,—he was free then, as he has always been. They could do nothing to him."

"Who are you?" said James.

The man did not seem to hear.

He said, "A little dust in a gold box,—what has that to do with him? Women cannot see that. They cling to anything that will link the loved one to earth. Your cousin, the Lady Elizabeth, Lord Napier's wife, she is weeping over the stockings he wore at his execution, and will not have the bloodstains washed out. Another niece is making a little shrine of coloured marble plaques for his portrait in miniature. Bits of stone and silk, a little dead dust, these are the things they make live for ever,—they will hand them down through their families to show—what do they show?—the devotion of his womenkind. The Lady Elizabeth risked her life to steal his heart from his enemies and send it to you."

"Are you one of her servants? I do not remember your face, but it is long since I have been in Scotland."

"No, no, no," said the man vaguely, pushing away these questions with fat hands on which the red hairs glistened in the clear light of the room. He began perfunctorily to tell his story,—the servant sent with the heart had been attacked and robbed; the gold case carried off, passed from hand to hand, but he himself had at last tracked it down, stolen it in his turn, and now brought it here.

" Why did you? " asked James.

The man shrugged.

" A little dead dust," pursued James, his interest in this odd character suddenly awakening, and his sense of logic outraged by his conclusions,—" in a precious box which you might have sold,— and I imagine you are not rich."

" No, no," said the man, " I thought of it, of course, but what is the use? One does these things again and again, and nothing comes of them."

So bleak and blue a look had stolen up behind the crimson of his cheeks that James suddenly saw that the slightly swaying movement he had made from time to time, shuffling a little on his heavy feet to meet it, was not drink, as he had half suspected, but faintness.

He made him sit down, sent for food and wine, then, since he was an unconventional young man, and it was nearing his dinner time, decided he would dine with him. Food revived his guest. He was greedy but discriminating, prompt to discern the best dishes, and drank copiously, but all the time he ate and drank, though at first faint with hunger and then engrossed in his satisfaction, he talked amusingly, discursively, with the practised ease of a man who had long recognized that this is the payment he must give for his meal.

James, who had at first felt only repulsion, was moved to wonder and even envy;—this man had been everywhere, done everything, seen everyone.

Again he wondered if he had spoken aloud. The man was nodding his great head at him across the table.

" What does it all amount to? " he said. " I have satisfied every lust that itched me, I have gratified every prick of curiosity, I have juggled with the fates of great men as though they were a pack of cards,—and what does it all come to? Curiosity and pride, you get knowledge by the one and power by the other, but what else do you get? A vision of the whole world, yourself included, as a mass of wasps struggling in a honey jar, pressing each other down into the sticky sweetness, so as to stand on their sinking bodies and suck their own advantage, until they too sink, on those sinking bodies, to their death."

James said, " I have thought that too. These men's very greed for success prevents it. They rush from one side to the other of the boat until they sink it and are all drowned together. There was a man called Sir John Hurry who took me prisoner when I was a boy—he had already turned his coat twice over— then he joined my father after his last victory at Kilsyth, and in the end was executed with him."

" I know, I saw him," said the man gruffly, and fell into his first long silence since the meal began. James too was silent, and wished he had not spoken so unguardedly. Had this man then seen Montrose himself die? He could think of nothing to say that would pull them away from the subject that he dreaded, yet wanted to approach. But his guest did not notice his embarrassment; his own silence was the deeper one of absorption. At last his words came.

" Beauty was there," he said, " and a pleasant way of living, and what has happened to it all? I may have helped to destroy it—I don't know. It was long ago, in your father's youth. If he had made friends with his King early enough, so that Charles had trusted him instead of Hamilton, who always hoped to be king himself,— well then, it might all have been prevented. Who knows? Who knows? Anyway, Montrose lost his chance to do so. And now he is dead, and I go on living, crawling betwixt heaven and earth."

James watched him pulling at his thick underlip, and looked away, then said rather awkwardly,

" Argyll and Warriston brought my father to death. Now they are under Cromwell's heel. They say Warriston skulks through the streets in terror, because he hears Montrose's Highlanders have sworn vengeance. And the people shout ' Traitor ' at Argyll. If the young King ever comes into his own, the first thing he will do is to cut his head off."

He leaned forward to fill up his guest's slender wineglass yet again, and saw the sunk head staring up at him.

" I saw Montrose," he said.

Again there fell silence, this time deep and heavy on them both, so that James could hear his companion's thoughts. Slowly there began to form in his unwilling mind the picture that he had tried to drive out as he played on the spinet that very afternoon,—the picture of the houses of the Canongate in Edinburgh, and all the souls in them craning out to see his father go by to die.

He could avoid that picture no longer.

" You saw him—then? "

" I was in the crowd. I was back in Scotland—some matter of pounds and pence—maybe my instinct to be in at the death. I was one of those whom they paid to throw stones and filth at Montrose as he was led to his death. There were women who had been brought from all over the country, women whose men had been killed by his Highlanders. No need to pay them to take vengeance. The streets were buzzing with fury.

" Then he came. He was wounded, feverish,—he had been led for days through the country on a horse with no saddle, his feet fastened under its belly—now he was in the hangman's cart, his arms bound behind his back, that he might not defend his face. He was wasted with loss of blood, ragged, unshaved. And on his face there shone a look of peace,—no, of happiness.

" There was a grand wedding party going on at Moray House, just opposite where I stood: Argyll's son, young Lorne, was being married, and some of the guests came out on the balcony to stare at the sight below. Now the shouting would begin, they thought, and stones and dirt flying. Not a sound or stir. All those crowds struck still as the dead, except where some fell on their knees, praying. The only noise was the tramp of men and horses, and the hangman's cart rattling over the cobbles. I saw a shadow behind the window, Argyll himself,—behind him, Warriston. For one instant I saw Argyll's yellow face looking down on his enemy, then it hid itself."

James felt his hands shaking. His mouth had gone very dry; when he began to speak, there was no sound. He poured himself more wine, and after a moment was relieved to hear his voice say in its most dispassionate tones :

" I heard that Huntly's daughter, the Lady Jean, was one of the party on the balcony, that of all those crowds she was the only one who shouted an insult at my father."

" We'll all be under the sod in a few years," replied his companion, " and what difference will it make then which goes first? Lady Jean can spit her venom,—her brother Aboyne died abroad, of a broken heart they say,—Lewis is Huntly now, and busy making his peace with his uncle Argyll. They speak more of Gordon now than of those still alive."

" He was the only one who did not fail him," cried James in sudden passion,—" and the King he fought for, failed him."

" He fought for more than that. He fought for all men. They will try to hide themselves from it,—to throw mud at him for centuries after his hands are bound in death. They will cloud his name, let the sour droppings of their minds fall upon him. But these die, and he will live."

The resonant voice had ceased. James had leisure to consider a practical minor point. He could not have this man the poorer for bringing him the gold case that held his father's heart. If he gave him all that he now had, it would mean that he must part with another and more valuable possession than the Persian rug. Reluctantly, when the stranger rose to leave him, James looked at his spinet.

As he pocketed the money his host gave him, the old man's little light eye flicked out at the young man in a sudden gleam of curiosity and pride. He said—" You won't know my name, I expect. And yet I once had a considerable effect on your father's career. You were not born when—My name is Carlippis."

James shook his head.

" No," he said, " I have never heard it."

" I did not think you would," said Carlippis, with an attempt at jauntiness, but he looked disappointed. He shambled out, and James stood looking after his bent back.

Printed in Great Britain by T. and A. Constable Ltd.
at the University Press, Edinburgh